SISTER OLIVE WOULDN'T HURT A FLY

Gill Calvin Thomas

First published in 2025 by Blossom Spring Publishing
Sister Olive Wouldn't Hurt A Fly © 2025 Gill Calvin Thomas
ISBN 978-1-917938-26-6
E: admin@blossomspringpublishing.com
W: www.blossomspringpublishing.com

From childhood's hour I have not been
As others were; I have not seen
As others saw; I could not bring
My passions from a common spring.
From the same source I have not taken
My sorrow; I could not awaken
My heart to joy at the same tone;
And all I love, I loved alone.

Extract from 'Alone' Edgar Allen Poe (1829)

'It is a man's own mind, not his enemy or foe, that lures him to evil ways.'

Buddha

'No, I can't bear it, not again.' Will was hallucinating, and knew it, but its pull was too strong for him.

He saw his mother: watched her knuckles whiten as she gripped his father's leather belt.

'Liar, liar!'

He wriggled, trying to get away. 'I wasn't lying. Please don't hurt me!'

He heard his professor's voice. 'Your final warning, Will.'

His wife Miriam and son Oliver materialised. 'Why should we believe you? You knew it was your fault all along.'

He tried to reach out to his son. His voice cracked. 'Don't leave me! I can't transform without you.'

Miriam shook her head in despair as she led Oliver away.

'Miriam, come back! Don't go!'

He laid his head on the pillow and closed his eyes, trying to shut out the visions. He could still hear Miriam's voice repeating, 'No more. I won't take any more.'

He whispered, 'I'm sorry. I thought I could control it, but it's too late. My mother was right. I *am* an abomination.' Tears ran down his cheeks as the darkness led him into unconsciousness.

PART 1

Chapter 1
Chester
28 December 2021

The house was freezing. Will had allowed the wood burner to go out again. Miriam found him huddled in his study, books and papers stacked high on his desk. As soon as he saw her, he closed the lid on his laptop.

Despite being irritated by her husband's behaviour, Miriam set about lighting the wood burner. She scrunched newspaper, placed kindling on it, and then set a well-seasoned log on top. She shivered, and her hands shook as she struck a match against the side of the box. It broke. A second flared, and she placed the flame underneath the paper, hoping it would take. The evening was dank and still, with no updraught to help it ignite. She leaned over and blew underneath. At last, she saw a flicker of flames as the kindling began to take. She shut the wood burner door and sat back, thinking about the last few days.

She had tried to make Christmas special; instead, it had demonstrated a family falling apart. On Christmas Day, Will had accepted the presents he was given, although he had none to give. He placed his unopened gifts on the floor beside him. Ollie, their ten-year-old son, offered to unwrap them for him. Even then, Will barely glanced at Ollie or at his presents. Shortly afterwards, he left them without saying a word.

Three days later, Miriam heard loud voices coming from Will's study. What she witnessed horrified her – Will stood waving his arms around as he directed a torrent of incomprehensible words at Ollie. When Ollie saw her, he sprang up and ran to her, relief flooding his face. She guided him out.

'Why was Dad shouting like that?'

'Dad's gone a bit funny.'

She didn't press him. Ollie would confide in her when he was ready. However, one thing was certain: Will had not just 'gone a bit funny'.

After supper that night, Miriam stood outside Will's study door as she summoned up courage to confront him. Whether he sensed her presence, or whether it was that he was going out anyway, he flung the door open and they stood facing one another.

'What's the matter with you? How dare you shout at Ollie!'

A dark shadow descended around him. The man she had once loved had disappeared. He had the same features: his dark hair swept back from a high forehead, an aquiline nose and dark eyebrows that nearly met in the middle, but his eyes, light grey and normally kind, were different – darker somehow. The mouth she had once liked to kiss was no longer full and inviting. He was tight-lipped, austere.

'Will, we need to talk. This has to stop.'

'Yes,' he repeated mindlessly, 'it must stop. Let me be. We are nearly one, and the demon must fall.'

She watched him walk down the hallway and out of the front door, then vanish into the night.

When Will reached the corner of the road, he paused beneath a sycamore tree. He slowed his breathing, counting his breath in, holding it, before breathing out again. He let his breath control him: felt how the cool air entering his nostrils calmed him. He understood now how

Miriam drained him of his power. He needed the icy cold air so that darkness could soak into him. He raised his arms towards the night sky.

Meanwhile, Miriam was left to puzzle over Will's words: 'We are nearly one, and the demon must fall.' She didn't understand what he meant. He was clearly in a dark place and in need of professional help, because she felt powerless to help him.

She recalled how his slide into mental ill health had begun when he had lost his post at the university. He told her it was because he had breached professional boundaries. When Miriam learned he had involved two of his students in private research and that one of those students had committed suicide, she was horrified. The shouting match that ensued between them resulted in a rift that neither of them had been able to overcome.

***

Ollie's bedroom was on the third floor; it took up all the attic space. Light spilled in from a large sash window, and when Ollie looked out, he could see an ancient oak tree, with its branches spreading towards the house and over the road. The room was spacious enough for his model railway to be permanently set up and ready to go.

Miriam liked to go up to say goodnight. Sometimes, when he let her, she would tell him a story. Tonight he was sitting up in bed in his navy dressing gown, fresh after his shower. He had inherited his father's straight dark hair and grey eyes, but his features were softer, more like hers.

She sat on the antique velvet chair beside him.

Ollie looked startled. 'Didn't you see the woman

sitting there?'

Miriam was puzzled. 'What woman?'

His eyes twinkled and he smiled knowingly. 'You can't see her, can you?' Miriam looked around but saw nothing. 'What are you talking about Ollie?

Alright, go on; tell me.'

He had a wicked grin on his face, and Miriam could not help but smile as she settled down on the chair to listen.

'It was the night before Christmas Eve. I woke up, and she was sitting where you are now. I asked her who she was, and she said her name was Agnes and that she would protect us from the darkness.'

Miriam had some difficulty understanding what he had just said. She took a deep breath. 'Okay. What does Agnes look like?'

Ollie hesitated for a moment. 'She wears a white cap and a long black dress with a white collar. She sits on that old blue chair as though she's part of it. When she reaches out to me, I can see her hand on the bed, but I can't feel it. And when I wake in the morning, she's gone.'

'Did she tell you where she came from?'

Ollie bit his lip and shook his head. 'No, but she told me she's our friend and there's no need to be afraid. She will keep us both safe.'

Miriam didn't know what to say. Will had turned their lives upside down, and now Ollie was saying he had seen a ghost. She tried to stay calm and hide her anxiety so as not to frighten her son. She felt lost. Fatigue enveloped her. She did not want to give in, but she had an overwhelming desire to lie next to him and go to sleep. She rose from the chair and sat down on the bed beside

Ollie, her hand gently resting on his arm. She stayed with him until he slept, then went downstairs.

Chapter 2

The following day, Miriam and Ollie spent the afternoon at the cinema, watching the new *Star Wars* film. Afterwards, she dropped him off with her best friend Pat while she went home to pick up a book he wanted. The wood burner had gone out yet again. Well, it could stay out. If Will wanted to be warm, he could light it himself.

Despite her mounting fear of him, she knocked on his study door. There was no answer. She forced herself to open the door. Will was sitting with his back to her. He looked around and stared, his face pale and thin. Although he appeared to look at her, she was sure his gaze went straight through her. He turned back to his papers without speaking. For a moment, she wondered whether she should go to him, put her arms around him, and ask if there was anything she could do to help. But the distance between them was too great. She fetched Ollie's book, left Will in the house, and hurried back to Pat's.

Pat stood at her front window, observing Miriam as she walked up the driveway. Her dark, curly hair seemed to bounce with each hurried step. She was wearing a tweed coat and brown sheepskin boots, a blue woollen scarf tied loosely around her neck.

They both worked at the same school: Miriam as a talented and popular history teacher, and Pat, the recently promoted deputy head. In her new role, Pat had seen less of Miriam, but what she had seen rang warning bells. Miriam was clearly worried about something.

Pat left the window and strode out through the hall to the door. A huge smile lit her face. 'You look cold. Come on into the warm.' She watched as Miriam unbuttoned her coat to reveal a petrol-blue dress, pinched in at the waist with a wide black belt. Miriam sat on the hall chair, unzipped her boots, and put on the pair of slippers she had brought with her.

Pat felt a little envious of the way Miriam had with clothes. Despite her present worries, she looked stunning. She carried off her generous figure with panache. High cheekbones gave her an exotic appearance, whilst her nose and wide mouth looked perfectly in proportion. Beauty, however, was more than skin deep. Her hazel eyes told a tale of compassion and curiosity. They were smiling eyes. They crinkled at the corners when she laughed.

They were both tall, but Pat thought of herself as far too skinny. No matter what she ate, she remained as slim as ever. However, her long legs made skinny jeans and jumpers look great, and with her long, dark, shiny hair worn loose, she looked carefree and younger than her years. Her blue-green eyes were short-sighted, usually hidden behind brightly coloured glasses. She thought herself plain, but that was not how others saw her. Because she rarely looked in the mirror or at photographs, she had no idea how wonderfully expressive her face was. When she smiled, her face lit up with joy, and her laughter was infectious.

'How's Ollie? I hope he's not being a nuisance.' Miriam bit her lip. Ollie could be demanding. He asked a lot of questions.

'He's upstairs, chatting away to himself. He had something he wanted to sketch, so I've given him a drawing pad and some charcoal.'

'I'll just nip up and see him.'

Pat went into her kitchen-diner to lay the table. When

Miriam returned, she remarked how good the food smelled.

Pat grinned. 'We've steak casserole for supper. But first, how about a glass of wine?' She walked over to a well-stocked wine rack, picked a bottle of Chilean Merlot, and poured a generous amount into two large crystal wine glasses. 'Don't stand on ceremony, Mimi' – Pat's pet name for her – 'That's better, you're smiling. Ollie will be happy doing his own thing for a while. Let's go into the lounge.'

Pat had kept her Christmas decorations to a bare minimum: no tinsel or display of cards, just a small tree standing in the corner, which she had decorated with gold and silver baubles and a string of white lights. Miriam sank down with a sigh on the cream leather sofa.

Pat handed a glass to her and sat beside her. 'I'm delighted you're here. Are you going to tell me what this is all about?'

Miriam lifted her glass and sipped. 'This is good. Thanks, Pat.' She sighed. 'I'm not sure where to start.'

'Well, Mimi, my love, start at the beginning.'

'It's Will. I hardly recognise him. His whole personality seems to have changed, and weird things are happening to the house; even the lights seem to have a mind of their own.'

Pat grimaced.

'I know what you're thinking, but it's not the house. Ollie tells me he has seen a ghost in his room. Well, that's not what he calls it. He sees a lady called Agnes, who has come to keep us safe, but I don't think we are. I don't understand what's happened to Will, and I can't trust him to be alone with Ollie. I caught him shouting nonsense at Ollie the other night, as if he was talking in tongues. When I confronted him, he walked off, gabbling something about fighting a demon.'

Pat sat upright. 'I was expecting you to tell me he'd found another woman.'

'Don't worry, if I had evidence of an affair, I would consult a solicitor. But I don't think that's the reason for his behaviour. What really hurts is the way he looks at me. I swear his eyes have darkened with hatred. I don't know what I've done, and I don't know how to respond to him.'

'Why should it be something *you've* done?'

Miriam took a large gulp of wine. It went down the wrong way, and she coughed as Pat thumped her on the back.

'You could both stay here, you know. Give yourself time to think.'

Miriam, close to tears, looked away.

'Look, I'm going to insist. Stay here tonight with Ollie. You can go and get some clothes in the morning.'

Facing Pat again, Miriam drained the last dregs of her wine. Pat reached over, picked up the bottle from the coffee table, and refilled her glass. 'I'm going to put the vegetables on. Think about it, Mimi. You shouldn't stay with Will. If he's losing it, he could hurt you both.'

Miriam settled back further into the sofa, luxuriating in the comfort and warmth. Pat was right about Will, and she was right about the house. Her house wasn't just old and quirky; it was cold, with a malevolence she had never felt before.

Pat returned. 'We've got some time before dinner. You said Ollie has been seeing a ghost. Well, I think I've seen her too. Before you arrived, I was upstairs and heard Ollie talking. I went into the bedroom and saw something

11

out of the corner of my eye. Just for a moment. Ollie smiled and said, "You saw her, didn't you?" When I asked who, he said, "My lady."'

Miriam frowned. 'Oh, hell's bells – you think she's here with him?'

'Yes, as extraordinary as it sounds, I believe she is. I'm pleading with you, don't go home. At least stay a couple of days and see the New Year in with me. Come on, what do you say?'

By now, Miriam's face was drained of colour. 'But then what, Pat? At the risk of sounding pathetic, I can't just run away.'

Pat snorted. 'Well, if you want my advice – leaving might just help Will come to his senses.' She reached over and laid her arm on Miriam's shoulder. 'Why don't you go and fetch Ollie? Supper should be ready by now.'

This time, Miriam's legs felt heavy as she climbed the stairs. She found Ollie sitting on his bed sketching and went over to look. He had drawn a woman in a long dress, her arms outstretched. Her face looked blurred. He had blended the charcoal in swirls, then drawn in eyes, nose and mouth.

He had printed *AGNIS FIGHTS THE DARK* at the top of the page.

'Is this your lady?'

He nodded.

'This is how you see her?'

He shook his head. 'No, not really. I'm not very good at drawing. She's pretty, kind of like you.'

Miriam smiled at him. 'Can you see her now?'

He shook his head again. 'No, not now she knows you're here. Pat saw her before you came. Agnes didn't know if she could trust Pat, but I told her she's my godmother, and she smiled such a nice smile. She wears a silver cross on a chain. She put her hand to her neck and touched it, then she sort of faded away.'

Miriam stared at her son. 'That's extraordinary. And you're not frightened?'

'No.' His voice trembled. 'It's the dark that scares me. She keeps it away. I wish she'd keep it away from Dad. It's all round him.'

Miriam wrapped her arms around her son and kissed the top of his head. 'Sweetheart, I'm going to do my best to find out what's going on. We're both going to stay with Pat for a while to give us some time to sort things out.'

Although Ollie loved and trusted his mother and wanted to believe her, he looked doubtful. That was the point at which it struck Miriam that he seemed to accept the changes in his father. Whatever else he had done to Ollie, Will had drawn him in, and at the same time, he had excluded her.

'Don't worry, Mum, Agnes will help us.'

She pulled him close to her again. How could this be happening? Tears formed in her eyes and she blinked them away. 'Pat has our supper ready. We'd better go down.'

If anyone had looked through the kitchen window on that cold December night, they would have seen two women and a boy sitting at a pine table, tucking into a hearty supper. A pleasant family gathering. They might have imagined laughter and cheerful conversation. But if they looked more closely, they would have seen it was the boy who supported the others. It was he who lightened the atmosphere.

After supper, Miriam went upstairs to run a bath for

Ollie while he carried the dishes from the table to help Pat load the dishwasher. When his mother called him, he kissed Pat goodnight and ran upstairs. She stared after him. He was a joy. A bit small for his age, but he would soon have a growth spurt. Apart from those strange grey eyes of his, he was so like Miriam.

***

With Ollie reading in bed, Miriam switched off the main ceiling light, leaving a warm glow from the bedside lamp. She left the bedroom door open and went back downstairs, to find Pat sitting in the kitchen. 'Discussing Will's behaviour has helped me realise how serious our situation is.'

Pat was pleased to hear her friend beginning to own the problem, and simply replied, 'You must get yourself a solicitor.'

It was as though Miriam hadn't heard. 'I was so busy writing online tutorials and teaching Ollie, I didn't notice how ill Will had become.'

Her answer irritated Pat, but she kept quiet, until Miriam said she would ring the doctor.

Pat snapped, 'You need a solicitor, not a doctor. Wake up to what's happening and stop making excuses for him.'

Miriam went over to the window, pulled back the curtain, and looked out into darkness. 'I wish it was that clear cut. We've been married a long time; we loved one another once, and he's Ollie's dad.' She drew the curtains closed once more and turned to face Pat. 'He was so deeply affected by the loss of his job and the suicide of his student.'

Pat interrupted, 'I notice you stress the loss of his job before the death of his student. Remind me what happened during that period.'

Pat's words broke through Miriam's defensiveness. 'Will set up some research in his own time – to study religious communities and changes in belief systems through the ages. He involved two of his tutor group without seeking permission from his supervisor. It all came to a head when a link was made between his research and the student who died. But she had been accessing material on suicide at home, and in the end, no blame was attached to him. Then when Covid struck, he shut himself away. I had a hundred and one things to think about, and I couldn't cope with him as well. Living through lockdowns was difficult enough with school and everything else.'

Pat maintained a serious expression. 'You are right to be worried about Will's state of mind. Suppose he's dabbling in the occult or something. Do you think he might want to use a young, innocent boy for a particular reason?'

The two women stared at one another.

Pat continued gently, 'I don't want to frighten you, Mimi, but you must agree, it's a possibility. Think about what we have here. A young woman compelled to take her own life, and a father who is trying to influence a ten-year-old into his way of thinking.'

Miriam cried, 'Will included Ollie in his world while he excluded me, but surely he wouldn't harm him! When I asked Ollie about his father, he just said, "Dad's gone a bit funny."'

Pat frowned. 'One thing's for certain; you're going to need time to sort this whole mess out. Set something in motion now, before term begins. I can arrange cover.' She got up and joined her friend, laying an arm on her shoulder. 'We've talked this over enough. My prescription for you is another glass of wine, then a hot bath and bed.'

Miriam sighed. 'I'll just go and check on Ollie.' She tiptoed into the spare bedroom, to hear Ollie breathing steadily. She pulled the duvet up over his shoulders and kissed him on the top of his head. Then she looked over at the chair where Pat said she had seen 'something'. Despite herself, she whispered, 'Thank you. Thank you, Agnes, for looking after my boy. Please keep him safe.' She took Ollie's drawing downstairs with her.

Pat studied the drawing. 'It's rather good, isn't it? And I believe him. Let's face it, neither of you are safe with Will. Whatever happens, promise me you'll not take Ollie back there.'

Miriam took the drawing from her friend, placing her hand over the image. 'I promise.'

***

Will was concerned that Miriam had not returned home with Ollie. His son was paramount to him, because without him, he might not be able to complete his life's work. He had no feelings left for Miriam. Ever since their son had been born, she had ceased to be of interest to him. Ollie was everything. He guessed she had taken him and sought refuge with one of her friends. Well, no matter, she could not conceal herself for ever. His companions would find them and bring Ollie to him. They were due to arrive within the hour to help him pack and to transport him to the rented house in Castle Terrace that they had prepared for him and Ollie. Miriam's home was stifling him; he could not bear to remain many moments longer.

Sometimes he only retained a hazy memory of life before he had begun his journey and become the keeper of truth. He understood how he was being pushed forward to surrender this life and fight the enemy within. He welcomed the cold and darkness. It lingered around him, investing him with authority. He could feel power waiting to burst out of him, and for this his son was vital. Their blood must be joined together for him to transform from this life. As one being, they would become sovereign. Miriam was mistaken if she thought she could hide the boy.

***

Will's two companions helped him pack his laptop, books and papers. He went upstairs and bundled some clothing into a bag. When he looked around him, he recognized that he was leaving his old life behind him, but it meant nothing to him. He walked to the front door with his two friends. The smaller of the two stopped and looked behind her. 'I have something I must do. You carry on.' As soon as she heard the front door close, she felt in her robe for a piece of paper. She laid it on Will's desk, smoothed it out with care, and smiled to herself.

Chapter 3
30 December

Miriam stood beneath the oak tree at the front of her house in Rope Lane, trying to spot any movement through its dark windows. It was silent; nothing stirred. She searched in her bag for her keys, then strode across the road, the front door key ready in her hand.

The heavy front door creaked. She stood and listened. She could hear nothing; even the old grandfather clock in the hallway had stopped ticking. Will hadn't bothered to wind it up, but to be fair, neither had she. She stepped over the threshold. It was cold. She cried out in exasperation, 'Why can't you at least keep the wood burner going?'

She walked down the hallway towards Will's study. The room was empty. The papers and books that had been strewn across every available surface were gone. One solitary piece of paper remained. She picked it up and felt her heart thump as she read the message.

WOMAN – YOU ARE NO LONGER NEEDED, BUT THE BOY IS MINE. YOU MUST LEAVE HIM WITH ME, OR I CANNOT VOUCH FOR WHAT WILL HAPPEN TO YOU BOTH.

Miriam sat in Will's chair, staring at the note. She had an overwhelming urge to run, to grab some clothes and get back to the safety of Pat's house. She was half-way down the stairs, a bag of clothes in each hand, when she heard banging on the front door. Nervously, she shouted, 'Who's there?' No-one answered; instead, the knocking began again. Taking a deep breath, she stepped in front of the door and slid the chain in place, opened it a fraction, and peered through the gap at two people wearing black cloaks. Their hoods cast their faces in shadow.

'What do you want?' she stammered.

The taller of the two figures pulled his hood back a fraction. Dark eyes stared at her. 'You saw the note.' He had a high-pitched voice and a Welsh accent.

The other cloaked figure spoke. A woman's voice this time, with the same sing-song accent. 'The marshal requires his boy.'

Miriam banged the door shut and slid the bolt over. Her skin prickled. They continued to knock on the door. She picked up her bags and ran through to the kitchen. She slipped into the yard and locked the back door behind her. Her hands shook as she tried to find the key to the padlock on the back gate. At last she located it on the keyring and fumbled with the lock. It was stiff, and the gate, infrequently used, opened with a loud creak. She looked around. No-one in sight. She closed the gate, snapped the padlock, grabbed her bags, and ran down the back alley.

She thanked her lucky stars that, as usual, she had been unable to find a space to park close by. She reached for her key fob and pressed it, saw her car lights flash, and ran for it. She wrenched the passenger door open and threw in the bags, making sure the doors were locked before leaning forward on the steering wheel, breathing heavily.

The two dark figures appeared at the top of the road just in time to watch Miriam drive away in her small green Volkswagen.

***

'You were quick!'

Miriam dumped her bags by the stairs before turning to face her friend. 'Will wasn't there.'

Pat studied her face. She knew Miriam had dreaded confronting Will, but she didn't look relieved.

Miriam whispered, 'I don't want Ollie to hear us talk. Is he upstairs?'

Pat shook her head. 'He's in the kitchen. We've been making Rocky Road.'

They found Ollie at the sink, his sleeves rolled up, washing all the utensils. Pat's face broke into a huge smile. 'You're going to have to come and stay with me more often!' She handed him a towel to wipe his hands.

He grinned at them both. 'I've put the baking tray in the fridge like the recipe said. Can we have one later when they're set?'

Miriam smiled. 'Of course we can, and I think you deserve a treat for all your hard work. How about watching a history programme on iPlayer?'

With Ollie happily watching *Kingdom of Conquest,* Pat and Miriam went through to the kitchen and shut the door. 'So, what happened that you don't want Ollie to hear?'

Miriam ran her fingers through her curly hair. 'Will was gone. His study was empty except for this.'

She handed over the note, and as Pat read it, her expression changed. 'Good grief! You may have thought Will wouldn't hurt Ollie, but this note is threatening you both.'

Miriam agreed. 'It frightened me. I ran upstairs to pack a few things, and I was about to leave when someone banged on the door. I put the chain on, opened it, and saw these two dark figures: one tall and thin, much taller than me, and the other small and chunky. They were both wearing dark cloaks with the hoods pulled up, so I couldn't make out their faces.'

Pat raised her eyebrows. 'I'm guessing that neither of them was giving away *The Watchtower*.'

'I'm trying to remember what they said. Something about the note, then the woman spoke in a sing-song voice.' Miriam mimicked her: '"The marshal wants the boy." She was a sturdy woman. She stood with her arms folded across her chest.' Miriam looked across the table at her friend. 'She looked absurd, but I was still terrified.'

'What was the taller one like? It wasn't Will, was it?'

'No, but he was tall like Will. Dark eyes, very pale. I slammed the door and ran round to the back and hoofed it to the car. And here I am. What on earth has Will got himself mixed up in? They called him "the marshal". A play on words because, of course, it's not just his surname, but a marshal can mean head of a household.' She laughed nervously. 'I wonder if Will has talked to Ollie about the first William Marshall. He does seem interested in that period, and I wouldn't think it's on the school curriculum. Ollie must be protected from all Will's nonsense. I'm just going to check on what he's watching now.'

Ollie was immersed in his history programme about Beaumaris castle and barely registered her, so Miriam said nothing. When she returned, Pat had two mugs of coffee in front of her.

'I was thinking, you could report Will, you know, show the police the note.'

Miriam sat down. 'I can imagine what they'd say. "When did you see him last?" "Well, yesterday." "He's hardly missing, then, is he love?" Even if I show them the note, they'd say, "Some sort of prank, I daresay, love."'

'Yes, but we know it's not a prank. The note is threatening you and Ollie.'

Miriam put her mug down. 'Why? It doesn't make sense. What do I do now? I can't just run away.'

'You can, and you must. It's you and Ollie who matter. Will is dangerous; he's possibly part of a death cult. His student committed suicide, and now he wants Ollie for something nasty. We also know he is able to get others to do his dirty work.'

Miriam was shaken by what Pat had said. 'But what can I tell Ollie? I can't believe this is happening to us!'

***

Will lay in an upstairs room in the house in Castle Terrace. With blackout blinds on the windows, he could not to tell whether it was night or day. He felt himself beginning to drift away into another dimension as the ayahuasca brew that Sister Olive had administered began to take effect. His body shook as he went deeper and deeper into a new and altered state.

Chapter 4

A hot bath should have helped Miriam sleep. It hadn't. In the early hours, she resorted to listening to the BBC World Service. She dropped off eventually, but jerked awake at around 6.30, feeling as though she was choking. She looked over at the twin bed beside her. Ollie was still fast asleep. She swung her legs out of bed, pushing her feet into her slippers. She shivered in the cold of the morning and padded down the stairs, to find Pat already up. 'Couldn't you sleep either?'

Pat reassured her, 'I'm an early riser. Why don't you get yourself a cup of tea and join me?'

Miriam sat opposite Pat with a steaming mug in her hand. 'I'm so full of rage, I feel like I'm going to explode. I tossed and turned most of the night thinking about Will.'

Pat responded swiftly, 'Right then. Do you want my advice? Stop faffing about. Will's an adult. He's big enough to sort himself out. Whatever he's mixed up in, he's brought it on himself. I don't see why you or Ollie should have to suffer.'

'I can't just abandon him.'

'Oh, for goodness' sake, Miriam!' Pat's voice had become sharper. 'Don't be an idiot!'

Miriam stammered, 'Ollie knows there's something wrong, hence his imaginary friend.'

Pat shook her head in disbelief. 'Give Ollie some credit. Why don't you believe in his ghost? He's a sensible young chap. You baby him too much.'

Miriam was silent for a moment. Pat's comments hurt. She murmured, 'I'm fighting on all fronts. Will has just about broken my spirit, but I'm trying to find my way through. Don't be cross with me.' After a pause, she continued quietly, 'I left the front door bolted yesterday. I'll have to go through the back to unbolt it, otherwise Will won't be able to get in.'

Pat snorted, 'Good! Why don't you change the locks for good measure?'

Miriam ignored the comment. 'I must get in the house and unbolt that door.'

Pat seemed annoyed, although, grudgingly, she admired her friend's loyalty. 'You shouldn't go on your own. Why don't we all go?'

'I don't really want Ollie to go back into the house. Let's try and do something normal. Why don't you go into town with Ollie this morning? He's dying to use his Christmas gift vouchers. I can go to the house, then meet you afterwards at that pub on the canal. I'll buy us lunch.'

***

Miriam drove past the house a couple of times. The mysterious pair, if they were still hanging around, had hidden themselves well. She went round the back. The padlock securing the back gate opened more easily. She unlocked the back door and let herself in. Everything was as she had left it. She entered Will's study, found some paper, and tried to write him a note, but after three attempts, she gave up. She simply didn't know what to say. It was best to say nothing.

She shivered. The house felt unnaturally cold. She recalled how excited Ollie had been on Christmas Day, opening his presents in the lounge. The Christmas decorations they had put up together were still there but were already gathering dust. The bright rugs on the floor looked moderately cheerful, and the cushions were colourful, but the heart of the place had gone. It had become a sad, empty shell.

She climbed the two flights of stairs to Ollie's room and sat on his bed, looking across at the old chair where he said he had first seen Agnes. 'Hello, Agnes. Are you there? I wish you could tell me what to do.'

She gazed out of the window at the oak tree across the road. She could see the entrance in the wall where people cut through to the canal, and she imagined them sauntering down the towpath, enjoying the winter sunshine. Everything seemed normal, until she heard a noise behind her. Turning round, she saw one of Ollie's model trains trundling around the track. It came to a halt under a bridge.

She felt a draught, as though something or somebody had glided by. The ceiling light came on, flickered, and then went out. Her heart thumped. 'Is anyone there?' She jumped up and looked around, but nothing happened. Her logical mind told her it must be the electrics, so she pulled every plug she could see from its socket before she unbolted the front door and left the house.

Just before she reached the junction of the road, something told her to stop. She stood behind a wall and peered round the corner. What she saw made her gasp. The same two mysterious figures in black were standing near her car. Luckily, they were facing in the other direction. In her mind's eye, she saw herself striding towards them, shouting, 'Get away from my car and leave us alone!' She wanted to hit out at them, to threaten to call the police. Instead, she turned and hurried towards the canal and the safety of the pub, thinking it was no good; they must leave Chester and seek refuge.

She felt relieved when she entered the pub and scanned the room for Ollie and Pat. It was crowded and noisy, but that was normal, and it felt safe. She spotted them sitting at a table in the corner. Pat waved. Miriam pushed through the crowd and sat down beside them.

'Good, you made it. We haven't ordered yet. Was everything alright?'

Ollie wanted to show her his new books, and Miriam tried to act normally. 'That's a great choice of books. We could read your new Harry Potter together.'

Pat raised her eyebrows, and Ollie's expression made it clear that he was nearly eleven and quite able to read for himself.

Pat went straight to the point. 'Tell me. Did you see Will?'

'No, and I'm relieved he wasn't there.' She turned to Ollie. 'I'm sorry, love, but Dad wasn't at home.'

'That's alright, Mum.' He grinned at her. 'Agnes told me not to worry.'

Miriam sighed. 'Oh, Ollie.'

Pat covered her friend's hand with her own. 'Did you see anyone? It's OK. Ollie knows. He's been telling me about two dark figures.'

Miriam stared at her son. His expression was now open and innocent, but his grey eyes, so like his father's, tried to reassure her. 'They won't hurt us. Agnes won't let them.'

'Oh, goodness me, Ollie.'

'Honestly, Mum. She'll fix it. Can we order now? I'm ever so hungry.'

Well, Miriam thought, *that's the end of that. I can't*

hide what's going on, although I don't know what's going on, and my son doesn't seem bothered by whatever it is. She was surprised by how calm she felt. As she looked at her son's bright face, she suddenly knew that whatever the future held for them, they would cope.

'Good idea. Shall I guess what you want to eat? Could it be a double cheeseburger with chips and oodles of tomato ketchup, I wonder?'

His big grin said it all.

When Pat left them to order, Miriam slipped her arm around Ollie's shoulders. 'I think you and I must stick together like glue. You, Pat, and I will come up with a plan, just like Baldrick in *Blackadder.*'

Ollie's face lit up in response.

***

By the time they left the pub, the light was fading. They went home in Pat's car, leaving Miriam's where it was. The sky was clear, and it was going to be a cold night. They hurried in, locked the doors, and drew the curtains. The house felt warm and welcoming. For the first time in ages, Miriam felt herself relax.

'Why don't you have a catnap, Mimi? You look done in.'

'I might not sleep tonight if I do. I'll just sit quietly for a bit.' She settled down on the sofa and let her head fall back on a cushion. Despite feeling warm and comfortable, it was impossible to rest completely.

Pat could see that she was still anxious, so she asked her what she was thinking. Because Ollie was sitting on the floor, reading one of his new books, Miriam replied ironically, 'I was thinking, what if Agnes could wave a magic wand?'

Ollie heard her and piped up, 'I don't think Agnes can do that. She's only my guardian. Maybe she has a friend who could.'

'Sorry, Ollie, I was joking. I didn't mean it literally.' She turned to Pat. 'You've given us shelter, and we will always be grateful, but we both know now that it's too risky for us to remain here.' She looked down at Ollie. 'Shall we go away and have an adventure together? Would you like that?'

Ollie grinned; he liked the idea.

Pat was relieved. 'That's a good solution. Take a break. I wish I could come with you. I must stay here, but you can tell me what you're doing, and if you're not too far away, I can come and visit. Now, how about a little bit of tea?'

Despite having polished off an enormous lunch, Ollie wolfed down beans on toast with an egg on top, followed by an apple, a banana, and a large piece of cheese. When he had finished, he took himself upstairs to read his new book.

It was an opportunity to continue their conversation. Pat mused, 'I fear Will may be experimenting with dangerous ideas. It's a good thing Agnes has appeared to protect Ollie. She may always have existed in the old house but only appeared because of whatever Will is doing.'

Miriam gazed at her friend. 'We can only pray that Agnes will protect him from anyone who tries to harm him. And from now on, that includes his father.'

***

They saw the New Year in together. Ollie could barely keep his eyes open, but he was determined to watch Big Ben as it struck twelve. When the firework display had finished, Miriam had to wake him and help him to bed. She and Pat stayed up for another hour.

'Your life is going to change,' Pat murmured, very tired. 'But that's not quite right, is it? It's already changed.'

Miriam could think of nothing to say. She felt numb and lifeless. She kissed Pat goodnight. 'Let's talk about it tomorrow. We both need sleep.'

Chapter 5

Will felt as though he was lying on a bed of warm, slippery mud. When he tried to move, he felt himself sliding. He couldn't get a grip on anything solid. He couldn't open his eyes. He had spent New Year's Eve with the others. When they had retired, he remembered lying down and falling asleep immediately.

Waking, he felt panic taking over and wasn't sure how long he had slept or what day it was. It shouldn't be happening again. It must be a dream. That was it: he was having another hallucinatory dream. Stop. Go with the flow. If it had a beginning, then it would have an end. It was some sort of test. He tried to breathe slowly, but his limbs were contracting. He could hardly breathe. He was going to drown . . .

***

It was a new year, a new beginning, and Miriam was aware that her fear was ebbing. When Ollie had come thumping down the stairs and burst into the room, crying out 'Happy New Year!' and 'Pinch, punch, the first of the month!' Miriam and Pat had not been able not resist his enthusiasm. They had wished each other a happy new year and tucked into a huge breakfast, deciding that they would try as best they could to put any worries aside for the day; and since Ollie was clearly in need of some new clothes, they would go to the January sales.

***

Ollie was kitted out; Miriam's bag was overflowing. 'Can

I borrow your keys, Pat? I'll take this lot back to the car. Ollie, stay with Pat. I won't be long.' Miriam set off for the car park, and Pat called out to say they would wait for her near the library. As they walked towards the centre, Pat stopped to look in a clothes shop window. Ollie could see she wanted to go in, and he wanted to please her, so he promised he would stand outside whilst she had a quick look. However, he soon became bored, and when he recalled how his mother had promised to buy him a penknife, instead of waiting as promised, he strolled down the street, thinking he might see a shop that sold one. He was just thinking about going back when he looked across the road and thought he saw his father. He suddenly wished he could talk to him and explain why he and his mum had to go away. Without thinking of the consequences, he shouted out, 'Dad! Dad! Wait!'

He watched until the road was clear before running over. He could just see his father striding away in the distance. He ran after him, shouting his name, but instead of stopping, Will seemed to pick up speed. Eventually, Ollie found himself running up a road he didn't recognise. He stopped for a moment and looked around. He was alone, and he still couldn't see his father. He decided to walk round the next corner and then, if he couldn't find him, he would turn back. As he did so, he felt his arm being grabbed, and he came to a sudden halt. He looked up into a stranger's face.

The man was wearing what looked like his father's coat buttoned up to the neck, but he wasn't him. This man was taller. His hair was dark, his skin very pale. He had a high forehead accentuated by a short fringe of hair shaped round his face and bushy dark brows over eyes that appeared black. His face looked bony – Ollie could see his cheekbones – and his mouth was thin and mean. Thin wrists and grubby white cuffs poked out of the sleeves of his coat. His tight grasp on Ollie's arm hurt.

He smiled and spoke in a Welsh accent. 'Got you at last, my boyo. I'm taking you to your father.'

Ollie stared up at him. 'Okay, but first you must tell me where he is. What have you done with him?' He felt the man relaxing.

His thin lips parted as he grinned at Ollie, revealing discoloured teeth. 'He's not far away. He's waiting for you.'

Ollie was far more streetwise than his mother could ever have dreamed. With a truly angelic look on his face, he smiled, and as he smiled, he turned and kicked the man between his legs as hard as he could. Doubled over in pain, the man let go of his arm. Ollie ran round him, kicked the man's bottom for good measure, then sprinted back down the road. He heard the man behind him shout, 'I'll get you for that, you little bastard!'

Ollie could hear the man's limping footsteps behind him. He burst out onto the main street and slowed down to a walk as he joined the crowd of shoppers. He spotted a group of teenagers and tagged on to them, but when he looked back, he saw the man was still following. He thought he recognised one of the girls. 'Can you help me? See that man behind us in the black coat? He's trying to kidnap me.'

The three teenagers looked at Ollie. The girl with long blonde hair spoke first. 'Is that man a paedo or something? Look, he's spotted us watching him. He's walking back the other way. You two – follow him at a distance, see where he goes.' Her friends nodded in agreement, crossed over the road, and went off in pursuit.

'Now, young cub. Who are you and what's going on? Spill!'

'I'm Oliver Marshall. My dad's missing, and that man grabbed me. He said he'd take me to my dad. But he was creepy, so I kicked him in the goolies and ran.'

'What a clever, brave cub you are. I'm Sandy. I think I've seen you before. You're the son of my history teacher, aren't you?'

'Yes, I'm Ollie, and I'm not a cub!'

Sandy grinned back at him. 'I reckon you are. But what are you doing in town on your own, Ollie, when there are creepy people like that man out to get you? That sounds risky to me.'

Ollie looked embarrassed. 'He fooled me. He was wearing my dad's coat, so I followed him thinking he was Dad. I've got to get back to the library. My Aunt Pat will be wondering where I am.'

'Okay. I'll come with you and help you find her.' She cuffed his head gently and smiled at him. 'Come on, let's go. My friends will tell us what they find out about the creepy man, then you and your aunty can decide what to do.'

Ollie stopped. 'I don't think I should worry them.'

Sandy looked at him. He reminded her of her brother, always up to some sort of mischief. 'Alright, but if we do find out anything important, I'll make sure I find you.'

They walked up the road until they reached the entrance to the library, where Ollie spotted Pat. When Sandy saw who she was, she broke into a broad smile. 'You didn't say your aunt was Miss James from school!'

Ollie winked at her. 'She's my godmother, but I call her Aunt Pat. Thanks for helping me, Sandy. I won't forget it.'

Sandy looked after him as he ran over to Pat.

Aunt Pat was very stern. 'Where did you get to? Your mother's out looking for you!'

Shamefacedly, Ollie confessed. 'Sorry, I got a bit lost. I thought I'd find a shop that sold penknives, and I forgot the time, then I was up a road I didn't recognise. I had to ask the way.'

Pat raised her eyebrows at his explanation and looked thoughtfully at the teenager who was now walking away. She decided to say nothing. 'I said to your mum that we'd wait for her at the coffee house. I knew you'd come back. But don't do it again! You know how worried she gets. The sooner you two can get away from here, the better.'

She said the same to Miriam once they had found each other. Miriam was so relieved that Ollie was safe that she did not have the heart to scold him. As they got back into Pat's car, Miriam suggested that they drive back via her old house so that she could pick up various papers and other things she would need.

They drove around the block to make sure no-one was watching the house and parked in the adjacent road, near Miriam's car. Visiting the house was depressing: the front porch had already been used to dump empty beer cans. Pat began to clear them while Miriam opened the door. Gone was the familiar homely smell of family living; instead, it smelled damp, stale, and unwelcoming.

Ollie wrinkled his nose. 'It smells of sadness. Can I go up and see my room?'

Miriam collected what she and Ollie needed, whilst Pat, ever practical, busied herself emptying the recycling and the kitchen bin into containers in the back yard. She washed the few mugs left in the sink and cleared away plates. As soon as they were both finished, Miriam called out to Ollie.

He looked dejected as he walked down the stairs. 'Agnes wasn't there. She may not like us leaving.'

Pat put her arm around his shoulders. 'If you need her, she'll find you, don't worry. Don't lose your trust in her, or you might lose your connection.'

Ollie sighed and moved to his aunt's side. As Miriam watched them together, she recognized the strong relationship they had developed. While she had clung to her own ideal of childhood for Ollie, Pat valued him for what he was fast becoming. In that moment, Miriam vowed to herself that while she would find it difficult to let go of her idea of him as her little boy, she would listen more to what he said and stop making assumptions about his age and his abilities.

They shut the front door behind them. Miriam was struck by a profound sense of sadness as she and Ollie turned and walked away. They were leaving their home and everything they knew. They had no idea what might lie ahead. Miriam realised that she could not map their future; it was impossible for her and for Ollie to know what might happen to them in the days ahead.

***

Sandy's two friends had followed the tall man wearing Will's coat: watched as he turned into a small front garden and opened the front door of a house. Of course, they had no clue as to what or who else was there.

'I have told you previously, Brother Oswald. Please knock on the door and wait.' The man looked at Oswald and inquired why he was wearing Marshal William's coat.

Oswald responded uneasily, 'He gave me permission, and I nearly caught the boy. I had him within my reach.'

The man repeated, 'You had him within your reach? What have you done?'

The man addressing Oswald was dressed in a black tunic. A hood obscured his face. He struggled to rise from his chair. Oswald may have been tall and thin, but his superior was even taller. His tunic, which covered his upper body, did not hide the amount of flesh that lay beneath, or a glimpse of khaki twill trousers that tightly hugged his massive thighs and calves. On his large feet, he wore a pair of sheepskin slippers.

He raised his arms, and as he did so, his hood fell back. Long white strands of hair clung to his face. His left eye was unseeing and milky white, while the right eye was deep brown and glowering with rage. His fleshy nose favoured the left side of his face, where the skin appeared puckered, as if it had previously been burned. In contrast, the right side was smooth, accentuating the disturbing difference between the two halves of his face. His lips, although drooping to one side, were red and full, and sneering now as he glared at Oswald.

'Are you telling me you allowed a ten-year-old child to get the better of you? And did you intend bringing him here?' He looked closely at Oswald, who was shrinking away from him. 'You did, didn't you? You were going to bring the child into my home! Why do you think we constructed a secure room for him in the Castle Terrace house? We don't want any trail leading here.'

He glared at Oswald, and when he spoke again, there was no mistaking the anger in his voice. 'What happened?'

'It wasn't my fault,' Oswald whined. 'The marshal was here this morning, seeing Sister Olive. I told him about my plan, and it could have worked. I saw the boy walking around on his own. He was across the road from me. He called out, thinking I was his father, and I walked away as quickly as I could. He followed, and I led him into our road. I had hold of him, but he wriggled away and kicked me.' He reached down to the tender spot still throbbing between his legs. 'Slippery little bastard. By the time I caught up with him, he'd joined a group of youngsters, so I came back here.'

'Were you followed?'

'No, I don't think so. Look, Brother Leofric, I'm sorry. There's nothing to stop me using my own initiative, is there? And the marshal agreed.'

'Oh, for God's sake, stop snivelling. Ring Sister Enid and tell her to bring the car here. Summon our members. We must plan. And Oswald, check with me next time. I'm the leader of this group now. You take your orders from me, not the marshal.'

Oswald hesitated. The idea of Brother Leofric issuing orders was anathema to him, but he said nothing.

Chapter 6
3 January

Before the weekend, Miriam had arranged to see her doctor. She wanted to reassure herself that she had done everything she could to help Will before she left. As she expected, the doctor explained that her hands were tied. Will would have to come to her himself if he wanted help. She listened patiently to what Miriam chose to tell her about her marriage breakup before suggesting she sign Miriam off work with stress.

Miriam felt tears form in her eyes. She had not expected the level of sympathy she received. She had no means of knowing that she was not the first patient to ask for help. The stresses and strains of the Covid outbreak had taken their toll on front-line workers. The doctor understood that if Miriam needed some time off to recover, she should receive her due.

Miriam had some savings, and armed with this extra financial security, she and Ollie trawled the internet together for accommodation. They found a reasonably priced flat in the town of Flint that was immediately available. Flint would be just about far enough from home to help them feel safe, yet it would be easy for them to travel the thirteen miles back to Chester if necessary. By Monday evening, they had somewhere to stay, so tomorrow their new lives could begin.

***

Pat stood at her front door and continued waving until Miriam's car disappeared around the corner. Ollie, who had turned in his seat to wave back, now sat with his face averted, trying to hide his tears. Miriam didn't know how to comfort him. Whatever she said would sound hollow, and she knew that she, too, was at risk of crying. So she leaned over to touch his knee, hoping her action would convey her love and understanding. Ollie watched the GPS on his mother's phone, and Miriam watched the traffic ahead. When they reached the motorway, they made good progress. Ollie called out when their exit was close, and soon they arrived on the outskirts of Flint.

Ollie guided them to their new address, on a main road near the centre of the town. They saw an old three-storey terraced house, its brickwork a dull reddish brown, the downstairs windows grubby from dust thrown up by traffic. They had chosen the flat because it was within walking distance of Flint Castle, which Ollie was keen to visit. Miriam now feared the location would be the only thing in its favour. She suggested they leave their luggage in the car while they found which flat was theirs.

Ollie punched in the code for the front door. The hall was dark and unwelcoming, with brown linoleum on the floor. Miriam located the light, and they saw Flats 1 and 2 on either side of the passage. Two more flats were located on the first floor. They walked up the next flight of stairs and saw their flat, Number 5, straight ahead of them. It was the only flat at the top of the house. Following a tussle with the keypad and with the key in the lock, Miriam turned to Ollie. 'Well, here goes. Fingers crossed.'

She opened the door and reached for Ollie's hand, and they walked in together. It was warm and it was compact. The front door opened straight into the living area. The walls and carpet were blue. There was a round white Formica table in one corner, with two white dining chairs. A blue tweed sofa was lined up in the centre of the room in front of a white dresser, on which sat a small flat television and a WIFI router.

The kitchen space was in the opposite corner, a curved worktop delineating it. Behind the bar, they could see white cupboards housing an oven, a washing machine and a sink. Miriam looked in one of the cupboards and drew out a red kettle and matching red toaster. Another cupboard held four bright-red plates, in different shapes and sizes, and four thick red mugs. A wall cupboard contained four sets of different-sized glasses. The cutlery drawer included four of each utensil, all with red handles. The owner clearly liked bright colours.

A door at the far end of the room led to a large bedroom with twin beds, and beyond that, a small bathroom. Velux windows let light into both rooms.

'A bit small, but it's nice and clean. I guess there's everything we need here for a few weeks.' Miriam endeavoured to show a brave face, whilst Ollie tried not to look unhappy.

But she couldn't disguise the wobble in her voice. 'I'm sorry we had to leave home, love. We're going to miss Chester, but it won't be forever.' She smiled at her son. 'Let's go and get our luggage, set ourselves up, then we can go and do some shopping. We can cook something special for tea. At least it's not raining. Come on, let's see who can get to the car first! Time to explore.'

***

Miriam set them a routine, and the days passed peacefully. They spent some of Miriam's savings on a phone for Ollie, although Miriam felt uneasy about him having one, but she wanted him to be able to contact her when he went out on his own. They rang Pat most evenings. All was quiet in Chester. Pat had the keys to Miriam's house, but as Miriam had redirected her post to Pat's address, there was no need for Pat to go into the property. She had driven past it and noted the curtains were still partially drawn, as she and Miriam had left them. There was no sign of Will.

***

On day eight, Miriam could see Ollie was getting restless. He wasn't used to living in a small flat with just his mother for company. When she said, 'We're lucky to have such good weather. Why don't you wrap up and go out?' She thought he would leap at the chance, but he hesitated. 'You'll feel better after some fresh air. We've been cooped up here for too long. Go and explore the castle again. You may see the boys you made friends with last week. Have a look at the architecture; you might see an interesting feature you haven't found before.'

***

Ollie walked through the inner gatehouse to the green and imagined himself as a Norman knight defending the castle. Lost in a world of his own, he didn't see the boys. It was only when he shaded his eyes to look up that he spotted them sitting at the top of the great tower. They shouted something he couldn't hear. He walked to the bottom of the tower and began to climb the metal spiral steps. It was tall, he thought, maybe fifty feet from the ground. The tower was empty now, as the separate floors and stone stairs had long since crumbled away with time. When he reached the top, he stood and looked across the estuary towards the land on the other side. It was called The Wirral. He liked that word: it rhymed with squirrel.

He looked over to the other side of the tower. The boys were sitting on the edge of the wall. Lewis, the ringleader of their little gang, grinned at him and called out, 'Scaredy-cat, scaredy-cat, what do you think you're looking at?' Identical twins Gareth and Huw joined in the taunting.

He would show them he was no scaredy-cat. They were on the opposite side of the tower, so he would walk along the wall to join them.

They watched in silence as Ollie clambered over the railing. He tested the stones on the wall. They felt solid. He started to walk, but when he looked down, he trembled. The ground was a very long way down. He could just make out the long grass at the bottom of the walls, and despite his growing anxiety, he noticed the grass was a different shade of green where the salt water crept into the ditch at high tide. He stood still for a moment as he felt a gust of cool air on his face, then froze as he heard a sound carried on the wind. It seemed to whisper in his ear, 'Come to me, my little lord.' He began to panic. He felt compelled to jump. He shook his head and cried out, 'Go away!' He felt darkness sweep over him.

A familiar voice broke the enchantment. 'Depart, foul wraith! GET OUT!'

He instantly felt lighter. He let his arms float down to his side and stood very still, eyes closed. The demon had vanished. He became aware of shouting. 'Ollie, you idiot, come here!' Lewis was waving his arms, his mouth wide open. Gareth and Huw stood on the rampart, hands outstretched towards him, beckoning him.

***

Ollie burst through the front door, hurried over to his mother, wrapped his arms around her, and hugged her tightly.

Miriam laughed. 'What's brought this on? I'm pleased to see you too!' She hugged him back, but as he drew back from her, she could see something was wrong. 'What is it, love? What's happened?' She held him at arm's length, concerned with how pale he looked.

'I was walking on the castle wall, and I went all dizzy. It was scary.'

'You mean you were afraid because you were up high?'

Ollie replied. 'I'm not sure. I'm usually OK, but when the wind blew, I heard a voice, and then I felt strange. It was as if the voice was trying to make me jump.'

Miriam drew her son to her and held him tight. Although she was puzzled, she remembered the promise she had made to herself – *Trust what Ollie says; don't make assumptions*. She let him continue without interrupting him.

'Lewis and the twins saw what happened. Afterwards we left the castle and walked through the woods. It felt ancient in there, but there was a good feeling. The castle has too much darkness.'

Startled now, she did interrupt. 'Do you mean the same sort of darkness you felt back in Chester?'

Ollie's face said it all. He was clearly scared. 'I think the darkness found me because I was afraid.'

Miriam felt lost. She knew she couldn't fool her son by pretending to understand. She had to find the right words to show she believed him.

'Ollie, love, be patient with me. I want to understand.' She hesitated. 'I remember something strange happening to me when I was about your age. I was with my father in Avebury. We were in a field of standing stones. I rested my hand on a tall stone, and I told my dad how weird it felt, as though I'd gone back in time. He laughed at me. I could see by his face he thought I was being stupid. I don't want you to ever feel like that.'

Ollie could see his mother was struggling. 'Don't worry, Mum, you never put me down. It's just sometimes you treat me like a very little boy.'

'I'm sorry, Ollie. I know I do it. Just give me a little nudge when you catch me. It only comes from my love. I want you to grow up to be confident and independent, to live your own life, and most of all to be happy. I want you to have good memories.'

'But Mum, not all memories can be good, can they?'

Miriam was startled by her son's insight. It was time she accepted that he was indeed growing up, and growing up to be thoughtful and perceptive. She felt a flash of pride. 'I think we might be able to turn uncomfortable memories into good ones. Just then, when I remembered my father's response to me, I learned something about myself I hadn't thought of before.'

'So, one day, when I think of Dad and the darkness around him, I might understand what's happening now and where I fit in?'

'Let's hope so.' Miriam hesitated, weighing up whether it was the right time to ask him what had happened with his father. She decided it was. 'Are you able to tell me what happened in Chester between you and dad?'

Ollie fell silent. His father had told him things which he said must remain a secret between them. Ollie had kept silent, but since then, all their lives had changed. The time had come for him to tell his mum at least part of what his father had shared.

'It was during the last lockdown. Sometimes when you went into school, I was alone with Dad. That was when he told me how he had made new friends and said I mustn't tell anyone. It was top secret. Only I didn't understand why, and when I asked questions, he'd become angry. That's when I first saw the darkness all around him. It was weird. It was like a dark mist descending on him, and after I had seen it once, it stayed there, all round him. You came back that day and heard him talking in his strange voices. I'm sorry, Mum, I wanted to explain what was happening, but I didn't want to tell on him.'

'What was he trying to teach you?'

'At the beginning, it was all about witchcraft and what he called supreme forces. It was like a Harry Potter story with Voldemort, but worse, because he believed in it. He said he was making it come true. When I asked questions, he shouted at me and turned mean. After that, when you had to go out, I tried to keep away from him, but on Christmas Eve, he shouted at me again, and Agnes appeared. I don't think he could see her.'

Miriam shivered.

Ollie, his small face very serious, continued, speaking softly. 'I don't want us to live with him anymore. He's nasty; he frightens me.'

'Oh, Ollie, I'm so sorry I left you with him. I should

have protected you. I promise we're not going back to him. I don't want us to hide, but I think right now that we must. You felt darkness this afternoon, so whatever that darkness is, it's found a way to us. Before we left, you said Agnes warned you about the 'dark strangers' but said she would protect you. Maybe the best explanation for your feelings in the castle was that the strangers have found us, and maybe they were near you in the castle but you didn't recognise them. We need to leave here, go somewhere where we can feel more secure.'

'Will we have enough money? Perhaps we could do the lottery or something.'

Ollie's idea broke the tension, and Miriam smiled. 'Don't worry, love. We have enough to get by. Let me think about this. We'll have a look on the internet tonight, to see if we can find somewhere else away from here – unless you would rather go back to Pat.'

'No, not Chester. Sorry, Mum, but there's something else I should have told you.'

Seeing how stressed her son had become, Miriam interrupted. 'Is this about the day you wandered off, when you'd promised to stay and wait for Pat?'

Ollie blushed. Perhaps she knew. 'I didn't want to say anything to worry you.'

Miriam left the silence for a bit longer. She used her teacher voice to say, 'I'd much rather know.' Her voice softened. 'So, can you tell me what happened that day? You know your way round Chester. Why did you need Sandy to be with you?'

Ollie explained how he had followed a man wearing his father's coat and how the man had grabbed him and said he would take him to his father.

'Oh, Ollie, the man was going to kidnap you! How did

you get away?'

'I kicked him and ran. He was one of the men Agnes warned me about, so I wasn't going to go with him.' He grinned at Miriam. 'I wasn't afraid, but after I ran, he followed me, and it seemed like a good idea to be with other people, so I found some girls who looked after me.'

Miriam shivered. Her fear for Ollie's safety had just increased a hundredfold. She understood how much she had underestimated him. However, although he might be feisty, he was still a little boy.

Ollie could have been reading her thoughts. 'I'm nearly eleven, Mum, and I'm strong. Please don't worry about me.'

'I think I'll always worry. It's what mums do. But we need to get away from here. It's too close to home, and they may already have found us.' Miriam wasn't at all sure who 'they' were, but she knew that the time had come to move again.

Chapter 7
Chester

Pat was busy checking through paperwork and nearly missed a quiet knock on her front door. She looked up from her task and listened. There it was again. She opened the door and peered out. She was just in time to see a girl with long blonde hair disappearing up the road. She called out, 'Is that you, Sandy?' The girl turned around and walked back towards her. Pat smiled as Sandy came into focus.

'Hello. I'm sorry to disturb you. Can I speak to Ollie, please?'

'I'm sorry, Sandy, he's not here. But you could tell me. Why don't you come in?'

Sandy bit her lip. 'I should really talk to Ollie.' She hesitated for a moment, then followed Pat through into the kitchen.

Pat pointed to a chair, rearranged the papers she was working on, and sat down opposite her former student. 'What's so important that you need to see Ollie?'

Sandy didn't answer straightaway, and Pat could almost see her thoughts whirring around in her head. Eventually, she spoke. 'Ollie didn't tell you and Mrs Marshall, did he?'

'Tell us what?'

Sandy pushed her hair back from her face. Pat thought she really was a very pretty girl, with her tawny-coloured eyes and straight little nose. But she was frowning now, her face screwed up in concentration. 'The day I brought Ollie to you at the library, he had been following a man he thought was his dad. Only when he caught up with the man, the man was wearing Mr Marshall's coat, but he wasn't his dad. He tried to kidnap Ollie, but he managed to get away.'

Pat raised her eyebrows. 'How did a ten-year-old tackle a grown man?'

Sandy looked rather embarrassed. 'It's true, it really is! He's brave. He turned round and kicked the man in the nuts.'

Pat was confused for a moment. 'Oh, I see! Then what happened?'

'The man recovered and was running after Ollie. That's when Ollie came up to my friends and me. We saw the man clearly. He was tall, very pale, and had dark, wispy hair. We thought he was a paedophile, so I asked my friends to follow him. He walked back up the road and disappeared into a house.

'About fifteen minutes later, some people went into the house. Then a silver-grey car pulled up. The driver jumped out, and two of the men came out of the house. They looked around to see if anyone was watching.' Sandy grinned. 'My two friends are very good at concealing themselves. A third man came out. He didn't seem very well, and he stumbled, so the woman who'd been driving took his arm. The other man opened the back door of the car, and the driver helped him in. The man we think was Mr Marshall turned and waved towards the house. He shouted, "See you in Castle Terrace", before he slammed the door and drove off. My friends took some photos, made a note of the address, then came and told me what had happened. Afterwards we thought it was odd that there were so many people coming and going to an ordinary house, so we thought we'd see if the address was linked to an organisation.'

Sandy gazed at Pat as if considering how much to tell

her. She continued in a quiet voice, 'If the man who was helped to the car was Ollie's dad, and he's a member of the organisation, I reckon he could be in trouble. But when I left Ollie, he said he didn't want to worry anyone, and that's why I'm here. I thought at the time he was playing games. But he wasn't. I think this could be deadly serious.'

Pat frowned. 'What did you and your friends find out?'

'The address is linked to an organisation called Family of Hope and Rebirth. It sounds alright, but when we dug further into it, it's weird.'

Pat took her glasses off and looked intensely at the girl sitting opposite her..

'We think it must be some sort of cult. They write about the oneness of humanity and how they'll renew and transform themselves through rebirth. They say on their website that they have "garnered a supreme force that will transcend the past". Their aim is to restore "unity through purpose, making whole that which has been sundered". They don't say what's been sundered, or how they'll restore unity, or what unity is, only that by summoning rebirth, they'll heal the conflicts from the past. We thought they might mean human sacrifice because they say how a blood covenant can rescue us from demons. Then they talk about purity of the blood, and how England is being polluted by the devil's people. It's crazy stuff.'

Pat swallowed back a feeling of panic. 'Have you got the photos you mentioned?'

Sandy felt in the pocket of her jacket for her phone.

After looking at them, Pat sat back in her chair and grimaced. 'It's Mr Marshall alright. I don't know who the others are. They all seem to be friendly enough. He's certainly not there against his will.'

'But Miss James, the tall man in the photo frightened Ollie. Why was he trying to snatch him? Sorry, I shouldn't ask. It's Mrs Marshall's business, not ours.' Sandy hoped Miss James would know what to do. She liked Ollie. She thought he was lion-hearted, a brave little cub. In her opinion, if his father was trying to abduct him against his will, something needed to be done. Mrs Marshall should be told. Her thoughts spilled over into speech. 'And where is Mrs Marshall? Have they split up?'

Pat was startled by the question. She shivered as she thought how close Ollie had been to being snatched. Sandy had mentioned human sacrifice. Was Will really planning to harm an innocent child? She murmured, 'Thank you for coming to warn us.'

Sandy frowned again. She repeated, 'Have Mr and Mrs Marshall split up? Is that what this is all about? I promise we won't say anything.'

Pat contemplated the serious young woman sitting opposite her. 'I don't believe you would. Yes, they have split up, and Mrs Marshall has gone away for a while.'

'I'm glad she and Ollie have got away. I showed my mum the website. She was shocked. I didn't understand why at first, then she told me about Mr Marshall's student Sara – the one who committed suicide. My mum thinks, no matter what was said at the time, that he must have encouraged her. But this website was only set up 18 months ago, when Sara had already passed away.'

Pat took a deep breath. 'I'll go and see Mrs Marshall and Ollie this weekend and explain to them what you have found out so far. Promise me, Sandy, no more digging. We don't know what we're dealing with here. '

Sandy looked across the table at Pat. 'Yes, I promise, and I won't breathe a word about this to anyone.'

Pat's expression was grim. 'One more thing. Can I share the photos with Mrs Marshall?'

Sandy nodded. 'I can forward them to you.' She saw Pat frown. 'It's OK, I'll keep your number secret.'

'Thank you, Sandy. I'm very grateful for the way you looked after Ollie, and I'm sure Mrs Marshall will be too. You said you had discussed the website with your mum. Does she know you've come to see me?'

Sandy stood up. 'Yes, Mum drove me over here. She doesn't like me going out on my own at night. She's outside.'

Pat was relieved. 'I should have asked you before. With your permission, I was going to ring your parents. I'll come out with you and have a chat with her. Then I must finish my preparation for school tomorrow.'

***

Meanwhile, in Flint, Miriam and Ollie were searching the internet, looking for somewhere to go. Miriam's phone pinged. Ollie jumped up. 'It's a text from Pat. She's coming down to see us tomorrow evening. Brilliant. She can help us plan our next move.'

***

The Venetian blinds were drawn, allowing dim light to filter through the slats. Will opened his eyes. He was lying on a beanbag in the middle of an empty room. He moved his head from left to right, right to left, trying to unlock his neck. How long had he been here like this? He remembered leaving Leofric's house and Oswald driving him to the house in Castle Terrace. But surely that was a long time ago? Since then, everything seemed to have gone blank.

He called out, but his call was only met by silence. He tried to move. His head was splitting. He groaned, closed his eyes again, and thought, *I'm nearly there. I can almost taste it*. He heard footsteps approaching. He whispered, 'I must have more. Please, I'm so close now.' He felt his head being lifted.

'I'm here, Brother William. Just relax now. Drink this.'

A glass was put to his lips. He drank all the bitter draft, barely conscious of Sister Olive smiling down at him.

Chapter 8
14 January

Pat was about to leave work when the head walked in and sat down opposite her. 'I understand you're seeing Miriam this weekend. She's a valued member of staff, but you know as well as I do, the school needs stability after the disruptions we've had with lockdowns. I don't wish to sound unfeeling, but she's not the only one with marriage problems. We need to know what her intentions are.'

As deputy head, Pat understood the school's needs, but as Miriam's friend, she also wanted her to have some time to sort her life out. She listened respectfully but said nothing.

On the way to Flint, Pat thought about her conversation with Sandy and the photos she had seen. She thought about Will's fall from grace and the student who had committed suicide. Did Will see himself as a fallen angel? Lucifer, cast out and able to summon demons into his darkness? Maybe it made sense of the last words he had spoken to Miriam, mumbling something about a demon. She grappled with the idea of Will as a fallen angel: Satan, deluded and dangerous. Almost unconsciously, she increased her speed.

As she reached the outskirts of Flint, she spoke out loud. 'I hope Ollie's told Miriam. They can't come back to Chester, not with a mad man out to kidnap him.' She shook her head. The problems seemed insurmountable. If Mimi gave her job up, how would they live? Renting accommodation wasn't cheap. If she decided to sell her house, there would be all sorts of complications with Will. What was he entitled to? How would Mimi pay for lawyers?

She pulled up near their flat and spotted Ollie at an upstairs window. She drove on until she found a parking space, and as she was leaning over to grab her overnight bag, airbed, and sleeping bag, Ollie appeared at her side.

'Aunty Pat, let me help you.' He took her bag from her while she struggled with the airbed, which seemed to have a mind of its own. She stood a pace away from Ollie. 'Let me look at you. I'm sure you've grown at least an inch. How have you been?'

'Good.'

She challenged him. 'Have you? The last conversation I had with your mum was that you were missing your friends.'

'I am a bit. Can I talk to you before we see Mum?' He looked so serious, far too serious. 'I've told Mum I don't want to go back to Chester.'

'Let's take my luggage up, Ollie. There may be quite a lot to talk about, and best to talk with Mum too.'

He nodded, and clutching her bag, led the way through the front door.

By the time Pat had climbed three flights of stairs, she was gasping for breath. 'Is this it? I hope so. You didn't say we had to climb Mount Everest!'

***

Pat and Miriam sat together on the sofa, Ollie on a cushion on the floor.

'Shall I tell you what happened to me in Chester, Aunty Pat?'

Everything he had shared with his mother came out in a rush. He looked shamefaced when he told Pat how he had mistaken the kidnapper for his dad and how Sandy had rescued him. Then he told her how he had felt darkness creeping over him at the castle.

'I don't think I'm a scaredy-cat, but I don't want to go back to Chester, not if Dad's there.' He bit his lip, then said in a quiet voice, 'He's not my dad anymore.'

Pat sighed, 'Oh, Ollie. You've had a hard time keeping secrets. Sandy came to see me yesterday. That's why I'm here. I could have phoned, but I thought we needed to talk it over together. Sandy's friends followed the man who tried to kidnap you. They saw your dad and took some photos.'

She passed her phone to Miriam, who looked at the photos intently, then passed the phone to Ollie. Ollie identified the man who had tried to kidnap him.

His mother looked thoughtful. 'What shall we do now? The man who tried to take you looks as if he's helping your dad, and your dad isn't objecting.'

Pat scratched her head. 'I don't know. I've been thinking about it. I think you have two options: take time out, get far away from here; or go back home, report the attempted kidnap, and start divorce proceedings.'

Ollie's eyes filled with tears. 'I don't want to go home. It's too dark. Please don't make me.'

Miriam reached for him. 'Come here, sweetheart. We're not going home. We'll find somewhere where we can start again.' She looked over at Pat. 'Ollie must be my first priority. I'm going to have to resign. I'm sorry if it's going to be a problem for you and the school.'

'Oh, come on. That's the least of our worries. It's where you're going to go to be safe that's worrying me.'

'I lay awake last night thinking.' Miriam put her fingers under Ollie's chin, tilting his head up to hers. 'Do you remember the holiday you and I once had with my cousin Martin? I could ask him if we can stay for a few weeks, just until I find another job and somewhere for us to live.'

'I remember,' Ollie responded. 'It was Studland, wasn't it? While we were there, we went to Swanage, to an arcade, didn't we? I won lots of tickets, and afterwards we played crazy golf. Yes, please, let's go there.'

'Oh, well,' Pat said. 'Two run wild in Dorset! Enid Blyton eat your heart out! But listen, I've got some other news. Well, it's not news; it's a bit of history. After you two left Chester, I was thinking about your ghost, Ollie. Your description of the dress Agnes wears got me thinking about the people who lived in Chester in the 1600s. I came across a story about a woman called Agnes Howe who lived in Rope Lane, and I think she must be your Agnes. She was born in 1620 and died in 1647. It's a tragic story. She was a widow with a son called Matthew. When Matthew was ten, she married a man called Samuel Howe. It seems Samuel killed Matthew in a fit of jealous rage, and he accused Agnes of being a witch.' She looked over at Ollie and said in a gentle voice. 'They were bad times then. Folk really believed in evil spirits and witchcraft. Samuel Howe spread a rumour that Agnes had killed Matthew during a blood sacrifice.'

Ollie remained silent, so Pat continued. 'People believed witches practised dark arts. Innocent women were used as scapegoats and wrongly accused. Poor Agnes was no exception. She was tried and publicly executed. The story goes that she maintained her innocence throughout and swore revenge.'

'Oh, poor Agnes. She must be so sad.' Ollie frowned. 'She knew I was in danger, and she saved me. I wish we could help her.'

Miriam smiled at his reaction. 'Maybe one day, when we've sorted everything out, love, we'll go back and help her rest. I hope she is your Agnes. It makes sense, doesn't it? After what happened to her own child, she's been protecting you.' She turned to Pat. 'You are clever. Thank you. I'm glad we have a name and a story.'

Pat looked very pleased with herself. 'Come on, you two, enough of the sadness. I'm going to take you out for a meal. I'm starving, and there's only room for two at your table. I daresay there will be room at the inn.' She raised her eyebrows at Miriam, who didn't seem to have got her weak joke, and went on, 'I'm so relieved you've decided. And I'm hoping you will take Agnes Howe to your hearts! Now let's get out of here, gang.'

***

With Ollie in bed, fast asleep, Pat and Miriam talked into the early hours. Pat revealed what Sandy had said about the cult and its aims but decided to say nothing about her anxiety that Will meant to harm Ollie. As they continued to discuss the cult, they thought about how during Covid, people had been drawn to crazy ideas posted on the internet. It wasn't just anti-vaxxers; there had been countless intrigues and irrational notions doing the rounds. They speculated on whether Will had joined the ranks of conspiracy theorists to become the ringleader of a cult, and how he appeared to have cast Miriam in the role of a witch to belittle and threaten her. But Miriam found it hard to imagine Will, who had once been a kind man, being drawn into such a cult. She held onto her belief that he was mentally ill. Help was a word she kept repeating.

'No, Mimi, he would have to want to leave the cult. You won't be able to talk him out of it. It doesn't work like that. You can't rescue him. He's a grown man and must make his own choices. Take time out. Get far away from here. Live a quiet life for a while and then decide what you want to do. I'll keep an eye on things and contact you if I hear anything at all about Will, and I'll see if I can find out any more about this cult.'

Chapter 9
17 January

Miriam and Ollie were packed and ready to leave the flat by 10 a.m. Ollie had mapped the route down to Dorset. It would take about six hours. As a treat, Miriam had booked them a room in a pub near Oxford, where they would stay the night.

Once they were on the motorway, Ollie stopped checking the GPS and appeared to drift off to sleep. In truth, he was thinking. Eventually, he broke the silence. 'Can you tell me some more about your cousin Martin? Why don't I call him Uncle?'

'I suppose he just likes being called Martin. When we were growing up, he was like a big brother to me.'

Ollie thought for a moment. 'I remember Studland. There was a long beach. I was sitting on a pony, and he walked beside me, holding onto the pony's bridle. He was tall, but I can't really remember what he looked like.'

Miriam grinned. 'How can I describe him? He's taller than me. He has dark auburn hair and blue eyes. I've always thought him rather handsome and dashing.'

'What does 'dashing' mean?'

'Daring, I suppose. He likes sailing and mountaineering and the outdoor life.'

Ollie smiled. 'I remember his funny jokes. And he taught me about aeroplanes.'

'Flying is his passion. He works in the aircraft industry in Bristol. Do you remember his girlfriend, Janey? She and Martin shared a flat in Bristol. She came to stay a few times that summer we were last in Studland. She taught at Bristol University but had just started a job in New Zealand before Covid struck. Then New Zealand closed its borders. Martin plans to fly out to see her as soon as the border opens. He's asked us to stay in the house while he's away.'

Ollie wanted to know more about Studland. Then he started to count how many red cars he could see. Eventually, he drifted off to sleep.

Some miles further on, Miriam was not sure where she needed to leave the motorway, so she pulled into a service station. She turned to look in the back seat for a map, and as she did, a silver-grey car pulled up behind them. It looked familiar. She frowned but forgot about it, concentrating on memorising the road they needed to take. A few miles further and she could exit the motorway. She preferred country roads.

Ollie woke up, and they strolled into the services for a comfort break.

She was in the process of washing her hands when she looked in the mirror. A woman had come in. She was short, and her brown hair was styled perfectly, as if she had just come from the hairdresser. She had rosy cheeks and lips painted with red lipstick. Miriam noticed her anorak was open to reveal a generous upper body and recalled the cloaked woman in Chester. She had been wearing pink lipstick then.

Miriam dropped her head over the basin as the woman entered one of the cubicles, then hurried out, drying her hands on her jeans as she went. She looked around for Ollie. Nowhere in sight. She could feel her heart pounding as she began to panic. Then she spotted him looking at books in the forecourt and called, 'Are you ready, love? Let's go. Race you to the car, but mind the traffic!'

Within minutes, they had driven away. No-one

seemed to be following, and Miriam slowed her breathing. She was imagining things. She kept her eye on the mirror, watching for a silver-grey car. Sure enough, she saw it behind her in the distance. She wasn't imagining it. A sign told her that the Oxford exit was a mile away. She kept to a steady speed in the inner lane. The silver car was three vehicles behind. They were almost upon the exit she wanted. She kept her nerve, making it look as though she was going to drive on, then at the last minute, she swerved, taking the exit at speed.

'Mum. That was bad. You got beeped.'

'I know, I'm sorry, love.' She was shaking and felt sick. She saw a layby, indicated, and began to brake. 'I'm afraid we were being followed. When we stopped at the services, I spotted one of the strange people who came to the house in Chester. It took me a while to remember that photo of Will being picked up in a car, a silver-grey car, and a silver-grey car has been following us. It pulled in behind us at the motorway services. I saw them a mile or so from our turn-off. That's why I took this road at the last minute so it would be too late for them to follow us. I'm sorry I frightened you. I sure frightened myself!'

Ollie stared at his mother. 'They must have followed us from Flint. What shall we do now?'

'The pub we're going to isn't far from here. We'll drive straight there and tuck the car away – keep our fingers crossed they won't spot it. Then we'll watch for a while to make sure we've lost them. They'll probably take the next exit off the motorway. Let me just have a look at the map.'

Miriam looked at the route. It was a main road, so they could be going anywhere in the area. She pointed at the map. 'This is the route we'll take. Let's hope luck is on our side. Hold on, Ollie! I'm not going to hang around; we need to get out of sight.'

They were in a line of fast-moving traffic when they spotted the pub Miriam had booked, The Doghouse. They had no option but to pass it, and at the first opportunity, Miriam turned into a farm entrance, reversed, and drove back at a slower speed. The pub was a little way back from the road, with several free parking spaces in front. Miriam ignored them and drove round the back, tucking the car in between a large white van and a red estate car. Their green VW was well concealed.

They checked in and went upstairs to find their room. It was an airy twin room looking out over open fields. 'Let's go downstairs, Ollie, and see if we can get something to eat.'

The dining room was quiet. They ordered and found a table in an alcove where they couldn't be seen from the entrance. Despite their ordeal, they were both ravenous.

'Now we know for sure, Ollie – they really are looking for us. They haven't given up. But how did they know where we were?' Miriam frowned. 'Either, as we suspected, they already knew, or they followed Pat.'

'Or maybe it was the demon at the castle. I heard the voice, then Agnes came and told it to get out.'

Miriam looked up. Although she had not intended it, her response was sharp. 'I've told you, Ollie. You mustn't hide things. It's important you tell me everything. Otherwise, how can I protect you?'

'Sorry, Mum. I didn't want to worry you. I was happy Agnes was there with me; I thought I'd lost her. But I guess the more sensible explanation is they followed Aunty Pat when she came to visit us. It was your skill at driving that lost them.'

She grinned. 'In a way, it doesn't matter how they found us. The important thing is that we know we must look out for them. I'm glad we're here in one piece, and I'm glad your Agnes is still looking out for you, but now we need to lie low, just in case. Martin's not expecting us until tomorrow afternoon, so we can have a nice, relaxed breakfast and leave when we're ready. We'll stick to side roads as much as we can. Once we get to Martin's, we'll be safe.'

***

Oswald, the driver of the silver-grey car, swore. He carried on swearing for some time. His wife, Enid, sitting beside him in the passenger seat, pursed her lips. 'There's no need for that, Oz. I told you: you should have got closer to them.'

Oswald growled back at her, 'You didn't say anything of the sort. If you hadn't had your nose in that fucking phone, we may not have lost them.'

'Oh yes, blame me, why don't you?' Enid's sing-song voice rose to a crescendo. 'And stop swearing at me.'

To his credit, Oswald apologised. 'Okay, let's take the next exit and double back. I don't think they knew we were following. The silly bitch just missed her turning.' He was about to let out another string of expletives, but when he looked at his wife's face, he just muttered, 'Women drivers!'

Enid raised her eyebrows. 'No comment. Anyway, what does Leo expect? We're not detectives.'

'Whatever he expects, he's going to be furious. We can't fail again. Just pray luck is on our side and we catch up with them. They could be heading for Oxford or carrying on towards the South.'

They drove on for some miles, watching all the time for a small green VW. They slowed down as they passed through villages. It was past lunchtime. They pulled into several pub car parks, searching for the green VW, but by now, they were getting tired and even more disgruntled. They stopped in the front of The Doghouse pub, gave it a cursory glance, then drove off again.

'This is useless. They could have gone anywhere. I'm hungry; we'll stop in the next place we see and eat. Then you can ring Leo.'

Enid glared at Oswald. 'Why me? You're the one that lost them. You do it.'

'Don't start again, Enid. We both lost them.'

They sat in silence, not knowing that they were heading away from their target.

They stopped at the next pub and had something to eat, then Oswald rang Leo from the car while Enid used the Ladies. He held the phone away from his ear, glad that he was not in the same room as Leo. His friend had a temper, and he certainly showed it now. If Enid thought *his* curses were bad, she should listen to Leofric, the leader of their group.

'How many times have you let them slip through your hands? Just get back here. Go to the safe house; the marshal trusts Enid. Tell her to ask him if he has any idea where they might head. Then get back here with some answers.'

Oswald thrust his phone back into his pocket and started to bang his right fist repeatedly on the steering wheel. He stopped, let out a deep sigh, and rubbed his hands together. He moaned, 'I've had it with this play-acting. Who the hell does he think he is? I'm out of here.

Where's my wife? Why does she always take so much time in the toilet? Bloody woman! Gets on well with the marshal, my arse! Of course she does, always creeping around him.'

He was still muttering to himself when Enid walked out of the pub entrance. Oswald glared at her. 'I hope you're satisfied with yourself. I've just had to listen to one of Leo's tirades. He's told us to get back. You must talk to the marshal. Hurry up, woman.'

'Leo's got you in a good mood, then.' Enid laughed at his frustration. 'Oh, let's go along with Leo's game. Back into the world of make-believe – *Brother* Oswald.'

She grinned at him, and despite himself, his good humour returned. He chuckled. 'Right you are, *Sister* Enid.'

They hit Chester right on rush hour, crawling through the centre and arriving at the Castle Terrace house just after 6 p.m. They opened the front door to an eerie silence and walked from room to room before they found Will curled up on a camp bed upstairs. Enid squatted down and spoke softly. 'Brother William, it's us. We're back. I'm sorry we've been so long. We lost them on the motorway. They headed off towards Oxford.' She shook him. 'Come on, now, wake up. Did you hear what I said? We lost them heading off towards Oxford. Do you know where they could be going?'

Will opened his eyes and stared at Enid. He looked puzzled, as though he had no recollection of who she was.

She took his hand. 'Come on, Brother William. It's me, Enid. Listen to what I'm saying.'

He clutched at his head. 'Get me a drink. I'm so dry. My head's splitting.'

Enid turned to Oswald. 'Go on, Oz, make yourself useful. Get some water.'

Will sighed and struggled to sit up. 'You lost my son near Oxford? The address book. I must go back to Rope Lane.' He grimaced. 'Oh, my head! Ring Sister Olive. I need something for my headache first. I can't think.'

Enid contemplated the man they called the marshal. When they had first encountered him, he was glamorous, energetic, full of ideas. He inspired them to become part of the Family of Hope. Back then he was father to them all, that is until Olive got her hands on him and he began to take drugs. Olive said they would aid his journey to self-realisation. Because of her meddling, he was no longer the patriarchal, messianic figure they had followed. Now they were stuck with Leo bossing them around. 'Let's get you home, then. I'll ring Sister Olive. She can meet us there.'

Oswald handed Will a glass of water. His hand trembled as he lifted the glass to his mouth. He drank the whole glass, tipping it back with both hands. 'I need Sister Olive now,' he rasped.

Oswald regarded Will with disgust. 'We'll leave immediately. I'll help the marshal out to the car. Enid, you ring Olive.' He squatted down, eye to eye with Will. 'Think you can manage that?'

Enid jerked round. 'Don't talk to the marshal like that! Come on, Brother William. Let me help you up.' She glared at Oswald. 'Remember our place in this. You must show respect.'

Will sat in the back seat, his head lolling forward. As Enid leaned over and fastened his seat belt, he whispered, 'Her cousin. She may be travelling south to him.' He let his head slump forward again.

They parked in front of Will's house, helped him out, and stood with him while he unlocked the door. He walked unsteadily towards a dresser in the hall and opened the drawer, throwing bits of paper, Post-It notes, old coupons and pens onto the floor. 'It's not here. She's got it.' He staggered towards the stairs, pulling himself up using the banister. Enid followed him into a double bedroom. He sat on the bed, then with a sigh, lay down. 'I've told you; I need Sister Olive now. I'm so tired. My head's bursting.'

'She's on her way.' She tried to get his attention. 'Please think. Is there anywhere else we can search? Anything you might remember?'

Will opened one bloodshot eye. Since his search for truth had begun, his face had become skeletal, his bone structure in sharp relief, his skin deathly pale. 'Go away. Leave me alone.' He turned away from her to face the wall.

Enid covered him with a duvet and went downstairs to fetch a jug of water. She tiptoed back into the bedroom and laid it on the bedside table. They waited until Olive appeared and left, closing the door behind them.

Oswald sat in the driver's seat and slammed his door. His wife sat down beside him. 'What's the matter now?'

'I've had it up to here.' He reached up and struck his brow. 'Enough of this play-acting, kowtowing to *the marshal*. It's ridiculous. He's just a man called Will, with crazy ideas. I've had enough. You mark my words; he's gone too far. He and Leo will destroy the lot of us. We should get out now, while we can.'

'You know we can't leave the group, Oz. Not yet. We must stick with it. We agreed, we must find what we're looking for. We can't do it on our own, and besides, we're in too deep.' She shrugged her shoulders, and in a voice that clearly mocked, muttered, 'Maybe all will come to pass as the marshal pronounced.' She gazed at her husband. 'In all seriousness, we can't leave now. You know what happened to Harold.'

Oswald looked askance. 'What do you mean, what happened to Harold? That was an accident.'

'My dear, you are so innocent sometimes. Look, let's just toe the line: ride it out.' She winked at him and murmured, 'It can't last. We will get what we want, and that unholy trio – Will, Leo, Olive – they'll get what they deserve, you mark my words.'

Chapter 10

Miriam and Ollie had had a peaceful evening in the pub, and now Ollie was asleep in the twin bed beside her, his breathing even and steady. Anyone looking on them might assume Miriam was calm, but just like a swan floating serenely on a lake with its feet beneath the surface, Miriam was paddling furiously. She felt out of control and desperately lost. Although she knew it might lead to a sleepless night, she searched for The Family of Hope and Rebirth on the web. She shivered at what she read. The words *transformation* and *blood covenant* leapt out at her. Pat was right. It had all the hallmarks of a death cult, and Will could be the ringleader. She shut her laptop, not wanting to read any more.

Instead, she began to daydream about their honeymoon in Wales. She had been happy then, and Will had been loving and attentive, but he was so youthful, and his ideas could make him euphoric. She would tease him and gently bring him back to reality. She had a vivid memory of them standing on Pembroke Castle green, arm in arm. He pretended he was *the* William Marshal, Earl of Pembroke. She was his lady, the Lady Isabel de Clare. Afterwards, they spent hours scouring bookshops in the town for local history.

He was sweet, and it was fun making up stories together. She had thought of it as his dreamworld, made of dungeons and dragons. But maybe it was no longer a game to him; it had become real. He had lost his job because he had been conducting private research into ancient beliefs and his young student had committed suicide. It was too much of a coincidence. It made sense of the words on the website – *summoning rebirth by transcending the past.* Something ancient, something pure. What was he trying to do and why? And why did he want Ollie?

When she was pregnant, he was convinced the baby would be a boy. After their son's birth, the passion he had once had for her seemed to vanish. Their relationship became one of friendship, until he had lost his job and she had lost her trust in him.

When news began to leak out about a deadly virus sweeping a faraway city in China, he acted as though it was Armageddon. Despite her protestations, he insisted they stockpile necessities, adding to the mounting chaos in their home. Inevitably, global travel allowed the virus to escape, so it arrived unbidden just about everywhere in the world. Hundreds of people were dying every day, and Will became fanatical about keeping safe. Lockdowns came and went, vaccines were discovered, yet his obsession with death was unabated.

As she lay in bed thinking, it dawned on her that his fear might have arisen because he didn't want to die before he had fulfilled his destiny. The wording on the Family of Hope and Rebirth website could have been written by him. And he wanted Ollie: Ollie, who had once trusted and loved Will, until his father had so frightened him. Miriam looked at Ollie again. She felt paralysed by the growing realisation that her husband was dangerous and almost certainly insane.

Her thoughts turned to Ollie's ghost. Pat believed Agnes Howe existed, perhaps had even lived in or near Miriam's house. Poor Agnes, burned as a witch in 1647, wrongly accused of causing the death of her son. Miriam had bought the house because she had fallen in love with it. At the time, it was run down yet comfortable – an old, friendly house with its own history and personality. She had thought it was a good place to raise a child.

But the house began to change. Will complained that she moved his papers, although she knew that she hadn't touched them. Eventually, they converted a downstairs bedroom into a study for him, and he began to spend all his time alone. She could not remember the last time he had spent a night with her.

And Agnes, had she always been in the house, only materializing when Ollie became troubled by Will's behaviour? Of course, Agnes would never have trusted Will. She must have sensed he meant harm. It was history repeating itself, and Agnes meant to stop it. She whispered to herself, 'Thank you, Agnes. I'm sorry I doubted you. Please stay close and protect my son.'

She tossed and turned, and sometime in the early hours, she fell into a troubled sleep.

***

She felt a hand stroking her hair and woke with a start.

'It's okay, Mum, you're just having a dream.' Ollie sat on the bed beside her, a worried frown on his face. 'What was it about?'

Miriam felt as though she was in a different reality, her dream still alive within her.

'It's alright, Mum, I want you to tell me. It might help us understand.'

Miriam was shaken. Her face wore a hint of revulsion. 'I was dreaming of your dad. He was lying face down on something dark, maybe earth. No, it was mud. It was soft under my bare feet. I don't know how I knew it was him, but I did. I leaned over and touched his shoulder, thinking he was dead. He moved, but as if in agony. His face was white, his eyes almost black. They pierced mine. I felt excruciating pain. I tried to close my eyes, to shut him out, but I couldn't. I was rooted to the spot, so I tried to turn my face away. I heard him laughing; he was laughing at me. That's when I woke.'

She put her head in her hands, and when she looked up, she had tears in her eyes. 'I know it wasn't real, but it felt real.' She sighed. 'It was just a nightmare. I shouldn't have told you.'

'Mum, of course you should. You want me to tell you everything, so that's what you should do with me too. Dad's in a dark place, and we can't do anything about it. I think Agnes is somewhere close by him. She was in my dreams last night, but she's not here with us. I don't think Dad knows where we are; that's what she wanted me to know. But we've not really escaped his darkness.'

They stared at one another. Miriam reached out for Ollie's hand and squeezed it. They sat quietly, both deep in their own thoughts.

Some minutes later, Ollie broke their silence. 'I'm quite hungry, Mum.'

Miriam glanced at her watch. 'Oh my goodness, it's nearly 9! We'd better throw some clothes on and go down for breakfast. They finish serving at 9.30.'

By 11.00 they had packed their small overnight bag and were ready for the road again. They drove off, somehow feeling lighter despite Miriam's dream.

Ollie, who rather liked *Wind in the Willows*, sang in what he thought might be a toady voice, 'Parp, parp, we're on the open road and ready for an adventure!'

Miriam smiled at him. 'Yes, I think we are. We're going to get on with our lives. I thought we could go via

Wareham. It's a nice old town. We can have some lunch there, perhaps drop into Corfe Castle, then we should reach Studland by five. Martin has promised to be home by then.'

***

Will woke from his dreamlike state. He had encountered Miriam in his dream, but he couldn't reach Ollie. She had stood in the way, protecting their son. Next time he would find him. He reached for his water glass. It was empty, as was the jug of water Enid had left him. He struggled to sit up. He felt weak, his head still pounding. Dressed in pyjamas and dressing gown, he swung his legs out of bed, his bare feet touching wood before he gradually forced himself to stand upright. He stumbled out to the landing. Despite keeping a firm hold on the banister, he nearly fell as he began to descend the stairs. By leaning his back against the wall in the hallway, he managed to slide himself crablike towards the kitchen, found a glass, ran the tap, then gulped the water down. Within seconds he choked and vomited the water back. He breathed deeply and tried again, this time sipping the water. It stayed down. He found a packet of cookies on the worktop and started to chew on one. It was stale, but he continued to grind it between his teeth. He tried to swallow but began to choke. He spat the mess out onto the floor.

He leaned over the sink again, ran the tap, and splashed his face with water. His skin felt foreign to his touch, his chin rough. He grimaced at his own smell. How long was it since he had washed and shaved? No matter, none of it would matter soon. He turned and leaned back against the sink, then slowly slid down to the floor. This would not do. He must ring Sister Olive. He was so nearly there; it was within his grasp, almost tangible. He crawled out of the kitchen to the hall table and reached for the phone.

***

Miriam and Ollie arrived in Wareham in the early afternoon. She saw a sign for a public car park and drove in. Despite Ollie's reassurances that they were no longer being followed, she parked at the far end, between two high-sided vehicles.

It was one of those rare winter days when the weather felt almost springlike. A gentle south-westerly breeze blew wispy white clouds across a blue sky. She took a deep breath of the cold, fresh air. 'I would have been a bit younger than you are now when my father told me about these walls.' She pointed at what looked like a man-made grass embankment in front of them. 'Look, those grassy mounds are what's left of the Wareham Walls. It was once a Saxon settlement. I think the walls may have been built at the time of Alfred the Great because of the Viking threat.'

Ollie spotted a path winding up the grass embankment and ran to the top. He looked around, shaded his eyes with his hand, and shouted, 'I can't see any Vikings. Alfred must have chased them away!' He laughed and ran back down, stopping to look at a display board. 'Yuck! Come and look at this. This is called the Bloody Bank. They've got a drawing of severed heads.'

Miriam joined him. 'That was another time. They were the Duke of Monmouth's men. There was a rebellion against King James in the late 1600s. James was the brother of Charles II, and heir to the throne, but he was Catholic. The Duke of Monmouth, a Protestant, tried to take the throne. He was defeated, and so all those poor men who supported him were put to death.'

Ollie looked back at the picture. 'I'm glad we can't travel back in time. It was very nasty then.'

'Yes, it was brutal. People were tried in courts – these men were tried in the Dorchester Assizes. But today, if people do something very wrong, they're put in prison. Come on, let's walk over to the river and find somewhere to eat.'

They strolled down the road and crossed over, walking as far as the bridge so they could look upriver. From there, they could see boats moored along the bank. They wandered down to the quay. On their side of the river, they had a good view of the magnificent old bridge, with a causeway over the flood plain on the other side.

Two people sat on a bench eating a picnic. Ducks waddled around them, hoping for food. Miriam pointed at the pub at the far end. 'That looks nice. Let's go and get a snack.'

Whilst they waited for their order, Ollie asked his mother for more stories. She recounted what she remembered about King Stephen and the Empress Matilda and how Matilda's men had been besieged in Corfe Castle by King Stephen's men. Ollie's eyes shone with excitement. 'We're surrounded with history here.'

Miriam ruffled his hair. 'Yes, everywhere we go, our history goes before us.'

Their sandwiches arrived, and when Ollie had finished, he fired more questions. 'How come you were here with your dad? Did your dad like history too?'

Miriam shook her head. 'The house Martin lives in now used to belong to our grandparents. They had two children, my father and his brother Stan, Martin's dad. They were both born and brought up in the village. Then when Martin and I were small, we used to come and stay with Granny and Grandad. We had our summer holidays and Christmases at their house. My dad was an engineer, but he loved history. He died before I got my history degree, but I think he'd have been proud and happy with my choice.'

She reached over for Ollie's hand. 'I'm glad we're here. It's a bit like coming home for me. When our grandparents died, Martin inherited the house, and I inherited some money and had just been offered a job in Chester. That's how I came to buy our house. I used my grandparents' inheritance. You know what came next. I married your dad, and we had you, and no doubt we would still be living together in Chester if ...' Her voice tailed off and she sighed. 'Maybe one day we'll understand. I'll just go and pay for our lunch, then we had better make tracks.'

They drove through Studland village, turned off, and carried on down a long tarmac road until she reached a rutted lane, where she slowed down to avoid the potholes. She stopped in front of a green gate. Swallow Lodge had been built in the 1930s. It was painted cream, with a flat roof and large windows giving it an art deco look. It was encircled by a neatly trimmed yew hedge. The gates were open, so they drove in and parked on the drive. A magnificent magnolia tree stood in the middle of a mossy lawn. Underneath the tree, snowdrops were in flower, and together with purple cyclamen, they made a carpet of colour.

They walked up the uneven stone path towards the front door. Miriam reached out for the knocker, and as she did, the door was flung open.

'At last! Here you are.' Martin was tall, his dark auburn hair held back in a ponytail, and he held his arms out wide to gather them both to him. He hugged them, then stood back. 'Miriam, you look as beautiful as ever. And you, young Oliver – how you've grown! I haven't seen you since you were a young sprog this small.' He held his hand close to the ground, then laughed. 'I can see you're growing into a fine young man. Come on in.'

They followed him into the hall, where he took their coats and hung them up. It was evidently the place to dump boots and bags. Ollie asked his uncle whether he should take his shoes off, but Martin shook his head. 'No need. Shoes off only if you've been walking on the muddy moor. Sorry, it's a bit chaotic in here.' He picked up a rucksack and hung it on a peg, a sheepish grin on his face. Miriam reached out and squeezed her cousin's arm. 'I'm glad you haven't changed. This house was never meant to be a showcase. It was always a home. I remember our granny scolding Grandad for being untidy, but she never meant it'.

Martin's blue eyes shone with pleasure at the memory. His face was plumper than Miriam recalled, and he seemed heavier than when she had seen him last. He was dressed in a navy-blue Guernsey sweater and navy walking trousers, his feet slipped into a pair of bright yellow crocs. He noticed Miriam looking at his feet and grinned. 'They're practical, my love.'

As he listened to the two of them, Ollie felt himself relax. Even though his mother had done her best to be cheerful, she had been constantly on edge. He smiled to himself as he followed them out of the hallway and into a large kitchen.

Miriam gazed around. 'Gosh, this has changed. It's modern!'

Martin grimaced. 'Yes, it's a long story. I miss the old Rayburn, but Janey said she wanted all the mod cons if she was going to live here. Then she buggered off to New Zealand.' He covered his mouth with his hand. 'Sorry, beg your pardon, excuse my language. What I should have said was, before she took herself off.'

'It's okay, Ollie's not that innocent!' Miriam giggled. 'I guess it makes life easier for you, and you always enjoyed cooking. I can smell something delicious. What are we having?'

'The fatted calf, of course!' He looked at Ollie's face. 'No, I don't mean that literally. It's a nice organic free-range chicken roasting away. There'll be roast potatoes, vegetables and lots of gravy. Oh, I suppose I should have asked, but you do both eat meat, don't you?'

Miriam nodded. 'We both love chicken, and it's kind of you to cook for us.'

He grinned at her. 'Let me show you your bedrooms. Then we can fetch your luggage and settle you in.'

After dinner, Ollie went upstairs to get ready for bed. Before he drew the curtains in his room, he stared outside at the darkness. His room overlooked the back garden, and there were no lights he could see, but the windows at the front overlooked the bay. He had stood in the hallway at the top of the stairs and watched a ship make its way towards Poole Harbour, its lights shining brightly in an expanse of dark sea. It was a clear night, and he could just make out outlines of buildings on the other side of the bay. The moon looked as though it was waxing. It would soon be full. He thought how his father was somewhere underneath the same moon as him. He shivered, remembering him.

***

Miriam and Martin cleared the table and sat down with their coffee. Martin began to talk about Janey, how he was missing her and felt abandoned. Although she had assured him her contract was for eighteen months, he was convinced that she wanted to make a life in New Zealand.

'I need to see her. I'm just waiting for the New Zealand borders to open, then I'll book my flight. We were together a long time, and I miss her; and I want to know she's happy. We both own the flat in Bristol. I'm hoping she'll agree to sell.' He sighed. 'I've been reconsidering my life. I've decided to find a job closer to home. I don't mind what I do. If I learned one thing during the pandemic, it's that life can so easily be cut short, just like that.' He snapped his fingers. 'I yearn to be content in myself. I'm fed up with commuting up and down to Bristol. I don't want to be trapped in the rat race for the rest of my life.'

Miriam took a sip of coffee. 'We're both going to be looking for new jobs, then.'

Martin frowned. 'I think you'd better tell me what's been going on. Have you left Will?'

It took all of Miriam's courage to describe again why she and Ollie had fled. Martin didn't interrupt. He sat with a grim expression on his face. When she had finished talking, he got up from the dining table and opened a cupboard, from which he drew out a bottle of brandy and two glasses.

'That's an extraordinary story. You say you were followed from Flint by members of a cult who you think are trying to abduct Ollie.' He walked over to Miriam, handed her a glass, and sat down opposite her, warming his glass in his hands. He avoided eye contact, looking down at his glass.

Miriam remained silent. Her hands were shaking, so she put her glass down in front of her. She wasn't sure now whether Martin believed her. She didn't blame him for his reaction, but she wanted comfort. He still avoided her gaze. She brushed away the tears in her eyes.

Eventually, Martin sipped his brandy and looked up. 'This cult, you say it's something to do with being reborn. What's Will intending to do?'

'I don't know. But you understand now why I had to get Ollie away. Tonight was the first time I've seen him looking really relaxed.'

'But Miriam, Will isn't stupid. He'll guess where you are. It's only a matter of time. It's not safe for you here, particularly as I'm probably going to travel to the other side of the world.'

Miriam dropped her head. She looked up as tears flowed down her cheeks.

Martin sighed, got up, walked around the table, and put his arm around her. 'Let's go and sit in the lounge. Come on.'

He helped her up, and with his arm still round her shoulders, took her into the lounge, a room which was so familiar to her. There was the same picture of Old Harry Rocks hung over the mantlepiece; the same chintz-covered chairs and sofas were lined up in a semi-circle round the open fireplace. He led her to one of the sofas and sat beside her.

'I may seem unfeeling, and I'm sorry if I've upset you. But you know I'm right, don't you?'

She pulled away from him and nodded in agreement. 'I promise we won't stay long, Martin, but being here will give us some thinking time, and Ollie needs some stability. I think he misses Will, despite everything that's happened. I can only give him so much reassurance, and lately he's been trying to reassure me. We need a calm head and some good advice.'

'Drink your brandy, my love. You and I always made a good team, and I think I know the very place for you to go. Trust me. It's going to be alright.'

***

A few miles away in Swanage, Martin's friend, Caitlin Rose, had failed to hear her phone ring, and it was only after she had taken her daughter Kirsty to school that she saw she had missed his call. Even then she did not ring him back immediately because, as so often happened, when she opened the front door of her home, her eyes were drawn to the stairs, where the man who had tried to kill her many years ago had fallen to his death. Sometimes she could bury the memory of it, but she had had a restless night, plagued by a recurring dream of a ringmaster making her dance to his tune.

In those days, there had been an antique mirror at the top of the stairs. When the man had fallen, the mirror had fallen too and shattered on the tiles below. She had replaced it with a modern full-length mirror which now hung near the front door. She turned and looked up to where the old mirror had hung, reflecting in its time countless images of the people who had lived in Rock

House and who were now gone.

She turned back to study her own reflection. She saw a tall, slim woman. Her hair, which had once been dark, was now silver. She kept it short and swept back from her face. She looked pale this morning. She stared at herself. Her eyes were her best feature. Remarkable blue eyes, someone had once said. She had tried to conceal the dark shadows under them, but she couldn't disguise how tired she looked. She smiled at herself. 'Come on woman, pull yourself together. You've got things to do and places to be. But coffee first!'

She strode into the kitchen and switched on the coffee machine, then settled down at the old pine table and picked up the newspaper. Her phone rang. 'Morning, Martin. Sorry, I meant to return your call. How are you?'

She listened for several minutes, a smile slowly spreading across her face. 'Of course I'll help. The flat's empty now. Sally's away, enjoying some winter sun. She'll be back next Saturday. I'd love to meet Miriam and Ollie. Maybe Miriam and I could have a chat in private, then when Sally's back, we could all have Sunday lunch. We can make a party of it. It's just what I need.'

PART 2

Chapter 11
Chester
24 January

A woman on a bicycle rode up to Miriam and Will's house, dismounted, and propped the cycle against the front wall. Olive Lander was an imposing figure: five feet nine inches tall, with a muscular body beginning to turn to fat. She wore a belted black rain jacket, dark trousers and heavy black lace-up shoes. A scarf was tied round her head, and on top of the scarf perched a red cycle helmet. When she took the helmet off, the long red pashmina-style scarf was revealed. She threw each end of the scarf over her shoulders before bending over to attach a lock and chain to her bicycle. Then she tucked her helmet under her left arm, reached into a wooden box on the back of the bike, and picked up a dark brown leather bag. She pulled out a set of keys from her jacket pocket and opened the front door.

She shivered. It was a cold winter's day, but the temperature inside the house was several degrees colder than outside. She looked on the floor for post, but as usual, there was none, just a few leaflets advertising local services. She called out, but there was no response. The house was eerily silent.

She was no stranger to the house. Unknown to Miriam, Olive had been inside many times before. She left her helmet on the hall table and looked around the downstairs rooms before ascending the stairs. She expected to see Will in bed, but he was slumped on a chair, looking out of the window.

'You took your time.' His voice was feeble.

She stood and stared at him. Her eyes glinted behind purple framed spectacles. She reached up and pulled her scarf from her head, dropping it on the bed. When she turned round, her face radiated kindness, tinged with expectation and twisted pleasure.

The contrast between them was stark. Whereas Will's face, with its dark stubble, was almost a death mask, Olive's was rosy cheeked and full of life. 'How are you, my lord? I see you managed to go downstairs. We should get you into bed now, before you have your brew.'

She leaned over and grasped his arms, almost carrying him over to the bed. She looked at the bedclothes with distaste. They smelled of his unwashed body. She shook her head, unsure what to do. Her instinct should have been to wash him and change the bed, but now all she felt was revulsion. She must leave him as he was. When it happened, it must look natural.

He grimaced as she removed his dressing gown and helped him lie down. Once his head settled on the pillow, she pulled the grubby duvet over his emaciated body. 'I'll fetch some more water. I won't be a moment.'

He sighed and lay still.

When she returned, he was lying with his eyes half-closed, looking strangely calm. He endeavoured to smile, but his dark eyes showed desperation, the eyes of an addict in anguish. Olive poured him a glass of water and helped him sit up, telling him to sip slowly. His eyes never left her as she opened her bag and took out a syringe. She drew up clear liquid from a bottle, then smiled at him. 'Easier this way, lord.' He nodded his head as she rolled his pyjama sleeve up.

Will shut his eyes and lay back on the pillow. Olive

sat beside him, holding his hand until he slipped into unconsciousness. When she withdrew her hand, she leaned over to touch his head, smoothing his dark hair back from his face.

She sat very still and watched him. He looked at peace. She was tired herself and could have fallen asleep if it hadn't been so cold. Shivering, she shook herself awake, reached for her bag, and walked out of the room, glancing back once more before she descended the stairs. She picked up her helmet from the hall table and went out, locking the front door behind her.

As she put her helmet on, she realised her head was bare. No matter, she would pick her scarf up next time. She glanced around to see if anyone was watching her, but the road was deserted.

* * *

Two days later, the morning was clear and cold, so Olive delayed leaving home until the early morning frost had melted. Just as before, she rode up to the house, dismounted, and left her bicycle propped against the wall by Will's front door. She grasped her bag and reached in her pocket for the front door key. As she did so, a woman walked by, pulling a tartan shopping trolley. She stared at the extraordinary sight of Olive, dressed entirely in black, hair covered in a bright blue scarf with a red bicycle helmet perched on top. That woman would remember Olive's pasty, moon-like face with its large pair of purple spectacles. As Olive disappeared into the house, the woman stopped and stared at the closed front door. She shook her head in puzzlement, wondering who the strange people were going in and out of Miriam and

Will's house. She decided it was none of her business, and putting it out of her mind for now, crossed the road to enter the path leading to the canal. She saw her neighbour sitting on a bench and went over to join him.

Meanwhile, Olive did her usual circuit. She checked the kitchen, Will's study, dining area and front room. Then she took off her helmet, folded her blue scarf with concentrated precision, and placed it inside her helmet. She went back into the front room and peered out of the window. No-one there. It was a pity she had arrived so late and been seen.

She had left Will alone for two days, with hardly a thought for his welfare. Her step slowed as she began to climb the stairs. She stood on the top landing, listening for any sound. There was none. She opened the bedroom door and tiptoed over to the bed. Will lay under the duvet where she had left him, his eyes open but unseeing.

She reached down to touch his forehead. He was cold. Rigor mortis had set in. She raised her open hand to her mouth and kissed it, laying her palm back on his forehead. 'Goodbye, my lord'. But in the face of his death, she was light-hearted and pleased with herself.

Her nose wrinkled. The room smelled of Will's unkempt body and of death. She walked over to the sash window and pulled it up to let cold air into the room, although the window slid down shut again. She needed something to prop it open. Will's square hairbrush lay on the dressing table. She picked it up, raised the window again, and inserted the brush into the gap.

Gone was the caring, nurturing persona she had adopted when administering the drugs to Will. In a cheerful voice, she trilled, 'There, now your soul can fly out. You can go back into your other world. Fight those demons and see if you can make your wishes come true. All will be well, Will.' She giggled and said it again. 'All will be well, Will', and then to herself, 'Oh, that's neat'

She took her glasses off, breathed on each lens, and rubbed them clean with a tissue. She looked exultant, as if Will's death was a remarkable achievement. When she left the room, she shut the door firmly behind her. Lucky it was so cold in the house. He would keep.

Back in the front room, she half closed the curtains. The room was furnished very simply, so it would be easy for her to move all the furniture, creating enough space for Leo to perform one of his conjuring tricks. She would summon the group to this very room. How they loved to dress up and pretend! She chuckled. She would feign surprise that Will was absent but would explain that he was transformed. He'd be there in spirit, when all the time he would be upstairs in bed, 'transformed': that is, as dead as a dodo, and she would be the only one who knew. It was her secret. She covered her mouth with her hand and giggled again.

She set to work, tearing down the sad-looking Christmas decorations and dumping them in the kitchen bin. She pushed all the furniture back against the wall. Satisfied with her handiwork, she went back out into the hallway and shut the lounge door behind her. Before she opened the front door, she wrapped her scarf round her head, put her helmet on top, and fastened the chin strap. As she cycled towards the town centre, she remembered she had left her red scarf somewhere in Will's house. She would find it next time.

She felt no remorse over Will's death. It did not trouble her conscience one iota. She had only enabled him to achieve what they had both desired. But it had also cleared her path to leadership of the group: once she had got rid of her husband.

***

Olive's association with William Marshall had begun three years before. She had been leafing through a local paper. Half of one page was taken up by a picture of a young woman called Sara Olivia Lawrence. Olive had looked at the image closely. Sara was smiling. She looked jolly, with her round, plump face and large glasses: not a care in the world. Olive had thought she looked like a younger version of herself. In fact, she could have been her sister. But this beautiful, apparently carefree person had taken her own life. Olive felt Sara, like she herself, had been cheated of a life.

She had trawled the internet for further information. She had found the same photograph, this time in colour, and was struck even more forcefully by their resemblance. Sara's light brown hair was the same colour as hers. Both had blue eyes hidden behind a similar shade of purple glasses. The glasses were fun and clearly suited Sara's bubbly personality. As time passed, she copied all the information she could find about Sara, pasting it into a scrapbook. She began to truly believe that Sara had been her sister. Their initials were so similar. Olive's second name was Sarah – so they were Olive Sarah Lander and Sara Olivia Lawrence. It made perfect sense in her deluded mind.

She imagined how she had been like a mother to Sara, their own mother being a cold, unbending sort of woman who hadn't wanted either of them. Olive remembered how, as a little girl, her mother had habitually slapped her hard across the face and called her a useless article. She criticised everything little Olive tried to do, despite her anxious attempts to please. She had to wear ugly second-hand clothes. No pretty dresses for little Olive. No long plaits tied with pink ribbon. Instead, her mother had had her hair cut short like a boy's.

At the age of nine, her teacher had realised Olive was unable to read the blackboard, and poor Olive was forced to wear pink National Health glasses. The girls in her class laughed at her and called her four-eyes, and so she retreated, finding solace in books. As she grew older, she became sullen and disobedient. Her mother continued to beat her, but Olive refused to show any emotion.

As Olive's fantasy about Sara developed, she imagined how her mother had given birth to her baby sister. In this scenario, instead of leaving home at the first opportunity, as she had done in reality, she had remained to protect her baby sister. If her mother had tried the same tricks with Sara, she would have had Olive to contend with. She visualised how she and Sara had become a twosome, the best of friends, who were cruelly ripped apart. Her sister, who had been in the prime of her life when it was snatched away from her. She felt an overwhelming sense of failure that, in the end, she had been unable to protect her.

William Marshall's name had been linked in the press to Sara's death – he had used her in his research. Olive had found his university email and contacted him, determined to exact revenge. She knew in her heart that he was to blame and vowed that justice had to be served. She couldn't allow him to get away scot-free.

Information about William Marshall was child's play to find online. She discovered where he lived his perfect life, with his perfect wife and son, whilst her beautiful sister Sara was forgotten and lying dead in the ground. Well, *she* hadn't forgotten. She didn't know how, but William Marshall would pay for what happened to Sara. She began to stalk him.

He was so full of himself that he didn't notice her – a 52-year-old woman, past her prime. It was younger women, like her sister Sara, who interested him. She watched him, this tall, handsome man, striding around the town, dark hair swept back from his face, looking as though he didn't have a care in the world. He thought he could walk on water. Well, he couldn't.

When she wrote to him online, she asked if he was continuing with his research and asked if she could take part. He answered almost immediately, and they arranged to meet. She thought he talked a load of rubbish, but she smiled sweetly while he prattled on. He told her he had initially formed a group to study the rites and beliefs of ancient peoples. Now, he said, his voice awash with pride, they had progressed enough to shift their reality and experience life as it had once been.

He and his group had studied the old ways, when people worshipped God and feared the Devil. He believed that the world had been a better place then. She didn't agree but kept quiet. It was as though William thought all the progress that had been made over the centuries was worthless. He dismissed science and its rationalisations as a diabolical conspiracy against the true nature of the world.

When he spoke, William used his hands to illustrate his points. As he became animated, his face lit up with a strange light, and his grey eyes seemed to get larger. Olive admitted to herself that he made her feel woozy, and at times, she had to struggle to distance herself from him. She realised he was dangerous, seeing him as an adversary whom she must master. She may not have had his university education, but she was patient and she was cunning.

She met his small group for the first time in a musty old church hall. They were an ill-assorted bunch dressed in dark robes. They sat in a circle, each member droning on at length about their experiences of reality shifting. At the end of each session, they got up and linked hands, while Brother William, as they called him, intoned some sort of incantation. She was mesmerised by their antics.

When she told her husband Leo, he jumped at the opportunity of joining such a group. Leo had been badly injured in an industrial accident. His face had been disfigured and his personality had followed suit. Compensation allowed them to live comfortably, but instead of accepting his misfortune, he had been driven to look for cures, for signs and for portents that would lead him to a life where he was whole again. He attended a meeting with her, and that's how it had started. He was excited by the group's aims. He did not share the scepticism which she was at pains to keep hidden. She wanted revenge; he wanted healing.

Perhaps Brother William had spotted Olive's resemblance to her imagined sister, particularly as she wore the same purple glasses as Sara. He singled her out from the others to explain in minute detail about the world they could inhabit. He showed her techniques she could use to shift her own reality and share in his. The dreamlike time she shared with him became addictive for her, and she had to fight to retain her wish for revenge. In the beginning, she tried to link with Sara, but she could never make her materialise, and she became convinced that Brother William's proximity was the reason and was proof of his guilt. She hated him even more, particularly as she recognised she was allowing Sara's death to recede into the background. As the weeks passed, she knew she was no longer Brother William's favourite. Leo had begun to take her place.

Olive became one of the many, which didn't suit her at all. She and Brother William stopped going back into their other world as he became more and more absorbed by his need to seek self-realisation. He began to think of himself as some sort of Messiah leading his flock to the promised land. His change of attitude rekindled her anger – it was time for her to make William pay for the death of her sister.

In old Norse, Olive's name meant 'kind', but that didn't mean she was gentle or caring. She had some medical knowledge, having trained as a nurse. As a young nursing student, her supervisor had shamed her in public. Her assessment of Olive's practice was damning – she said Olive's values were at odds with the Nursing Code of Practice. What a load of rubbish Olive thought it all was, but that early experience helped shape her. She became adept at hiding her true character. She would never allow herself to be shamed again.

At first, it was incredible how Leo came to believe everything William told him. He was so easily fooled. It wasn't surprising, because she herself had fooled Leo for years. Leo's relationship with William was at first one of master and servant. Leo doted on him; when William discovered Leo's name was actually Leofric, which meant 'leader', William took it as a sign that Leo should lead the group, releasing William to continue with his search for enlightenment.

As the group worked through their dreams for an enlightened state of being, and as Leo settled into his leadership role, Olive worked out how she could take advantage of William's obsession with self-realisation. She made up a story of how she had once studied under a shaman in South America and had found a source of ayahuasca. William was jubilant. He believed she could supply him with a drug to unlock his mind. He was unbelievably gullible. What she had really done was source a supply of liquid oxycodone and mix it up with some magic mushroom extract. Sometimes she would mix it with other preparations, just to ring the changes. It was wonderful what you could find on the web.

As the drugs took over his mind, William began to withdraw from the group, and as he did, Leo lost interest in the initial aims of the group and instead began to dream up ways to feather his own nest. Of course the idea of transforming themselves was all nonsense; Olive knew it and Leo was beginning to realise it too. The other group members, however, remained as gullible as ever. Olive didn't interfere; after all, she would reap the benefits.

All this had happened before the Covid lockdowns began. It was only when the regulations were relaxed that the group could begin to meet again. Back in the same church hall, they sat around in a circle, each member so sure that their Brother William would guide them into another world that would change their lives forever. They each had a story to tell; they all had desires that they wanted fulfilled.

When Olive had first joined the group, she had noted how receptive a certain man, known as Brother Mark, had been to Brother William's ideas. During the first post-Covid meeting, Brother William announced the shocking news that Brother Mark had died, and had been transformed, as William put it, in his other world. He spoke with such joy that Olive could have spat at him. Brother Mark had clearly taken his own life, just as her sister Sara had done two years before. Another life had been cut short, and this time, it left a grieving widow and son. What Brother William was doing was dangerous. He must be stopped, and she was the one to do it.

As the year drew to its close, Brother William had begun to rave. He said he must have his child's blood to join with his own to reach a transformed state and find perfection as two became one. As he became more and more addicted, his marriage began to fail; his perfect family life was over.

Olive, remembering despite herself some of the biblical passages her mother would recite, believed the sins of the father also rested on the child. William's child bore the name of Oliver, so it couldn't be a coincidence that he had been named for her. Therefore, he was hers to do with as she wanted. She knew with certainty in her warped mind that she had come into the world to square the circle with her namesake Oliver. She would make William's dreams come true and inflict the perfect revenge on his whole family, in payback for her beloved sister's death.

Olive felt like a god, holding the power of life and death in her hands. William and Oliver, however, weren't quite enough to satisfy her newfound lust for power. She wanted also to be rid of her husband. She knew from her training and all those food programmes on television how highly processed food could harm the human body. She figured out that if she fed Leo food high in fat, salt and sugar, and at the same time, swopped his blood pressure pills for a placebo, it shouldn't take long for him to weaken and die. Once he was gone, she would be free, and Leo would have no-one else to blame but his own greedy self.

However, as she thought about her next move, she felt a frisson of anxiety. William was dead. She had caused his death. But who would miss him? There was no sign of the woman Miriam or her son. Two of the group members, Oswald and Enid, had been clumsy and had driven them away. She resolved to keep Will's death secret from the rest of the group, but she was going to find the boy.

It was fortunate that it was so cold. If Will's body wasn't discovered quickly, it would decompose naturally. When he was found, the authorities would probably put it down to another drug overdose. Nothing to do with her. She had time to complete her plan.

That night in bed, she shut her ears to Leo's snores. Enough of thinking. It was time for more action. She turned over, shut her eyes, and drifted into a dreamless sleep.

Chapter 12

Olive argued with Leo that the group were losing cohesion with the marshal's absence, and despite her husband's misgivings, persuaded him to hold one of his incantation ceremonies in Will's house. She said it would bring them all back together. He agreed, so five days later, Olive summoned the group to meet at the marshal's house. She told them to come one or two at a time, since it was a quiet neighbourhood and they did not want to arouse the curiosity of the neighbours.

She arrived at the house an hour early to prepare for the ceremony. As she unlocked the door, she immediately stepped into role: Sister Olive, wife of Brother Leofric.

Although she had dressed warmly in thick trousers and a fleece, she shivered. It was still very cold in the house. She tilted her head back to look up the stairs and smiled. She held the key to Brother William's destiny, and it was she, and she alone, who was in control. It gave her a feeling she had never experienced before.

She called out, half-mockingly, but now half-believing it herself, 'We've come to transform you, Brother William, but we won't wake you, not just yet.' She reached into the small case she carried and pulled out a long black robe. Lifting her arms, she pulled it down over her head. She walked around the downstairs rooms, ensuring nothing had been disturbed before going into the front room. She went to the window to draw back the heavy dark-blue velvet curtains. They would have to be partially drawn again, but she needed some light to set up the room.

She rolled up the rugs and pushed them against the wall, leaving the floorboards bare. She picked up all

Miriam's brightly coloured cushions, carried them to William's study, and threw them on the floor. She unplugged the television and carried it through to the study, placing it on the empty desk.

She returned to the front room and looked around, satisfied with her preparations. It was just right. Now for the finishing touches. She took out a small pottery vase from her case and placed it on the dresser, then felt in her pocket and drew out a box of chalk. She got down on her knees and concentrated on drawing a pentangle on the floor, giggling and muttering to herself, 'How Leo loves play-acting. One day he'll summon up some false gods, then he'll be sorry.' She pushed herself up and stood straight, stretching her arms above her head, easing out her muscles. She was ready.

There was a knock at the front door and Olive hurried to open it. The tall, overweight, figure of her husband Leo stood there, dressed in a heavy brown tweed coat with a brown felt hat pulled down over his face. He favoured his right side and was leaning on a stout wooden walking stick which he gripped in his left hand. He stepped into the house, and as he did so, he pulled himself up straight, every inch the leader. Bold, devious Leofric. He might not be as loved as William was, but he, like William, had developed a mesmeric hold over the group.

'The marshal not here yet?' He had no clue of what Olive had been up to.

Olive hastened to shut the door behind Leo, hiding her smile. Leo dropped his shopping bag on the floor, unbuttoned his coat, and took off his hat. Was it just her wish for him, or had he put on a lot more weight? His stomach bulged over the khaki twill trousers he habitually wore, and the cloth strained across his enormous thighs and calves. His brown polo shirt was open at the neck, revealing bushy white chest hair. He had used generous amounts of greasy hair cream to slick his wispy white shoulder-length hair away from his face, his poor scarred face. But Olive was used to his appearance.

She answered him. 'No, my love, the marshal's not here yet. You know you have to summon him.'

Olive was fairly tall for a woman, yet she had to stand on tiptoe to kiss his smooth right cheek. As she did, she reached up, stretching her fingers out to pick at the puckered skin on his left cheek.

'Don't do that, woman. It's not seemly. Leave me alone.' He turned away from her, as though ashamed of his disfigurement, but also trying to show his authority over her.

Olive folded her arms over her chest and wrinkled her nose, but quickly resumed her usual bland expression as he turned to face her.

'Help me with my robe. The others will be here soon.'

She picked up his shopping bag and pulled out a purple robe that Leo had had made for him, for what he called 'conjuring up the essence of the spirits'. It was like an ecclesiastical cassock, the sort a bishop might wear.

He stooped as Olive reached to pull the robe over his head, bending down slightly so she could do up the buttons before she passed him an embroidered piece of red and gold cloth, which he placed like a stole around his neck.

She gazed at him in what she hoped he would take to be admiration. 'Very regal, my love.'

'Show me the room. I must ready myself.' He picked up his bag, and leaning on his stick, followed his wife into the front room. He frowned as he saw the bare window. 'Draw those curtains across, but leave a gap. We must have some natural light for the forces to enter and continue their work.'

Olive raised her eyebrows, thinking, *Who does he think he is, bossing me around? He's becoming insufferable.*

He looked down at the chalk pentangle and nodded in approval. 'Help me with the candles.' He emptied them out on the floor, and Olive sank down once more, crawling on her hands and knees to place them in a circle around the pentangle: nothing fancy – they were long-lasting night-lights. She drew out a gas lighter from the bag and lit each one.

Leo looked at them with satisfaction. 'Now we wait for our brothers and sisters. Tell me who has confirmed their attendance. I hope we get a bigger gathering this time.'

'Our Welsh contingent are coming.'

Leofric glared at her as she imitated Enid's voice. She shrugged and laughed, then listed another five members.

'I see, and where, pray, is Brother Harold?' Leo rather pompously asked. 'Missing again?'

'I've told you, Leo. He had an accident on an escalator in that shop.' Her eyes glinted behind her glasses. She beamed at him.

'I don't remember you telling me. Have you been …'

He was interrupted by a loud knock on the front door. Olive hurried out of the room to let in the next person. Three people stood there. Four others were ambling up the road, chatting together.

Olive glared at them. 'Hurry up! Come in quickly – you were told not to draw attention to yourselves.'

A blond-haired man of medium height, with a cheerful face and a wispy moustache, stepped through the doorway. 'Sorry, Sister Olive. We met down the road. Leave the door open; the others are coming.'

'Out of the way, Brother Henry. Quickly, all of you get in here!'

Henry's blue eyes twinkled as he moved to one side to enable Oswald and Enid to enter. They strode in but kept their heads down as they tried to hide their amusement. Despite Olive's continued protestations, Henry went to the front door and called out to the others to hurry.

'For God's sake, Henry, don't be an idiot! Go in there and get changed.' Olive pushed him into the front room before turning to Oswald and Enid. 'You two as well. Hurry up. Leofric's waiting to start the ceremony.'

The others arrived, calling out as they came in. *What a strange bunch they are*, thought Olive. Oswald, Enid and Henry were followed by a young man and his mother, then an elfin woman, no taller than five foot, even in the high-heeled boots she wore, and a tall grey-haired female, who appeared to be permanently stooped in order to converse with her friend. A strange group indeed!

***

Eight figures in black robes, their hoods pulled up over their heads, stood in a circle just outside the pentangle. The night-lights burned steadily. A sliver of light shone through partially drawn curtains, drawing attention to the impressive figure of Leofric, who stood in the middle of the pentangle. His voice resonated around the room. 'Master, we summon you. Our marshal is transforming and welcomes you.'

All was silent in the room except for the sound of deep breathing. The group, although not aware of it, were breathing in unison. The temperature inside the room was so cold, their breath condensed in the air, giving the impression of mist emanating from featureless faces.

Leofric, who stood in the middle of the pentangle, raised his right arm above his head and called out, 'I command thee.'

Eight voices responded in unison, 'We command thee.'

The nightlights began to flicker. There was a crash. The vase on the dresser beside Olive had shattered on the floor, and as it did, the ceiling light came on, illuminating the whole scene. The bulb began to flicker. A nervous giggle escaped from one of them.

Leofric cried out, 'Lord, we are ready,' and then groaned as though in pain. Olive thought his act was impressive. But Leo let go of his stick and it dropped to the floor with a clatter. He reached out as if to clutch at something, at anything, to keep him from falling. His face was a mask of pain. He collapsed on the floor, extinguishing and scattering the night-lights, which began to roll away. The robed figures stood in silent shock, the only sound the rolling nightlights. The ceiling light stopped flashing and shone steadily.

Henry was the first to break the silence. 'Well, you've excelled yourself this time, old boy. The trick with the light was bloody good.' He kneeled and tapped Leofric on the shoulder. 'Come on, I'll help you up.'

Leofric was unresponsive.

Henry peered at him. 'He's out cold.'

The others crowded round. Olive pushed them out of the way and knelt beside her husband. She felt for a pulse and said authoritatively. 'He might have had a heart attack.'

Someone muttered something indistinguishable.

Olive turned round. 'What did you say, Oswald?'

'I said one of the demons has fallen.'

She shook her head. 'How could you, and you his friend? Can't you see he's ill?' She stared down at Leo. 'We've got to get him home. Get him to bed. Don't just stand there, everyone! Help me lift him.'

One of the women knelt beside Olive. 'We might hurt him. Wouldn't it be better to call for an ambulance?'

'No, he wouldn't want that.' Olive's expression changed. She was no longer pleading, but she sounded scared at the enormity of what had happened. 'What's the matter with you all? Come on, get him up. He can't be found here. We shouldn't be here. We've got to carry him out to the car.' She leaned over and shook her husband, trying to get him to respond.

No-one moved.

Enid watched Olive. 'How exactly do you think we're going to lift him? He'd be a dead weight and he must weigh a ton.' She appealed to the others. 'We can't move him. We should put him in the recovery position and call for an ambulance. I don't want his death on my conscience, thank you.'

'No, no, no!' Olive shook her head violently. 'He hates hospitals. No ambulance.' She murmured quietly to herself, 'It shouldn't have happened here.'

The group remained motionless. They stared at Olive in their bewilderment.

'We have to get him home. He would want to be in his own bed. Please, help me lift him.' She knelt beside him and tried to sit him up, but it was impossible. Instead, she sat and heaved his head onto her lap.

The elfin woman was the first to move. She pulled her robe over her head and tucked it under her arm, and as she turned to leave, said, 'It looks to me as though he's had a stroke. If the medics treat him quickly, he has a good chance of recovery. I'm going to call 999, whatever you say, Olive.' She had her phone in her hand as she wove past them all to the door, closing it quietly behind her.

Oswald nodded. 'She's right, Olive. I've read about strokes. We should get him to hospital. He looks really bad.'

Henry leaned over once more to peer at Leofric, then he held his hand out to Olive. 'Come on, we must put him in the recovery position. Get up off the floor now.'

Realising she was beaten, Olive wriggled away from her husband, letting his head drop to the floor with a slight thud.

Henry watched Olive's face as he helped her up. 'You two have surpassed yourselves this time. I saw you knock the vase to the floor, but you must tell us how you managed to get the light to come on, then flicker on and off. That was good – so good, it's just about finished poor Leofric off.'

The other group members were surprised by Henry's flippant tone, but Olive ignored him. 'No, no, this wasn't meant to happen.' She looked up at the others. 'What are you all doing?'

One by one, they were pulling off their robes. Oswald knelt and blew out the remaining night-lights. He started to pull Leofric's robe up, but Olive slapped his hand away. 'What are you doing? He'll get cold. Leave him be!'

Oswald sighed. 'Have it your own way, Olive. But it'll look very odd when the ambulance arrives. It must be on its way. If you think for one minute that we could allow Leo . . .'

He didn't finish, as Olive screamed and launched herself at him, scratching at his face. Oswald put his hands out to protect himself and pushed her away. She fell back, sobbing in frustration.

Enid went to her, put her arms around her and held her until her sobs started to subside. 'Come on, love. It's over. You're in shock. Look at me.' She held her at arm's length. 'We must get help. Hurry! Get that robe off Leo! When the ambulance comes, we don't want them to think we're weird, do we?'

The tall grey-haired woman looked at the tableau in front of her. She had always thought that what they were doing was nonsense. She had joined because she found this small group of people fascinating, a rich source for her story-writing, and she had to some extent grown to like their company. It had all seemed so harmless. Now she wished she and her friend had never got involved. It occurred to her that she might now be questioned by the police. She didn't want that.

Henry's tone was sombre. Leofric's collapse had shaken him. He had always thought Olive and Leofric's shenanigans were play-acting, but it looked as though something had really happened here, something outside their control. Had they really summoned a spirit?

The young man and his mother had remained silent throughout. They had joined the group in an effort to contact her dead husband, the young man's father. She was convinced by William's theories about transformation, believing her husband would reappear to them. She looked puzzled now. 'I don't know what's happening. Where's Brother William? Why isn't he here?'

Her son reached for his mother's hand. 'We should leave now.' He looked at the others. 'We should *all* go. This is wrong. It's always been wrong. We didn't really go back in time; we were just shifting our own realities. My father died for nothing.' He looked at his mother and smiled. 'Sorry, Mum, this can't work. It really is time to go.'

As they left, they found the woman who had gone to ring 999 sitting on the stairs. She had covered herself with her robe but was still shivering with cold. 'I've rung for an ambulance. They should be here soon.'

The young man led his mother towards the front door. He looked back before he opened it. 'There's something very wrong here. We should all make ourselves scarce. It might get awkward if we have to talk to the police.' He opened the door. 'I'm sorry, we have to go. I've got to look after my mother.'

The elfin woman on the stairs was thoughtful. They were in a strange house, and the only ones who had known who it belonged to were Olive and Leofric. It was freezing and clearly was a house that wasn't lived in. She and her friend should leave. If Leofric died before the ambulance came, the police would have to be called. She got up and opened the door to the front room, beckoning to her friend. 'Come on, we shouldn't get involved. When the ambulance comes, Olive must sort things out. Sorry, Olive, it's your responsibility, not ours. You've got our numbers. Let us know how Leofric gets on.' She bit her lip and frowned. 'I think we're trespassing. Henry, you had better come with us.' She raised her voice. 'Come on!'

Henry whispered something as he walked away, which was difficult to hear. It sounded like, 'Farewell, Leofric. Looks as though you'll soon be on the other side.'

Only Olive, Oswald and Enid were left with Leo, now stripped of his robe and lying motionless on the floor in the recovery position.

Enid went out to the kitchen and came back with a damp cloth. 'Help me move him over a bit. Let's get rid of these chalk marks.'

Olive looked on in silence. Oswald picked up the nightlights and took them through to the bin in the kitchen. Olive sat quietly, rocking back and forth, watching the activity around her.

Enid patted her shoulder. 'Come on, Olive. It's time to stop the play-acting. We must have a story ready. If the ambulance men ask who the house belongs to, you must tell them the owner is away and we were here to water the plants.'

Olive looked up.

Enid went on, 'Yes, that sounds good. It would explain why the heating isn't on. Tell them Leo wasn't feeling too good before we arrived.'

Olive's hands trembled as she touched her husband. 'I'm sorry for everything, Leo. I wanted them to take you home. It wasn't my fault. I had no say. You'll hate hospital.' She looked at Enid and Oswald, her voice changing to one that was harsh and monotonous, almost robotic. 'We are the custodians of the marshal's work now. We must ensure it continues. We will deliver the boy to him as we promised.'

Enid got down on her knees in front of Olive. She grasped both her arms, forcing Olive to look at her. 'Remember, Olive, I am your friend, and so is Oz. Let's have no more "Brother this" and "Sister that": no more talk of the group and finding the boy. We don't want this to look suspicious, do we? We did our best to help Leo, didn't we? He's very poorly. He has to go to hospital now, doesn't he?' Her Welsh lilt rose at the end of every sentence, and her voice reverberated around the room. 'His power over us has gone. He can't harm any of us anymore, can he? You might even be free.'

***

After another ten minutes or so, the ambulance pulled up at the house. Two female paramedics assessed Leo and immediately called in for more help. 'I'm sorry, Mrs Lander. He's too heavy for us to stretcher him safely to the ambulance. We're asking for assistance from our fire service colleagues. They won't be long.'

Olive shivered. In one way, it was what she wanted, to get rid of Leo. But she was aware of the body upstairs and did not want anyone poking around, especially when one of the paramedics said, 'It's very cold in here. I'm sure your husband would be more comfortable in a warm blanket.' She had to remember to look traumatized, but also to remain calm. 'You said they won't be long. This isn't our house. We only came to water the plants.'

The faint sound of a siren sounded in the distance. A look of relief flooded Olive's features. Oswald studied her face. He was puzzled, and later, once they had been left alone to lock up and he and Enid had returned to the front room, he said, 'I think we should search the house.' He looked worried. 'Did you notice Olive and Leo didn't offer any explanation for why William wasn't with us today? Normally, Leo would be moaning about his absence. Where is William? You stay here. I'm going to look round.'

Enid objected, 'No, Oz. Whatever happens, we're in this together. I'm coming too.'

The house was deathly quiet. Enid shivered. 'The house is brooding. It's waiting for something to happen. It's creepy. Maybe we should leave it be. What we don't know can't hurt us.'

Oswald swallowed nervously. 'Did you notice how desperate Olive was? There must be a reason she wanted us to get him home and why she didn't want us to look for a blanket.'

'Yes, I did notice.' Enid took a deep breath. 'She didn't want any strangers poking around. She's hiding something. We should look in the bedroom. That's where William was the last time we saw him.'

Enid led the way to the stairs. Halfway up, she turned round and called to Oswald, 'Don't just stand there, Oz. Come with me!' She stepped onto the landing. 'There's a horrible smell.' She sniffed. 'Oh God! It smells as though there's something rotting in here!'

She waited for Oswald to join her. They stood together outside the bedroom door, where the smell had become stronger. She hesitated before pushing the door open. A deathly odour enveloped them. There was a body in the bed, a dark head on the pillow. They looked at one another in horror. Enid slammed the door shut and stumbled back down the stairs.

'Oh God, I'm going to be sick!' Enid covered her mouth with her hand, but it was too late. 'That's vile!' Enid panted, holding her stomach. 'I'm sorry, Oz. I'll clean it up.'

He shook his head. 'It's okay, my love. I'll sort it. You

go and sit down.'

She went back to the sitting room. Too nervous to sit still, she looked at the remnants of the chalked pentangle, and she got down on her knees, spitting on her fingers, trying to rub out the faint outline.

'Whatever are you doing down there? Leave it now.' Oz helped her up and sat down beside her. He put his arm round her shoulder, pulling her to him. 'I've never smelt anything so disgusting.' He swallowed. 'I thought Leo was just playing his power games. What has he done? William must have been dead for weeks.'

Enid looked up at him. 'We've all been playing Leo's game. He's not the only one who should take the blame. Olive must have known William was up there. And we're guilty too. We cheered William on with all that transformation nonsense.' She looked around. 'We've got to get out of here. If the bedroom door remains shut, it might contain that dreadful smell. It could be months before he's found. The boy and his mother are unlikely to return any time soon.'

Oswald looked at her in horror. 'Are you suggesting we just leave William here in that state? Leave William's wife and son to find him? Have you lost your senses?'

'Well, yes,' Enid retorted. 'We've got caught up in something that's gone wrong. We both lost our moral compass years ago – or are you choosing to forget? Maybe we can start again now Leo is no longer with us.'

'He's not gone yet. They may save him.'

They stared at one another. Neither of them wanted him to live, but neither of them wanted to say what they thought.

Oswald patted his wife's hand and stood. She looked up at the tall, thin figure leaning over her. 'I'm just going to make sure everything is as it should be. We don't want to alarm the authorities when they come, because they *will* come, and we must be ready. We've just got to keep our heads.'

Enid smiled weakly and nodded in agreement. 'Let me help put the furniture back. And we'd better take Leo's robe for safekeeping.'

It was dark when they left the house, and they were relieved to sit quietly for a while in their car.

Enid turned to her husband. 'Should we go to the hospital? Poor Olive will be all at sea without Leo. I just hope he's passed by now. Maybe she can start to have a life, poor woman.'

'Are you sure you want to go? Yes, I feel sorry for her, but not that sorry. She was part of this. She was meant to be looking after William. What's she been doing? Feeding William poison, I daresay. I suggest we go back to Leo's house and look for anything linking us with him.'

'No, there's plenty of time for that. We should go to the hospital to offer Olive some support. She is a sort of friend, after all. It wasn't her fault she was married to that man.'

Oswald reached over and ruffled his wife's hair. 'You sentimental old thing. Let's do it, then. Keep your fingers crossed that this will soon be over. No more puppet master. No more anything. We'll soon be home, soon be free.'

PART 3

Chapter 13
Studland

Ollie was beginning to feel at home in the bedroom he occupied in Swallow Lodge. He wished he and his mum could stay forever, but it seemed they would have to move to a place called Rock House. Today was the day his mum was going to see the house, and Martin was going to take him to visit the Tank Museum at Bovington.

He swung his legs out of bed, padded over to the window, and pulled the curtains back.

Although they were miles away from Chester, he stood away from the window, just in case someone was lurking in the back garden. It was impossible to forget how the man dressed in his father's coat had nearly kidnapped him. He had been fearless at the time. The girl called Sandy had called him her 'brave little cub', but as the weeks passed, he began to appreciate how much danger he had been in. It could be the same man who had followed them down the motorway. He shivered as he thought how the man might be getting closer.

The day looked dreary. His mother had told him about sea frets, and today, misty low cloud hung over the sea. Ollie gazed out of the upstairs window: no sign of land on either side of the bay. Afraid that the trip would be cancelled, he checked the weather forecast. By mid-morning, the sun would break through. He felt pleased. He had been looking forward to a day out with Martin.

He wished his mum could have given him a dad like Martin. Martin was fun and would have looked after him.

He remembered how he had felt, left alone with his dad when his mum was at work. After she had left the house, his father, who normally remained in his study, would seek him out to tell him about his 'breakthrough' into a different world. His father would become animated, and his voice would rise in volume. Ollie tried but couldn't understand what he was saying. He hadn't hurt Ollie, but he had worried him, and Ollie, who was close to his mother, felt torn between both parents. He felt as if he was betraying his mother by keeping his father's secret.

Miriam waved Ollie and Martin goodbye, and once they were out of sight, she let her mask slip. She dreaded the prospect of meeting Martin's friend. On the drive over to Swanage, she was over-cautious on the winding, narrow roads, braking far too frequently. She imagined there might be walkers or cyclists around every corner and almost slowed to a stop. As she came down the hill and headed towards the town, she could just see the tops of the hills blanketed in mist. It chimed with her mood.

She pulled into a parking spot on the seafront and tried to think positive thoughts, a tall order in her present state of mind. However, the sea helped calm her as she watched gentle waves washing onto the shore. The tide was halfway out, and she could see several people trudging across the beach with their dogs, their heads down, wrapped up well against the winter chill. She would have liked to join them, to inhale the clean, cold sea air. However, Caitlin was expecting her, and it wouldn't do to be late.

She headed away from the beach, through the town centre and up a long, steep hill. Turning right into a side road, she saw a wooden sign for Rock House. She stopped in front of a tall wrought-iron gate. She had instructions to punch five numbers into a keypad. As she did, she wondered why the people in the house wanted to lock themselves away. The gate swung open. She drove through, and as she glanced in the mirror, she saw the gates swing closed behind her.

There were tall trees on each side of the driveway, still bare of their leaves. The grass verges were tidy, the road smooth. She rounded a bend and slowed down to view the house. It was on high ground and was partially hidden in a light mist, almost in cloud. It looked ghostly. She blinked and focused on the building. She saw a three-storey stone house, with large windows on its frontage and steps leading up to a solid wooden door.

She parked and took a deep breath before she opened the car door. As she levered herself out, she looked around, allowing herself time to take in the atmosphere of the place. It was cold and damp outside, but to her, the house seemed to radiate light. She saw a figure in one of the front windows. Caitlin must be watching out for her. She walked up the steps to the front door and rang the bell: heard a dog barking and stepped back. The door opened, and a tall woman stood framed in the doorway, a broad smile on her face.

'You must be Miriam. Come on in out of the chill. I'm Caitlin, or Cat if you prefer.'

The hallway felt warm and welcoming. Miriam looked down at the red Victorian tiles on the floor, then as she looked up, her eyes were drawn to a wide staircase carpeted in red, a smooth wooden banister on one side. The stairs were in keeping with the size of the house, and as she studied them, she experienced a strange feeling of disorientation.

She jumped when Caitlin, with a light touch, laid both hands on her shoulders. She and Caitlin were of similar height, so they faced one another, barely eighteen inches apart. Caitlin studied her face with quiet concentration. Her gaze disconcerted Miriam. What was this woman doing? But Miriam didn't try to break Caitlin's scrutiny of her, for all she saw in return were a pair of bright blue eyes, full of kindness, and a gentle smile of welcome.

Caitlin reached out and touched the side of Miriam's face, and as she did, Miriam felt herself unwind.

She smiled back at the woman in front of her and broke the silence. 'Have I passed your test?'

Caitlin smiled. 'Yes, of course you have. And have I passed yours?'

Miriam pushed a loose curl away from her forehead, uncertain how to respond.

'I'm sorry, Miriam, I was very forward. I've invaded your personal space. A bit much? Yes, it was, wasn't it? Be honest.'

'Nobody has ever held my attention in that way – eye to eye, with such concentration.' She thought for a moment before continuing. 'It felt intimate, as though you were looking into my soul. Tell me what you saw.'

'I saw a woman in the prime of her life. Dark, curly hair, hazel eyes, high cheekbones. Her face might speak of ancestors from other lands. Her expression told me she is anxious and under strain, but her eyes told me she is honest and will fight for what's right.'

Miriam, who was well out of her comfort zone, found herself oddly attracted to this tall, self-possessed woman smiling at her. There was something other-worldly about her. Something pagan.

Miriam burst out, 'I feel discombobulated. You have

discombobulated me!'

Caitlin chuckled at Miriam's reaction, put her arm around her shoulder, and steered her out of the hallway into a large kitchen. It was a light and airy room: a comfortable space to cook, eat and live in. Caitlin led her to a large pine table and pulled a chair out. A bright yellow cushion covered its seat. 'I'm sorry, Miriam. It was instinctual. At that moment, I wanted to be close to you.' She grimaced. 'My friends will tell you how kooky I can be. Come and sit down and relax. I'll make some coffee.'

Caitlin, her back to Miriam, reached up to take mugs out of a cupboard. 'Martin told me a little about your circumstances. Did he tell you anything about me?'

'Only that you often help people and we would be safe with you in this house. I didn't know what to expect. I guess I was apprehensive when I saw the gate and then the house. My front door opens onto an ordinary street in Chester. This house looks unique. It looks imposing. In the mist this morning, it was also sort of atmospheric and ghostly.'

Caitlin, who had listened to Miriam with her back to her, turned to face her. 'I think I should tell you something about me before you decide whether you might like to come and stay with us. The 'us' is my daughter Kirsty and my friend Sally, and sometimes, Bob. Sally is on holiday, and Kirsty is at school. Bob is Kirsty's father. He has his own place too; he's not here all the time. So today we can have some peace to get to know each other.' She opened the fridge, took out a carton of milk, and put it on the table. 'Do you take sugar?'

Miriam shook her head.

Caitlin pulled out the chair opposite Miriam's. 'I've lived here over twenty years. It was my mother's home and her parents' home before her. My mother died when I was very young; I was fostered out and only inherited when my stepfather died. It's interesting that your first impression of the house was that it looked ghostly. When I moved here, I was in an unhappy relationship and became very anxious, and I began to see a ghost. I was sure the ghost was my mother and she had come to warn me of danger.'

Caitlin stopped talking for a moment to observe Miriam's face. Miriam gave nothing away, so she continued.

'You see, there was a conspiracy to cheat me out of my inheritance. They didn't succeed, thanks to my friends. So here I am, older and maybe a bit wiser.'

'Do you still see your mother's ghost? And who are "they"?'

Caitlin took a sip of her coffee before replying, ''Yes, I think my mother is still here, should I need her, but I haven't seen her for a long time. The "they" were an unscrupulous lawyer who was brother-in-law to my stepfather, and my stepfather's grandson. The lawyer's dead now, and my stepfather's grandson confessed and showed some remorse for his part in the conspiracy. I've no idea where he is, and I have no wish to ever see him again.'

Miriam asked, 'Why did you tell me about your mother's ghost?'

'When you came in, I wanted to hold you. You looked so lost. It took me straight back to how my younger self felt. Come with me a minute.' She got up and went back into the hall. Miriam followed her. Caitlin pointed to the stairs. 'The crooked lawyer fell to his death there. Sometimes my mind plays tricks and I see him still lying there. Wicked deeds can leave a deep mark, though the memory of those dark days has faded. This is an old house. Discord tried to find a way to wrap itself around the fabric of the place, but it didn't succeed.'

'Is that why you give people shelter? Are you making amends in some way?'

Caitlin bit her lip and frowned. 'Maybe it's something like that.' She looked away as though she had been caught out.

Miriam was anxious in case she had caused discomfort. 'I'm sorry, that was uncalled for. Ollie and I would be grateful if you could offer us refuge. How much did Martin tell you about us?'

'He told me a lot about Ollie and how Agnes the ghost had come to rescue him. I'm sure Ollie's experience is linking us. You were meant to come here.' She stopped and closed her eyes, as though gathering her thoughts, before continuing in a quieter voice. 'Martin's worried about Ollie, as I'm sure you are. He told me Ollie's father tried to kidnap him so he could be with him in a mysterious cult.'

Miriam bit her lip. 'Yes, that's it in a nutshell. Members of the cult followed us as far as the outskirts of Oxford, but we managed to lose them. I fear they are still looking for us.' She turned away from Caitlin, walked over to the window, and gazed out. 'We stayed in a pub on the way down. We were sharing a twin bedroom when I had my first nightmare. I woke up with Ollie sitting beside me. After I described the dream, Ollie said Will could no longer hurt us because his ghost had told him so. He has absolute trust in her.' She turned back to face

Caitlin and sighed. 'Since then, I've had recurring nightmares. Will is always present. I think he's in mortal danger, and I feel powerless. I was no help to him when we were at home, and then it was too late.'

Caitlin frowned. 'Sometimes people don't want to be helped, and if he plans to seek custody of Ollie, he's going to have to fight for him through the courts.' She reached for Miriam's hand. 'Can you tell me – has he abused you or Ollie?'

Miriam faltered for a moment. 'Not physical abuse, although I think the reason he didn't strike me was because he was being controlled by something. My fear of him was based on his growing power. His whole persona changed. His eyes were blank, but when he stared at me, they seem to burn into my soul. Ollie says he sees darkness all around him, like an aura. Then there's the cult. At first, Will told Ollie stories, but then he began to frighten him, talking in strange tongues. Will finally walked out on us, but we don't know where he is, what he's doing, or what he plans to do.'

Caitlin sat very still. Her quiet manner encouraged Miriam to continue.

'I've talked it over at length with a good friend in Chester, who encouraged us to leave, but I'm afraid there's no doubt we were followed. I recognised one of the cult members in the motorway services, and I don't believe it was a coincidence. When they tried to kidnap Ollie, he was brave and managed to get away. Following us added a new dimension, and I don't mind telling you how frightened I've become. I'm convinced they will try again.'

Caitlin frowned. 'Well, they are not going to find you here too easily. The house is secluded and secure, and there's always somebody around. You could tell your story to a couple of private investigator friends of mine. They helped me years ago, and in my experience, it's no good hoping things will just resolve themselves. It's better for you to take charge. If you like, I'll call them.'

Miriam sighed. 'I'm frightened, not knowing what the cult is all about. I'm worried I'll be called on to rescue Will, to face evil, when all I want to do is bury my head and hide. I wish someone could wave a magic wand and take it all away.' She looked up. 'I'm not sure I have the strength, but I know you're right. In the end, I must face the truth, and I can't do it on my own. I'll find the money somehow. Please call them before I change my mind.'

Caitlin nodded. 'Look, don't worry about the money; we'll work something out. Charlie and Sam are good friends of mine. Hopefully, they'll be able to find some answers for you.' She reached out and took Miriam's hand. 'Now, let's think about happier matters. Kirsty and Ollie are about the same age. You never know how children will react, but I bet they'll like one another.' She grinned. 'And there's someone here I haven't introduced you to. Come and meet our dog. She's waiting patiently. Are you OK with dogs?'

Miriam frowned. 'If they're gentle, yes.'

'That's good. I'll go and fetch her.'

Caitlin came back into the kitchen with a tall grey standard poodle walking at her heel. 'This is Frida. Come to her, put your hand out, and she'll give you her paw.'

Miriam got up and walked towards the dog. 'Oh, she's beautiful! Hello, Frida.' She stooped over and held her hand out to the grey poodle and was indeed rewarded with a paw. She held the paw for a moment, then released it and stroked Frida's head instead. 'Her fur is so soft. I thought it would be wiry.' She stood up. 'Is she yours?'

Caitlin grinned. 'I think it might be the other way round; we belong to her. We gave Frida to Kirsty for her ninth birthday. Frida was a little bundle of fluff then, full of mischief until she grew, then she became the dignified dog you see now. Her intelligence is awesome. If she could talk, I reckon she'd boss us all around. Wouldn't you, Frida?'

'I was bitten by a wire-haired terrier when I was quite small. I've been wary of dogs since. But I think I could get on with Frida.' Miriam sat down again. 'Thanks for making me so welcome, Caitlin. I was dreading leaving Swallow Lodge, but now I'm beginning to think we will be safe here with you. Martin's right: Will would guess where I am, and although I love Martin's house, it is very isolated. When he goes to New Zealand, I'd be nervous being alone with Ollie down there. Afraid of my own shadow.'

'That's sorted, then. I suggested to Martin we all have Sunday lunch together. Sally will be back, and Ollie can meet us all. I'd love to offer you and Ollie a home. Fingers crossed Ollie likes us. Shall we go and see the flat?'

***

Faced with their imminent move, Ollie had been unable to unwind. Both Ollie and Miriam tried to hide their fears from each other, but Miriam noticed how nervous Ollie had become. It seemed to be building day by day. If they went out in the village, he frequently looked over his shoulder, anxious that someone might be following. When night fell, he pulled the curtains across before putting the lights on. He only wanted to go out when Martin could accompany them; she feared he was becoming dependent. He looked to his uncle for protection. It was a bad sign, particularly as Martin had booked his flight to New Zealand and would be leaving in ten days.

Miriam discussed moving with Ollie, but despite her assurances that he would make new friends, he wanted to cling to the safety he had found in Swallow Lodge. They had been invited to lunch in Rock House; Ollie would see his new home tomorrow. Miriam remembered how nervous she had felt at the thought of moving, and she sympathised with her son. Fingers crossed. If the two children got on well, it might all progress smoothly.

For the first time in months, Miriam worried about what she could wear. They had only packed warm, casual clothes. Martin suggested she order something from Amazon, but she wanted to try clothes on; ordering online seemed wrong to her. He suggested shopping in Swanage, but she felt too exposed. If cult members were around, she didn't want to lead them to her new home. In the end, she left Ollie with Martin and drove over to Dorchester. With a long Puffa coat turning her into a shapeless blob, and with a hat pulled down, partially hiding her face, she felt safe enough to venture up the High Street.

She was sad to see many of the shops closed and boarded up. It seemed Covid had hit the town centre badly. She went into a large shop she remembered from years ago. The smell of perfume and makeup greeted her at the door. She hurried straight upstairs to the women's clothing department and began to look through rail after rail of dresses. After much indecision, she ended up buying a light-grey trouser suit. When she tried it on, she admired herself in the changing room mirror. Stress was good for something. She had lost weight, and the suit fitted perfectly.

In a better mood, she went in search of a coffee shop. She chose a table by the front window and sat staring at passers-by. What was she thinking? Strangers could mean danger. She had let herself be lulled into a false sense of security. She would never forgive herself if people from the cult were close and Ollie was harmed. She drank her coffee quickly and paid her bill.

She pulled her hat down, buttoned her coat up, and hurried down the High Street towards the car park, looking neither right nor left. She breathed a sigh of relief when she reached the car, got in, and locked the doors. What was happening to her? She was becoming afraid of her own shadow.

Chapter 14
Rock House, Swanage
30 January

Caitlin woke early and lay in bed planning the day. She had Sunday lunch to prepare for nine people. She counted them on her fingers: *Kirsty, Sally and Bob, that's four of us, then Miriam, Martin and Ollie, seven, and finally, Charlie and Sam.* She sighed with satisfaction.

She was particularly pleased Charlie and Sam were coming to meet Miriam in informal surroundings. Caitlin remembered how she had struggled with the idea of strangers helping her, but if she hadn't, she would never have met Charlotte Taylor, of Charlie Bond Investigations, and gained a trusted friend. Caitlin and Sally could offer sanctuary, but they couldn't hide them for ever. The people threatening Miriam and Ollie had to be stopped.

***

Sally stretched and yawned. She was happy to be home and comfortable in her own bed. She had spent a fortnight with Ann and her family in their home in Cyprus. Sally and Caitlin had formed a friendship with Ann when she helped Caitlin search for the truth about her mother Cessie's life and death. They missed her, but it was the right time for her to be with her family, where she felt happy and secure.

Sally often reflected on where life could take people. If she and Caitlin hadn't become friends whilst studying on the same course in college, their lives would have been very different. They had been friends ever since, their friendship strengthening over the years. They had never been inseparable, which was probably the secret of their continued affection for one another. They both had other relationships. Caitlin with Bob, and she with a variety of men who had passed through her life.

Caitlin and Bob seemed to have the perfect relationship. He was still living in his cottage in the High Street, but he shared his life with Caitlin and Kirsty, and they with him. Sometimes he stayed over, and then, in the quiet way he had, he would go back to his cottage. Kirsty had her own bedroom in the cottage and sometimes would choose to be there with her father. She had known nothing else in her short life and saw it as perfectly normal. She was lucky to have two loving parents, something neither Sally nor Caitlin had experienced.

Sally loved Kirsty. She loved her curiosity and her quirky sense of humour. She was doing well in school, and it seemed she might become an accomplished sportswoman one day. She seemed to be good at everything. *Unlike me*, Sally thought, *the ugly duckling, unpopular and never picked for team sports*.

When Caitlin had first come to Rock House, she had converted the attic into a self-contained flat for Sally. However, Sally spent most of her time in the main house, so they decided it would be more use as accommodation for people in need. As far as Sally knew, no-one before had been fleeing kidnap and witchcraft.

Caitlin had also helped Sally buy a property in Swanage, so Sally's ambition of running a café had become a reality. Sally had spent the next twenty years building up a successful business, but at the age of fifty-five, she had sold the business and taken early retirement. So now she could lie in bed, planning each day as it came.

Sally's reflection was interrupted by a small face appearing round the door. She called out, 'Come on in, Kirsty.' A long-legged sprite stepped into the room, a mug held at arm's length, careful not to spill a drop of the tea she had made. She was the spit of her mother, with her father's gentle nature thrown in. Her hair wasn't as dark as her mother's had once been, but her eyes were the same remarkable blue, and this morning they twinkled with fun.

'Come on, Sal, you old lazy bones. Mum's been in the kitchen for hours. Cooking up a storm, singing away at the top of her voice.'

Sally sat up straight and held her arms out for the tea. 'Thanks, Kirsty. You're a hero. It's Sunday and I'm feeling lazy. I didn't think I needed to get up yet. Our guests aren't due to arrive until midday, are they? Is your dad here?'

'Yes, he's in the garden. He wanted to check on some of his plants, but I think he's trying to avoid Mum in the kitchen. She plans to make apple pie. Come on, Sal, get up! Come and rescue the situation.'

Sally smiled at the thought. Despite her best efforts, Caitlin had never mastered pastry making. Cakes she was brilliant at, but pastry – she just didn't have the light touch needed. She would either make the dough too wet or too dry. Then she would roll it out with enthusiasm, giving it a good stretch.

'OK, you win. Give me twenty minutes. Go and tell your mum I'm on my way.'

***

By 11.00, lunch had been prepared. A leg of lamb spiked with rosemary and garlic was roasting in the oven.

Potatoes had been parboiled and left to cool, ready to be added to the roasting tin. Vegetables were prepared and in the steamer. An uncooked apple pie sat on the table, brushed with egg, its edges crinkled.

Bob leaned against the kitchen worktop, coffee in hand. Age suited him. He still had a full head of light brown hair peppered with some grey. As he had worked out of doors for much of his life, his skin was weathered, and the laughter lines around his eyes had deepened into wrinkles. As usual, he was dressed in a clean pair of jeans and a check shirt. However, in honour of the occasion, he had worn his best blue cashmere jumper, a Christmas present from Caitlin.

He looked over at her now, the woman he loved. They had been lucky to be able to choose a way of life that suited them. They both needed space, but they also needed each other. Each time they came together, he found himself admiring her long, supple body, still slim and beautiful. But despite his love for her, at times he needed the peace and quiet of his old cottage to practise his guitar and to dream.

He remembered when Caitlin had first told him she was pregnant: the joy it had given them. At first, he found it hard to understand why Caitlin hadn't wanted to marry him. He thought he might not be good enough for her. Then he came to realise she didn't want or need marriage. She was drawing a line through the past.

She had been born to Cecilia Roberts, who had married George Rose for the sake of her unborn child, a relationship that had led to Cecilia's death. But times had changed: couples weren't pressured to marry when there was a child on the way. For Caitlin, marriage was unimportant.

When Kirsty was born, he had been fascinated by her tiny features. Then when her eyes took on the same hue as her mother's, he fell hook, line and sinker for her. He had no idea that such love could exist. When they were all together, he liked to think Kirsty had inherited some of his features too. Her face was rounder than her mothers, and when she grinned her cheeky little grin, he saw something of his own mother in her. In his opinion, he and Caitlin had made a perfect human being.

Caitlin stood with her back to Bob, muttering as she piled plates onto the worktop. 'Where on earth has that serving platter gone?' she sighed as she started to put the plates back.

Bob recognised the stress in Caitlin's voice. She could be cool, calm and collected, then suddenly something would unnerve her.

'Sal and I can take over now, love. Leave the plates; I can tidy up. Go and relax. Our guests will be here soon, and it'll be all systems go, with you fussing over them.' Bob walked over and took her hand. 'Come on. Everything's ready.'

She allowed her head to rest on Bob's shoulder, relaxing against him. Then she turned to face him, wrapped her arms around him, and kissed him.

'Sorry, I'm trying too hard, aren't I? It's because I think Miriam's in danger, and it's brought back memories of unscrupulous people threatening me.'

'Sweetheart, if you're worried and decide it's too much for you, we can find them somewhere else to live. Don't go taking on too much. You can't put the whole world to rights.'

'I know. Well, let's see what happens today. It'll be nice to see the flat being lived in again, and Kirsty and

Ollie are the same sort of age. They might become friends.'

***

Sam Huxley stood by the window. He was contemplating how easily the man Caitlin had invited for lunch fitted in. Martin was dressed casually and had an easy charm which Sam wished he could imitate. He and Sally were obviously old friends, and now they were deep in conversation.

Martin had left his cousin Miriam to her own devices. She looked rather lost, standing by the fireplace, occasionally sipping from a glass of Prosecco. Sam tried to hide his gaze but couldn't stop his eyes being drawn to her. He thought she looked exotic, with her high cheekbones and dark, curly hair. She noticed him staring and smiled at him. To his horror, he realised he was blushing.

He had been invited to lunch as a friend, but Caitlin had also asked him to come in his capacity as a private investigator. He had therefore decided to dress in a dark suit. He was a modest man and so wasn't aware of how attractive he looked. His white shirt was crisp and newly laundered, his blue silk tie loosened at the collar. His dark hair, once styled to emulate a young Paul McCartney, was cut short and beginning to show grey at the sides. It gave him a distinguished air. As he looked at Miriam, his face creased into a smile.

She walked over and held out her hand. 'I know you're Sam, but we haven't been properly introduced, have we?' She gazed directly at him. 'You were looking at me just now. Have I fascinated you, or is it my story that intrigues you?'

Sam stuttered, 'I'm sorry. No, no, not at all. I was just thinking how lonely you looked.'

She smiled wryly. 'Oh, I see. Then, I'm sorry. I'm not lonely. I was just feeling awkward on my own and wondering whether I should offer to help Caitlin.'

Sam grinned. 'Best not to. We could do the washing up together afterwards if you like.' He realised what he had just said and felt himself blushing yet again.

She burst out laughing. 'I've never been asked on a washing-up date before! You're on.'

Their laughter made Sally look up. She turned to Martin and whispered, 'Gosh, I think Sam's about to pull!'

Miriam and Sam chatted on, oblivious to the others. 'By the way, I *am* intrigued by your story. When you and Ollie are settled, we must talk. See what we can resolve.' He looked at her, a serious expression clouding his face. 'Charlie and I will only act on your instructions. That's how we work. When Charlie gets here, we'll sort out a meeting.'

'Thank you. I'll accept your help with gratitude, but we'll have to work out a budget.' She looked away. Sam reached out and touched her shoulder. 'Don't worry about that now; it will all work out. Would you like me to freshen your drink? There'll be more Prosecco in the fridge.'

The kitchen was deserted. Sam found an open bottle and offered it to Miriam. 'I shouldn't really. I'll get tiddly on an empty stomach.'

'Go on. You're not driving, are you?' They smiled at one another as he tilted the bottle to fill her glass.

'And what about you, Sam? Are you driving?'

'Afraid so. I was born and brought up here in

Swanage, but our office is in Poole, so it's more convenient to live there. Private investigation work comes and goes. Sometimes it's good, sometimes not. Charlie does quite a lot of work as a civilian investigator with the police, but I prefer not to, even though it's lucrative if you can get it. Did Caitlin tell you Charlie and I were both in the Force?'

He noticed the worried expression on Miriam's face and apologised. 'Forgive me. I get carried away. It's because I love my job.'

'It's OK. I love my job too. I was a history teacher in a comprehensive school in Chester, but I had to resign when we came here. I'll go back to teaching when I can; I miss the children. But that's what I meant when I mentioned working to a budget ...'

Caitlin appeared in the doorway. 'OK, you two, what's all this? Enough of that sort of talk today. Oh good, Sam's filled your glass. Be a love and pour a glass for me. We're just waiting for Charlie now, then we can eat. Ollie and Kirsty have gone out in the garden with the dog. Bob's with them and all's right with the world. Live for the moment, my lovelies; tomorrow we'll think about the serious business.'

Miriam bit her lip. She looked embarrassed. 'Sorry, Caitlin.'

'Right, first, you don't have to call me Caitlin. Call me Cat – all my friends do. Secondly, if you wish it, this is going to be your home, and I want you to make yourself at home. You don't have to look embarrassed. Oh, and my bark, when it comes, is much worse than my bite. Come on, follow me – let's break up Martin and Sally's little tête-à-tête; they've been on their own too long. Bring the bottle, Sam.'

Whenever she had the time on a drive to Swanage from Poole, Charlie made a point of parking in the National Trust car park at Corfe Castle. Today was no exception. The walk round the castle would help her leave her work life behind her.

When she had first met Caitlin, she had been driving her father's old Rover. She always swore that being in his car with a client was as good as the client sitting in a psychiatrist's chair. It didn't feel like that in her Volvo C40. A big, comfortable, business-like car but, in her opinion, it lacked soul. She parked, and dressed warmly in a black woollen coat, a white woolly bobble hat and black leather gloves, she crossed the main road towards the castle. Keeping to the lower track, she crossed the little bridge to the Church Knowle Road. She walked through the next gate into her favourite part of the walk. The castle mound was on her left, and to the right of the path was a meandering stream with overhanging trees. She was alone on the path, and she stood still to allow the peace of the place to wash over her. She whispered some of her favourite lines:

'What is this life, if full of care,
We have no time to stand and stare—
No time to see in broad daylight.
Streams full of stars, like skies at night.'

Charlie knew having quiet time on her own was essential to her wellbeing. She needed to separate her police work from her personal life. By the time she arrived at Rock House, she wanted to feel relaxed and enjoy being with the people she loved most in the world. Cat and Bob, Sal and Kirsty, not forgetting Frida the dog, who thought she was human, or Sam, who had planned to turn up early so he could begin to assess Miriam's situation. They had agreed, if there was an investigation, Sam would take the lead role, with Charlie acting as backup.

She could hear footsteps approaching, which shook her out of her daydream, and she carried on walking until she reached the square. Despite the cold, there were tourists milling around. She made straight for the café. No cake today. There was always a groaning board at Rock House. She heard her tummy rumble, but her inward voice was stern – no cake, no biscuits. Think about your weight.

Yes, she had to think about her weight. Since she turned fifty, she had felt her waist thickening. At first, she turned to looser clothes, then came to realise she was on a slippery slope towards middle age. She wasn't ready for it, and maybe she never would be. In her job, she felt she must maintain a good level of fitness. No cake, no biscuits. Her new mantra.

She pulled up outside Rock House at 12.20. Sam had parked his Land Rover Discovery to the side, leaving enough room for a small VW, which she presumed belonged to Miriam. She parked beside it. It had just started to rain. She raised her face, feeling the raindrops on her skin. Dark clouds were gathering; it was going to be a wet afternoon. She hurried to the front door and knocked before letting herself in.

She hung her coat on the rack and made her way into the sitting room. Frida, who had heard her knock, was at the door waiting for her. Charlie bent over to stroke her.

When she looked up, she saw the six others in the room. 'I hope I'm not late!'

Caitlin sprang up from her chair. 'Excellent timing. Join us for a quick drink before lunch.'

Charlie smiled at the two children sitting together on the window seat. The dark-haired boy sitting next to Kirsty had unusual light-grey eyes, serious now as he studied her, summing her up: friend or foe? He looked nervous, which was hardly surprising in a strange place with all these adults. 'Hi, Kirsty, and you must be Ollie.' She grinned at them both. 'Come and give your Aunty Charlie a big kiss, Kirsty!'

She was pleased to see Kirsty had taken Ollie's hand in hers and was drawing him over to greet her. She put her arms round both, kissed Kirsty on the top of her head, and then held her hand out to Ollie. 'Very nice to meet you, Ollie. I'm Charlie. How are you?'

Ollie looked up at her, took her hand, and smiled. 'I'm very well, thank you, Charlie.'

'Pleased to hear it. And this lovely lady must be your mum, Miriam. It's OK, don't get up. I hope they've all been looking after you.'

Charlie's words triggered an unexpected emotional response in Miriam. To her horror, she had an overwhelming urge to cry. Teardrops ran down her cheeks. Not trusting herself to speak, she hung her head and reached in her pocket for a tissue.

Caitlin was sympathetic. 'I'm sorry, Miriam, I should have had more sense. Meeting us all at once today was a lot to ask of you.'

Miriam mopped her eyes to stop the tears which were still running down her cheeks. Her voice trembled. 'I'm sorry. I'll be alright in a minute. Your kindness has made me emotional, that's all it is.' She noticed the worried look on Ollie's face and tried to grin. 'Everybody just ignore me for a few minutes.'

Caitlin, diverting attention away from Miriam, said, 'I see some empty glasses. There's another bottle of Prosecco in the fridge – Bob, be a love, go and fetch it.'

Kirsty asked, 'Can we have a little bit of fizz with orange juice, Dad?'

Bob looked at Miriam. 'It's just a wee drop. Is it OK for Ollie to have some?'

Kirsty had managed to lighten the mood, and Charlie watched admiringly. This small, sensitive godchild of hers was looking after Ollie and trying to break the tension for his mum. What a girl!

***

Ollie and Kirsty knew the adults wanted to talk about serious matters, so when they finished lunch, they disappeared with Frida. Sam insisted he and Miriam could clear up. Charlie looked at him in surprise but didn't interfere. Maybe this was a new way of getting information. Who knows what could happen over a dishwasher! She supposed it might be like standing and chatting with colleagues around the photocopier in the office.

Sally winked at Martin and suggested they take her car for a spin. Charlie was puzzled. What had she missed? Strange goings-on. So, when she and Cat found themselves alone, she asked. 'Spill the beans, oh, wise one. What have you engineered?'

'That's a bit cutting. It's nothing to do with me!' Caitlin's expression was one of pure innocence.

'You can't get away with that, Cat. If I'm not wrong, Sam appears to be making eyes at Miriam. A vulnerable married woman with a child.'

'Don't be an old fuddy-duddy, Charlie. She's left her husband, and from what I hear, she won't be going back.'

'Yeah, well, I've heard that before. Battered women go back to their man time and time again. And Sam's been through enough.'

Caitlin shook her head. 'No, not this woman, not after what's happened.'

'How can you possibly know that, Cat?'

'For a start, she's not a battered woman.'

Charlie detected sadness in Caitlin's eyes but was unprepared for her next statement.

'My mother's ghost has reappeared. I saw her standing at the window when Miriam first came to see me. It's the same thing again: a woman threatened and in danger. No good will come of this if we don't intervene. Cessie's warning us and wants us to help. I know it.'

Charlie sat down on the window seat with a bump. Was it really happening again? Cat stared out at the rain, perhaps mimicking how she had once seen her mother's ghost standing there.

'Oh, my dear. Do you really want this? Can you cope? It nearly destroyed you last time.'

'Of course. I can't turn them away. Cessie will want us to help, won't she?' Caitlin sat next to Charlie and took her hand.

'You and Sally have always believed in me. We must do this, or that poor woman will be lost. Ollie says he sees evil around his father. He calls it 'the darkness'. He and Miriam are in danger and Cessie knows it. I don't understand it yet, but I will.' She stopped speaking and gazed at her friend. 'They are obviously comfortable with each other, and she needs friends.' She reached up to push her hair away from her face, her expression grim, her eyes sorrowful. 'If it wasn't for you, my friend, I wouldn't even be here now.'

Charlie sighed. 'I think I understand. When are they moving in with you?'

'Martin's flying out on Wednesday, so I hope tomorrow or Tuesday. I think it would be a good idea if Sam did a formal interview with her at Martin's on Tuesday morning. Kirsty and Ollie have made friends already. I don't think Ollie will mind staying here with me.'

Charlie frowned. 'Why interview her at Martin's? Why not here?'

'I don't know, to be honest. I just think it might be best to keep the whole sorry story out of Rock House. I've heard part of it from Miriam, but I suspect there's a lot more. Do you remember when Sally and I came to your old office and you let me talk and talk? I don't think I could have been so open in my own home.'

'So, you don't want Cessie to hear. Is that it?'

They both chuckled, the tension broken. 'No, silly! Ghosts only feel. They don't hear. Or do they? We'll never know.'

'Alright, enough said. When they've finished in the kitchen, let's put the plan to Miriam. Where's Bob, by the way?'

Caitlin smiled. 'You know him; he can only stand so much company. He's probably out in the shed. He'll come back in for tea. And promise, not a word to him about Cessie. He'll worry about me.'

Chapter 15
Swallow Lodge

'How are you feeling now?'

Sam wished Miriam could relax. She was sitting in a leather armchair in Martin's lounge. Sam sat opposite her, notebook in hand. She couldn't stop fidgeting, tapping the fingers of her left hand on the wooden arm of the chair, with her right knee jerking to the same rhythm. She seemed unwilling to make eye contact. 'Miriam,' he repeated in a gentle voice, 'tell me how you're feeling.'

'I've been taken over.' She scowled at him. 'I've lost control. We left our lives behind in Chester. There's nothing of ours here, nothing familiar.'

'And Ollie. How is he?'

She scowled again. 'He's with Caitlin. He loves Rock House. He loves Kirsty. He loves the dog. I feel as if I've lost him too.' She put her head in her hands. 'I feel so angry.'

Sam observed but remained silent. Eventually, Miriam lifted her head and looked at him. She took a deep breath. 'I lost Will a long time ago, but I loved my life, my home, my friends, my job. When we left Chester, I thought it would be for a few weeks. That we'd be able to go back home, resume our lives. Waking up this morning in Rock House, I realised it's final, and I'm so fucking angry.'

'OK, tell me why you think it's final now. What's happened to make you feel like this?'

Miriam pointed at the fireplace. 'See that picture of Old Harry Rock? It's hung there as long as I can remember. This was my grandparents' house, and when we sought refuge with Martin, it almost felt like coming home – it gave us continuity.'

She gazed around the room. 'But now we've even had to leave here, and it's all because of Will.' Her voice rose. 'I hate him. He haunts me; he screams at me in my dreams. My whole life has become a nightmare.'

Sam put his notebook down on the floor, very slowly eased himself up, and knelt beside Miriam. He took both her hands in his.

She looked up at him. For a moment she thought he might pity her, but his eyes only showed concern. 'I'm sorry. I didn't mean to swear at you, but you asked me how I felt. God, I hadn't realised how angry and upset I've been. It's like a tsunami. Waters are pouring in, and I'm sinking.' She repeated, 'I didn't realise.'

Sam gazed at her, his face serious. He chose his words carefully. 'You've given everything up, but you are still you, and Ollie is still Ollie. You'll both find a way through.' His smile was compassionate; he already felt an affinity with her, and he knew what it felt like to cope with almost unbearable loss. He wished he could have reached up to hold her, but despite and maybe because of her vulnerability, he knew he must maintain boundaries.

Miriam gazed back, feeling as if something had changed between them, but what was she thinking? There was no 'them'. She could not allow herself to dream. Her reverie was broken when she heard him say, 'You know, you are a truly remarkable woman.'

She did not know what to say. She looked away and eventually broke the silence by simply thanking him. He moved back to his chair. She wasn't sure what had happened and found herself murmuring, 'There's evil waiting for me in Chester. Any life I have here won't be real, not until I know what I have to face. I don't feel in control, and it's getting worse. It's swallowing me up.'

Sam picked up his notebook again. 'Shall we begin at the beginning? I'll take notes. Afterwards, if you wish to, we can decide how to proceed. Is that acceptable?'

Miriam took his lead and nodded. She sat still, thinking for several moments before she started to speak in a soft voice.

'We were alright back then, Will and I. Affectionate rather than loving, but he was a good dad. In hindsight, I think there may have been a long steady decline in his mental health, I just hadn't noticed. Then, when Covid struck, he became fixated and fearful.

'Our home in Chester is old, a bit cranky. Things would go missing. Lights would come on and off. For a long time, I thought Will was gaslighting me, then I came home one day to hear him lecturing Ollie. He could have been talking Esperanto for all the sense he made. When I confronted him later, he muttered something about fighting a demon and simply walked out of the house.

'It was then that Ollie told me he had seen a ghost. He called her Agnes: said she had come to look after us. I thought he was being fanciful, until we were staying with my friend Pat, and she said she had seen Agnes too. That's when I began to believe Ollie.

'It was becoming clear that it wasn't safe for Ollie and me to be at home with Will. We accepted an invitation from Pat to stay with her until we decided what we should do. We only had a few things with us, so I had to go back home. I packed up and was just about to leave when I heard loud knocking. A strange couple stood on the doorstep and demanded I give Ollie up. They were both wearing black cloaks with the hoods pulled over their heads, so I couldn't see their faces clearly. I suppose they were trying to appear mysterious, and I was frightened and ran away through the back door.

'I forgot to say, Will had left by then. His things were gone, but there was a note demanding Ollie, threatening dire consequences if I didn't give him up. After that, the strange couple were like shadows following us. At the same time, Ollie began to know things he shouldn't have known, things he had learned from the ghost, and I became more fearful.

'We decided we would have to leave Chester. What Ollie hadn't told Pat or me was that during a shopping expedition, a man had tried to kidnap him. Somehow, he got away. When he did eventually tell me, he said he hadn't wanted to tell us in case it worried us.'

Miriam faltered and stopped. Sam wished he could give her some words of comfort, but he waited for her to resume her narrative.

She closed her eyes and took a deep breath before speaking.

'We rented a flat in Flint, not far from Chester. I was thinking then, when things were more settled, we'd be able to go back home, but that was before Ollie had a bad experience in the castle. He was standing on the castle walls and felt as if something was willing him to fall. He said it was the darkness, the same darkness he used to see surrounding his father. After that he told me about the attempted kidnap, and I realised we had no option. We would have to seek refuge further away, where they couldn't find us.' She hesitated. 'I'm just going to get some water.'

She came back carrying a glass and resumed in a voice devoid of emotion, 'A few days later, Pat came to see us. Some senior girls from school had helped Ollie after the attempted kidnap, and one of the girls knocked on Pat's door in search of Ollie. When she realised Ollie wasn't there, she told Pat what had happened and recounted how they had followed the man. They thought he was a paedophile. They kept watch on the house and saw a man being helped into a car by a couple of men. They all drove away together. Pat showed me the girl's photos. I'm afraid the man being helped into the car was Will. He wasn't being restrained. They were all friendly; he even waved as they drove away.

'The girls continued to keep watch and were surprised by the number of people going in and out of the house. They found the address was linked to a website. That's when we figured out Will had got himself caught up in some sort of cult, and I decided to ask Martin for help. It was when we were travelling down to Martin's that I realised we were being followed. It was the same silver-grey car I had seen in the photo. I think they were Will's friends. We lost them on the motorway, and we reached Studland undetected.

'Since then, Ollie has been getting more and more nervous. I'm not much better. I'm having terrible recurring nightmares. Ollie says his father can't follow us or hurt us now because Agnes has told him so, but how on earth can I put my trust in a ghost?'

Sam looked puzzled. 'You said a moment ago that Ollie thinks his father can't hurt you now. Has he hurt you?'

She shook her head. 'Not physically, no. He's hurt us both psychologically. The note Will left said I wasn't needed but Ollie was, as though he had a part to play in Will's new life with the cult. Sorry, I know it sounds bizarre.' She looked over at Sam for some sort of reassurance, but he remained impassive.

'You took it as a threat to Ollie's safety?'

She snapped, 'Yes, of course I did! How else would I take it? He had frightened Ollie when we were at home. There's no way I was going to allow Will anywhere near my child.'

'You call him your child, not our child. Is Will his father?' He saw how his words had shocked Miriam. 'I'm sorry, I have to ask these questions.'

'Yes, of course he is our son. Ollie was born out of love. I became pregnant in the first year of our marriage. Will was fun, but I hadn't realised how irresponsible he was then; that came later. Ollie looks very like him. They have the same grey eyes, long eyelashes and straight dark hair. But, thank goodness, Ollie's nature is entirely different to his dad's.

'Our issues started because of Will's lack of accountability. He would have sudden enthusiasms. He'd dream up schemes, draw people in, and when nothing came of his plans, he'd simply drop whatever it was. He didn't care about the impact his actions had on others. I was the serious one, earning a living to keep us all, because by then he'd lost his job. Luckily, we don't have a mortgage.'

She stared over at Sam, who was busily scribbling notes. He seemed to feel her gaze and looked up. 'Does the house in Chester belong to you both?'

'It's in my name. I bought it with cash my grandparents left me. It's a lovely old house in an old part of Chester. After Ollie's revelations about the ghost, Pat did some research and found that a woman called Agnes Howe had lived in our lane and had been burned as a witch. The story is, her son was killed by his stepfather, and then he spread the rumour that his wife had caused the child's death. When Will started frightening Ollie, Pat thinks the ghost materialised to protect him. Parts of the house are very old, so the ghost could indeed be Agnes.'

Sam needed time to figure out how to deal with another ghost. He remembered his first reaction, twenty years ago, when Caitlin had talked about her mother's ghost. Instead of commenting on Miriam's ghost story, he began to sum up what she had said.

'So, there you and Ollie were, living your lives in Chester. You had a job you enjoyed, teaching history. You said Will was sweet at the beginning of your relationship, and he was a good dad. He was irresponsible, but at what point did he begin to frighten you and Ollie? Can you tell me what it was that became so frightening?'

'That's just it, Sam. It's difficult to pinpoint any one thing. I wasn't frightened at the beginning – I don't think either of us were. That came afterwards. It started with Will's fear of Covid. It became an intense fixation. He began to isolate himself, consumed by the thought he would catch the virus and die. He locked himself away, rarely came out of his study. We shopped online, as most people did then, but he insisted on having his own order and would squirrel everything away in his room. His order seemed to consist of a mountain of bacterial wipes, bottles of water and boxes of biscuits and crackers. By that time, we had stopped eating together as a family.

'He did agree to have dinner with us last Christmas. It was a dreadful trial, for us and for him. Maybe that's when we began to be frightened. Frightened of a monosyllabic man who blanked us out. He wore a mask and latex gloves throughout and proceeded to clean everything around him with bacterial wipes. His table mat, his glass (he brought an unopened bottle of water in with him) and his cutlery. He looked at the dish of food I gave him as though I was trying to poison him. He played with it, shifting it round on his plate. I took it away in the end and put it in the food bin.

'Our house is a bit cold in winter; we're used to putting on extra sweaters. As he sat at the table with us, I was able to really observe him for the first time in months. He was in the room with us, but his thoughts were elsewhere. The bulky clothes he wore couldn't disguise how emaciated he had become. His face looked thin, austere. His whole personality had changed. He wasn't Will anymore.'

As Miriam delved further back into her memory to try to explain how it had been, her face drained of colour. She sat with her arms folded closely against her chest, as if trying to protect herself. When she finally unfolded her arms, she reached up to cover her mouth with her left hand, gnawing on one of her knuckles.

'I sound like an uncaring bitch who's making excuses for neglecting her husband's mental and physical wellbeing. But he had pushed us away. I didn't know what to do, and quite frankly, by that time I didn't know what I was feeling. Maybe I just didn't try hard enough, and when I did try, it was too late.'

Sam didn't attempt to reassure her, but he maintained eye contact and asked her another question. 'You said before that he had frightened Ollie, lecturing him in a strange language. I got the impression you meant he had raised his voice at Ollie, thereby frightening him. Later, when you confronted Will, he walked out. It was after that incident that Ollie told you he had seen a ghost. A ghost that would keep the darkness away. Was that the trigger for your fear, you and Ollie?'

'Yes, that's how it started. I had come to believe Will had either been taken over by some sort of demon or that he was quite insane.'

Sam looked up from his notes. 'As I listen to you, I'm hearing some guilt. I'd like you to consider your husband's part in this. You said you have nightmares and fear he is in danger. I wonder if you think it's the same danger you and Ollie ran away from? Maybe your feelings of guilt are based on thinking Will is unable to control his life, that someone or something else is orchestrating it for him. That appears most powerful to you. Of course, he may also be mentally unstable and in need of help.'

Miriam stared at him. 'You think he might be a puppet? I'm not sure, Sam.' She pushed her hair back from her forehead, deep in thought. 'He's always had strange ideas. He was convinced once that he could find a way to go back in time. The website the girls discovered is called Family of Hope and Rebirth. It's about renewal and transformation of self through some sort of resurrection.' She closed her eyes. 'I can see the words on the website now. *They will restore unity by making whole that which has been sundered.* It's really a whole load of twaddle.' She shook her head. 'Well, I think it's nonsense. The sort of vague, dreamlike notion Will would be attracted to. But there was a tragic incident when he was working at the university. A young student of his committed suicide. Although it wasn't proven, I always had a sinking feeling it had something to do with him. Losing his job because of what happened certainly pushed him over the edge, and now he's living in a different reality. It's as though he's in a weird make-believe place, somewhere beyond our help.'

'Would that be a good spot to start?' He smiled. 'I don't mean the make-believe place; I mean start with researching the website and find out who is behind it?'

'Oh Sam, I don't know. What if something happens to you? It's malevolent. It might try to draw you in. Maybe I should just hide: hope Will never find us and it will all go away.'

'Do you think it will go away?'

She looked up at the ceiling and shook her head. 'No, I don't. But what if we unleash something we can't control? No, please put it off for now. It won't hurt to wait a few weeks, will it?'

Sam smiled. 'Let's go for a walk on the beach. Chew this over. Then we'll head off for Rock House. I agree, no action yet. Give it a few days. A few days will give you and Ollie time to settle down. You'll be safe in Cat's world, particularly as Charlie and I are part of it, and if we need to act, we will do it together.'

Chapter 16

The attic in Rock House had been an important element of Caitlin's story. When she had first inherited Rock House, the main part of the house had been almost empty. However, whoever had cleared the house had not cleared the attic. The abandoned papers she found there had been the key to discovering the truth behind her mother's death.

The house had what would once have been a servant's staircase, accessed from a hallway leading from the kitchen. It had been altered to allow comfortable access to the first floor and beyond it to the attic flat above, without encroaching on the main house.

The flat itself contained a large, open, airy studio space, as well as a small bedroom, a shower room and separate bathroom. The walls were painted white. The kitchen within the studio space was small but perfectly adequate for tenants to be self-sufficient. Caitlin had furnished the space simply: a grey sofa fitted in one corner, a television mounted on the wall opposite. Shelves had been built along the other wall. A repository, it seemed, for all the books the family had read. She had also provided a small square wooden dining table with four chairs.

As the house was built on a hill, the second floor provided wonderful views of the garden and the hills of Nine Barrow Down on one side, and on the other side, views of the distant sea. On a clear day, it was possible to catch a glimpse of the Isle of Wight.

Miriam had insisted Ollie have the bedroom in the flat to himself, while she slept on the sofa, which converted to a bed. She had been afraid to be separated from him at first. Their flight from Will had caused them both to be fearful, but now she thought it was time to let go, and as the weeks passed, she and Ollie began to feel more relaxed.

The tenth of February was Ollie's eleventh birthday. They had a small party that evening, but on the following Saturday, they fulfilled one of Ollie's dreams – to visit Monkey World. Kirsty had told him about the orangutangs, her favourite ape.

Miriam and Ollie had kept in regular contact with Pat, and she travelled down from Chester for the birthday outing. Thankfully, she had little to report. Miriam's mail had been redirected to her home, so she had no need to go to the house

She had worked a half-day on the Friday before the outing and managed to reach Rock House by 7 p.m. She had brought her trusty blow-up mattress with her, so she turned down Caitlin's offer of a spare bedroom on the first floor. She and Miriam talked far into the night. When they discussed school life, Miriam understood again how an important part of her had been ripped away. She missed the children and the joy of teaching a subject she loved. She thought how Ollie must be missing his school friends, despite saying he liked their home study.

They talked about Will, surmising what he might be doing with himself. Miriam thought it all seemed rather ordinary. Could it be ordinary? Had she exaggerated what happened and got things out of all proportion? Then she remembered the attempted kidnap and the experience of being followed. No, it was real, alright. Strange, nonetheless, to think about her life in Chester. It all seemed such a long time ago as she reflected how swiftly she and Ollie had been absorbed into life at Rock House.

The conversation about Chester left her feeling flat. Eventually, they felt exhausted and settled down for the night, Miriam on the sofa bed and Pat on her mattress. Neither of them slept particularly well.

When morning came, they were called downstairs for bacon butties cooked by Bob – another of Ollie's birthday wishes. Kirsty had sung her father's praises beforehand. He couldn't cook much, not like her mum, but his bacon butties were heavenly. She was quite right, of course. Bob grilled the bacon to perfection: the fat was crispy, the meat succulent. He had bought big floury baps fresh from the baker that morning and spread them with thick farmhouse butter. It melted slightly as the hot bacon lay on the butter, and Ollie thought they were indeed heavenly, particularly with tomato ketchup.

***

They were ready for the outing by mid-morning. It was a calm but cloudy day. Miriam drove her car, with Pat in the front and Ollie and Kirsty in a world of their own in the back. She followed Caitlin, Sally and Bob in his work van. They arranged to meet Sam and Charlie at the entrance to Monkey World.

As soon as the adults had paid the entrance fee, Kirsty and Ollie scampered in to study the map. When they had established where they were, they made a beeline for the orangutang area. Miriam watched as the pair of them stood gazing in wonderment. One of the orangutangs rested on a frame close by them. He observed them with a wonderfully wise expression. No wonder Terry Pratchett had transformed the librarian in his *Disc World* books into an orangutang. Miriam wondered what sort of violence and hardship the apes had experienced before they were rescued. Then she was struck by a sudden thought. Will's website talked about transformation. What was Will trying to transform himself into? She had a sudden vision of an orangutang with Will's face. She made herself snap out of it. This was Ollie's birthday treat; she must not dredge up such fancies.

It was a full day. The children wanted to see everything, listen to the keepers, and watch the animals being fed. They had lunch in the café together. They needed a large table – Pat, Miriam, Caitlin, Sally, Bob, Charlie and Sam, and the children – nine of them all together.

After their meal, Kirsty grabbed Ollie's hand and led him off to the children's climbing area. She had been teaching Ollie how to cartwheel. Miriam laughed out loud when she saw them both cartwheeling down the path, one after the other.

The climbing frames were very high, a copy of the frames that had been erected in some of the monkey enclosures. Miriam watched Ollie climbing to the top and was thankful he had not developed a fear of heights after his experience at Flint Castle. The adults sat together at a picnic table, chatting to each other while they watched the children playing.

Throughout the day, Pat observed Miriam and Ollie with the others. If she hadn't known, she would have thought they were all old friends. They had formed a cohesive group in a very short space of time. Furthermore, Kirsty and Ollie could have been brother and sister – except for their eyes. Kirsty had her mother's beautiful blue eyes, and Ollie had inherited his father's strange light-grey eyes. Both children had extraordinary eyes. She thought how weird and wonderful the world was sometimes.

It turned out that Charlie had agreed to come back to Rock House to give Sam an opportunity to discuss progress with Miriam. Pat watched them both with interest as Miriam agreed to go out for a quiet drink.

Kirsty hopped up and down. 'Please, Miriam, don't worry about Ollie! I've got a spare bed in my room for friends' sleepovers. Please can he stay with me?'

What could she say but yes? Despite Miriam's concern about it, she was going to be alone with Sam again.

Chapter 17
28 February

It was early morning a couple of weeks later when Miriam hurried into the Rock House kitchen.

Caitlin was startled by the scared expression on her face. 'Whatever's the matter?'

'I've just had a text from Pat. She says she wants to talk urgently. I'm to come to Chester and bring Ollie with me. Something awful must have happened!'

Caitlin walked over to Miriam and held her hand out for Miriam's phone. 'Give us a look.' She scanned it. 'Have you tried ringing her back?'

'Yes, but it just keeps going to voicemail. Something must have gone very wrong!'

Caitlin shook her head. 'Not in the way you think, *Mimi*.'

Miriam looked at her and frowned.

'All the time Pat was here, she never once called you Miriam. So why is she calling you Miriam in this text?'

Miriam gasped and covered her mouth with her hand. 'Oh my Lord, Cat, it's one of them! It's got to be! What have they done to her?' She went across to a chair and sat down with a heavy thump. 'If they've hurt Pat ...'

Sally placed the last of the cutlery from the dishwasher into a drawer and shut it with a bang. 'Stop panicking, Miriam. Think about it. What's the most likely explanation? I'd say they've stolen Pat's phone.'

'Or . . .' Miriam snapped, '. . . they could have forced her to send a text and she's given us a clue. They could have kidnapped her.'

'Well, there's one way to find out,' Sally snapped back. 'Phone the school. You mark my words; she'll be safely at work.'

Miriam bit her lip. 'Sorry, sorry! I'm sorry, Sal. I'm being melodramatic. Yes, I'll ring the school now.' She looked at her watch. 'She may be in the staff room for the mid-morning break. I'll call and pray she's in today, safe and well.'

Caitlin and Sally gave each other a knowing look. Sally raised her eyebrows, then pointed at the coffee machine and nodded her head. She switched the machine on, checked the coffee bean and water levels, then took three cups from the cupboard and placed them on the kitchen table.

They could hear Miriam talking in the hall. When she came back in, she had a look of relief on her face. 'She's OK. She's in school. She went shopping last night. When she came to pay, she found her phone had disappeared. She remembered putting it in her shopping bag ready for the checkout but left it in the trolley while she browsed the shelves, so anyone could have nicked it. The shop manager rang the police straight away and then let her ring the bank to cancel the card. They thought it was the action of an opportunist, a petty thief.'

'Well, there you are, then. It could happen to anybody.' Sally patted Miriam on the arm. 'Nothing much will happen except those people will be trying to trap you. They're not very good at it, are they?' Sally screwed up her face, deliberately distorting her features.

Caitlin remonstrated. 'Sal, what *are* you doing? This is serious! Miriam, you need to check your texts. I hope no mention was made of Rock House or Swanage. It's no good trying to hide and hope all this will go away. I'm going to ring Charlie now. And Sal, for goodness' sake, keep your feelings under control.'

Miriam scrolled through her texts. 'It's OK. There's nothing here to give us away. Luckily, I gave Pat directions to Rock House when we spoke on the phone.' She suddenly became aware of Sally's watchful face. 'Have I done something to offend you, Sal?'

'No. I'm sorry, Miriam. I should have realised Cat doesn't miss a thing. It's jealousy. I've always been close to Sam, and I've seen how he looks at you. It's made me feel old and discarded. I'm so selfish.'

'Gosh – is that what it is?' Miriam frowned as she began to recognize the impact she had been having on the household. 'I've insinuated myself into your home with all my troubles, usurped your friends. I'd be jealous too!'

Sally muttered, ignoring Miriam's apology. 'Cat knew. She damn well knew. I don't know how she does it. I thought I'd hidden what I was feeling.'

They stared at each other. Sally saw a woman in the prime of her life, not a grey hair on her dark, curly head, and large hazel eyes which had looked so terrified a few minutes ago. Now those eyes, defined by their long, dark eyelashes, looked completely sympathetic. Miriam's skin glowed; its olive texture seemed to highlight her youth, and there was not a wrinkle in sight. Sally felt ashamed of herself.

Miriam, on the other hand, saw a tired, middle-aged woman who was beginning to lose her youthful looks. Her red hair had faded into a sandy colour, and she had pulled it up into a tight bun on the top of her head: not a very flattering style. Her face, free of makeup, was freckled, her blue eyes tired and red-rimmed. Fine lines were beginning to form above her top lip. She carried herself well, but Miriam could see she was overweight. She looked so demoralised. Miriam felt ashamed of herself for causing her pain.

'To tell the truth, Miriam, I'm feeling old. I used to sleep all night long, but now I can't get to sleep, and when I do, I wake a few hours later. The trouble is, I've no purpose in my life. I sold my business a few months ago. I've gone from being busy to having too much time on my hands, and I'm not sure what to do with myself. I liked being active and having a team working with me and customers to talk to.'

Caitlin appeared at the door. 'I thought you'd have the coffee ready. Do you want me to make it?'

Sally shook her head. 'Sorry, I got distracted. I'll do it.'

'I overheard what you were saying, Sal. You could get a part-time job. Charlie's always complaining about keeping her books up to date. You could do them for her, easy.'

Sally sat down next to Miriam and sighed. 'I'm not qualified for anything like that, and why would she want me anyway?'

'Sal, you look, but you don't see. Of course she'd want you! Give it a try at least. If she says no, you haven't lost anything.'

Sally stared at her. 'What do you mean, I look, but I don't see?'

Caitlin raised her eyebrows. 'Think about it. I'm not explaining it to you. Now, make that coffee, and I'll tell you what I've learned so far. Charlie's out on a job, but I spoke to Sam.' She looked pleased with herself. 'I told him about the text. He'll come to see us tonight. He's made some progress with the website. Luckily, he contacted them some days ago, so they're not going to link his interest in the website with you, Miriam. He apologised. He said he knew he'd promised to leave it for a few days but didn't think it would harm to stick his toe in the water.'

Miriam added a spoonful of brown sugar to her coffee and stirred it vigorously. She looked annoyed. 'I trusted him. Sam said he would only do what I instructed, and instead of leaving it as I requested, he's done what *he* wanted to do. How can I have confidence in him?' Her face was a picture of dejection.

'No, no, no, Miriam!' Caitlin leapt to his defence. 'Imagine how it was. He knows how to access the website. With just one click, he could find out what Will was up to.'

'Well, he's not in my good books, and I shall tell him so.' Miriam smiled wryly at Sally. 'This is great coffee, by the way.' She swallowed the last of it and put her cup in the sink. 'I'd better go back and find out how Ollie's getting on. He's working his way through Kirsty's last maths test. I'm going to have to think about getting him into a school soon.'

***

'I know what you're going to say, Miriam, and I'm sorry. My curiosity got the better of me.'

Ollie and Miriam were upstairs in their flat when Sam knocked. Ollie opened the door, and when he saw who it was, his face lit up with delight. Not so his mother. Miriam was busy trying to give him the cold shoulder. 'You promised, Sam. A promise is meant to be kept.'

He looked shamefaced for a moment. 'Sometimes I go with my gut instinct. It's a curse. But look – it's a good thing I did. We don't want to alert them. They won't link the two things together, and when you fail to rush off back to Chester, they'll know you've rumbled them.'

Ollie hopped up and down. 'Brilliant! I want to be a detective like you when I grow up!'

Miriam pretended to be offended. 'Great, two of you against me, that's all I need.' She blew a raspberry at them both. Her sudden change of mood caught them by surprise.

Sam chuckled as he stood with his hands in prayer position, a beseeching expression on his face. 'So, am I forgiven?'

She giggled. 'I can't keep this up. Tell me what you've found out.'

They sat down together.

'There was a contact email on the website, so I emailed to ask for information about the group. I didn't get a reply, so I rang the contact number. A woman picked up. She called herself Sister Olive. When I said I was keen to join, she went silent. I thought that was a good sign. She was at least thinking about it. I asked if I could come and meet them. I said it was just what I'd been looking for.

'I began to think she'd put the phone down, then in a little girly voice, she said, "Yes, alright. Come and see Sister Olive. See what I can do with you. That would be lovely."'

Miriam frowned. 'But won't they figure out who you are, from your name? They'll google you. That's what I'd do.'

'No, I used my stan43 address, not my own name. It's a useful name, that one. I respond to Stan quite easily!'

Ollie piped up. 'So, are you going to Chester, Sam? I wish I could come with you.'

'Oh, Ollie.' Miriam shook her head. 'Definitely not. Of course you can't.'

'But Mum, who is going to look after Sam? I could introduce him to Agnes. She would keep the darkness off him.'

'Thanks, Ollie. But you know, the whole idea is that you and your mum stay here, where you're safe. Instead of them setting a trap for you, I'm going to set a trap for them.'

'Are you going to be a spy in the group. An undercover spy?'

Sam ruffled Ollie's hair. 'Maybe. I don't know what I shall do yet, but I will promise to come back with some answers for you and your mum. Now, I was told to come up to fetch you down for supper. I don't know about you, but I could eat a horse, or maybe a cow, or maybe even a little boy.'

Ollie shrieked, pretending to be afraid. 'No, no, Mr Wolf, please don't eat me!'

'Alright then. I think there's spaghetti bolognese downstairs. Probably taste better than you. Let's go, gang.'

PART 4

Chapter 18
Chester

Olive Lander was feeling pleased with herself. The doctor had been very kind as he told her there was no more they could do. Her husband Leo's life was ending. He had looked so sad, as though he had failed her. She mirrored his expression, smiling sadly, and managed to force a few tears into her eyes by imagining how a soon-to-be widow should feel.

As Leofric, leader of their group, her husband had been a powerful figure. He had thought he was invincible until that moment during the ceremony in Will's house when he had crashed to the ground. It may have happened in the wrong place, but it had been a very satisfying finale to her plan, and as his control had drained away, she imagined it had entered her instead. When he died, she would be ready to receive all his power.

She had filed Will's death somewhere in the deep recesses of her mind, but she had also convinced herself that for him to enter the other world he craved, she must find his son. In return, she was certain Will would give her an even more powerful role in his universe. She had not forgotten her original mission. Will and his son must pay in this world for her sister Sara's death. Her job was to ensure the appropriate punishment for them both.

She had enjoyed the cloak-and-dagger business of following Pat. Stealing her phone had been as easy as taking candy from a baby. She hadn't even password-protected her phone, and now she, Olive Lander, had set a trap. In her topsy-turvy mind, it was just a matter of time before she had the boy in her grasp.

Now she knew for certain that Leo was about to die, she had decided to spend the afternoon sorting through his paperwork. When he and Will had first started to forge their special bond, they had marginalised her. They treated her as a little woman and refused to share information. Well, after reading the files, she had a pretty good idea what the group had been about all along. It wasn't reality shifting or Leo's silly hocus-pocus; it was far cleverer. If only they had shared what they planned to do, she would have helped them. She had been resentful, but now she knew what they had been up to all along, she felt smug and almost laughed with joy. She was going to be a rich widow.

What had come as a surprise to her was the depth of feeling she held for Oswald and Enid. Since Leo had been in hospital, they had been a constant support and even brought her little meals. She wasn't used to having such friends, but in the circumstances, she was quite willing to be friendly too. What a strange pair they were, with such a ghastly secret. She had phoned them to tell them about Leo, and they were due to arrive at the house at any minute. She was prepared.

When the doorbell rang, she leapt up from her chair and strode over to look at herself in the mirror. She stared at her reflection as she conjured up a picture of the saddest occasion she could recall seeing – the TV pictures of the crowd at Princess Diana's funeral procession. Such an outpouring of grief. With that thought uppermost in her mind, she opened the door to the mismatched figures of Oswald and Enid Hughes.

Oswald was tall and thin, always obsequious, and with

his habit of stooping, he looked like a stretched-out chicken. And there was Enid, small and rounded, always perfectly coiffured and made up, with her bright lipsticks and eyeshadows, and so willing to please. Well, they were both from Wales. The English had conquered them and taught them to be submissive. She was quite sure her new friends would do her bidding.

She welcomed them. 'Thank you so much for coming over. It means the world to me. Poor old Leo isn't expected to last the night. I was going to go over later to sit with him so he doesn't leave this world alone.'

'Oh, my dear.' Enid put her arm around Olive. 'We're so sorry, but you know, he would have hated being disabled. It's for the best.'

Olive turned her head away and spoke in what she hoped was a grief-stricken voice. 'Life must go on, and we have things to discuss and decide. I know Leo would have wanted you to be part of any future planning.'

They looked at one another in puzzlement before following her into the lounge. She pointed to the sofa and sat down in the chair opposite.

Enid and her husband had been regular visitors to Olive and Leo's home, and Enid had frequently been struck by how unhomely it was. The lounge was no exception. There was a uniform drabness about it. Magnolia paint, dull greyish-cream carpet. There were no pictures or photographs, just a few seaside-themed ornaments, purchased, she presumed, on summer holidays. The sum of their sad lives

Enid frowned. 'What do you mean by future planning? I thought we'd all agreed the group was finished.'

'Not quite. You must realise there are loose ends. The website is still up. I had an interesting conversation with a young man just two days ago. He's keen to join us.'

Oswald interrupted her. 'Well, say no to him! Surely without Leo, the group has no future?'

Olive smiled what she hoped was a sad but sweet smile. 'He whispered something to me a few days ago. Told me we needed the boy. At least I think that's what he said. He was difficult to understand.'

Enid shook her head from side to side. 'That's ridiculous. It was bad enough when Leo ordered us to follow them. We're not going down that route again. No.'

Olive trilled, 'It's OK. Calm down. We're not going to do anything bad – no travelling involved. We'll do it here.'

By now, Oswald was becoming bad-tempered. 'We don't mean travelling down a road to find them, we mean *no*, we're not doing any more!'

'Don't be like that. I've set a trap. They will come to us. You've got to help me now I've started it. Please, I can't carry out Leo's wishes without your help. He'd want you to help me, I know he would.'

Olive gave them an ingratiating smile. 'I found his files on everyone yesterday. He wouldn't have liked anyone else to read them, so I thought we could have a nice big bonfire. Burn it all up in the garden. Get rid of it. But you must agree to help me tie up this tiny little loose end first.'

Oswald and Enid stared at her.

Oswald spoke first. 'Alright, we will try to help you, but only if you promise the boy will not come to any harm.'

'Of course not! What do you take me for? I don't want to hurt anyone. It's what I said: a loose end. I just want to talk to him.'

Although Enid smiled, her eyes told a different story. She knew Olive was up to no good. 'Tell us about this trap.'

'I pinched the teacher's phone when she wasn't looking. I found Miriam Marshall in her contacts and pinged off a text to her today, asking her to come to Chester and to bring the boy with her. There were some very interesting photographs on it as well.'

Enid scowled. 'What have you done with the phone?'

'I chucked it in the river. Now, here's what I want you two to do. You must keep an eye on the teacher's house and alert me when Brother William's wife and son turn up. They should be on their way soon. I'll do the rest.'

Oswald raised his voice. 'The rest of what, Olive?' He looked at his wife. 'We don't want to be part of it. We're finished!'

'If you help, I'll let you burn all the files, including your own.' Her sly expression told Oswald all he needed to know. 'You'd like that, wouldn't you? Then we could seal the deal with a glass or two of Leo's single malt. Come on, it's just a loose end, that's all.'

Enid, who up to that point had been unaware that Leo kept files on group members, nevertheless had a good idea what might be contained within them. Although she knew better than to trust Olive, the idea of setting light to their secrets lifted her mood, and she began to feel more sympathetic towards Olive. 'Alright, we'll do it. But it's the last time. It's not good for you to carry on with this, Olive. You'll be free soon. Leo was a controlling man. He could be an absolute bastard; we all know that. That's why we're willing to help now. But you must remember, Brother William asked us to concentrate on meditation and reality shifting, not to indulge in superstition and magic. There's been enough harm done already. If the boy and his mother come ...' She stared at Olive for a moment. 'You do know what happened to Brother William, don't you? We've said nothing, but if the woman comes, she will go to the house.'

Olive fixed her gaze on them both. Oswald looked away, unable to deal with what he read in her eyes.

'Well, poor Brother William can't stay there forever, can he?' Olive said in a cheerful voice. 'With Leo dead, the secret dies with him, and we are all bound by our secrets, aren't we? Now, come on, cheer up. We can burn the paperwork and toast Leo's life. If the woman and the boy turn up, we'll manage it together.'

Enid rose from the sofa. 'If they fail to turn up, you should thank your lucky stars. I for one will have my fingers crossed that they stay wherever it is they're hiding. I hope we never see them again. Now show us the files, Olive, and let's get that fire underway.'

They drank a lot of Leo's whisky as they watched the files burn, and then thought they might as well finish off the bottle. Enid used the time to try to persuade a very tipsy Olive to stop her pursuit of the boy.

'I am Leofric's alter ego,' Olive slurred. 'His last breath will enter me and then I'll know what to do.'

Oswald stared at her and shook his head. 'What d'you think you're going to be? The leader of the pack or something? Dream on, Olive.'

She hung her head, and they thought they heard her whimper. It was, in fact, fury bubbling up inside her.

'Oh, Oz, you've upset Olive now. Look, we can keep on with the group, love, if you really want to. Brother William was our mentor. He hypnotised us and drew us all into his other world. But we can't get there without him. Leo thought he was a great leader, but he was a bully. If you really want the group to carry on, we could make it fun without him lording it over us. We could have lectures and do experiments. I know! We could be water diviners. That would be fun and useful too – finding water.'

Enid was beginning to sound excited, but in Olive's mind, she was humouring her as she might a child. If Enid thought there would be fun, she could think again.

Enid continued, 'But no more black magic. It was too stressful. Remember how upset members used to get? And look what happened to Leo. We can't risk it.'

In the end, with much drunken hugging, Olive pretended to agree with them. The three friends shook hands and watched as the files turned into a pile of ash.

Olive giggled. 'Look how paper transforms itself in the flames. All gone!'

***

They had to order a taxi to get to the hospital. The nursing staff were surprised but looked on them with pity. Poor things, they had had to summon up Dutch courage to see them through the night. Who could blame them? It was hard letting a loved one go, and after all, they were quiet and weren't hurting anyone.

When Leo breathed no more, Olive cried out, 'He's gone!' She almost felt grief for the man who had passed from her life. Her thoughts became kind. After all, hadn't they supported each other, and hadn't he left her with a very good pension, a mortgage-free house and a lovely nest egg? She had nothing to complain about. She had conveniently forgotten how she had deliberately hidden his blood pressure pills and fed him all the unhealthy food he could eat.

***

The three of them returned to Olive's house in the early hours. Oswald and Enid slept downstairs in armchairs, while Olive went to bed. Olive, unlike Oswald and Enid, woke up feeling refreshed and full of hope.

'It's St David's Day, a fitting day for Leo to have drifted away from this earth, don't you think?' Olive smiled at Enid. 'When the time comes, we must have daffodils for his coffin. They're so jolly and yellow. A host of golden daffodils. He would have liked that.'

Enid wasn't so sure. 'He was English to his core, Olive, not Welsh. Why would he want daffodils?'

'He liked your accent. He was always remarking how musical you sounded.' Olive had a way of simpering when she tried to ingratiate herself.

Enid wasn't fooled. 'We should look through his papers to see what his instructions were. Did he make a will? Oh Lord, we didn't burn his personal papers yesterday, did we?'

Olive shook her head. 'No, of course not, and there was no will. We talked about it but never got round to writing one. We weren't thinking of dying. Not quite yet.'

Enid thought, *No, I bet you weren't*, but masked her thoughts, asking in a soothing voice, 'Do you know what his wishes were? Cremation, burial? Church, humanist, pagan – what would he have wanted?'

Olive smiled. 'I'm sure he would have chosen cremation. He wouldn't have wanted much. Not to cause too great a stir. He didn't like to spend money either.' She stopped for a moment, then brightened up. 'No funeral, but we could have a wake, couldn't we? We could invite the group to say goodbye. We could have a finger buffet and a glass of fizz. He would have liked that.'

Enid was surprised by Olive's reaction. She had imagined Olive wanting to display Leo's coffin in a carriage drawn along by four black horses. A fitting end for Leofric the leader. Instead, she mumbled, 'Well, if you're sure, talk to the funeral director.'

'And,' Olive interrupted, 'Leo could wear his purple robe and the embroidered thing he liked to wear round his neck – to go into the flames. He'd be like a Viking warrior. Only it would be in the oven in the crematorium, not in a boat. We couldn't float him out on a lake or anything.'

She clapped her hands. 'Oh, but maybe I'll keep his purple robe. He wouldn't want a perfectly good robe wasted.' Her face lit up. 'I can hear him now. He wants us to throw his ashes into the sea. That's what he wants. We could make a holiday of it. You, Oz and me, a holiday by the sea. Yes, that's what Leo would have wanted. He loved going to the seaside, and I know just the place.'

By this time, Enid was gazing at her so-called friend, wondering if she had gone mad with grief. Either that or she had become euphoric at the idea of her husband being dead and disappearing from the earth before finally being swallowed up by the sea. She decided it was probably the latter.

Chapter 19
5 March

When Sam arrived in Chester, he checked into his hotel and rang Pat. His first task was to shadow Pat and find out if anyone was following her. He parked opposite her house in the afternoon and watched. His patience was rewarded when he saw the pair Miriam had described walking along Pat's Road. He took photographs of them and sent them via WhatsApp to Miriam. She called back and confirmed their identity.

'It looks as though they might be waiting for you and Ollie to turn up. But they're half-hearted about it. They've walked up and down the road twice. No sign of them now. Perhaps they've gone. Pat and I are meeting at my hotel later. I'll be watching until she leaves to make sure she's not followed.'

'I wish I could be there with you, Sam. I feel so powerless here. Are you sure you wouldn't like me to come up so I could help?'

'No, that wouldn't be a good idea. I'm the private investigator, remember. This is my job. Your job right now is to look after Ollie and stay safe. To be honest with you, surveillance can be very boring. I don't think you'd like it.'

Being on the end of a phone gave Miriam courage. 'I'd just like to be sharing the experience with you. It's lonely without you. I've got used to having you around.'

'Good! But right now I must concentrate, or I might miss something vital. The sooner I get this done, the better, then I can come home. I'll call you tonight.'

Sam sat back in the seat of his hired car. He wanted to jump out, do a fist pump, and let out an exuberant cry of triumph. She cared and wanted to be with him. However, he was pleased he had controlled himself, for there was the couple again, this time in the silver-grey BMW Miriam had described. He noted the registration number. The light was fading, and with luck, they would soon give up and go home. It must be time for Pat to leave for the hotel soon. He would follow, and tomorrow he intended to tail her on foot to look out for anyone who might be watching.

They had gone by the time Pat left her house, looking neither left nor right, walking straight to her car, and reversing out onto the road. Driving some distance behind her, Sam watched her park her car and disappear through the hotel entrance. He drove around a few times to make sure no-one was following before parking on the opposite side of the car park.

She was sitting in reception. By this time, he was as sure as he could be that she wasn't being watched. As he went towards the lift, she got up and followed him. They didn't speak until they were in the safety of his room.

'Well, this is exciting! How nice to see you again, Sam.'

He grinned and leaned over to peck her on the cheek. 'Nice to see you too, Pat. I must say, you're taking to this like a duck to water. The pair Miriam described have been watching your house, but they got fed up and left. I made certain they weren't following when you drove away, and no-one else appeared to be. I suggest, though, to be on the safe side, that we have room service.'

'Oh – the hotel staff will think we're up to no good!' She laughed in delight. 'By the way, how are you and Miriam getting on?'

Sam responded, 'I think I know you better than to say

anything at all about Miriam.'

'Spoilsport! To be honest, I've been telling her for years to dump Will. He's never been any good for her. But she's very loyal. Anyway, tell me what our next move is.' She looked at him in expectation and was rather disappointed when he simply said, 'I'm going to phone reception with our meal choices. Then we'll eat.'

Pat frowned. 'Stop teasing, Sam. I want to know what you plan to do here in Chester.'

Sam had booked an executive room with a desk and a table. He pulled out a chair for Pat and they sat down opposite one another. 'Tomorrow morning, I want you to walk around the town, window-shopping. As you walk past the library, I'll follow you on foot, see if I can spot anyone tailing you. The person who stole your phone and sent the bogus text to Miriam was opportunistic, but they must have been watching you. It's not likely to have been the pair who've been cruising outside your house, or you might have recognised them from the shop. I've got their car registration number, so we should know who they are before too long. Charlie's sorting it out.'

'That's good.' Pat had been concentrating on his every word. 'You aren't worried about me, are you? I can look after myself.'

'I'm sure you can, Pat. But if there is someone out there, I want to know who they are. So, that's tomorrow, and you won't see me much. I'll stay in the background. Did you spot me when you drove away tonight?'

She shook her head.

'Good. Well, I'm driving a dark-blue Ford. I followed you here.'

'Are you trying to show off your snooping skills, my man?' She laughed. 'Obviously, I'm not as vigilant as I thought I was.'

He grinned. 'I'll ring you tomorrow evening with any news. We should stay away from one another just in case.'

Pat's eyes were bright with excitement. 'So, what comes next?'

'I have an appointment on Monday with a woman who calls herself Sister Olive. She's asked me to meet her in a café in town. I'll see what that brings, and I'll go from there. Miriam has been ringing the landline in her house in Rope Lane. No-one has picked up, so she thinks Will has gone for good. She's given me the house keys. I'm not planning to go there until I've investigated this cult business. With luck, members of the cult will trust me enough to let me into their ranks.'

'You must find out what they want with my godson, Sam. I was shocked when I heard about the attempted kidnap from one of our sixth-form girls. Oh, silly me, of course you know; Miriam will have told you.'

'It's okay, Pat. I'd always rather have too much information. Now, let's have a look at that menu. I'm starving!'

***

The next morning, Pat followed Sam's instructions and walked past the main library. Sam, who had been waiting for her on a bench nearby, shivered with cold despite his anorak. He could have kicked himself for forgetting how much colder it could be away from the south coast. The skies were dark with cloud, although according to the forecast, rain was supposed to hold off until the afternoon. Sam hoped so, as there might be a greater chance of their thief being out and about. He rose from the bench and began to walk in the same direction as Pat.

He watched while she browsed in shop windows all along the length of the street. It was getting very cold; he breathed a sigh of relief when she finally walked into a large bookstore. Several people followed her in. Once inside, he tucked himself into a far corner, in the language and travel section. When Pat joined a queue at the coffee shop, he stood well back and watched.

He focused on a tall woman wearing a long black raincoat. He had noticed how she kept glancing at Pat. She was currently hanging around a table displaying three-for-two offers. When Pat moved towards the coffee counter, the woman remained where she was until two people joined the queue behind Pat, at which point she joined the queue herself.

Pat picked up her coffee from the counter and sat at a table for two. When the woman's drink was ready, she walked over to Pat's table and spoke – Sam was too far away to hear what she said. He watched Pat nod in agreement. The woman sat down opposite her and began to sip coffee. He observed them having a brief conversation, after which Pat pointedly began to scroll through her phone.

Pat looked up when the woman spoke again. They chatted for several minutes, and then Pat left. The woman's eyes followed as Pat made her way to the front entrance. Once she was out of sight, the woman moved quickly. She almost brushed against Sam in her haste as she rushed past him. Sam tailed them both at a safe distance.

As Sam had instructed, at midday Pat turned for home, unaware that the tall woman was behind her. When she reached her house, the woman watched as Pat disappeared inside. The woman then walked a short way up the road and drew out what looked like a key fob from the pocket of her raincoat. She clicked it and the lights flashed on a white jeep. She opened the driver's door and folded herself into the seat, where she remained, watching the house.

Sam ducked round the corner and noted the registration of the jeep. Another job for Charlie. He waited until he was out of sight, then rang Pat. 'What did the woman who came to your table talk about?'

'She just asked if she could sit with me. Afterwards she asked if I was shopping on my own. She said she was waiting for a friend, but she didn't think he could be coming. That's about it.'

'Well, she's parked near your house. She's sitting in a white jeep watching you. If you go up to your front bedroom window, you should just about be able to see her.'

'That's creepy. She was a bit weird. Her eyes seemed to glint at me behind her purple glasses. I don't remember ever seeing her before.'

'We will find out who she is soon enough. I've sent a WhatsApp to Charlie. She should be able to identify her if she's the car's owner. So, Pat – you know you're still being watched. Make sure you keep your door locked. Are you planning to go out this evening?'

Pat was silent for a moment. 'No, I've prep for school tomorrow. Can you ring me and let me know when she's gone? I suppose the cult are still hoping Miriam will come. Surely they can't keep it up much longer? It reminds me of when they were hanging around Miriam's house, waiting for her. I thought then that they're very stupid.'

'They're persistent, I'll give them that. Hopefully, they'll realise before long that Miriam hasn't taken the bait. Take care, Pat. You know where I am if you need me.' He rang off.

Chapter 20

Sister Olive had asked Sam to meet her at the cafeteria in Harper's store at 9.30 a.m. He arrived on time and travelled up to the second floor in the lift. It was a large area, and the tables were well spaced out. A few couples were eating breakfast, and other people stood in a queue waiting to be served.

Sam stood at the entrance and looked around for a single woman. He could see no-one obvious, and then he felt someone brush past him. Startled, he turned to face the tall woman in the long black raincoat who had been following Pat the day before. She raised her eyebrows as if to question him, thought better of it, and instead walked over to a table near a window.

Once there, she shrugged out of her raincoat and placed it on the back of the chair. Sam noticed she was dressed in black trousers and wore clumpy black leather lace-up shoes, but her jumper was bright orange. It looked like the sort of jumper his mother would have knitted: a substantial garment, with a large red and green embroidered flower which drew attention to the rise of the woman's breasts. She placed her shopping bag on the table and rummaged within, drawing out a newspaper. She looked pleased with herself as he walked towards her.

'I thought so. You must be Stan.' He nodded, and she indicated the chair opposite her. 'So nice that you managed to get here on time. Come and sit down.'

So, this was the woman who had stolen Pat's phone and tried to set a trap for Miriam. He observed her eyes glinting behind her purple glasses, just as Pat had described them. Her face was round and pale, yet her rouged cheeks gave her an appearance of health and wellbeing. Her nose was small and straight, but her lips were thin, and when she smiled, he could see gaps between her small, sharp teeth. He observed lines above her top lip and thought she might be a smoker, although he couldn't smell tobacco.

'And you must be Sister Olive. Very pleased to make your acquaintance. May I get you anything?'

She rewarded him with a coquettish look. 'Oh no, I couldn't possibly accept a drink from someone I have barely met. Let's go Dutch. I thought I might have a fry-up. How about you?'

'You go ahead, Sister Olive. I'll just have a drink.'

She got up, scraping her chair across the floor. 'You wait there, then.' She delved into her bag and drew out a large brown purse. 'I'll go and order – keep an eye on my bag.'

Yes, Sam thought, *beware of thieves. Is she tempting me?* He smiled at her and watched as she sauntered to the counter. She came back with a pot containing a knife and fork, a serviette, and a wooden spoon with the number 6 on it.

'Now, let me guess. I specialise in accents.' She peered at him. 'I think you are from the West Country. What are you doing up here?'

'Right first time, and it's work, Sister Olive. There's not much work to be had where I come from. How about you? Do I detect a Yorkshire accent?'

She clapped her hands. 'Yes, I used to live in York, but I've been living in Chester for twenty years or more now. What sort of work do you do?'

'IT mostly. I've some temporary work here, which might lead to a permanent post. I'm the person they call when something goes wrong.'

'Well, I never. You could be useful to us, Stan. My husband used to run our website. He can't now: he died a short while ago.'

'I'm very sorry to hear that.'

'Yes, well, these things happen. Best not to dwell. Now, where were we? Oh yes, the website. You called me about joining our group.'

A waiter approached them carrying a tray. She clapped her hands again. 'Yes, I'm number six. A full English. Oh, it looks lovely!' She pulled the serviette out of the pot with a flourish and tucked it into the neck of her jumper. As the waiter put the plate in front of her, she placed her knife and fork on each side, eyes full of anticipation. Without another word, she began to eat. Sam couldn't help but watch in consternation as she attacked the food. She tore at the bacon as though starving. It repelled him. He imagined what it must have been like for her husband; he probably died to get away from her.

He stood. 'I'll just go and get myself a coffee.'

She ignored him and carried on eating. When Sam returned, she was mopping up the remnants on her plate with a piece of bread and butter. 'My, that was good! I like indulging myself occasionally. No-one to stop me now.' She changed the subject. 'So, Stan – why do you want to join us?'

He sipped his coffee before answering. 'I liked what I saw on the website. I'm looking for something different. Forgive my curiosity, but are you a nun?'

She tittered. 'No, not a nun. It's one of our group's quirks. We call ourselves "Brother" and "Sister", and I suppose I've got into the habit of it. Our first names usually reflect who we are, and mine's an old Norse name for "kind". I used to be a nurse. Ursula is another member. Her name's Latin for "little bear", and she's a tiny woman; says she's a teddy bear! Isn't that strange?'

'That's interesting. Gosh.' He tapped his fingers on the table, as though thinking. 'You're not a women's group, are you?'

'No, of course not. Our friend William started the group, and there were four other men too. My husband Leo was one of them. His full name was Leofric, which in old English means "leader". So he became our leader. It was all meant to be, do you understand?'

'I'm afraid I'm just plain Stan.' Sam opened his eyes wide and smiled, hoping he was charming the strange woman.

'Well, if you want to join us, you could choose another name. Wouldn't that be fun?' She delved into her bag and drew out her phone. Using her index finger, she typed into a search engine. 'Here – have a look at this list of names. See if you can find a name that suits.'

Sam reached over and took the phone from her. 'Here, this would be a good name for me. Pascal – it's French for "Easter born", and I was born at Easter. What do you think?'

She clapped her hands once again. 'Oh yes, that's a lovely name! So, you're an Easter bunny. Pascal – well I never!'

He laughed with her.

'I think we're bonding already, Pascal. That's wonderful!'

'Does that mean I can join you? I lost hope after my divorce. You remember that old country song "Me and Bobby McGee?"'

She shook her head.

'It goes, "Freedom's just another word for nothing left to lose" – well, that's how I've been. Maybe taking a different name will give me a fresh start – and I could make new friends in the group.'

'Oh yes indeed. You'll make friends and have fun. But we must have the wake for my husband first; you will be invited, of course. Then we're going to set off on some new ventures.'

Sam frowned. What did Sister Olive's sudden change of direction say about her mental state? 'A wake, you say. So, your husband's death really was recent. Are you sure you want me there?'

Olive took great pleasure in saying the new name Sam had chosen, emphasising the end of the word. 'Yes, of course, Pascal.' The sly expression on her face changed into a beaming smile. 'You will be transformed. You have a lovely new name now, and soon you will grow into it.'

They gazed across the table at one another.

'I'll email you the details of the wake. Think of it as though you are coming to a West End play. I'll send you descriptions of our individual members and all the names, and you can guess who's who. What fun!'

Suddenly, Sam wanted to laugh. He found it difficult to contain himself. Wide-eyed and smiling, he let out a big breath. 'I can't believe how kind you are. The name Olive really suits you.' He managed to look serious by thinking about Ollie. They had tried to kidnap Ollie. Sister Olive, or whatever her name was, might come over as absurd – but she wasn't. It was acting, pure and simple. Yes, she was simpering now; she liked being flattered. He asked, 'You said you are going to set off on new ventures. Can you tell me a little about them?'

'Well, you see, now Leofric and William have transformed, we thought we needed a new direction. After the wake, we'll all get together and plan. Sister Enid, you'll like her, she's very Welsh and an innocent soul. She thought we should learn how to do water divination. Would you like to be a water diviner, Pascal?'

Oh no, he felt the need to laugh bubbling up again. This time he could hardly stop it. 'Marvellous, yes, I'd like that!' He gulped down the rest of his cold coffee, switching his mind back to how Sister Olive had just used the word "transformed". Although he couldn't grasp her meaning, he decided not to question her. 'Well, I'll wait for your email. I'd love to join the group if you'll have me. It sounds interesting. right up my street.'

The little girly clap came again. This time she even bounced up and down in her chair. 'I'm so pleased. You do promise to help us with the website though, don't you? It will need a bit of work now we're going to pastures new.'

He nodded. 'When you're ready, let me know what you want, and I'll be happy to help.'

'We're sorted, then.'

They both stood. He leaned over to shake her hand, a hand that felt dry and rough to the touch.

'You're not working today then, Pascal? You can come and go as you please.'

Aware that she was fishing, he looked straight into her eyes. 'I can work from home any time, don't you worry.' He took his phone from his pocket. 'This little gadget alerts me to any incoming.'

'Very handy, Pascal. I can see you are going to be a great asset to us. I'll be in touch.'

Sam helped her on with her raincoat. He caught a slight odour of sweat covered up with some sort of musky scent.

She buttoned up the coat, pulling the belt tightly round her middle, which made her belly protrude. She patted it. 'Such a good fry-up they do here. You should try it.'

He watched as she walked away, swinging her shopping bag from side to side. He didn't attempt to follow her. Charlie should have her name and address from her car registration by now.

He left the store and walked further down the street, looking for the anonymity of a franchise coffee outlet. He found a large Costa, went in, and ordered a flat white and an almond croissant. It was some hours since he had visited the hotel breakfast buffet. He felt empty, but the emptiness wasn't just hunger; it was something deeper. He had been touched by malevolence. Everything was wrong about the woman who called herself Sister Olive.

***

When Sam arrived back at his hotel, he switched on his computer and saw Sister Olive had already emailed the date and venue for the so-called wake. He emailed back, accepting the invitation.

Charlie had come up trumps. He now knew the identity and address of the registered keepers of the BMW tourer and Sister Olive's Suzuki jeep. The BMW was registered to Oswald Hughes and the jeep to Leo Lander, both living in the centre of Chester. He settled down to think. The wake was tomorrow evening in a church hall on the other side of the town, some way from his hotel.

Sister Olive, as promised, had sent him a list of the eight names of the group members attending and had attached descriptions of each. He looked at the list with growing concern. To put it mildly, her description of each member was condescending. She showed no feeling for any of them.

He spent the next hour writing his report. Charlie was a stickler for paperwork. She noted everything, no matter how small. He gave himself time to reflect on what he had written. He always did this; he would often spot details he had missed. They were in his head but somehow didn't get transferred onto the page, so he read the report slowly and with great care.

He had a feeling he was missing something. Why had Olive accepted him so readily? Was she setting a trap for him? What had she said that was niggling him? He read through the report again whilst visualising himself sitting opposite her. He frowned. Got it. It was the way she had used the word "transformation". She had inferred he would become transformed because of his new, assumed name. He had thought her comment strange at the time.

He wasn't sure why he had chosen Pascal. He was an atheist, and therefore, in his personal life, he dismissed superstition. Olive could be using "transform" to mean death. He went back to the Family of Hope and Rebirth website and read through their objectives: *The aim is to make whole that which has been sundered: to gather the supreme forces that will transcend the past.*

He shook his head. They seemed to be into transformation and rebirth, but there was no explanation of how. Did they mean resurrection? A thought about the early Judeo-Christian faith popped into his head. Olive had clapped her hands in delight at the name he had chosen. Pascal – Easter birth. It was the time when Jesus was supposed to have risen after three days.

Had he stumbled on something? Resurrection came after death. He shivered. She said her husband, Leofric, had died. However, at one point in their conversation, she had used the word transformed to mean death. Try as he might, he couldn't get the context in which she had mentioned it. He wished he had secretly recorded their conversation. That was a major slip-up when dealing with a complex individual like Olive. Was this woman dangerous? Yes, he believed so. Was this some kind of death cult? He wasn't sure.

So where did Ollie and Miriam figure in all this craziness? They wanted Will's son for some twisted reason of their own. But Will was no longer in the group. Sensible man: maybe he had become disillusioned with the group and left. While Miriam and Ollie were fleeing in one direction, Will might have been going in the opposite direction. He hoped so.

He would meet the group tomorrow. If he couldn't find out where Will was, his next task would have to be to locate him. He could only hope finding Will wouldn't lead to Miriam resuming her life with him in Chester. He was Ollie's father, and in the end, Miriam might put Ollie first. He also had to acknowledge that her friendships, her job – they were all in Chester. His heart sank as he thought it through. He had admitted to himself some time ago that he was attracted to her. She was such good company when she relaxed. Her dark eyes bubbled with fun. He wanted to be with her and Ollie and was determined to make his move when he thought the time was right. He even thought if push came to shove and she and Ollie wanted to return to Chester, he would follow them.

Chapter 21

The GPS told Sam that he was in the vicinity of the church hall where Leofric's wake was being held. He just couldn't see it, so he parked and went in search of the hall on foot. He had walked past it several times before he spotted a small plaque by an entrance in a high stone wall. He peered at the faded writing: he had reached his destination.

He gained entry through an ancient wooden door. The metal drop handle looked original, probably several centuries old. Sam examined it with interest. As he shut the door behind him, the metal latch dropped back neatly into its groove.

He found himself in a courtyard, where he almost fell. The stone flags, with moss growing in between each one, were slippery under foot. A tree, which he thought must be a yew, nearly obscured the door. The combination of high walls, old stone flags and the tree gave the building an air of mystery. He wouldn't have been surprised to hear the chanting of monks.

The entrance to the hall was through another old door, but this time the door handle was modern. He turned it and stepped into a small dark antechamber.

Sam took a deep breath of musty air. It took him straight back to his childhood, when, every Sunday afternoon, instead of him playing with his friends, his mother bribed him to attend the local Sunday school. It had had the same sort of stale smell. He had hated Sunday school. Casting his mind back now, he couldn't remember what he had learned or who had been there. He just remembered the sinking feeling he always had as he walked through the door..

Here he was again. But this time he was going into a situation with a job to do. He heard the inner door creak. He blinked hard. A tall monk in a black robe stood in the entrance, staring at him. They gazed at one another, both with puzzled expressions on their faces.

Almost simultaneously, something clicked in the minds of both men. The monk, who Sam now realised he had spotted outside Pat's house, was apparently Brother Oswald. Oswald called out in an unexpectedly high-pitched voice, 'Oh, you must be the new man Sister Olive has been telling us about. Welcome.' His thin face broke into a smile. 'Come on in.'

Sam followed the man into a small, brightly lit hall. He had to blink again. The people standing around were all dressed in similar black robes, except for one flamboyant figure. Sister Olive was dressed in a purple robe with an embroidered piece of red and gold cloth draped round her neck. The robe was far too long for her. It rustled as she strode over to greet Sam.

'Pascal, how wonderful! You've made it.' She turned to the group. 'Come on. Come and greet our newest member.'

Each one shook his hand. He also recognised Brother Oswald's wife, Sister Enid, but the others were strangers. Their black robes gave them some uniformity, but there was a stark disparity in their overall appearance.

When he had greeted everyone, Sister Olive put her arm through Sam's and led him to a long table on which were laid a variety of pies and sandwiches. At the far end, a giant chocolate cake had been placed on a glass cake stand. It had small birthday candles stuck into the top at odd angles. For a moment, Sam wondered if he had come to the wrong place. The wake was more like a bizarre birthday party.

Olive thrust a plate into Sam's hand, then turned to the others and called out, 'Come on, Brothers and Sisters, now our new brother Pascal is here, we can tuck in. We're here to celebrate Leofric's life and transformation. Don't be sad; remember he's in a better place. A miracle has happened, and in his new life, he will be whole again.'

Sam chose to keep quiet, and plate in hand, looked down at the table holding the food. He crossed his fingers, hoping it was all hygienically prepared. Two large tables had been laid with cutlery and condiments. As he had been given the privilege of being first to choose his food, he helped himself, then walked over to the furthest table with his plate of savouries. Sister Olive went next. *Oh no, she was walking towards him, with her plate piled high*. She sat down opposite him. Sam recalled Sister Olive's sharp little teeth barely chewing yesterday's breakfast in the café, and he shuddered.

She smiled at him. 'We have a present for you, Pascal. Don't start on your meal yet. I'll just pop out and get it.' Her robe whispered along the floor behind her. Sam found himself imagining Miriam in a wedding dress, walking down the aisle: how she would lift her veil and tilt her face up to his. But it wasn't Miriam he saw; it was Sister Olive, her round face and small eyes masked by the purple glasses. He shook his head to dispel the vision. These weird people were really getting to him.

Brother Oswald and Sister Enid were now walking towards his table. Sister Enid sat down next to him. Unlike Sister Olive's plate, hers was sparse: two small chicken wings, a scotch egg and three cherry tomatoes. Brother Oswald's plate was similar, with the addition of a large slice of pork pie.

'Tell us a bit about yourself, Brother.' Sister Enid's voice, in her North Wales accent with its sing-song cadence, brought him back down to earth.

'There's nothing much to tell, I'm afraid. I'm originally from the West Country. I work in IT. I'm a boring computer nerd and I spend all my days sorting out software.'

She smiled at him. 'Are you married? Do you have children?'

'I was married, but we didn't have any children and we're not together now.' Sister Enid looked sympathetic. 'Oz and I always wanted beautiful children. But it's just us two. Together forever, inseparable, aren't we, Oz?'

His wife gazed at him with sorrowful eyes, and he immediately changed his bland expression to one of sadness and nodded. 'Yes, dear.'

The door opened. Sister Olive glided back towards them, carrying a green supermarket bag. 'Here we are. We have a robe for you. It was Brother Harold's, but he's no longer with us. You're about the same size.' She pulled it out of the bag and held it out.

Sam started to reach for it, but instead of giving it to him, she held it to her face and sniffed. 'I washed it myself. I've put that smelly softener stuff on it. It's lovely. I get the whiff of a fine summer's day in the garden, just like they say on the adverts.' She chuckled at the thought, then scowled. 'Brother Harold used to smoke. I told him it would be the death of him. I don't believe you can transform smelling like an old ashtray.'

Sam remained silent. He was being given a dead man's robe. Sister Enid, seeing his expression, patted his hand. 'Don't worry, he's not dead yet. He had an accident, that's all. Fell down an escalator, poor man. He's recovering in a nursing home.'

Sister Olive handed the robe to Sam. 'Come on, Brother Pascal. Up you pop. Put it on and let's see you in it. I think it will suit. If you like, you can wear a jolly scarf with it, brighten it up a bit. I've got lots, all different colours. You can come round and borrow one.' Olive beamed at him.

'Thanks.' Sam tried not to show his distaste as he slipped the robe over his head and pulled it down to his ankles. He had to admit, it did smell rather nice.

Sister Olive clapped. 'Oh yes, just the right size. I thought it would be. That'll keep you nice and warm. Now, come on, let's eat. I'm starving!'

'Wait a minute.' Sam pulled out his phone. 'Can I take a selfie in my new robe first? Better still, how about a picture of you and me together, Olive?'

Olive looked at her food with regret. 'Good idea. Let's do it before we eat. Oswald, you take the picture. A lovely picture of our new recruit Brother Pascal with his dear friend Sister Olive.'

They stood together with broad smiles on their faces. No need for them to say 'cheese'; they already had their poses prepared.

Oswald took several photographs and handed the phone back to Sam. 'There, you should get one good one out of those.'

Sister Olive licked her lips, her eyes fixed on her plate. She ignored Sister Enid, who had pulled out a packet of wet wipes, and while the others wiped their hands, Sister Olive started to tear into her food. Their reaction to her bizarre behaviour was simply to nibble at theirs, but Sister Olive made short work of hers and went to refill her plate.

Enid whispered, 'Since her husband died, I'm afraid Sister Olive has become rather obsessed with food. Part of her grieving process, I expect.'

Sam whispered back, 'Strange reaction. But I suppose grieving takes all sorts of forms.' He tried not to grimace as Olive plonked herself down opposite him, her plate piled high again. 'Come on, everyone, there's loads left. Go and have seconds!'

No-one in the hall moved.

'I'm leaving room for the delicious cake you've baked.' Sister Enid tried not to show her disgust as Sister Olive tore at a chicken leg. 'You know I can't eat too much. I haven't got the height like you. It all goes straight to my middle.'

'Well, you'll have to wait, Enid. We must finish our firsts before we can go to seconds. It's all got to be finished. My mother would never allow …'

Sam stood. 'I thought I'd move round the tables. Get to know people while you finish eating.' He picked his plate up and walked over to the other table. The pretty elfin woman looked him up and down. 'That was quick. Where did the robe come from?'

'Someone called Brother Harold.'

Five pairs of eyes stared at him.

She replied, 'Oh dear. Poor Brother Harold. He hasn't transformed yet, and you're being given his clothes.'

The robed figure who Sam remembered was called Brother Henry had initially welcomed Sam, but now his warm demeanour disappeared. 'Hardly his clothes, Sister. Just his robe. It looks as though Brother Pascal is going to take his place. You'll have to watch your step, Brother. Anything could happen.' He gazed up at Sam. 'Sit down,

Brother Pascal, why don't you. Take the weight off your feet. Don't worry, we'll look after you.'

The elfin woman bit her lip. 'Harold nearly died. He's not well, and he's very confused.' She muttered, 'Still thinks someone pushed him, does he? Well, he could be right.'

The others stared at her.

Brother Henry turned to Sam. 'Are you sure you want to join our merry band? Strange things do seem to happen.' Unaware that Sister Olive had walked over to their table and was now standing behind him, he whispered to Sam, 'Careful, old boy. Olive has you in her sights.'

'What mischief are you cooking up now, Henry? Leave Brother Pascal alone. I know what you're doing. I assure you, I'm not looking for a replacement for my beloved husband. I see him all the time. He is with me in his spirit form and a great comfort to me.'

Brother Henry rose from his seat and reached out for Olive's hand, and gazing at her the entire time, kissed the back of her hand with reverence. 'Oh, my dear, dear Sister, I'm so happy for you. So, he has transformed already. It is indeed a miracle.'

'You never cease to surprise me, Brother Henry. Sometimes so frivolous, but this time, you have got it in one. Indeed you have. Now, how about cake? I baked it myself this morning.' She turned to face the room. 'Come on, everybody. We each have a candle to light for Leofric. Then we can say a little prayer for him before we let him go to another realm.'

With her robe held out in front of her, she led the way. She picked up a plastic gas lighter, brandishing it before her as if she held a magic wand. 'Line up like you did before. I'll go first, followed by our newfound Brother Pascal, then everyone else can follow on. Say a little prayer to Leofric when you light the candle, then pass the lighter to the next person.'

So, the ceremony began. Each person lit a candle, then bowed their head in silent prayer before handing on the lighter.

The oldest of the members looked tearful. She murmured a prayer in a quavering voice that everyone could hear. 'Go into that dark night, Leofric, and find my husband like you promised. Tell him I must speak with him. I'm still waiting.'

Her son put his arm around his mother, took the lighter, and laid it back on the table.

Sister Olive glared at mother and son for a moment. 'It is *I* who command my husband's spirit, not you. I am going to blow all the candles out now, and afterwards, he will obey my commands.'

Her smile revealed her sharp teeth, and Sam was immediately reminded of the fairy-tale wolf about to eat Red Riding Hood. He shivered.

'If you are nice to me, I'll ask him to search for your husband. But he may have more important things to do.' She leaned over, breathed in, then blew hard at the candles. They kept burning. She had another go. They kept burning.

The elfin woman (for that is how Sam now thought of her) said in a loud voice, 'I know what you've got there. Everlasting candles. Where did you get them from Olive, a joke shop?'

For the first time, Sam saw Sister Olive lost for words. The wolf had disappeared; the inward struggle she was experiencing was visible on her face.

A nervous giggle escaped as she lifted her hand to her mouth. 'They were in the drawer. They were part of Leofric's kit. He must have wanted it to be like this. No matter, we'll wait for them to burn out. Then I'll do the command.' She turned to each of them. 'Yes, I can hear him. It *is* what he wanted. Soon they will burn out and we can finish the ceremony. Then we can each have a slice of cake and a glass of wine. It will be our communion; it will bind us all together.'

Her face brightened, and she beamed at them all.

***

As they were about to leave, Brother Henry sought Sam out. He stood square in front of him. He seemed to have an involuntary tic as he winked and bobbed his head. 'It's been wonderful to meet you, Brother Pascal. Let me shake your hand.' He grasped Sam's hand in his own and shook it with vigour. 'Yes, old boy. Great to meet you. No doubt we will meet again before too long.'

Sam felt something being placed in his hand. He made a fist of it as he smiled at Henry. 'Thank you for making me so welcome, Brother Henry. Until the next time.'

Sam thrust his hands into the pockets of the robe. Whatever he had been given was slightly sticky; it clung to his hand. He brushed his palm against the pocket until it was released.

The group changed in the antechamber, stuffing their robes into the bags Sam had noticed when he first entered. Sister Olive handed Sam the bag in which she had brought his robe. He disrobed too, folding the robe up neatly, mindful of the item in the pocket.

They all looked so ordinary without their robes. It was

surreal; Sam felt as though he had been carried into a parallel reality. The floor had turned into quicksand. It threatened to pull him down until his head disappeared and he would no longer be able to breathe. He looked down at his feet. The stone flags were moving. Time had slipped. He put his hand on the wall to steady himself and saw Sister Olive's eyes glinting at him. She turned from him, a triumphant expression on her face.

They were about to leave when Sister Olive cried out and raised her arms towards them. They stared at her as she removed her glasses. Her eyes were filled with tears. 'Oh, how wonderful. Leofric has revealed himself to me.' Her voice trembled. 'He wants me to scatter his ashes into the sea, in our special place.' She turned her head from side to side, as though listening to a far-off voice. 'He wants Brother Oswald and Sister Enid to be with him at his new beginning too. What a wonderful revelation! I'm so happy.' She raised her arms to the heavens and called out. 'Husband, I hear you and will do as you ask.' Then she clapped her hands and turned to beam at them all.

All the members of the group stared at her. Sam glanced over at Brother Henry, who was barely able to keep a straight face. Sister Enid was the first to embrace Sister Olive, after which, lined up again, they took it in turns to hug her.

As Sam walked up the road in search of his car, he shook his head in amazement. He had rarely witnessed anything so preposterous.

***

Back in his hotel room, Sam shook out the black robe and felt in the pocket. He found a piece of serviette smeared with sticky chocolate icing. He turned it over. Scrawled on the underside was the name Henry Parker and a phone number which was just about decipherable.

He was relieved that the fuzzy feeling he had had outside the hall was beginning to go, but he made himself a cup of mint tea to dispel the indigestion he had. Settled at the table with his tea, he rang the number.

'Hello, *old boy*. Thanks for getting back to me.' Apart from the emphasis on 'old boy', the voice had changed. There was no jocularity in it now.

Sam remained silent.

After a moment, the voice began again. 'OK, I understand. I don't know who you are, but I know where you are.' He laughed. 'That surprised you, eh?'

Sam still chose not to speak.

'So, can we meet in reception, or shall I come to your room?'

'Come up – it's room 403.'

Sam opened the door and ushered Henry in. They stood eyeing one another suspiciously. Sam was surprised by the change in him. Gone was the persona he had presented in the hall. Here he stood up straight; he looked taller and older. His facial expression had changed. He was serious, no more winks, just steady eye contact.

'How did you find me?'

Henry smiled. 'Followed you from the hall, of course.'

'Why did you follow me?'

'Look, Sister Olive is cunning, but she's not too clever. I asked myself why a new member would suddenly turn up to revive the group, when we all thought the group was finished.'

'Alright, you've caught me out. But why are you here? Are you Sister Olive's minder or something? Are you reporting back to her?'

Henry burst out laughing. 'Are you kidding! No, I'm a mole. A spy.'

'Who are you spying on?'

'I'm Harry Townsend's grandson. Harry Townsend is Brother Harold; you have his robe. Cards on the table. I'm with the group to find out what happened to him. Poor Grandfather joined the Family of Hope for friendship – I felt bad, because initially, I showed him how to attend their zoom seminars, then when Covid lockdowns relaxed, he started going to their meetings. My mother noticed a change in him, went along with him to one of the meetings, realised it might be a cult, and tried to persuade him to leave. By then she thought they had some sort of hold on him. He refused to leave, so I joined instead to keep an eye on him, swearing him to secrecy. He played along brilliantly. Then he had his accident. Now we're sure they did have their hooks in him, and we're certain his savings have been raided.'

'How do you know?'

'It was the so-called accident. He survived the fall down the escalator, but he's suffered a brain injury, as well as broken bones. He's in a nursing home, and he's unlikely to be able to go home. The social worker asked my mother to be with him while the admin people went through his finances. He's got to pay, you see. Anyway, there's a lot of money missing, and he's unable to tell us where it's gone. So, you see – I'm a mole. I'm on the case. Now you know who I am – who are you, *Brother Pascal*? Why are you here?'

Sam had been sipping his mint tea all the way through

Henry's revelations. He hadn't decided whether he could trust this man, not yet. 'Have you got any ID on you?'

Henry stared at him. 'You are one careful person. Let me see.' He pulled his wallet out and handed Sam several cards. 'Satisfied? If I was spying for our Olive, I would have told her you're not what you seem. Come on, *Pascal,* come clean. Are you the police? You have that look about you.'

Sam, elbow on the table, hand on chin, contemplated Henry. 'Sam Huxley, private investigator.'

'Aha! I knew it! You're investigating Will's disappearance, aren't you?'

'What makes you say that?'

Henry scowled, enunciating his words very slowly as though Sam was an idiot. 'It might be - because he's disappeared! Come on, *Sam,* I've been straight with you. Tell me.'

Sam decided he had no option but to trust Henry. 'I'm investigating the Family of Hope and Rebirth on behalf of Will's wife. She's worried about her husband.'

Henry's eyes widened. 'I knew it. Behind the mumbo jumbo, all the prancing around in robes, there lies danger. I've done quite a lot of ferreting – Olive's full name is Olive Lander, and I think she's evil. I hope you didn't eat too much of her chocolate cake. She put cannabis in it.'

'Interesting. That accounts for my wobbly feeling. I thought time had slipped for a moment back there.'

Henry carried on, 'The first thing I noticed when I joined the group was the fuss Olive made of my grandfather. It made my stomach churn to see her being all girly and flirty with him. Silly man was flattered. I think she got what she wanted out of him, then tried to dispose of him. He's been a wonderful grandfather to me.

It's terrible to see him as he is now.'

'I'm sorry, Henry. It's a bad business. My advice to your mother would be to apply for power of attorney. If he lacks capacity, it should be straightforward. Then, if your suspicions about his finances are correct, you can involve the police. As a vulnerable adult, your grandfather would have certain protections. Is there anything else you can tell me? Do you know something about Will, for example?'

'Not much. He was a shadowy figure – always robed, with the hood obscuring his face. By the time I joined, he had almost removed himself from the group.'

Sam interrupted, 'How do you mean, removed?'

'He stopped coming to the meetings. We were told he was very close to finding the secret of transformation. I remember someone asking what transformation was, and our dear leader sneering. He said, "How do you expect me to tell you?" Meaning, I suppose, we had to wait for Will's revelations to find out. They seem to have a lot of respect for him. They called him the marshal. But he was mostly in the background. It was Leofric, Olive's husband, Leo, who was the leader. A powerful man. Tall, very heavy, legs like tree trunks and with a face that had been badly disfigured.'

Henry stopped speaking for a moment, looked over at Sam, and grimaced. 'Yes, it was a bad business. All of it. I thought it was finished when Leofric died, but it seems Olive has other ideas. I think she's skating on thin ice. As I said, she's cunning, but not particularly bright. She's likely to trip herself up. Then we'll have her.'

Sam nodded. 'Possibly. What happened to Leofric? Do you know?'

'I was there!' Henry cried. 'It was all very intense. He

was having one of his ceremonies. We were all invited over to Will's house. When we got there, Leofric was lording it over us in his purple robe – the one Olive's wearing now – he had a pentangle drawn on the floor, and all these night-lights placed round it in a circle. He stood in the middle and cried out to the so-called Supreme Being. Totally nuts, but this time, it was weird: the lights started to flicker, and it felt as though something was moving in the room. Then the light stopped flickering, came on properly, and went off and then on again. There was a crash. I think Olive engineered that – shoving a vase onto the floor. The whole thing was too much for the poor old boy. He made a weird, guttural sort of sound, then collapsed. He was out cold. Olive didn't want him to go to hospital. She wanted us to carry him out to the car. As though we could. You would have needed a crane to lift him. It was ambulance or nothing. We decided to leave before the medics arrived.'

Sam listened attentively to Henry's testimony. 'You said this all happened in Will's house.'

Henry nodded.

'Was he with you at the ceremony?'

'No, he didn't come. Quite frankly, if he has any sense, he will have got as far away as possible from the mayhem Olive and Leofric had been causing. Olive seemed quite at home in his house. I bet she'd been after him as well. The woman's man-mad.'

Sam shook his head. 'She does seem to latch onto men. You called her cunning. I'm sure you're right, but she's also an arch manipulator. Everything she does will be for a reason. I think she exploits people, uses them for her own ends. I've never met Will, but from what his wife has told me, he's erratic and impulsive. Olive will undoubtedly have a purpose for him if he hasn't got away.'

'So, what shall we do?' Henry's serious face reminded Sam of himself, when, as a young copper, he had been thrown in at the deep end. Henry, with no training or skill apart from his obvious talent for acting a role, would be a liability. He tried to let him down gently. 'I must contact Will's wife. I need her instructions before I act. But there's no "we", Henry. There could be danger.'

'But you need me, Sam! What about me taking you to see my grandfather, for instance? He's lucid sometimes, and he might tell you something he hasn't told me. He still thinks I'm a young kid.'

Sam smiled. 'Yeah, I can do that. But that's all. We don't know what we're dealing with. Arrange for me to meet your grandfather tomorrow, and we'll go from there. There's a possibility Olive and the others have gone away by now. You remember her pretend vision after the wake telling her where to scatter Leo's ashes. If they have gone to do his bidding, there's not much I can achieve here, and I might be needed back at base.'

Henry was more cheerful. He had something to do, and Sam might change his mind. 'Alright then. Let's swop details now and I'll leave you in peace. We might get some new insights tomorrow.'

Sam raised his eyebrows. 'Remember what I said. There's no "we". I'm being paid to do a job. I can't be worrying about you.'

***

Sam looked at his watch. It was 10.15, maybe too late to ring Charlie now. He wanted to talk to Miriam but knew hearing her voice would distract him. No. Report writing first. He sat staring at his laptop. He had no idea how to start.

His phone rang at 10.35. It had to be Miriam.

'Hello, Sam, is that you?'

Not Miriam, but a voice he didn't expect.

'Hello, Cat. This is a nice surprise. How are things in Rock House?'

'We're OK. Kirsty and Ollie are now blood brother and sister – literally! Miriam is moping but trying not to show it. We've had a few nice days' weather.'

'So, why the phone call?'

'I've been meddling. It's Sally. She's been negotiating with Charlie. When you come back, she may be your new office angel.'

'That's good news, Cat, but why did you really ring?'

'You know me too well, my darling. I'm worried about Miriam. Ollie has settled in well. He's happy. Miriam doesn't seem so happy. You will have to tread carefully with her, Sam. She's frightened of her husband. She's haunted by him. She's a loyal person, and despite all that's happened, she still thinks it's her place to help him.'

'I might be able to come back in a couple of days, Cat, but in the meantime, all you can do is give her your support. Could you tell her I was late in tonight, but I'll ring her tomorrow?'

Caitlin ignored his request. 'Are you going to try to find her husband?'

'In good time, Cat. I've joined the group. I haven't found out where he is yet, but I'm getting closer. Whatever has happened to Will is not going to be good, not if Sister Olive is involved.'

Caitlin's voice sounded trancelike. 'Miriam's haunted. There are things going on we don't understand. Be very careful, Sam. My mother's ghost is restless. I can feel her here – watching over us.'

Sam knew how seriously Caitlin took the sightings she had of Cessie, long since passed away. 'You think she's warning you again?'

'Yes, I'm quite sure she is. Be very careful, dear Sam. I'm sorry I've rung you at night – dumping this on you, not a fair thing for me to do. Come home soon. We all need you.'

'I'll try, and I will be careful. You be careful too, Cat.'

After the phone call, Sam sat in the quiet of his hotel room, trying to make sense of his conversation with Caitlin. He didn't really believe in the existence of ghosts. Caitlin knew how he felt, but she had absolute belief, and maybe she had been right all those years ago. Her mother's ghost had warned her. But that didn't mean he had to believe the same.

Caitlin said Miriam was haunted by Will. But they were just dreams. Why did Caitlin think dreams were causing a resurgence of ghostly activity in Rock House? It made no sense to him. Of course, Ollie would be convinced. He believed in the ghostly Agnes Howe and thought she had saved him from falling from the walls of Flint Castle.

Then he remembered how Henry had alluded to 'mayhem', a phrase which he hadn't followed up. He must ask him tomorrow whether the group ceremonies they performed were based on some form of black magic. He chided himself. There was no such thing. The paranormal did not exist. It was more likely the group were role-playing. He bet, if he visited Olive's house, he would spot some old Dennis Wheatley novels on a dusty bookcase. Dennis Wheatley had been a favourite of his father's, alongside books about beings from other worlds. All of it daft, he thought, but harmless. From what he had learned about the Family of Hope, it was far from harmless.

His mind was in overdrive. The conversation he had had in Harper's café with Sister Olive came back to him. She had said that both her husband and Will had been transformed. Yes, that's what he had tried to remember before. He struggled to think in a logical way, but he kept going back to the same thing. It was beyond his understanding because it was supernatural. He felt he was being trapped into thinking in a way that he would normally reject. However, he had to remind himself that twenty years ago, in Rock House, he had come to believe in Caitlin's ghost. He shook his head. *No!* He had been right yesterday. It was preposterous. He must put away all these random thoughts about the supernatural. He was an investigator, not a ghost hunter.

He knew he had put no real effort into finding Miriam's husband, maybe even avoided it – but tomorrow, he could put it off no longer. First the visit to the nursing home to see whether Brother Harold/Harry had anything to tell him. Then he would knock on doors in the vicinity of Miriam's house.

No chance of writing his report now. It was too late to ring Miriam. He'd send her a text and promise to contact her tomorrow. Little chance of sleep either. Good old Caitlin; she had dumped on him good and proper.

Chapter 22

The following afternoon, Sam met Henry at the nursing home. It was a modern building. None of the cabbage or toilet smells he remembered from visiting his own grandfather. This home was clean and brightly lit. The staff were dressed smartly in blue uniforms.

Henry led him through the lounge. None of the residents were watching the large TV but were dozing in their chairs, lulled by a gameshow host. It was very warm in there. No wonder their heads lolled forward. Sam was sure his would too, given half a chance. He had had a bad night. Sleep would have been very welcome.

Henry's grandfather, Harry, had a comfortable single room. He sat looking out of his window into the garden, where the wind moved the bare branches of trees, but the flower beds beneath were bright with narcissi and hyacinths, and the sky was a brilliant blue.

Henry called out, 'Hello, Grandad! How are you feeling today? I've brought Sam to visit you, like I promised.'

Not only did Henry talk at his grandfather loudly, but he didn't give him time to answer his question. Sam wondered if it was always like that when people grew old.

Harry Townsend looked alert. His back was straight. His hair was still quite dark, and he sported a moustache, giving Sam the impression that he might have been in the services. The army, maybe. The walking frame in front of him, however, told a story of broken bones.

'Your moustache isn't getting any better, son. Told you, shave it off. You won't get a woman like that!'

Henry leaned over and kissed his grandfather. He

grinned. 'I know. Soon, I promise. Maybe next time I come in, it'll be gone. Sam, come on over, grab a chair.'

Sam held his hand out. 'Very good to meet you, Mr Townsend.'

'Please, son, call me Harry. No Mister this or that in here. We're all on first name terms, like it or not.'

Sam listened as Henry and his grandfather chatted. He noticed how Harry repeated himself. Henry was patient and good-humoured, answering but also deflecting him when his grandfather became confused.

A nurse came in to enquire if they all wanted tea. It was served with a piece of chocolate sponge (not laced with cannabis this time!), and when they had finished, Henry moved the conversation to his grandfather's accident. 'Do you remember your accident, Grandad? Do you remember where it was?'

'Of course I remember. I was in that big shop, you know the one. I was tired. I was at the top of a ... what's it called, a moving staircase?'

'An escalator, sir?' Sam's gentle voice prompted him.

'Yes, that's it. I remember falling.'

'Can you remember if there was anyone behind you, Grandad?'

Harry closed his eyes. For a moment, Sam thought he was going to sleep. Then he opened his eyes and whispered to his grandson, 'I remember somebody breathing in my ear.' He shook his head from side to side. 'Sorry, I can't remember what happened next.'

Although Sam was concerned that the old man would become upset, he wanted to ask one more question. 'Harry – do you remember what you were doing in the shop?'

At first, Harry looked confused by the question, but

then he answered, 'What was it? There was someone there, someone to meet. I'm sorry, I don't remember. I bumped my head, you know. They tell me I'm lucky to be alive. I tell them you can't kill an old soldier that easy!' He winked. 'Sergeant Major Townsend at your service, sir!'

'Of course they can't, Grandad. You're a tough one.' Henry looked over at Sam and shook his head.

Sam had no more questions.

***

Henry joined Sam in his car. 'Do you know which shop your grandfather was in when he had the accident?'

"He was in Harper's. They called Mum when they were waiting for the ambulance. She had the impression the staff knew him quite well.'

'We can't jump to conclusions, but that's the same store where I met Sister Olive for the first time. Coincidence, don't you think? Trouble is, even if the staff can recall Olive being there with your grandfather, it won't prove anything. He's an old man; he could have tripped.'

'Well, can't we try? If she did push him, my grandfather deserves justice. All we need to get started is a photo of Olive. I can find one of my grandfather.'

'What did I say to you yesterday, Henry? No *we*.'

'Oh, come on. That's not fair. He's my grandfather, and I'm the one who led you to him. I've also told you who Sister Olive and Leofric really are. I'm quite good at this, you know. And I won't get in the way.'

Sam sighed. 'Okay, as he's your relative. We'll go together.'

Henry was about to say something, but Sam got in first. 'Right – if you are out with me, you do what I tell you. You will say nothing. I will do the talking.'

Henry nodded. 'Alright, boss.'

'In addition, everything we do is confidential. You don't talk it over with your mother, or with anyone else for that matter. Is that clear?'

Henry nodded again. 'I promise. When shall we start?'

Sam smiled. 'I want to make sure Olive has really gone away before we do anything, and I've got plans for the rest of this afternoon. So, why don't we go tomorrow? I'll meet you in the store at ten a.m. I suspect Olive is a frequent visitor; she remarked on how good their breakfasts were before she gobbled hers. Reminded me of a labrador I used to own, but not so nice.'

Henry wrinkled his nose. 'I can imagine. Alright, I'll be there.'

'Hang on a minute, Henry. Don't you have a job to go to?'

He grinned. 'All sorted. I asked for two weeks' annual leave yesterday. It's worked out well. I've been bidding for research contracts, so it's a waiting game now. I've got some work I can do from home, but I'm due a load of leave.'

Henry's answer wasn't what Sam had expected. 'What is it you do?'

'Medical research, but since we left the EU, research contracts are like hens' teeth. I have a feeling I might be looking for a new job before too long. Maybe retraining. Quite fancy the idea of teaching.'

Sam, who always thought honesty was the best policy, said exactly what was on his mind. 'I must apologise. I've been mixing you up with the rest of that group you belong to. You know, you are a fantastic actor. I've been treating you like a child. If you retrain as a teacher, my advice is to go for teaching drama.'

Henry burst out laughing. 'I'd make a brilliant Poirot, don't you think? And despite what Grandad says, I'd have to keep the moustache!' With that, he opened the car door. 'See you tomorrow.'

Sam watched him as he strode away. He must have guessed Sam would be watching – he jumped and clicked his heels together, then turned around and waved before disappearing up the road.

**

Olive and Leo Lander's small, unassuming house was near the town centre. Sam presumed this was the same house the group operated from. He parked and walked around. There was no sign of life. He took a risk and knocked. No reply. It seemed Olive really had gone away. He walked around to look at the back of the property. It was very close to the city walls; he could see people ambling along the top, taking in the views. He would be seen if he tried to gain entry in daylight. Next, he located Oswald's and Enid's house. No sign of them being there either.

Now to locate Miriam's house. It was situated in a residential area a mile or so away.

Much of the housing looked as if it had been built after the industrial revolution. The houses were close together, two-up two-down, each with a back yard. Alleyways ran along the back. He found her house, just as she had described it: larger than the other properties and situated on the corner of the road.

He parked and walked up the road to the house. Unlike the others, it had three storeys. Ollie had told him how he could look out of his window at an oak tree. There it was, and there was the entrance to the canal. He crossed and walked down the tow path as far as a bridge, then walked back and sat on a bench to think.

He remembered Miriam saying she had run out of the back gate to get away from the couple who were standing at her front door. There was always the possibility that Will had changed the locks to prevent Miriam entering. When divorce was in the offing, anything could happen. If necessary, he could break in via the kitchen. But first, he had some door-knocking to do. He checked the time. It was 5.15 already and would soon be sunset, maybe a colourful one, given the wispy clouds being blown across the sky by the southwesterly breeze.

He felt frustrated. The wisest action to take would be to go back to his hotel. Door-knocking could wait until the morning. It was not fair to expect older people to open their doors to a stranger when darkness was falling. He sighed. Another day had gone, and he wasn't sure what he had achieved. Okay, Harry may have been pushed, but there were unlikely to be any new witnesses, and no-one had come forward at the time. And Henry's involvement? Sam liked to work alone, but Henry was keen and had insider knowledge of the cult, so Sam didn't want to reject him. He figured it was worth the risk. He would give him the photograph of Olive in the morning and leave him to it. Now he must concentrate on finding what had happened to Will. That had to be his priority. He shivered. It was getting cold. He walked back up the tow path, hoping to find the pub where Miriam, Sally and Ollie had lunched on New Year's Eve. He was getting maudlin. He wanted to understand the life she had lived here in this little corner of Chester.

He craved company, so, after he had found the pub, he rang Pat and settled on a picnic bench by the canal to wait for her. When she arrived, the sun was about to set. Gentle greys and pinks bathed the sky with colour. Pat sat down beside him. Dressed in a chunky sweater, she didn't seem to feel the cold, but Sam shivered despite his anorak and scarf. As the sun sank below the horizon, he began to feel really chilled. She laughed and said the last few days had been unseasonably warm. It still didn't feel that warm to him. Pat called him a 'softy southerner'.

She could see he was feeling low. She had meant to have a quick drink and a chat, but instead they went inside and had dinner together. He was glad to have her company. When he asked her where she, Ollie and Miriam had sat for their New Year's Eve lunch, she raised her eyebrows. 'My, you have got it bad.' When he asked her what she meant, she shook her head. 'Well, if you don't know, I'm not telling you. Ring Miriam.'

When he returned to the hotel, he did just that. She immediately asked him about her husband. Had he found Will yet? Their conversation was friendly but impersonal, and he felt flat, thinking they were dancing around one another, neither of them voicing what they really felt.

After the phone call, he reassured himself – *just another few days, and I'll have this death cult in the bag. I'll have found out where Will has gone, and everything will work out*. If only. He knew from experience: life had a way of tripping him up.

Chapter 23

Sam woke to bright sunshine. He had been in a deep sleep, and for a moment wondered where he was. He grumbled out loud to himself – he was such an idiot. Why couldn't he tell Miriam what was on his mind? He grimaced. *Stop beating yourself up. You're not a teenager. Get up, get showered, get dressed and have breakfast.* He groaned. *Plan, that's what you've got to do: meet Henry, give him the photo of Olive, then leave him to question the staff in the café. You never know; he could get lucky.* Sam decided he would begin with door-knocking in the Rope Lane area.

He wasn't sure why he was in a bad mood. It was unlike him. What he was experiencing was an acute sense of foreboding. He swung his legs out of bed and reached for the kettle. Time to start the day.

***

Henry's moustache was gone, but he wasn't quite clean-shaven. Stubble had appeared, removing him further from his Brother Henry appearance. His face was surely thinner, his nose more pronounced. There were laughter lines around his eyes Sam had not noticed before.

With Henry's tasks agreed, Sam left him in Harper's store and set off for Miriam's house. He had to drive around adjacent streets until he found a parking space. It took him ten minutes to walk back to the end of her road and into the back alleyway. Pat had given him the front door key, but the gate at the back was padlocked. He had intended to climb over the wall for a quick look round before he tried the front door. Instead, he saw a policewoman, on tiptoe, already peering over it.

He called out, 'Excuse me!' He delved into his jacket to retrieve his wallet and drew out his ID.

The officer turned to look at him.

'Are you looking for Mr Marshall? I've been employed by Mrs Marshall to try and find him.'

The officer was tall, almost as tall as him, dressed in uniform trousers and jacket. She took his ID, pushing her short, wavy hair back from her forehead to read it. She looked him over and frowned. Sam guessed she was near retirement and world-weary. He had known officers like that when he was in the force. She had dark hair, and was dark of eye, with a square jaw, a straight nose and a very determined mouth. This one would not suffer fools gladly.

'Thank you, sir. You're in contact with her? We've been trying to locate Mr or Mrs Marshall to get into this property.'

'Yes. Do you want to talk to her? I have her number.' He scrolled down to Miriam's number and handed the police officer his phone. She wrote the number down in her notebook.

'OK, Mr Huxley, follow me.' She walked up the alleyway, tutting at the rubbish in one corner, and crossed over to a police car parked on the pavement under the oak tree. 'Wait here while I ring your client.' She got into the car, leaving Sam feeling rather like a naughty boy. Why did some women have that effect on him? He was confident in his job and his ability, but still, a woman police officer could make him feel guilty. *Guilty as charged, ma'am.*

The officer re-joined him. 'Mrs Marshall says you have the front door key, and she has given us permission to enter the property. Do you have the key with you?'

'Yes.'

She held her hand out. He thought she wanted to shake his hand and held out his own. She raised her eyebrows in amusement. 'I wanted the key, but yes, I should have identified myself. Constable Stuart. May I have the key now?' She reached her hand out again. 'Thank you. '

'Constable, may I ask you why you are here? Has a crime been committed?'

She shook her head. 'We've had complaints from the neighbours. Bad smell, clouds of flies. Possibly a biohazard – could be the plumbing or rubbish left in the house by Mr Marshall. I understand from his wife that it was all in order when she left the house approximately two months ago. So, shall we go and investigate?' She opened the door and stood back. 'Mrs Marshall tells me you were in the Met. What does that smell tell you?' She opened the door wide.

Sam screwed up his face in disgust. 'Putrescence of some sort. Decomposition, sweet smell of rotting meat.' He turned to her. 'Have you any masks in your vehicle?'

The constable went to the car and came back wearing a mask. She handed him a spare one and a pair of latex gloves. 'Okay, let's go in. Start in the kitchen, although I fear this stench is unlikely to be rubbish.'

It was clear that the house had not been lived in for some time. The worktops were dusty. There were grimy marks on the cream-tiled floor. A large bin held what looked like the remains of Christmas decorations and spent night-lights. No dirty dishes or cups on the worktops or in the sink. Sam noticed a cloth lying in the sink. He wrinkled his nose in distaste as he bent to examine it. Possible traces of vomit in the creases. They opened the back door to let in some welcome fresh air. The bins had been emptied. The drains were clear. Plumbing was not the source of the smell.

Sam tried to stop himself thinking about how Miriam would be feeling if she was with them now. The house was unkempt, unloved, and had an odour that was all too familiar. Furniture had been pushed against the wall in the lounge. Henry had said the cult had been holding a ceremony when the leader collapsed – it must have been in this room. He could just make out faint chalk marks on the floor.

The last ground-floor room they checked was at the back. It contained a desk, a chair and a single unmade bed: Will's study. It seemed to have been used as a storeroom. As he looked around, Sam realised why the lounge had been so empty. All the things that would have made it homely had been thrown in here.

'Okay. Nothing downstairs. Let's go upstairs.' The constable led the way to the hall landing. There were two open doors, and a third, which was closed, with steep steps leading up to it. The first two led to a large bathroom and a spare bedroom. Everything was tidy. Sam peered up the steps to what he guessed must be Ollie's attic bedroom.

The policewoman opened the third door. A cloud of flies flew into her face. She cried out in disgust. 'I'm afraid we've found the source of the stench, Mr Huxley.'

Sam entered the room and walked over to the bed to stare down at a body lying underneath a duvet. Constable Stuart remained in the doorway.

Sam carefully pulled the duvet back to reveal the decomposing body of a dark-haired man in pyjamas, one bony hand clutching a red scarf. Sam let the duvet drop and turned to his companion.

She walked over and stood behind him, her face ashen. 'I think we may have found your missing man. It seems he's been dead for some time.' She remained where she was, her hand over the mask, covering her nose. Sam hoped she wasn't going to be sick.

'How very sad. He must have died in his sleep. Come away now. We'll lock up and I'll report in. There's no more we can do here.' The constable turned from him and hurried down the passageway.

Taking one last look at the body, Sam left the bedroom, shutting the door behind him. He went downstairs and saw Constable Stuart standing on the pavement outside. He joined her, shutting the front door behind him.

She ripped her mask off. He could see her chest rising and falling as she breathed in large gulps of air. She scowled. 'Those flies. I hate flies. Worse than finding a body. If it is Mr Marshall, the lab will identify him soon enough. In the meantime, I'd better arrange for Mrs Marshall to be informed.'

She took her time talking to her police colleagues on the radio, and when she had finished, she opened the window and leaned out. 'Thanks for your help, Mr Huxley. Here's my card. Ring me if you have any further information about Mr Marshall. I think we can be pretty sure we've found the poor man.'

'You don't think we might have stumbled upon a murder scene, do you?'

She looked startled. 'What makes you say that?'

'The strange way the house was organised, as though there'd been a party.'

'Well, that would make sense of why a man should die

in his bed, wouldn't it? Too much alcohol, drugs, maybe. Heart condition – who knows? We'll get to the bottom of it.'

As she drove off, she called out to him, 'Nice to meet you.'

***

Sam stood under the oak tree, staring at the patrol car as it cruised down the road. *Wish I could say the same for you*, he thought. He shook his head. *No respect for the dead.*

He had deliberately left the kitchen door unlocked. He wanted another look inside the house. As an experienced crime-scene officer, he would be able to spot any irregularities the constable had missed or chosen to ignore.

He walked back to his car for a mask and gloves and hurried back to the alleyway. He climbed over the back wall into the yard, and the smell hit him again, but this time he was expecting it. He put his mask on, aware that breathing in polluted air could damage his lungs. He started in the lounge, taking several photographs. He looked more closely at the chalk marks, and as he did, he spotted a fragment of vase under one of the sofas, corroborating Henry's testimony.

He went upstairs. This time he examined the room in which the body lay. He took more photographs. He noticed a jug, containing what appeared to be water, on the bedside table. An empty glass lay on the floor. He picked it up and sniffed. There was no discernible odour. He pulled the duvet back and took a close-up photo of the scarf clutched in Will's hand. It looked remarkably like the sort of scarf Sister Olive would wear.

He noticed that the sash window was wedged open with a man's square hairbrush. He bit his lip and scowled. How long had Will been lying here? It could have been months. The wintry air blowing through the window would have kept the body cool, but the recent warmer weather would have accelerated decomposition.

He climbed the stairs to Ollie's bedroom and smiled when he saw the model railway taking up half of the room. It appeared nothing had been disturbed. This was where Ollie had said the ghost had appeared. She had sat in the old blue velvet chair beside his bed. In a soft voice, he said. 'Are you here, Agnes? If you are, knock three times.' Then said to himself, *Oh, very clever, Sam. Look what happened when Cat's ghost was mocked. Do not vex a ghost!*

He was about to hurry back down the stairs when a sound made him turn back. One of the little trains had activated. It was slowly rolling under a model bridge. Gathering speed, it circled the track before coming back to rest at the model station.

A look of amazement flooded Sam's face. He called out, 'Good on you, Ollie. You do have a protector. I'm here now, Agnes. Trust me, I'll help you look after the boy and his mother.'

Feeling ridiculous, he went downstairs and took one last look in the kitchen before he locked the back door. Then he let himself out of the front door and walked down the road without looking back.

He needed time to think. Miriam would be getting a visit from police officers, but probably not until tomorrow morning. First, he wanted to contact Charlie to tell her what he and the constable had discovered. He had chosen not to divulge anything about the case to the constable, but having re-examined the scene, he was unsure whether he had acted wisely. He tried Charlie's phone, but it was turned off. He rang Henry instead and asked him to come to his room at the hotel. He had to talk it over with someone.

***

Henry had been to Harper's to enquire about his grandfather. However, as Sam had predicted, the staff could remember the incident, but they could not be certain that his grandfather had met Olive Lander beforehand. They did recognise her as a frequent customer, but that was all.

Sam described his encounter with the police.

Henry was clearly shocked that they had found Will in the house and that he had been dead for some time. 'I never really got to know him, but the others respected him in a way they never respected Leofric.'

Sam explained how the police were likely to process Will's death and concluded with his suspicions. He wanted to move their own investigation on and made several suggestions, including gaining access to the Landers' house.

Henry nodded his head in agreement. 'As long as we don't get done for breaking and entering, I'm up for it.'

'At the moment, the police are unlikely to have made a link between the Landers and William Marshall. We're only going to be looking for written records, unless we have the luck of the devil and get into their computer. Meet me at the back of their house at seven p.m. this evening. If there are still walkers on the city wall, they

218

won't see us in the dark. We'll get in and out as quickly as possible. We need the details and contact numbers of all the group members.'

'Agreed. We could stage a coup in Olive's absence! Let's hope we find evidence linking Leofric and Olive to what happened to my grandfather. Great thinking all round, Sam.'

***

Although Sam and Henry searched the house that evening, they found no written evidence to link the Landers with financial gain, but Henry made a discovery. On opening the door to Olive's wardrobe, he wrinkled his nose in distaste at the odour of sweat and perfume, but he set about his task diligently and was rewarded when he found a small pile of files. After his initial excitement, he was to be disappointed. The information was scant: members' contact numbers, dates of birth and marked attendance registers. He took the paperwork downstairs, to find Sam feeling mounting frustration as he tried and failed to crack the computer's passcode.

Henry had returned to his search area to ensure everything was as he had found it when he heard Sam call out that it was time to leave. He had just spotted some loose papers hidden underneath clothing in a drawer he had failed to check the first time. He stuffed them into his rucksack and promptly forgot he had them.

The men left the house as surreptitiously as they had entered it.

PART 5

Chapter 24
Rock House
11 March

Caitlin had been vacuuming her bedroom and had not heard the knock at the front door. She noticed the security light had come on outside and went over to the window. Two police officers stood outside. She recognised the male officer who looked up at her; he had a daughter the same age as Kirsty. She immediately thought of Bob and ran downstairs to open the door.

'Good evening, Caitlin, we're looking for Mrs Miriam Marshall. I believe she's staying with you. May we come in?'

Caitlin felt sick. Bob was alright, but something must have happened in Chester. 'Yes, please come in.'

The female officer spoke calmly. 'Could you locate Mrs Marshall for us, please?'

Caitlin gazed at the officers. They had come with bad news; it was written all over their faces. She didn't pursue it.

'I think she's upstairs. Come and sit in the lounge. I'll go and find her.' Caitlin was aware that Ollie and Kirsty were in the dining room, working on Kirsty's history homework. She peered round the door; they were too focused on their research to notice her. She closed the door quietly behind her and hurried up the stairs to the flat. She knocked and called out, 'May I come in?'

Miriam had her back to Caitlin, and when she turned to face her, she looked distraught. 'Sam's just rung. He and a police officer found a body yesterday. He didn't want to worry me, not until the body had been identified, but it's Will.'

Caitlin walked over to Miriam and pulled her into her arms. Miriam allowed herself a few moments of comfort before drawing back. 'No wonder I saw him in my dreams. Sam said he was in bed, in his pyjamas, as if he was asleep. The poor man. His soul must have been in torment.'

Caitlin was stunned. It took her a moment to take in what she had heard. Poor Sam! He really was in the thick of the investigation. 'I am so sorry, Miriam. That's truly terrible news. That may explain why we have two police officers downstairs – they're waiting to inform you.'

Miriam stared at her. 'But what can I say to them? Sam hasn't told them anything yet. What should I do?'

Caitlin put her arm around Miriam's shoulder. 'I think they've simply come here with the news about Will.' Then she spoke without thinking, and almost as soon as the words were out of her mouth, she wished she could unsay them. 'He may have been murdered by those people.'

Miriam shook her head. 'No, I don't believe so. Will was easily led. It's more likely he went to his death willingly. He would believe he was going to be reincarnated. He had a thing about going back in time.' She shivered. 'I don't want my home to be known as a murder house. It's not fair, Cat. Will has already turned our lives upside down, and for what? One of his crazy ideas. I should have realised what he was up to.'

Caitlin sighed. 'I'm sorry, I shouldn't have mentioned murder. But honestly, how could you ever have foreseen what was going to happen to Will? None of this sorry mess is your fault.'

Miriam froze. 'Oh God, Ollie's down there with Kirsty. I must tell him.'

'Talk to him afterwards, in your own time, Miriam. Hearing it from police officers could leave him with a terrible memory. See the police on your own up here, and I'll stay downstairs with Ollie and Kirsty.'

They hugged one another again.

'I'll take them through the kitchen and show them the way up to the flat. Don't worry, I'll make sure Ollie's alright.'

***

'Mrs Marshall, we are so sorry for your loss.' The two police officers had chosen to sit on the dining chairs while she sat on the sofa. They had asked if they could make tea for her, but she had shaken her head in refusal. She had known what was coming, but shock had silenced her.

'Your husband has been formally identified by his GP, but because of the circumstances in which he was found, there will have to be a post-mortem.'

Miriam didn't respond, so the policewoman continued.

'After the post-mortem, the coroner will release Mr Marshall's body, and you will be able to register his death. You must register within five days of the release. Then you can arrange his funeral.'

The officers observed Miriam as she struggled to comprehend what they were saying. Miriam felt as if she was waking from a trance, and when her voice returned, words tumbled out, uncontrolled, without thought. 'My husband was mixed up with some very peculiar people. I was threatened by them, and they tried to snatch my son.

We ran away from home because Will wanted custody, but he was behaving so strangely that Ollie was frightened of him.'

The two officers stared at her. The male officer looked sceptical. What was she saying? Shock did strange things to people.

Reading the expressions on their faces, Miriam wished she had kept quiet. Why hadn't she left it alone? She must stop. 'I'm sorry. You must think I'm hysterical. He really was mixed up with strange people. I thought all sorts of things could have happened to him, but not this. Poor dear man. To die alone.'

She brushed tears from her eyes. 'Forgive me. Thank you for coming to tell me, but I need to talk to my son.' Miriam was barely holding herself together. Her hands shook. She staggered as she tried to get up and sat down again. Neither police officer moved. 'I'm sorry, I'm not thinking straight.'

The woman officer reacted first. She stood and spoke in a sympathetic tone. 'This has hit you hard, and we are so sorry for your loss. Would you like us to call anyone for you?'

Miriam shook her head.

'Are you sure there is nothing we can do?'

Miriam shook her head again.

'OK, we'll liaise with our colleagues in Chester and pass on what you have told us today.'

Miriam got up, relieved that the police were winding down the interview.

The woman officer handed her a card. 'Ring me if there's anything I can help you with. There's no need for you to show us out.'

After they had left, Miriam felt as if she had been

wrung out and emptied of all emotion. Strangely calm, she remembered how Rock House had seen its share of tragedy. Hadn't Sam told her he was first on the scene to find a man lying dead at the bottom of the stairs? She watched the police officers from the window, and when she had seen their car disappear down the drive, she went downstairs to find Ollie.

Her legs felt leaden. What can you say to a child when his father has died? Ollie had been frightened of what Will had become. But once, there had been good times, Will had been a loving dad, and they had had fun together.

That's what she would say. 'Hold onto the good memories.'

***

Back in the privacy of their flat, Ollie cried in his mother's arms. He didn't need her to remind him of the good times with his father. 'He was great once, Mum. But he couldn't help being sucked in by the darkness. It was too strong for him. You remember, Agnes told me he couldn't hurt us anymore.'

Somehow Ollie understood what his mother was thinking and found the strength to reassure her. 'He wasn't alone, Mum. Agnes was there with him. Dad got mixed up with evil people. Remember they tried to kidnap me. That's why we left. I don't think anyone could have saved him. The darkness had swallowed him up.'

'Oh, Ollie.' She gazed into his innocent grey eyes, then leaned back on the sofa and closed her eyes for a moment.

Ollie touched her shoulder. 'What are you thinking, Mum?'

'About the struggle between good and evil. I don't think I've come across real evil before. If good always wins in the end, it didn't help your dad.' She reached out for him. 'You're getting tall. Your face is changing too; I can see how you'll look when you're an adult. Remember how I said I didn't want you to grow up too soon? I wanted you to enjoy a carefree childhood.' She frowned. 'If you gave me marks out of ten for effort, I think I'd be at zero.'

'No, you wouldn't. None of this was your fault. You've protected me, and we can still be happy, but not yet. We have to say goodbye to Dad.'

Miriam smiled sadly, 'I'll have go back to Chester to sort things out, and I want you to stay here. Safe in Rock House. Will you do that for me?'

Ollie protested, 'I should be with you, Mum.'

'No, not this time, but in a few weeks, when arrangements have been made for the funeral, then we'll go to Chester and say goodbye to Dad properly. I promise I will talk everything through with you.' Her voice shook. She tried to smile, but in the end, it was the child who comforted the mother.

***

Later that evening, Charlie visited Rock House. In a businesslike manner, she explained the process the police would undertake, and that Sam was in contact with the police in Chester, who would keep him informed. She said that although Will's body had been identified, the cause of death had not been established. However, the police would allow entry to the house within a day or two. Sam had been in contact with Pat; their plan was to hire a firm to deep clean and to dispose of the bed in which Will had perished. Sam had not divulged anything about his investigation to the police.

When Miriam went back to the flat, she rang Sam. His message service kicked in. She left a message to ask him to keep quiet about the cult. 'Please, Sam, wait until I come. We can talk to them together.'

Chapter 25
Swanage
11 March

Choosing Swanage had nothing to do with the 'vision' Olive had had at Leo's wake. She and Leo had spent the few miserable days of their honeymoon in a guesthouse in Blackpool. No, she had chosen Swanage because the phone she had stolen from Pat James held some very interesting photographs. The device had even told her where and when the photos had been taken. She giggled to herself when she thought how she could rid herself of Leo's ashes and lay a trap for Will's boy in one fell swoop.

The day before she left Chester, she told Oswald and Enid that she would drive to Dorset on her own to make all the arrangements for a perfect holiday for them. It was to be a thank you for all their help and support during Leo's illness. However, when she rang them from Swanage, they discovered they would not be staying in a hotel, as promised; they would all stay in what she called a luxury lodge in a holiday park. So much for Olive's promises.

Oswald and Enid set off from Chester in driving rain. Rather than 'making a day of it' as Olive had suggested, Oswald drove at a steady 50 miles per hour all the way down the motorway. They only stopped for a late lunch in a service station near Gloucester, then carried on towards Taunton.

Enid was very bored. Oz always insisted on driving, calling her his 'ace navigator'. But there was no navigating to do. They had travelled miles on congested motorways, with lorries and cars speeding by them. She could hardly see anything ahead because of the spray thrown up by other vehicles.

Oz insisted on driving in the slow lane. 'Steady as she goes. We'll all get there at the same time.'

Well, she doubted that very much. She was becoming more and more irritated, until she burst out, 'I can't see the point of wasting petrol, travelling all the way down to Dorset. Why on earth couldn't we have gone to Colwyn Bay or Southport? More convenient and probably much nicer. Ridiculous bloody woman she is!'

'Maybe it's her way of grieving for Leo. Cut her some slack, love. What I can't figure out is why she wants us with her.' He sighed. 'I suppose, as the saying goes, no man's an island, and the same could be true of Olive, although it's hard to believe.'

Oswald continued, a frown of concentration on his face, 'We'll be off the motorway soon, love; it'll be better then. You can navigate us via Yeovil, then Dorchester, and then we're nearly there. Another two or three hours and we'll be with Olive in her luxury lodge.'

Enid groaned. 'Oh God, what a thought. It'd better be good, and I don't want to stay too long. You promise?'

'Yes, of course, love. Don't worry. A few days at the seaside will do us both a power of good.'

It was dusk by the time they reached Swanage. They got lost and drove round the town twice. In the end, Enid insisted they stop to ask directions. When they eventually managed to find the holiday park, the reception was in darkness, so they drove round and round the site, looking for the lodge in the dark. They were not in a particularly good temper by the time they found it, perched as high on a hill as it was possible to get. They struggled out of the car into what felt like a raging gale.

Enid tripped going up the steps to the door and banged her toe. Turning to Oswald in exasperation, she yelled, 'At least she could have put the bloody light on!' She banged on the door in a temper.

They saw Olive's moon face appear at a small side window, and then she was at the entrance. She stood there as large as life and beamed at them as she cried out, 'Welcome, one and all! Come in, come in!'

Oswald hung back for a moment and muttered to himself. 'She thinks she's welcoming us into a blooming pantomime.' But he only smiled. 'Hello, Olive, how lovely to see you.'

Oswald looked around the caravan, for that was what it was. He wasn't happy. 'Look, Olive, you said we would be staying in a luxury lodge. Alright, this caravan is big and should have a lovely view of the bay, but the wind is shaking the whole bloody structure to bits. What possessed you to book a holiday caravan at the top of a hill in March?'

'All the hotels were full.' Olive looked at them with an innocent expression which didn't fool either of them. 'Leo would have loved it up here, and look, when it's light, we will almost be able to see the pier. I went there yesterday to ask them about the ashes.'

'You still want to scatter them off the pier, then?' Enid, who felt a little better now they had reached their destination, chuckled. 'You could open the urn and we could let him go into the wind. Watch his ashes float off over the cliffs and into the sea.'

'You romantic old thing, Enid. The ashes aren't in some Egyptian looking urn. They're in a packet.' She got up from her chair. 'I'll go and get them.'

They watched her as she opened one of the kitchen

cupboards. She pushed back some crockery and produced a square green package. She held it out for them to inspect. It was about twelve inches in diameter and made of some sort of cardboard.

Oswald exclaimed, 'They fitted all of Leo in there! Such an enormous man squeezed into a little packet. It's extraordinary!'

Olive burst out laughing. 'They did cremate him first, you silly Oz. But you've made a valid point. I suppose they gave me the right ashes. I mean the ashes could be a small person, for all I know. I wouldn't have a clue who they've given me, would I?'

Enid examined the package and snapped, 'It doesn't really matter. You know he was a monster, don't you, Olive? I think it's a fitting end, sticking him into a little package. We'll have to remember to take scissors with us to get him out. It's well sealed.'

'Ah, no, no!' Olive cried. 'All we do is chuck him in, package and all. It's biodegradable. We don't have to scatter him. We could say a little prayer for him as he goes down into the deep. The package will simply dissolve in the seawater.'

***

Oswald groaned. It was early morning, and he lay on the edge of the pull-out bed beside his slumbering wife. He had had an uncomfortable night. He wasn't used to sleeping with Enid. She snored. Not only did she snore, but she also rolled over onto his side of the bed and kept pulling the duvet off him. He didn't think he could take much more.

Olive had provided supper the night before: pasties

from the local shop and baked beans. After a day of eating motorway food, baked beans were the last straw.

He now knew Enid farted in her sleep. It wasn't doing much for wedded bliss. He poked her. 'Do you want a cup of tea?'

She stirred and muttered something. He went over to the gas stove and fumbled around in several drawers before he found matches. He wanted to make as much noise as he could. Serve both women right.

With the gas kettle on, he peered out of the front window. Early morning mist still obscured the view. Typical, but it might turn out to be a fine day. Well, whatever the day held, they were going down the pier to do the business. One more night, and he was going home. That was definite.

***

Miriam wasn't looking forward to the journey back to Chester. Ollie was still asleep when she rose. She folded her bedding and placed it all in the box underneath the sofa. By the time she had showered and dressed, Ollie was awake and preparing toast for them both.

'Are you really going without me, Mum?'

For a moment, Miriam thought he would cry, but instead he turned away, opened the fridge, and poured himself an orange juice.

'Yes, I'm going soon. What are you and Kirsty going to do today? It looks as though it's going to be a nice day.'

'Kirsty says when the tide comes in, we'll go crabbing, and we're going to take Frida for a walk. Bob's going to cook us a Sunday roast for tonight.'

'Gosh!' Miriam said lightly. 'I wish I was staying now.'

Ollie's face lit up for a moment, until he realised she wasn't serious. 'No, Mum. Do what you said and then come home quick. Bring Sam too, and then he can tell me how he did the investigation.'

She looked at his anxious little face and could have wept, but instead she smiled. 'Yes, of course, and I promise I'll be back as soon as I can.'

By 10.30, Miriam was on her way. She drove slowly, remembering how she and Ollie had stopped at Corfe Castle and Wareham on their way to Studland. It seemed a lifetime ago. That Ollie had asked her to hurry home to Rock House hadn't been lost on her. Soon they would be able to start a new life. She sighed. Will, in death as in life, was causing confusion and disorder. She and Sam had had their first argument on the phone last night. In the end, she had put the phone down. She would not contemplate murder. She knew her husband had gone willingly to his death, no matter what Sam said.

Chapter 26

For Leo's last farewell, Olive had discarded her usual black apparel. She had dressed herself in purple: trousers and jumper of the same hue, and a woollen jacket in a slightly different shade. Pascal had complimented her when she wore the purple robe. The colour suited her. Pascal, her new favourite. She still wore her clumpy black shoes. They reminded Enid of the shoes worn by Rosa Klebb in *From Russia with Love*.

As they walked down the hill towards the town, Enid and Oswald managed to keep the conversation flowing by putting different ideas in Olive's head. They knew if one stuck, she would take it as her own. Despite their efforts, she was adamant they must continue with the group. She waxed lyrical about Pascal and the hopes she had for her new friend.

By the time they reached the pier, the mist had evaporated. The sky was a brilliant blue, with wisps of white cloud scudding by in the northeasterly breeze. It was cold and Olive shivered. 'Let's get this over and done with, then we can go to the pub for lunch.'

Oswald and Enid weren't going to argue. They had not been offered breakfast.

Olive took charge of the proceedings. She informed the volunteers at the entrance to the pier that everything was in order and marched straight past them, packet held out in front of her as though she was in a relay race. She walked with single-minded purpose towards the far end of the pier until she found a point she liked. Oswald and Enid walked slowly behind her.

When they were all together, they leaned over the railings to watch the sea below. It was rough away from the shelter of the bay. Waves were flowing rapidly underneath, blown in towards the shore by the wind.

Oswald thought the tide was still going in. 'Will it be alright to drop Leo in here? Look at the direction of the waves.'

Olive was ready. She wasn't going to wait because Oz thought the tide was rising. 'They told me the packet would dissolve and sink within minutes. Stop fussing. It will be fine. Come on, you two. Say a little prayer and I'll chuck him in.'

Olive leaned over the railings and threw the packet. The wind caught it for a moment, blowing it towards land, then it hit the water and began to swirl around. The three of them watched it in fascination. How could Leo, such a great big hulk of a man, be enclosed within this small green packet?

Enid hoped they were seeing the last of Leo, but what would happen during transformation? She imagined him appearing again in a puff of smoke, like a genie from a magic lamp. She blinked her eyes hard to rid herself of the image.

The packet really was swirling around now. It wasn't ready to sink. They watched a wave take it under the pier and hurried across to wait for it to appear on the other side. It was like playing a ghoulish game of pooh sticks.

It was floating towards the shore. Enid closed her eyes. There were children and dogs on the beach. It didn't bear thinking about. She whispered, 'Please sink, Leo.

You can't keep going.' Whether he heard her, or whether the packet had just reached its optimum saturation point, it disappeared. Enid breathed a sigh of relief.

Ever theatrical, Olive lifted her arms up and cried into

the wind, 'Hail, great warrior! Go out and conquer other worlds. We will meet again one day.'

Oswald scowled and turned away, muttering, 'Cloud cuckoo. As mad as a box of frogs.'

Olive smiled at him with cloying sweetness. 'Oh, dear Oz, you've just said a prayer! Leo would have appreciated that so much. Thank you, both of you, for sharing these precious moments with me. Let's go for a little walk. We can think about dear Leo, and then we can go and get a bite to eat. Your turn to pay, I think.' She set off, shoes clumping on the wooden boards of the pier.

Oswald and Enid followed her, wondering where they had gone wrong.

The three of them walked along the harbour. Children sat with their legs dangling over the wall, holding crabbing lines. Oswald couldn't help but notice a grey standard poodle waiting patiently by a brother and sister. Olive, who was feeling rather noble, having just said goodbye to her warrior husband, walked up to the dog and put her hand out to pat it. 'What a beautiful dog. What's your name, doggie?'

The dog growled.

Olive jumped. 'You should have that dog on a lead, little girl. It bared its teeth at me!'

Kirsty looked up at the old woman. 'Oh, I'm sorry. She's never done that before. Frida, come here.'

The dog continued to stand between the woman and the children.

Ollie got up. He had just had a crab tickle on his line, but he wasn't going to allow someone to be nasty to the dog. He called her. 'Good girl, Frida. Come.'

The dog trotted to his side, and he turned to smile at the woman. She stared at him, but he hardly noticed her;

she was just an old woman, and he wanted to get back to that crab. Kirsty had managed to catch three already.

Oswald watched Olive. She turned away from the brother and sister with a strange expression on her face. Did she have to be so nasty? He had a sudden compulsion to look at the boy. Dark hair, grey eyes. It couldn't be. Not Will's lad, here in Swanage of all places. If it was, thank God the boy hadn't spotted him. There was no reason why Olive should recognise him. He put it out of his mind.

The pub Olive chose was on the corner of the High Street. Despite the cold weather, people were sitting outside on picnic benches, chatting to each other. Some were smoking, and all had drinks in front of them. Oswald, once a smoker, would have given anything for a fag, a pint of beer and some sensible male company. He needed something to take his mind off the last twenty-four hours. He longed to pack up and get back home, away from this unbearable situation.

'Come on, you two. I've changed my mind. I'll treat you both.' Olive's mood had certainly improved. She stood between them and linked her arm through each of theirs to guide them across the road.

Although she was hardly aware of it, she had become Sister Olive again, and her brain was in turmoil. She knew now, beyond any doubt, that Leo was supreme, and by association, so was she. In her mind, there was no other explanation. She had forgotten all about the stolen phone. He was calling her from the deep and had guided her straight to the boy with those unmistakeable grey eyes. Somehow, she must rid herself of Oz and Enid, then she could go to work.

Chapter 27

Miriam reached Pat's house in Chester as the sun was setting. She stood in the driveway and marvelled at the salmon pink haze in the sky. It was good to be alive. Less than three months ago, she had come here to unburden herself and to seek refuge. She and Ollie had left Will to surrender himself to darkness. On the journey, she had continually asked herself the question – if this whole saga was a fight between good and evil, who had won? As far as she could work out, neither good nor evil had triumphed yet. Now she was here, having to confront the grim consequences of Will's behaviour, and she was mortally afraid. Maybe he and his darkness would win after all.

She had tried to banish Will's death from her thoughts, but it was impossible. The contrast between the living and the dead was too great. A grisly scenario appeared to her again and again. Although he usually slept alone in his study, she saw Will asleep in their old bed. She pulled the covers back to join him, only to see a skeleton dressed in his striped pyjamas – the old-fashioned pyjamas she and Will had once laughed about. Try as she might, she could not dispel the image.

Pat, who had spotted Miriam from the bedroom window, ran downstairs. 'Mimi, safe and sound at last! I've been worried about you. How was your journey?'

Miriam followed her into the hall before speaking.

'Slow. I drove up in a dream and can hardly remember the journey. I couldn't stop thinking about Will dying in the house alone. Of all the things I imagined happening, I never thought he would take his own life.'

Pat frowned. She wanted to challenge her friend but

instead kept the conversation at a safe level. 'Why don't you take your bag upstairs? The bed's made up in the spare room, and you must be hungry. Supper will be ready soon.'

Miriam leaned over and unzipped her bag. 'I've brought some wine.' She stood up, holding out two bottles of red. Neither of them moved. Miriam thought, *I'm always going to remember this moment. Two good friends, not quite sure what to say to each other anymore.*

'That's kind.' Pat took the wine, expecting Miriam to pick her bag up and settle herself in. Instead, she stood as if frozen. 'What is it? You look as though you've seen a ghost.'

Miriam came to and shook her head. 'Sorry, I was somewhere else for a minute. I'll go and freshen up.' At the bottom of the stairs, she hesitated. 'Have you seen Sam?'

She was rewarded with one of Pat's toothy grins. 'I promised to call him when you arrived. Shall I call him now?'

'I'm not sure I want to see him tonight. We don't really see things the same way.'

Pat spluttered and forgot all thoughts of safety or compassion. 'You know, you are an ungrateful so-and-so. Here he is, away from home, putting himself in danger, looking after your interests, and you're turning a few words you had with him into a quarrel.'

Miriam stared at her friend. She wasn't joking. What had Sam been saying? She managed to mutter, 'Point taken. I'm sorry, I wasn't thinking. I've been upset.'

'Of course you've been upset! Will's gone and got himself killed, but taking it out on Sam is just plain stupid. The next few days are going to be hard. You need his support, and he's a good man. Haven't you made enough mistakes in your life?'

Miriam didn't fully understand or appreciate Pat's sharp tone. They were friends, but what right did Pat have to say such things? She didn't want to provoke an argument, so she held her tongue, simply saying she would try and put things right. She hurried up the stairs, shutting the bedroom door behind her. She had made her best friend turn against her. What was happening to them? She had spent her life trying to be good. Evil had come in the guise of a man who had chosen death, with no thought for the person who would find his decomposing body. Will had wanted everyone to suffer. He had succeeded.

When Miriam eventually came down, she looked bereft, her eyes red-rimmed. 'I'm sorry, Pat. I'm not dealing with Will's death very well. It's the way he chose to die that's finished me.'

Pat picked up an empty glass and poured a generous helping of wine. 'Come and sit down. I should probably apologise to you. Tell me what happened with Sam. He's been very quiet. Whatever you said ...'

Miriam interrupted. 'I guess I lost it. I couldn't come to terms with the idea that Will cared so little for Ollie and me that he took his own life, without a thought for the impact his death would have. If we had gone back, we would have found him. Imagine how that would have affected Ollie. Afterwards, I realised people who commit suicide can't help what they do. They're not in their right minds.'

It was Pat's turn to interrupt. 'Why do you keep saying he committed suicide?'

'Sam seems to think he died of a drug overdose, so

what other explanation is there? He had a thing about re-creation. You remember Ollie saying he was looking for something ancient? I think in his twisted mind, he thought he was going back in time.'

Pat wasn't convinced. 'Maybe he did. But look, I want to ring Sam. He has a lot to tell you.'

'I don't think I can face him. He took my place. I should have found Will's body. He was in my bed. He meant us to find him, but coward that I am, I ran away.' She put her head in her hands. 'I'm ashamed.'

Pat gazed at her friend. 'Can I be honest with you, without you hating me?' Miriam looked up and whispered, 'I could never hate you.'

'Somehow or other, guilt has become engrained in you. You always see things as your fault when they're nothing of the sort. You can't take on the sins of the whole world any more than you can truly understand what another person feels. I'm not trying to preach to you, but try to let go. Don't think that way. You're not the centre of everything. You were certainly not the centre of Will's world, and you are not responsible for his actions. Keep an open mind; that's all Sam and I want.'

Miriam's self-pitying expression changed to one of surprise. 'You and Sam?'

'Aha – that got you! Yes, me and Sam. We're just like that.' She crossed her fingers. 'We're friends, you nitwit. I like him. And he hasn't confided in me; he's too loyal. We've only talked about the investigation, and he's got a plan. Him and his mate Henry.'

'Who's Henry?'

Pat chuckled. 'Now, he's a man I do warm to. He joined the cult to find out what was happening to his grandfather. He had me in stitches telling me about his experiences in amateur dramatics.'

Miriam looked confused.

'He said that getting into his character in the cult was his best acting job yet. Anyway, he's been helping Sam. Look, it's a long story. Why don't you hear what Sam has to say? I guarantee you'll both have a better night's sleep after you've given yourselves a chance to speak honestly.'

Miriam swallowed a large gulp of wine. 'I'll lay the table for three, then, shall I?'

***

Miriam and Sam had danced around one another all evening. They kept the peace by avoiding what was difficult for them, neither of them willing to voice their feelings or make eye contact. They both snatched glances before quickly looking away if spotted by the other. Pat simply observed. They needed time and space on their own to sort things out, but they were unlikely to get much of that in the next few weeks. They were each feeling lost, but unable to find one another.

After they had eaten, the two women gave Sam centre stage. He described how he had met Sister Olive and the other members of the group. He described his impression of how they functioned and operated. He made light of some of his recollections, but he remained steadfast in his belief that Will had been given dangerous drugs by members of the organisation, and they had to be brought to justice.

'No, Miriam, don't just dismiss it. Look at this.' Sam showed her the photograph of the scarf in Will's hand. 'Will was clutching this, and it's not yours, is it?' Sam's words were falling on deaf ears, but he would keep trying. 'It was under the duvet. Sister Olive wouldn't have known it was there. At least consider that he might have left us a clue!'

'It's true, it's not my scarf. Maybe he did fall for your shady lady – Sister Olive. Pat and I always suspected there might be another woman.' Miriam hoped Pat would say something, but she seemed determined to keep out of the discussion. 'None of this is making any sense to me, Sam. What are the police thinking? The scarf would have the Olive woman's DNA on it, wouldn't it? If they thought it was important, wouldn't they have investigated her by now?'

'I don't know what the police are thinking or doing, and my only contact is through Constable Stuart. As I said, we entered the house together. She immediately jumped to the conclusion that Will's death had been caused by alcohol and drugs; she couldn't get out of there fast enough. Consider this, Miriam – Will was a victim, and there may be more victims. We have a duty to stop them.'

Sam's statement hit home. Miriam gazed at him. 'I do get what you're saying, Sam, but I'm still convinced Will went into an unholy pact with members of the cult and made a choice. I agree others might be coerced. I can't help thinking of that poor student of his who committed suicide, but I honestly don't believe he was coerced. It's not logical. He couldn't have been a victim; he was the perpetrator. So, yes, let's go to the police and flag up how dangerous we believe the cult could be.'

At last, Pat joined the conversation. 'And the attempted kidnap. What about that? Surely I don't need to remind you – Ollie was threatened. He might still be at risk for all we know.'

Miriam took a deep breath. 'He's safe where he is now. Will can't want him; he's dead. That's a ridiculous notion.'

Pat disagreed. 'I don't think you can take anything for granted, Mimi. To my way of thinking, the cult members all have a screw loose, apart from Sam and Henry, of course.' She frowned at Sam. 'So tomorrow you need to begin preparing for what lies ahead. '

Miriam nodded. 'I know you're both right, and I appreciate what you're doing, I really do. But my heart sinks. I don't want my old home to be tainted with murder. It's not fair to it.'

Sam was restless. He rose and walked over to the window, and when he turned to face Miriam, his expression was difficult to read. 'When I went back to the house, I went up to Ollie's room. One of Ollie's model trains started to run, and the lights came on. Maybe Ollie's protector, his ghost, will want justice? The best thing I can say about Will is that he was a gullible fool. As he reached the point of dying, he might have regretted his actions. Hence your nightmares. Come on, Miriam – your home will survive. Ollie's ghost will still be there, guarding it. There's nothing to lose by telling the truth.'

For the first time, Miriam smiled, but the smile left her face as Sam outlined his and Henry's plan to get the group together one more time.

Chapter 28
Swanage
14 March

The day had barely dawned, and Enid and Oswald were already packed and thinking about their departure. It appeared there was no breakfast to be had in the caravan. Oz suspected Olive had a stock of food hidden in her bedroom. Luckily, they had had a good meal on Sunday evening and weren't hungry. The meal had been paid for rather grudgingly by Olive. She had gobbled her large plate of roast beef down rapidly, and before they had even finished their first course, she had ordered herself apple pie with cream, custard and ice cream. Then she became grumpy because Enid and Oswald went to the bar and chose a dessert as well. It crossed Oswald's mind, but only for a fleeting moment, that she might be short of money. No, she was up to her usual tricks. She was selfish and penny-pinching.

When it came to paying, she studied their bill carefully before stating, 'I'll pay for the food. You should pay for the drinks, Oz. I only had water, you had beer, and Enid had wine. I'm not paying for that as well. And leave them a little tip. Not too much.'

'Yes, Olive,' Oz said, but he thought, *You mean old woman.*

After the meal, they walked back. It was uphill all the way to the caravan. They had not brought a torch and consequently, Oswald trod in dog poo. He spotted some grass and did a strange dance, gliding around, trying to clean it off his shoe. The women's indifference to his predicament did not improve his irritability.

After the long trudge up the High Street and beyond,

they reached the caravan park. All was in darkness. March was clearly not a good time for renting.

'Why did you have to rent a caravan at the very top?' Enid panted. 'This hill's perpendicular!'

Olive snapped, 'I like it and I'm paying for it, so stop complaining. We're nearly there. Don't forget to take your shoes off. You can leave yours outside, Oz.'

Oz objected, 'Oh great. I'll have wet shoes to put on in the morning. Surely you can find a bowl and a spare cloth so I can wipe them clean? I don't want to be travelling all the way back to Chester with wet feet.'

It was pitch black, so they couldn't see the wolfish grin on Olive's face. Ever since she had seen the boy, she had been contemplating different scenarios to rid herself of the pair. She wasn't quite sure why she had asked them and only felt revulsion for them now, but she thought in the grand scheme of things they might still come in useful as scapegoats, and they were going of their own accord. It was all working out very well.

***

'We'll be on our way then, Olive. Are you sure you'll be alright on your own up here?'

Olive looked smug. 'Of course I'll be alright, Oz. I've got my Leo watching out for me and he's told me what to do. I'm to wear his purple robe up on the cliffs, and I'm to meditate, to draw him into me. He wants to help us map our futures.' She radiated self-confidence. 'He always had such good ideas, and now I'm going to be his alter ego. Don't worry, I'll be home at the weekend, refreshed and ready to go.'

Enid and Oswald stared at her. They had hoped that

now Leo was dead and his little green packet was at the bottom of the sea, her behaviour might change. But it appeared to have only spurred her on.

She waved as they drove away, and continued waving even when she could no longer see their car. There was a cold wind, but she barely registered it. She enjoyed flapping her arms around as if she might take off and soar away. It was a feeling of exultation. The sort of sensation she thought a saint would experience. She was jubilant. Sister Olive was back, and she knew exactly what she had to do.

Meanwhile, Enid and Oswald, creatures of habit, stopped at the same motorway services in Taunton, this time for breakfast. Enid stirred sugar into her coffee, a grim expression on her face. 'We should put our house on the market. Move right away. Buy a place somewhere distant like the Outer Hebrides. It's the only way we will ever be rid of that woman.'

Oz replied in a mild voice, 'I think I'd rather go to Spain. It would be warmer there.'

And in one voice, evoking stares from customers sitting at the table next to them, they cried out together, 'Yes, let's do it!'

***

Oswald had been right. Olive did have food in her room. Now she was on her own, she carried it through to the kitchen area and set to making scrambled eggs on toast for her breakfast. She smiled contentedly. She could do whatever she wanted, and what she wanted was to experience absolute power. She imagined herself dressed in the purple robe, standing on the edge of a cliff. Wasn't it King Canute who had commanded the sea? He must have possessed tremendous authority to have turned the tide back. Olive, who had such poor understanding and knowledge of just about everything, believed the myth. If King Canute could do it, so could she.

After her meal, she washed up and cleared everything away. She went through to the bedroom, took the purple robe out of a drawer, and smoothed the creases out of it with tender care. She slipped it over her head. An hour on the cliff, then she would change and go hunting. If the boy was here, she would find him.

**

From the back window of Caitlin's car, Ollie watched Kirsty hurry through the school gates. He waved, although she had already turned away and was about to walk through the entrance. Caitlin asked Ollie to sit in the front with her. He did so, and she observed him with concern as he buckled himself in. His mother had left some material for him to work on, but it wasn't the same. He should be in school, making new friendships, having fun. She would have to suffice instead.

It was as though Ollie could read her mind. 'Don't worry about me, Aunty Cat. Mum will sort things out when she's back. I'll be able to start school next term.'

Caitlin leaned over and ruffled his dark hair. 'Yes, I'm sure she will. You'll have to put up with me for a few days. I'll try and keep you amused. I've some errands you can do this morning, and I'm thinking this afternoon we could go to the museum. Would you like that?'

'Yes, please. Mum says there's a new book about Swanage. She's given me some money to buy it.'

'Good. Let's go back to Rock House, then. You've a worksheet to complete. Then you can walk downtown and get me a few things.' She smiled at him. 'Tomorrow, maybe we could go over to Poole, pop in to see Charlie and Sally. Charlie could show you the ropes and tell you what you need to learn to be an ace investigator like Sam.'

Caitlin wondered what he was going to say. He seemed grown up for his age, and she was aware she might appear patronising, jollying him along. He might prefer to simply read a book. But she felt sorry for him; he must be feeling sad and confused about his father's death. It was only natural, poor kid. She started the car.

'Aunty Cat, you don't need to worry about me, honestly. I'm used to being on my own.'

***

It didn't take Ollie long to complete the geography project his mother had set him. 'Are you wanting me to check it? Oh dear. Geography isn't my strong point.'

He chuckled. 'Don't worry. It was quite easy. I had to work with map references. I think it's mostly right. Can I go out now?'

'Yes, of course you can. I've made a list for you. If you take a rucksack, the things should be easy to carry.'

She handed him the list, and he looked at it and nodded. 'Okay, I've been in the supermarket with Mum. I know where it is.'

He set off, pleased to be outside. Kirsty had taken her gym kit with her. She had a football lesson this morning. He really fancied a game himself.

He loitered around town. He still longed to possess a

penknife. His pocket money would stretch to it. He had googled the sort of knives admissible for a young person to carry, but he was pretty sure he would need an adult to purchase one. There was nothing wrong with looking, though.

Olive spotted him early on and followed him. She kept her distance; she didn't want to spook him, but somehow, she had to find a way to trap him. There seemed to be no sign of his mother. Very careless of her to allow her child to wander around town aimlessly; he should be in school.

He left the town centre and began to walk up a long hill. He stopped to speak to a woman, who pointed to a junction at the top of the hill. He set off again. Olive was panting by now. The boy was walking swiftly, too fast for her, but she had to keep up. He reached the top, and she just managed to catch sight of him as he turned left. She broke into a lumbering run and then into a sedate walk behind him. She watched him punch numbers into a keypad on the post of a wrought iron gate. It swung open but closed again too quickly for her to react. She remembered the dog the children had had down on the front, and how it had growled at her. If the dog was outside, it would make things tricky. She would have to get rid of it. Poisoned meat came to mind.

'Excuse me,' Olive said to a passer-by, pointing at the sign for Rock House. 'I'd love to be able to visit this house. I believe my aunt lived here.'

The man stared at Olive. 'Are you one of the Roberts family, then?'

Olive nodded and tried to appear thrilled.

'Well, Caitlin Roberts and her family still live here.' He pointed. 'There's a buzzer on the post. Try it – she may be in.'

'Oh yes,' Olive simpered. 'I've just noticed the buzzer. Thanks. I'll try it later.' She looked at her watch. 'I'm on the way to the hairdresser, no time to speak to Caitlin now. Thanks ever so much for your help.'

Olive's face was a picture of innocence, or so she thought. The man thought differently. What a strange woman!

She schemed as she made her way down the hill. She had no intention of buzzing to be let through a gate. She could try to enter another way, but she didn't want to be caught in the grounds. The house wasn't the answer. She needed a plan, an encounter outside. Entice the boy into the jeep, that was it – and what child could resist chocolates?

She had blanked out the memory of the photographs on the stolen phone which had led her to Swanage in the beginning. She was convinced it was fate and part of her husband's plan. Leo had bequeathed her his power. It was meant to be. Now she had added the power she already possessed to his, she would be supreme. Her face lit up with joy.

***

Caitlin had been a little concerned when she suggested Ollie go into town on his own, but she believed in giving young people freedom to find things out for themselves. She had spent much of her childhood on an isolated farm, where she had been given free rein to roam the countryside. Living in Rock House, as she now did, was perfect for her and Kirsty. They both enjoyed just being part of nature and exploring the landscape through the different seasons, and now Kirsty was confident and competent to ramble around on her own.

However, when she heard the front door open, she breathed a sigh of relief. She called out, 'Is that you, Ollie? You were quick!'

Ollie deposited his rucksack on the kitchen table, and he didn't waste any time. 'When we go to the museum this afternoon, could we go and buy a penknife? I've found the one I want, and Mum said I could have one, but I don't think I could buy it without an adult.'

Caitlin smiled. 'What are you going to do with it? Carve wood?'

'Aunty Pat told me every boy should have a penknife, because you never know when you might need one. I was looking for one in Chester, but that was when the man tried to get me. Then I forgot, and I haven't been near any shops that would sell one since.'

'Of course, we can, particularly if your Aunty Pat says so. I wonder if every young person should have one? If so, Kirsty might need one too.' She raised her eyebrows, and he grinned, realising exactly what she meant.

***

Olive spent a couple of hours walking all the way from the Coastwatch station to the pebbly beach on the other side of the town. Now she was back in the square, and not in the least bit surprised to see the boy with the woman she guessed must be Caitlin. She watched them as they entered the museum.

Reassuring herself that they would be in there some time, she bought a large portion of fish and chips and settled down on a bench. She became fascinated by the herring gulls. She watched them watching her as they waited to pounce on her food. Nasty, fierce-looking birds. Then she studied them more closely and saw how big and handsome they really were. They were doing what nature intended, looking for something to eat. She lifted her head and watched them fly. How magnificent to be able to soar above all these dull people with their dull lives.

She had felt power enter her earlier that morning. She had raised her arms and allowed herself to sway in the wind. Now she felt an affinity with the gulls and imagined herself flying over the cliffs in her purple robe. She thought of Pascal. He had a lovely smile. Such clean teeth. A picture of him in his own purple robe came to her. He would reach out for her. She felt a delicious moisture forming and a tingle below. She put the chip paper between her knees and flexed her fingers in ecstasy. She would make him love her. Offer him a home.

She was getting carried away with her fantasy when she saw Caitlin and the boy exiting the museum. She heard the woman say, 'I don't think you've sampled the chips yet, Ollie. I know we've had a sandwich, but a small portion of chips to share would be rather fun, don't you think?'

They went inside and came out with the chips wrapped in paper. She overheard the woman say, 'I'm glad you liked the geology. There's lots of fossils on the Jurassic Coast. Tomorrow afternoon, instead of going over to Poole, I could drop you off at Durlston Castle. They have a huge rock there with an interesting audio recording. It tells you all about where it came from and what happened to it through each millennium. You can explore around the castle as well. It's an interesting building. Afterwards, if you follow the path around the castle, you will be able to see the Great Globe, then just walk up the hill and you'll be back to where you started at the castle entrance. I can pick you up from there after I fetch Kirsty from school.'

'I could walk back home, Aunty Cat. I think I can find my way, and if I get lost, I can practice using the GPS on my phone. Go on, let me!'

'Okay. I'll tell you what, though. If it's a nice day, I'll walk up to the castle with you, then you'll know how to get back home, and you must promise to be careful and ring me if you're worried about anything.'

Ollie took the last few chips, dipped them in the tomato ketchup, then offered them politely to Caitlin.

Grinning, she shook her head. 'No, go ahead. They're good, aren't they? Now, have you still enough pocket money to buy the penknife and the book?'

'Yes, I think so, and I want to try and read the book before Mum gets back, then I can tell her all about Swanage.' He sighed. 'I like it here. I hope Mum wants to stay. I suppose there's nothing to stop us going back to Chester, but I don't want to. I want to stay with you and Sally and Uncle Bob and Kirsty.'

Caitlin handed Ollie a tissue to wipe his hands. 'Well, we'll have to see how Mum feels when she gets back.'

They stood up, unaware of the woman who had listened intently to their conversation and who now gazed after them with a look of triumph on her face.

***

Olive had known Leo would make it all perfect, and he had. She would go to Durlston Castle and afterwards find just the right place for the boy to meet his father again.

Somewhere on top of a hill, where Will could soar down to meet him from on high. He could come in the guise of a bird to scoop him up. She chuckled. Oh, and she mustn't forget to buy some yummy chocolates. How delicious! The excitement she felt was physical. It was such a pity Pascal wasn't here to experience it too.

Chapter 29
Chester

The following morning, Miriam and Sam arrived on time for their appointment at Chester Police Station and were shown into a small interview room. However, they were kept waiting for over half an hour, and although Miriam kept her thoughts to herself, she suspected they were playing games with her. She had entered the police station in a positive frame of mind. She had nothing to hide, but the waiting was causing her to feel oppressed and defensive.

Two officers eventually arrived. Miriam guessed the tall, grim-faced uniformed officer was Constable Stuart. The plain-clothed officer appeared friendly. She was of medium height, dressed in a white polo-neck jumper and dark trousers. She had perfect pale skin, although her small nose had a sprinkling of freckles. Her hair was her most striking feature: shoulder length, very straight and flaming red. The contrast between her looks and the mediocrity of the room could not have been starker. Miriam felt as if she had been dazzled by a bright light.

After what felt like a long silence, she realised the detective was smiling at her in expectation. She stood and shook the officer's outstretched hand.

'Mrs Marshall, thank you so much for coming in. I'm Detective Inspector Wallis, and this is my colleague, Constable Stuart.' She turned to Sam, who had also risen from his seat. 'And you must be Mr Sam Huxley.'

He nodded and they shook hands. Once seated, the DI took the lead.

'The post-mortem report on your husband, William Oliver Marshall, has been recorded as a drug-delated death, caused by opiates. But I believe this may not be a shock to you. Can you tell me when you last saw your husband?'

'Yes, it was the 29th of December.'

No longer smiling, the DI sat forwards: alert, probing. 'That's very precise, Mrs Marshall. How come you remember the date so well?'

'It was the day I sought refuge with a friend. My husband Will had been behaving very erratically. He'd frightened our son Oliver. I'd tried to speak to him about his behaviour towards us, but it was like talking to a brick wall. He walked out of the house rather than talk to me.'

'What's your friend's name and address?' DI Wallis wrote Pat's details down, then turned to Miriam again. 'Was that the last time you were in the house?'

'I went back to collect some clothes on the 30th. He wasn't there then, but he had left me a note. It was to tell me he didn't want me, he only wanted our son, and if I didn't let him have Oliver, he wouldn't vouch for the consequences. A few days after that, I went back to the house with Pat and Oliver to pack some things we needed. That was just before we left Chester – around January 4th. The house was empty. Pat and Oliver can vouch for that. There was no sign of my husband on that day, and I had no idea where he was.'

'Are you saying, despite your husband leaving the marital home, you left Chester? Why?'

'I wasn't sure he had gone for good, and we didn't feel safe because he had threatened to take my son, and Oliver didn't want to be with his father. I've already said, his father had frightened him.'

The DI frowned. 'You could have asked for help. Instead, you decided to uproot your son, leave your job and your life in Chester. That's a big step to take. Where did you go?'

'We rented a flat in Flint for a few weeks. We didn't want to go too far because we thought we might be able to come home. But my son became frightened because he thought someone was watching him. He told me he didn't want to go back home because of his father, and so we decided to leave and go to Studland in Dorset, to my cousin Martin's house.'

'And all this time, you didn't have any contact with your husband? He didn't know where you were?'

Miriam was beginning to be irritated by the questions. 'No, of course we didn't have contact with him, but Oliver had a strong feeling he was being followed, and we were frightened. We were running away from Will. I had visited my doctor before we left Chester. My husband's behaviour was so strange, I thought he might be mentally ill, and I wanted someone to help him.'

'Which surgery are you registered with?' The DI wrote the details down. 'What advice did the doctor give you?'

Miriam felt boxed into a corner. 'The doctor said I couldn't just refer Will. He would have to agree to see a psychiatrist. She signed me off sick with stress, and it was after that Oliver and I left. Why are you asking me all these questions?'

The DI smiled. 'I'm trying to establish a timeline. You see, when your husband was found, he had been deceased for at least one month. Forensic science isn't infallible, and I'm afraid they can't give us a precise date. We know that an ambulance was called to your property on the evening of February 6th. A man was admitted to hospital.' She looked at her notes. 'A Mr Leo Lander, white male, aged 69. The ambulance crew recorded that his wife Olive was present, and two friends, Mr and Mrs Hughes. Do their names mean anything to you?'

Miriam was surprised. 'No, I've no idea who they are. Was Will with them?'

The detective shook her head. 'I'm afraid that's something we don't know.'

'Well, I can prove I was miles away, and I had no idea my husband was throwing parties. I told Dorset Police that Will was mixed up with some weird people.'

'Yes, you did, Mrs Marshall. They thought the story you told rather strange. Being threatened by a cult, was it?' She looked at her notes again. '*Family of Hope and Rebirth*. We are trying to establish the leaders of this group. They seem to have gone to ground. Can you help us locate them?'

Miriam swallowed. 'Why do you think I would know? I don't. They were Will's friends, not mine. If my husband died of opiates, find them, and you'll find the source of the drugs. People shouldn't be allowed to peddle drugs to innocent folk. You should stop them.'

Constable Stuart chipped in sarcastically, 'Well, yes, we do try to arrest drug peddlers, don't we, ma'am?'

Miriam looked across at Sam. She raised her eyebrows and frowned.

The DI turned to Sam. 'Now, Mr Huxley. Where do you fit into all this? A private investigator from Poole. You're a long way from home.'

'Mrs Marshall was worried about her husband. She wanted to know his whereabouts.'

'I see. That's despite the fact that Mr Marshall had threatened her, and you travelled all the way up here to find out what had happened to him. Anything else you want to tell me?'

'No, not really. I've found him – isn't that enough?'

Miriam felt Sam nudging her knee with his.

'There's nothing else to tell you. Are we free to go now?'

'You were always free to go, Mr Huxley. We're just establishing facts. Where will you and Mrs Marshall be if we need to contact you?'

Miriam interrupted. 'You'll find me at Ms James's house. Although once I've organised Will's funeral, I must get back to my son in Dorset. You have my phone number. Please contact me if there's any other news.' She stood up. 'Come on, Sam. Let's go, if these good people have finished with us.'

Constable Stuart looked quite sorry that they were allowed to go free. She smelled a rat. That pair seemed to be hiding something. There was something about them that didn't ring true.

***

Miriam sat in the passenger seat of Sam's hired car. 'My God, they think I did away with Will! Bloody cheek!'

'No, no, no. They must establish facts, and they always act like that. Trying to catch you out, make you feel guilty. It's part and parcel of the whole caboodle.'

'I'd forgotten you were one of them once.'

They were sitting in the station car park; Miriam gazed around at the marked police vehicles and scowled. 'It's another world to me. A world I don't think I like.'

'You're not going to hold my old role in the police force against me, are you?'

'Oh, Sam. I didn't mean it like that. Look, I'm sorry.

I'm sorry about this whole messy business. Neither of us knew we would be thrust into murder and mayhem.'

He leapt on her words. 'So, you agree with me? Will was, in essence, murdered. He didn't commit suicide.'

'In essence, maybe.' She bit her lip. 'I still believe he entered some sort of pact of his own free will. If he hadn't joined the cult, it might never have happened. That's what I believe. The two events added together may equal murder, but there's no evidence, is there?'

'There may be. Do you remember telling Dorset Police about the cult?'

Miriam shook her head.

'In that case, they've begun an investigation. That policewoman isn't very good at hiding her feelings, but I suspect DI Wallis is no fool. I think we can expect more contact with the police as the weeks go by.'

He reached across for her hand. 'I understand why you don't want us to find the evidence, but you must be prepared, because if it's there, the truth will come out. Henry is calling the cult members to a meeting this evening. I would like you to come and meet them.'

Miriam sighed. 'You're asking a lot of me. I can't think about anything else until we've registered Will's death and decided on a funeral director. Let's get out of here. I promise to think about the meeting later.'

**

Henry was about to thrust a note through Oswald and Enid Hughes's letter box when the door opened.

Oswald stared at him. 'What the hell are you doing here, Brother Henry? How did you know where we live?'

Henry tapped his nose. 'Yours to find out, Oswald.

I'm here to tell you the time for pretence is over. I'm Harry Townsend's grandson. You remember – the man you knew as Brother Harold. The man who I believe was pushed down an escalator, probably by Olive Lander – our dear Sister Olive. Wicked, don't you think?'

Oswald's face blanched. 'You had better come in.' He called out to his wife, 'Enid, we have a visitor.' He turned to Henry. 'Come in, come in. We won't bite.'

Henry spotted suitcases in the hall. 'Just come back from your idyll with dear Sister Olive? You didn't stay long.'

Enid snapped, 'No, it wasn't as promised.' She looked tired. She was usually well groomed, but now her hair needed washing, and her face, devoid of makeup, was drained. 'She booked a bloody caravan on top of a mountain.' She suddenly realised who she was speaking to and echoed her husband. 'How did you know where we live?'

Henry chuckled. 'I'm a mole, Enid. I find things out.'

Oswald was unsure of how to respond to Henry. With a hint of hysteria in his voice, he asked whether Henry wanted a cup of tea, then promptly forgot his offer as the meaning of Henry's words dawned on him. He took the path of least resistance. 'I'm glad you know about us. We'll be saying goodbye to everyone soon. Enid and I have decided to leave the group. In fact we have decided to leave the country.'

Henry scowled. 'I'm afraid it's not as simple as that; we have things to clear up. For instance, William Marshall's death. He was probably already dead when the group were summoned to his house for Brother Leofric's last gathering. But you and Enid knew that, didn't you?'

Enid whimpered and covered her mouth with her

hand. Eyes wide and innocent, she stared at him in dismay. 'You mean, when we were in Brother William's house, you think he was dead? That can't be. I don't believe you.'

'Okay, have it your way. You didn't know. Do you mind if I sit down? I would like a cup of tea, if you wouldn't mind, Oswald.'

While Oswald put the kettle on, Henry pulled out one of their kitchen chairs. He sat down, put his elbows on the table, rested his chin on the palm of his hand, and leaned over to smile at Enid. 'How Leo and Olive liked their secrets.'

She gazed at him.

'Yes,' he teased, 'Leo kept records. He wrote everything down.'

'When and where did you see these so-called records?' Oswald enunciated each word slowly.

Henry leaned back in his chair and folded his arms. He and Sam had found very little in the group's records; nevertheless, he decided to bluff.

'Oh dear! Did she try to buy you off to keep you quiet? We saw them yesterday at Olive's house, hidden in an upstairs cupboard. That's how we found contact addresses for the group. We couldn't crack the code on their computer – we'll have to leave that to the police. What did the old girl promise you?'

Enid sighed. 'I knew we shouldn't trust her. We thought we'd burned them all. She showed us the files, and afterwards we had a ceremonial burning. But she'd copied them, hadn't she?' She swore. 'Alright, let's assume Leo wrote everything down that he knew about us. It was a long time ago. What we did was a mercy.' Her eyes filled with tears, and suddenly she crumpled, collapsing forward, her head in her hands.

Oswald hesitated, unsure what to do. Time was suspended, until he gave her an ineffectual pat on the shoulder.

She looked up at him, and they gazed at one another. Enid's expression was sad but resolute. 'His name was Evan. Our son. He was disabled, mentally and physically. Fifteen years old, but still a baby. He had seizure after seizure the day he died. We should have called the doctor, but we didn't. We left him alone, and when we went back, we found him on the floor. We let nature take its course. That's what we did. We let our son die, and we've lived with the horror of it ever since.'

Oswald reached over, took Enid's hand in his, and said in a soft voice, 'We loved Evan, but he was getting too much for us to look after. He would have ended up in an institution. No life at all. Then along came Will. He promised to take us back to find Evan. He said we would find him in a different time and in a different body. He did take us back, but we didn't see Evan. That's why we stayed. We still hoped. And Leo knew everything we'd told Will.'

Henry frowned. 'Leo recorded something quite different. According to him, you allowed him to drown.'

Enid cried out, 'No, we never did! We let him go; that's all we did. We told the doctor. We had only been in here, in this kitchen. When we went back into the lounge, we found him lying on the floor. He'd inhaled his own vomit. It will be in his records. Leo Lander was a wicked, wicked man to say we had allowed him to drown.'

Henry was shocked. 'But you let him die alone. It's beyond sad. Have you ever thought he may have had a happy life looked after by someone else? Leo Lander may have been wicked, but what you did was worse.' His words hit home. They appeared as wretched, pitiful creatures to Henry. 'What I find hard to believe is that you carried on allowing Leo to manipulate you, or did you? Are you still playing his game?'

Oswald cried, 'No, of course we're not! We were devastated by what happened. We only carried on because of the fear of being judged, just like you're doing now.' He stared at Henry. 'What are you going to do?''

Henry's expression hardened. 'You've already given yourselves a life sentence of guilt and suffering, and you both deserve it. We'll give you your file to destroy – only make a better job of it this time.'

Oswald hung his head and murmured his thanks.

Not so Enid: she was furious. 'Don't judge others until you've been in the same position, young man. You haven't got a clue what we've been through.'

'Point taken, Enid, I haven't been in your situation, but I do hold life as sacrosanct. I hope I'm never put in a position where I'm forced to take a life. You made a choice. You weren't forced to do what you did. So, there we have it. Let's leave it at that.'

Oswald and Enid sat and glowered at him. Henry thought quickly. He hadn't meant the conversation to become so intense or heated, and he wasn't sure how to cope with it; he only knew he had to get them back on track. He must sound in control, although he didn't feel it. 'What I've come here to do is to ask for your help. Sam, who you know as Pascal, and I are calling a meeting of everyone. We've booked the hall. We want all the group there.' He stopped speaking for a moment to try to gather his thoughts, then found himself saying. 'It's time to terminate, or maybe I mean exterminate.' He said 'exterminate' in the voice of a Dalek.

Oswald and Enid watched his performance with horror. If he had meant to lighten the mood with his last remark, he had badly misread the situation.

Henry ignored their evident discomfort and continued, 'It's in the usual hall, 6 p.m. tonight. No robes, no hocus-pocus. Be there.'

Henry got up and left, calling back over his shoulder. 'Never mind about the tea, old boy. See you later.'

Chapter 30

The promise of a clear day in Swanage had receded. It was already beginning to cloud over. Caitlin, aware of her guardianship duties, had followed Miriam's instructions. School work in the morning, without fail – which meant they had missed the chance of good weather.

She called up the stairs. 'Are you ready, Master Oliver? Come on, best foot forward.' She glanced at her watch: 1.20. It was a thirty-minute walk over to Durlston Castle, allowing Ollie a few hours to explore.

Ollie hurtled down the stairs, his rucksack bumping on his back. 'Sorry, Aunty Cat, I'm ready. I was just getting myself one of Mum's energy bars.'

Caitlin laughed. They had already had lunch. Ollie was growing and had a hearty appetite. 'Here.' She held out a foil package and a water bottle. 'Piece of cake in case you get hungry, water in case you get thirsty. Now, it might rain later. Have you got a waterproof in your bag?'

He shook his head. 'No, I haven't, just this coat. I should be alright.'

'Hang on a minute, I'll find you one of Kirsty's.' She came back with a large waterproof and a bobble hat. 'That should do you. Those puffa jackets may be great for keeping cold out, but they're not much good in the rain. You can slip the waterproof on over your jacket. When you're hiking, you must be ready for anything. Let's go.'

Ollie stuffed his new gear into the rucksack, placing the cake on top. Caitlin opened the door. 'You've got your phone with you, haven't you? Remember what I said – I'm happy to pick you up, but if you decide to walk, you must leave Durlston by four thirty, so we'll expect you back by five.'

'I'll be alright, Aunty Cat. Once we've walked over, I'll know how to get back. Don't worry about me. It's an adventure!'

***

They walked up the drive together. Caitlin gave Ollie a note with the gate code written down, just in case he forgot it. He had already memorised the numbers, but he didn't want to upset her, so he put the note in his pocket.

As Rock House was near the top of the hill, their walk was level to begin with, but at the end of the road, they began their descent. Caitlin pointed out landmarks along the way. At the bottom, just before the road began to rise again, they entered the park.

Ollie wanted to explore the woods and the stream with its little bridge, and was enchanted by the variety of plants. Afterwards, when they began the walk up the track towards the castle, Ollie called out, 'Oh, look, this is called Isle of Wight Road! Will we see it from here?'

Caitlin wasn't sure. 'The weather may be against us today. Normally, there are clear views right across from the top of the track.'

They reached a tiered stone seat. Ollie clambered up it and could just see the outline of Old Harry Rocks. Caitlin pointed out where the Isle of Wight should be, but Ollie was disappointed to find the horizon obscured by cloud. There was something he liked about an island being stuck out there in the sea. His mother had told him it had once been part of the mainland, and he imagined it floating away.

At the entrance to the castle, Caitlin said goodbye and started to head for home. She heard footsteps on her left side and thought Ollie might have forgotten something. When she looked round, she saw a woman striding into the castle – but Caitlin thought no more about her.

***

Olive had spent the previous afternoon and evening working out how she would snatch the boy. She had found the perfect place to leave him as a sacrifice for his father – the man who had once been called the marshal, now transformed in his parallel life and waiting to be reunited with his son. In her twisted mind, her plan was foolproof and the perfect revenge for the death of her sister Sara.

She knew it would work because Leo had commanded it. He had been with her on the cliffs this morning. She had heard him call out, urging her to finish their work. Consequently, she had complete confidence. The boy would be there, she would track him at the castle, and then, when darkness fell, she would take him to the ancient barrow.

She had spotted a path near the castle which led into a wood, where there was a good view of the surroundings. She hid herself behind some bushes to wait for the boy to arrive. She didn't have long to wait, and she watched as he and the woman called Caitlin appeared. Olive remained hidden until she saw the boy wave goodbye to Caitlin. Olive strode briskly into the castle, arriving just in time to see the boy descend some stairs. She followed him, keeping her distance. She saw him step through a door, and she hung back to wait. She became restless; he had been in there too long, and she breathed a sigh of relief when, at last, she saw the door opening.

***

Ollie had enjoyed seeing the huge rock exhibit. An audio ran throughout, telling the story of the changes that had transformed the rock throughout the millennia. He admired the way different lights came on to shine on the spot where creatures had been engulfed.

When it was finished, he came out and looked around, wondering what to do next. He noticed a sign advertising an art exhibition. He walked down the corridor towards it, but before he got there, he saw an open space where a nature film was playing. He sat down and watched it all the way through. He wasn't sure whether he was allowed to eat there, but he was hungry, so he ate his cake and drank some water.

The film played on a loop, so he waited for a scene he had already watched and then left. He walked further down the corridor to find the art exhibition. The paintings were nice but not very interesting. He found an exit and walked out onto a path. By now, the clouds had blown away and the sky was much clearer, and he could see the outline of the Isle of Wight.

It was getting cold. He shivered. He saw a bench, put his rucksack down, and pulled out the waterproof. He had to push the sleeves right up. Kirsty's arms must be longer than his. He reached back into his rucksack for the black bobble hat. That was better. All zipped up, he was ready to explore.

As he walked down the track, he could hear the sea

below him. He found the Great Globe Aunt Cat had described, walked round to study it, and then began to walk back towards the castle. He glanced at his watch. It was nearly four. He would have to go home soon. He decided to have a quick look at the Learning Centre before he headed back and took what he thought might be a short cut through a wooded area. As he emerged back onto a road, he felt a tap on his shoulder. He looked round to see a woman in purple glasses smiling at him. Her round, pasty face looked familiar, but he couldn't think why. He had forgotten all about the incident with the woman who had caused Frida to growl. As with most young people, older folk all looked the same to him and became invisible.

'Hello, you're Ollie, aren't you? I wondered if I'd bump into you. My name's Olive. I live near Caitlin. She's told me all about you and your exploration of Swanage. I'm so pleased you like our town and you enjoyed our little museum yesterday. It's fun, isn't it?' She broke off to look up at the dark clouds forming above them. 'The wind's getting a bit nippy; it might rain soon. I'm about to go home – would you like a lift?'

Ollie had been taught about 'stranger danger', but this woman knew his Aunty Cat. She must be OK, and he was a polite boy. 'Thank you. That would be very kind of you.'

Olive beamed. 'Come with me. My jeep's over there.' She took him up a track onto a grassed area in front of a building which he thought must be the Learning Centre.

Ollie followed her into a car park. 'Can you go off-roading in your jeep?'

She giggled. 'Oh yes I can. It's great fun. Hop in.'

Ollie did as he was told, and they both fastened their

seat belts.

The woman who had called herself Olive started the engine. 'We'll sit here for a minute until the windscreen clears, then I'll take you home. Would you like a chocolate?' Olive handed him a box of truffles. 'Go on, have one.'

He looked at them, all thoughts of stranger danger gone from his head. He took one and tried to chew slowly, but it was soft and soon finished.

'Have another. One chocolate isn't enough for a growing boy.' He hesitated. Was it good manners to take two? He was tempted. They were delicious. A little bitter, but he supposed that was because of the dark chocolate. His mother had told him dark chocolate was good for him. He reached for another.

Olive watched him. It shouldn't take long for him to become sleepy. She started the jeep and began to pull away. She saw his head begin to droop forward, and she smiled. Perfect planning, indeed.

***

When Ollie came to, it was dark. He could hear the car engine and thought he must be lying on the back seat of the jeep. It was moving erratically, and it was very bumpy. Its angle told him it was going up a hill. He tried to move but couldn't. His wrists were tied behind him: no wriggle room. His feet were uncomfortable, placed one on top of the other and tightly bound at the ankles. He was blindfolded and there was something sticky across his mouth. Terrified, he tried to cry out. He recognised the voice calling out to him. It was her, the woman in the purple glasses.

'There, there, dear. Be quiet now. We're nearly there. I'll have you out in a jiffy.'

His head felt fuzzy. What had she done to him? It must have been the chocolates. His mother was going to be very cross with him. He shouldn't have accepted a lift.

The jeep stopped and he heard the woman get out. Then he heard a gate being opened, and she was back in, driving slowly now. They were going up a steeper slope. The car wheels spun, then suddenly they jerked forward and stopped on level ground.

He heard the woman muttering to herself but couldn't make out what she said. Then the door opened and she untied his hands. He tried to struggle, but she held him down while she undid his waterproof and his jacket. He felt a sharp prick in his arm. Now she was putting his jacket and waterproof back on, muttering all the time. She turned him and retied his hands behind his back. As he started to drift away again, he heard her say, 'Cosy. You'll be so cosy waiting for your father to come.'

He wanted to cry as he heard the jeep fading into the distance. He couldn't see or move, and he felt so sleepy.

***

Five o'clock came and went. Caitlin tried to reassure herself that Ollie would be back any minute now.

Kirsty joined her in the kitchen. 'Mum, it's nearly 5.30. You said Ollie would be back by now. He was going to help me with my maths homework. Should we go and look for him? We could take Frida. She'll find him.'

'I'll try his phone first, love. He might be walking down our drive at this very moment.'

272

Kirsty wasn't to be put off. 'But it's getting dark. Has he got a torch with him?'

Caitlin shook her head and tried Ollie's phone number again. She had been calling it every few minutes. It went straight to voicemail. She felt fear rising within her. What had she been thinking to allow a small boy to explore on his own? 'I'm going to ring your dad.' She rang Bob's number, which also went to voicemail. She left a message. 'Bob, please ring me back immediately. It's an emergency!'

Kirsty was very near to tears. 'Ring Aunty Charlie and Sally. They'll know what to do.'

Caitlin agreed. 'I'll ring the office.'

Sally picked up. 'Charlie Bond Investigations. How can we help?'

'Oh, thank goodness you're still there! You remember I was taking Ollie to Durlston this afternoon and he was going to find his own way back? He's an hour overdue now and I'm beginning to panic. It's dark and he's still out there.'

Sally reassured her. 'He's probably on his way back. I'll leave the office now. Charlie's here; we'll come together. Don't worry, we'll find him. If we catch the next ferry, we'll be with you in forty minutes. Ring me if he turns up.'

Caitlin and Kirsty looked at one another. Time was racing by and they were no closer to being able to find him. Caitlin's phone rang. 'Bob. Thank God! We must get a search party to look for Ollie. He's still not home from Durlston. Something has happened to him!'

'Don't panic, love. I'll drive over there now, see if I can find him. You stay put in case he comes back, alright?'

She wanted to scream. It was not alright. But she said nothing. She looked at her watch. It was now 6.10. If Sally and Charlie managed to catch the 6.20 ferry, they would arrive at Rock House in under forty minutes.

'Mum, Mum!'

Caitlin heard Kirsty calling out to her. She felt as if she was in a haze. 'We've got to tell Aunty Miriam. If Ollie really has got lost, he might be in danger. He could fall over a cliff in the dark.'

Caitlin groaned. 'Oh Lord, poor Ollie. Out there in the dark, all cold and alone. I'll ring her now.'

Voicemail. She could have screamed with frustration. She texted. She rang again. Voicemail once more. She left another message. She texted yet again.

Frida barked, making them both jump. The front door opened, and Kirsty ran out, shouting Ollie's name. Her face fell when she saw it was Sally, closely followed by Charlie.

'He's not back yet, then?' Sally and Charlie said in one voice. Charlie didn't hesitate. 'I'll ring the police. Something must have happened to him.'

Kirsty and Sally left her in the hallway while she phoned. When she came back, she looked grim. 'OK, here's what we do. Sally, you stay here with Kirsty. Cat and I will drive over to Durlston. The police are alerting volunteers. We'll have a search party organised within the hour.'

'But I want to come with you!' Kirsty shouted. 'Ollie is my friend. You can't make me stay here!'

'No, Kirsty.' Charlie was firm. 'You have a very important part to play. Ollie might be lost, but he might also be on his way back. Someone must stay here, so stay put. We'll keep in contact by phone.'

Sally put her arm around Kirsty. 'We can't all be out searching, love. They'll find him.'

Caitlin put her arms around both and held them tight. 'Be a brave girl, Kirsty. We'll find Ollie.'

Chapter 31
Chester

By 4.00 p.m., Sam, Henry and Miriam had arrived at Pat's house. Henry had only just been introduced to Miriam. There was something youthful about him, yet the conversation he recounted about Oswald and Enid told a different story. Miriam guessed he was older than he looked.

Sam interrupted Miriam's thoughts. 'Miriam. Did you hear what we just said?'

Miriam jumped. 'Sorry, I was miles away. What was it?'

'Henry has agreed to lead the discussion tonight. He's more familiar with the members of the group than me, and we both think it would be best if you and Pat were concealed. There's a stage in the hall. We can pull the curtain across but leave enough of a gap for you to see.'

Miriam frowned. 'That's rather melodramatic. I thought the idea was to get everything out in the open?'

Henry answered, 'Yes, but you see, if we introduce you at the beginning, it will affect what we want to do. We want them to have an open discussion and maybe come up with their own solutions. Above all, we want to find out the cause of Will's death. Remember, I was part of this group, but I had no idea what Will was up to. We want to know whether any of them did.'

'That's very noble, Henry, but why should they tell you? Self-preservation will click in, particularly if they think they could be complicit in murder.'

Henry nodded. 'We won't know until they start talking. There are four people in the group we know little about. Hopefully, they will tell us something about themselves tonight.'

Miriam hesitated for a moment. 'Okay, Henry. You've told me about the leaders – Leo and his widow Olive. The two others you've been discussing today seem to be close to them.' She thought for a moment. 'I've got to try and remember all these people – don't tell me. Oswald and Enid Hughes are the Welsh couple and probably the pair I encountered at the house all those weeks ago, who followed us when we left Flint. Who are the others?'

'These may not be their real names, remember. There's Maude. Probably in her forties, very reserved. I've no idea why she's in the group. Then there's Ursula – she's an anomaly. Maybe thirty, tiny build, well-spoken and intelligent. The other two are mother and son. Mother is called Eira, and her son, Paul. I had to persuade them to come tonight. They wanted nothing more to do with the group. Poor Eira was taken in by the idea that her dead husband could be brought back to life.'

Henry shook his head in sorrow. 'I think Leo and Olive gathered the sad and lonely to them. The Covid epidemic was a great time for them to prey on isolated people. They fed on their fears. I've told you about my grandfather's so-called accident, but we also discovered his life savings have gone down. I suspect they are in the Landers' possession.'

Miriam gasped. 'Oh no, that's awful, Henry! I hope Will wasn't part of their plans or aware that your grandfather was being cheated. Will lived in a different reality. He was obsessive. He believed powerful people controlled the world and hid the truth from us. Maybe he was right.' She swallowed. 'I guess he wanted to taste some of that power himself, but I don't think that ties in with theft. Theft of souls, maybe, but not money.'

Henry reassured her. 'I agree with you – he would be an unlikely thief. Olive and Leo were manipulating him, as well as the rest of us.'

Sam looked at his watch. 'Let's hope Pat's back soon, or our plan to conceal you won't work. Henry tells me the group are usually pretty prompt.'

Henry chuckled. 'She'll be here. Excuse me saying this, but she wouldn't want to miss this for the world. If it wasn't for Will's death, I think she'd be enjoying the whole thing. She's a bit of hoot on the side, isn't she?'

Miriam was alarmed. She realised she too had been enjoying the situation. She doubted whether Pat mourned Will. Pat didn't suffer fools gladly, and she had never liked him much. As for herself, the Will she had loved had disappeared from her life long ago, and she had already grieved his loss. However, surely she should still be unhappy. It wouldn't be decent to allow herself to recover from his death too soon.

She wished her last words to him had not been said in anger, and suddenly she had an overwhelming urge to share what she was thinking. 'I remember the last time I spoke with Will. As he walked away, he said, "We will become as one and then the demon will fall." I thought he was talking nonsense at the time, but now I'm not so sure.' She closed her eyes. 'Henry, did Sam tell you about my son's experience at Flint Castle?'

He shook his head. 'No, but go on.'

As she recounted what had happened at the castle, Henry appeared mesmerised. 'Will had become part of the demon, or the demon had become part of him. So, when he said, "Then the demon will fall," he might have been fighting it within himself. Maybe the voice Ollie heard telling him to jump was his dad's.' She stopped, fear mounting within her. '*We will become as one.* He wanted Ollie to be part of him to vanquish the demon.'

Sam faltered. He didn't want to upset Miriam by dismissing her theory outright. He chose his words carefully. 'You could be onto something, and if we swopped the word demon with the word evil, it might work. It's the old story – a fight between good and evil. Maybe Will's continual searching had infected him with evil, and he needed the innocence of a child to make himself whole again. I could go with that.'

Henry interrupted him to bring them back to reality. 'Or could he simply have been deranged? Come on, you two, you're getting carried away. You're letting yourselves be hooked into the fantasy. That's how cults work. If you want to dwell on evil, Miriam, wait until you meet Olive Lander. Now, that woman is without doubt a psychopath. She is evil personified. I hope we get her locked up!'

***

Pat arrived home and they were ready to go. Both women turned their phones to silent. By 5.30 p.m. they were outside the hall.

Henry led the way. 'Mind your step. The flagstones are slippery.' He fished in his coat pocket for the key to the inner door. It was a large, old-fashioned brass key. As Miriam watched, she wished she could turn around. Just walk away and forget everything. The door creaked open, releasing the musty smell of an ancient building.

Henry called out to them, 'Come on in. Leave the door on the latch. Let's get the hall set up for the meeting.'

Whilst Henry and Sam went into another small room

to fetch a table and chairs, Miriam and Pat climbed onto the stage and started to pull the curtains across. They were heavy red velvet curtains, evidently rarely used. Clouds of dust rose from the folds, making both women cough.

Pat grimaced. 'These old places give me the creeps. I wonder what they used the stage for. Careful, Miriam, don't pull so hard!'

Startled, Miriam looked up. The curtain had become unhooked on one side. She stopped. 'Now what do we do?' She jumped down and looked at the stage from the hall. 'It won't work. Unless we pull the curtains all the way across, you can see right onto the stage. Is there anything behind that screen?' She pointed.

Pat walked over to a tall wooden screen and shouted, 'There's a door behind here. Come on up and see.'

They found a small room behind the door. Miriam assumed it had been used for prompting. She imagined generations of pantomime audiences being entertained. Two dusty chairs lay on their side. Miriam righted one and sat down. 'Let's hope we don't have a Goldilocks moment and make a noise as these rickety old chairs collapse!'

Pat smiled. 'The best we can do is stay in here and leave the door open. We won't be able to see, but we should be able to hear. They'll start coming in soon. Quick, we should pull the curtains back to where they were and get ourselves in position.'

Miriam called down, 'Henry, the curtains are no good, but there's a room behind the screen. We'll be in there.'

He gave her a thumbs up.

Henry and Sam sat down to wait. It was not long before they heard someone call, 'Well, here we are, ready or not!' Tiny, elf-like Ursula was dressed in black leggings and high-heeled black leather boots. A short tawny fur jacket completed her ensemble. Her light brown hair was brushed away from her face. Sam thought that with her sharp features, she looked for all the world like a principal boy. He imagined her on the stage, slapping her thigh.

Maude followed behind. A good eight inches taller, she stooped as she stood next to Ursula. She too was dressed in black leggings, but she wore flat brown leather boots and an old-fashioned duffle coat fastened with toggles. She looked around. 'That's good. It's not too cold in here today. Do you want us to sit at that table?'

Henry nodded. 'I've just found out, all those times we've been here, freezing cold, we could have had the heating on. I found the switch, and bingo, it's warm already. See?' He pointed. 'Hot air ducts.'

Ursula dismissed Henry. 'I'm still not taking my jacket off. It's not that warm yet. How many of the group are coming, Brother Henry?'

'Four more. All will be here apart from Sister Olive. She's off on her seaside holiday.'

A harsh male voice could be heard from the doorway. 'Good riddance. I hope she doesn't come back.' Paul and his mother Eira walked in. Tall, ruddy cheeked and dark haired, Paul was dressed in jeans and a black leather jacket. He was evidently angry. He pulled a chair out for his mother and helped her sit down. Unlike her son, she was not a picture of good health. Swamped by a long navy woollen coat a couple of sizes too big for her, she appeared frail. White, waved hair framed a pretty but pale face. She blinked watery blue eyes and dabbed at her nose with a tissue. She sneezed. 'I'm sorry. I think I'm coming down with something. I should sit away from you all. Don't want to spread germs.'

'Don't worry, mother, you've only caught a cold.' Paul's voice changed as he faced Henry. 'I'm telling you now, Brother Henry. This is the last time we will ever set foot in this place.'

Henry held his hand up. 'I think we all feel like that. Have a seat, Brother.'

Paul sat and continued in a loud voice, 'Did you know our dear departed leader was a sham? There's a photo of him in the obituary column in the local rag. The blurb was singing his praises. He was a Rotarian. An upstanding member of the community. Huh – carried out charitable works, my foot.' He looked round. 'Did you see it? Leo Lander, failed bloody charlatan. May he rest in hell, after all he's put my mother through. If it wasn't for him, my father would still be alive.'

Sam was shocked. Had another member of the group died? 'Are you saying your father was a member of this group, and he died? And what did Leo Lander put your mother through? Sorry, Eira, I should have asked you.'

She shook her head. 'No, let my son tell you.'

'My dad believed all the bullshit Brother William spouted. During Covid, Dad isolated himself from Mum and me. We think he wanted to die because he locked himself in his woodworking shed, closed off all the sources of ventilation, and inhaled glue fumes. I found him slumped on a chair. We called an ambulance, but it was too late. Then today, after you rang, mother confessed to me. Our dear departed leader fleeced her out of my dad's retirement money. Told her Brother William had found a path back to find him, but they needed extra money to carry on with their experiment. Bastard –

double bastards! I hope Brother William is coming tonight. I'm ready to give him a piece of my mind, I can tell you.'

Paul thumped the table. 'Pair of bastards! I'd like to strangle both men with my bare hands!' He lifted his large, clenched fists, and Sam and Henry flinched.

Henry struggled to calm the situation. 'We're here tonight to try and find solutions, and we can include finding a way to get Eira her money back. Let's just wait for the last two of the group and we'll make a start. They should be here soon.'

Paul, breathing heavily, sat back in his chair. 'Okay, but be careful with that pair. Oswald and Enid were in cahoots. I saw all four of them once, wandering around the cathedral gardens together, as friendly as you like.'

'Are you taking our names in vain, Paul?' Oswald had just sidled in. He looked nervous.

Henry wondered if he and Enid had been waiting outside for Paul's tirade to pass. They sat down at the opposite end of the table. Oswald's smile was weak, barely a smile at all. 'Nice to see everyone.'

Henry began, 'I called you here tonight because it's time for us to face the truth. Three of our members have passed away. No more pretence. We could start by introducing ourselves and say a few words about why we joined.'

Ursula interrupted, 'Whatever are you talking about, Henry? Introducing ourselves? Where do you think we are, an AA meeting? And what do you mean by three members have passed away? I can only count two.'

He frowned. 'I'm afraid Brother William has died. He took an overdose.'

Ursula stared at the group members. 'So, he's joined

Leo Lander in hell. Helped along by dear Sister Olive, no doubt. Okay, then, Henry, let's pretend we're in a therapeutic group and introduce ourselves. That's bound to make everything better.'

Henry ignored her sarcasm and looked around the group. Silence. 'No volunteers?' he said brightly, 'Then, I'll begin. My name is Henry Parker, and I joined the group to keep an eye on my grandfather, only I'm afraid I was unable to protect him.'

Maude tapped her mouth with her index finger. 'I thought you and Brother Harold knew each other. So, what's his real name, and why did he join?'

'His name is Harry Townsend, and he joined because he was interested in fellowship. Then he fell under the influence of Sister Olive.' Henry looked at Paul. 'Yes, my grandfather too. His life savings have nearly gone. Would you like to go next, Paul?'

'Okay, my name is Paul Williams, and this is my mother, Eira Williams. We're still here because my father committed suicide eight months ago. He didn't even leave a note. Brother William claimed he would help reunite us, and Leo Lander has stolen part of my father's pension from Mother.'

'Alright, we'll go next.' Ursula sat up straight in her chair and looked around the others as if ready for a challenge. 'I'm Ursula, and this is Maude. My surname is Fischer. I was born in Germany but have lived in the UK most of my life. I teach German.'

Maude chipped in. 'I'm Maude Reed. Ursula and I met in Germany. I play the cello; our orchestra was touring Bavaria. Ursula was visiting family in Munich. We met there and we've been together ever since.' She reached out and placed her hand over Ursula's. 'We thought we'd rather enjoy the play-acting. You see, we thought it was quite a funny idea. I've been wanting to write a novel and thought it would be fertile ground, as indeed it has been.' She sat up, shoulders back. When she reached up to push her greying hair away from her face, they could all see how handsome she was.

Ursula smiled. 'I've not noticed you writing much yet, my love.'

Maude laughed and tapped the side of her head. 'Don't worry, I've stored all the information away in here, although I'm not sure I'll ever write about it. I mean, the hocus-pocus and the make-believe were great fun, but hardly believable. I don't think any of us banked on people dying, did we?'

Henry remained expressionless. He didn't want to comment on Maude's literary aspiration, although he thought it was a brilliant idea. He looked over at Oswald. 'Would you like to go next? You could say something about your friends.'

Oswald glared at him. 'They are not our friends.' His voice was solemn. 'Oswald Hughes, known as Oz. Enid, my wife. The pair whom Henry calls our friends – Leo and Olive Lander – we've known for a long time. We've tried to support Olive. We felt sorry for her after Leo collapsed, but her behaviour when we were away was outrageous. We want nothing more to do with her.'

Ursula dipped her head to one side to gaze at him. 'So, Oz – why did you join the group in the first place? You seemed to be number one henchman.'

He was clearly far from thrilled with her comment.

Enid cut in, 'Leo bullied my husband. Made him feel guilty about everything. Made him into his lapdog.'

Oswald tried to interrupt.

'No, I'm going to say it as it was. We joined the group because Leo threatened to disclose something we had done years ago.' She glared at the group. 'And no, we're not prepared to discuss details. However, we were fascinated by William Marshall's theories about life and transformation. Back then, we thought we might find our poor dead son in another world. We imagined him being whole and leading a normal, happy life.'

Husband and wife followed Ursula and Maude's example and held each other's hands. 'We really did believe. But as time went on, Leo made us do things we were unhappy with. I don't know why we didn't challenge him. But it's finished now.'

Sam had been quiet throughout, but it was time to reveal himself. 'I'm afraid it's not as simple as that, Enid. I was encouraged to take the name Pascal by Olive Lander, but my real name is Sam Huxley. I'm a private investigator working for Miriam Marshall. She wanted me to help her find her husband and to find out what was going on, because she was afraid of him and the harm he could do. Your cult had led him to a dark place, and she needed closure to get on with her life.'

Oswald interrupted. 'No, you've got that wrong. It wasn't a cult; it was a group. If it became a cult, then William Marshall was the instigator. It was his brainchild; he put it all together. He designed the website, and he organised our meetings until he became ill.'

Sam frowned. 'You're saying William Marshall initiated the group, and Leo and Olive latched on. Is that it?'

'Yes, and they turned it to their advantage. I swear we didn't know about Leo and Olive swindling money.' He shut his eyes for a moment. 'We have to report this to the police, don't we?'

Sam nodded. 'Yes, we do. There's also the matter of the attempted kidnap of William Marshall's son, and the strange nature of William Marshall's death. What have you all got to say about that?'

Maude and Ursula stared at Sam. Ursula's voice rang out. 'What are you talking about?'

Sam said bluntly, 'I can spell it out if you wish. William Marshall died of a drug overdose approximately six weeks ago. He died in his own home, in his own bed. I found his body a few days ago; and before you ask, I was accompanied by a police officer. In addition, someone in this room impersonated William Marshall to trap his son Oliver. I know it wasn't Henry, by Ollie's description, so do you want to say anything, Oz?'

Oswald put his head in his hands and groaned. 'Oh God. I'm very sorry. Will made me do it.'

'Oh yes?' Ursula cried out. 'Following orders, were you? The Nazis used the same excuse when they murdered most of my family. Well, let me tell you, you didn't do it in our name.'

Oswald cried out, 'We wouldn't have harmed him! Will just wanted his boy. He wanted him to become part of our mission.'

In the small anteroom, Pat put her hand over Miriam's mouth. She shook her head and whispered, 'No. Wait. It's too soon.'

Sam glanced over at the stage area and continued. 'You were trying to snatch Oliver, against his wishes, and force him to join his father. I call that kidnap. You also followed Mrs Marshall and her son when they left the area. You frightened them into fleeing from their home, leaving everything behind them. You've a lot of explaining to do.'

Oswald stood, pushing his chair back behind him with some force. 'We were told the boy wanted to be with his father. I was simply trying to reunite them. I admit we followed the boy, but we didn't do any harm. We came back, didn't we, Enid?'

'Oh, sit down, Oz. Let's face it, we lost them because they turned off the motorway. We must tell the truth.'

Sam looked sceptical. He wasn't sure they *could* tell the truth.

'Leo was furious with us. To be fair, Oz wanted to leave the group right away. I persuaded him we should stay and see it out. Come on, think how it was for us.' She looked around for sympathy. 'Can't you see? It was Leo. He had become so powerful and angry. We were terrified of him. We didn't know what to do. It was a relief when he died, and afterwards, we tried hard to persuade Olive to let the group go. But his death made her euphoric. She became more and more determined, and we didn't know how to stop her. When you volunteered to join the group, Sam, she took it as a sign. Maybe now, if we all agree, we can put a stop to it once and for all.'

Paul listened in silence; his face showed nothing but contempt. 'So, you and your friends frightened an innocent woman and her son so much they had to flee. Don't make excuses. There are none. If you are capable of that, what else have you done?'

'Yes, and when did William Marshall die?' Ursula's voice rang out as she turned to face Oswald. 'You knew he was already dead during that charade when Leo collapsed, didn't you?'

Oswald's voice was desperate. 'No, we didn't. After

the ambulance had gone, we were left to clear up and we found him. We didn't know what to do. Everyone would have been implicated. We tried to save you all, so we never said anything.'

This time, Pat was unable to constrain Miriam. She strode out onto the stage and shouted, 'Cowards! You left my husband lying there dead to save yourselves!'

Shocked by Miriam's sudden appearance, the group fell silent. She pointed at Oswald and Enid. 'It was you two. I recognise you. You started all this, banging on my door and demanding my son. I've left my home, my friends, and my job: uprooted my son, all because of you.' She jumped down from the stage and walked over to them. 'You frightened Ollie. It's unforgiveable.'

Pat watched Miriam from the front of the stage. She wanted to cheer her on, but she kept quiet.

'I've listened to what you've been saying. Quite frankly, it doesn't make sense. You didn't have to do any of it. Doubtless you were getting something out of it. What was it, getting your own back on life because my son is alive and kicking? Oh yes, he did kick, didn't he? Good.' The torrent of words subsided.

Oswald and Enid looked deflated. As was often the case with Miriam, guilt began to set in. She felt sorry for speaking out. After all, they were two fellow human beings who had got themselves into a situation they couldn't control.

She sighed. 'I don't blame you for everything. My husband and Leo Lander were pulling the strings, I acknowledge that. But you must tell me, do you know what happened to my husband? All the time I knew him, he never took drugs.' She walked over and sat down on a spare chair beside them. 'Tell me.'

Enid spoke quietly. Miriam strained to hear what she was saying.

'Olive was giving him a drug discovered in South America. She said it was harmless and would lead him towards enlightenment, but Oz and I think he came to depend on it. He wanted more and more. In the end, he didn't look very well. Olive had been a nurse, so we thought she knew what she was doing. She said she would look after him.' Enid rested her head on the palm of her hand and sighed. 'I'm sorry. We really didn't know what she was up to.'

Sam cut in, 'She was *up to* feeding him opiates, that's what she was up to. She certainly didn't give him a harmless drug from South America; that's just bullshit. You should have reported his death to the police immediately you found him. There may have been a chance to convict Leo and Olive of attempted murder.'

Oswald looked even more worried than before. He turned to Miriam. 'Are you going to report us?'

'No, I don't think I am, but how you're going to live with your consciences, I can't imagine.'

Paul Williams exploded. 'What! Not report them? That's criminal – they're criminals. They're all criminals!'

Miriam stood her ground. 'You may well be right, but what good would it do now? It's not going to bring Will back. On the other hand, it looks as though the Landers were swindling members out of their hard-earned cash. That should be easy enough to check out and recover.'

Paul thumped his fist on the table. 'And all this time that bitch is having a holiday at the seaside on our money. I'd like to go down there and wring her scrawny neck!' He glared at Oswald. 'Where is she – you know, don't you?'

'Tell him, Oz.' Enid patted her husband's hand. 'It's finished. It doesn't matter now. We need to get her back to face the music.'

He nodded. 'She's down in Dorset. It's a long way away, and she's promised to be back at the weekend. You might as well wait.'

Pat jumped down from the stage and cut in, 'Where exactly is she?'

He gave her a bitter smile. 'Swanage. She rented a caravan at the top of a bloody hill in the freezing cold wind. Can you imagine?'

Miriam leaned forward, arms folded over her stomach. 'I think I'm going to be sick. Oh God. I've got to ring Cat, warn her not to let Ollie out of her sight.' She fumbled in her pocket for her phone. Her hands were shaking so much she dropped it. She remembered it was on silent, switched it on, and stared at the screen in horror. 'Oh no. This can't be!'

Pat took the phone from her and cried out, 'Ollie's missing!' She handed the phone over to Sam. They stared at the screen with its list of messages.

Miriam was shaking, her face as white as a sheet.

Sam called to Pat, 'Can you take Miriam outside in the fresh air while I find out what's going on?'

Henry hovered. 'What time did the first message come through?'

Sam scratched his head. '6.15, and the last one was at 6.35. Nothing else.' He looked at his watch. 'It's now 7.50. If they haven't found Ollie yet, he's been missing for two hours. I'll ring Rock House.'

***

The house phone was picked up immediately.

'Hello, Sally Thomas speaking. Who's calling?'

'It's Sam. Have you found Ollie yet?' Sam listened to Sally for a moment, then continued, 'I'm afraid we have bad news. We've just discovered a member of the cult is in the Swanage area. She may have recognised Ollie. They've tried to kidnap him before. Are the police involved with the search?'

'Yes, they're out combing the Durlston Castle area now. I'm going to put the phone down, Sam. I need to update them. If you think it might be a kidnap, it changes everything.'

He waited for five minutes before ringing Sally back. 'Have you spoken to the police? Is Charlie with them? Where's Caitlin? I should speak to her.'

'Yes, the police are up to speed. They're going to ramp up the search. Charlie and Caitlin are out with the search party. Can I speak to Miriam?'

'She's outside with Pat. She's beside herself with worry. Look, we'll pack a few things and drive down as soon as soon as we can. Can you ring this number if anything happens?'

'Hold your horses, Sam. What's the name of this cult member? What do they look like? Where are they staying?'

'Her name is Olive Lander. Charlie has a photograph of her. She's staying somewhere in Swanage in a caravan high on a hill. That's all I know for now.' He looked around the room and cursed. 'The cult members who know the caravan's location were here a minute ago. I'll find them and ring you back.'

'Do that, Sam. It's vital we know where she is!'

Henry and Sam went out into the courtyard. Pat and Miriam were still there. 'Where did Oz and Enid go? Did you see?'

Pat answered, 'They just opened the door and hurried out.'

Henry called out, 'I know where they live. I'll go after them. Wait for me. I'll ring you.' He turned and nearly lost his footing on the flagstones. He fumbled with the door latch and then, with a wave, ran up the road towards his car.

'We must go right now, Sam, back to Swanage. We have to find Ollie.' Miriam's voice trembled.

Pat held onto her arm to keep her from falling.

'A few more minutes, Miriam. The others are still inside. I'm going to talk with them. They might know something that could help in the search. Pat, can you take Miriam back to yours? Pack a bag for her. I'll be with you as soon as I can.'

Although Miriam tried to protest, Pat led her out, and Sam went back into the hall. The four remaining cult members were huddled together. Eira Williams looked dreadful and was unable to stop herself coughing.

'Paul, you should take your mother home. She needs a hot water bottle and bed. There's nothing you can do here. Ursula and Maude – is there anything you know about Olive Lander that might help in the search?'

Maude hesitated, but Ursula spoke out. 'She likes drama and ceremony, having an audience. If she's got the boy, she may want to put on a show. She likes to feel powerful. I don't think she would kill him outright. We know from what happened to Will that she's likely to have a supply of opiates. If she follows the same pattern, she'll drug him and hide him somewhere. She may want to go back to check on her prey.' She stopped and looked at Maude. 'What do you think?'

Maude agreed. 'That's a good description; and if you're right, it might give us time. What we don't know is why she's doing it. Has she kidnapped him for a ransom or what?' She stared at Ursula. 'I think we should follow Miriam and Sam to Dorset. We might be able to help. Otherwise, we'll just sit around here worrying. Where's Henry gone?'

'He's trying to catch up with Oz and Enid. They've skedaddled, and they're the only ones who know where Olive Lander's staying.'

Paul began to help his mother up. 'Don't trust that pair to give you the right information. It shouldn't be too hard to find where Olive's staying. It's a small seaside town, isn't it? And you know it's a caravan and it's on the top of a hill. I'm sorry I can't help. I'm going to get mother to bed.' He reached in his pocket and handed Sam a card. 'You can reach me on that number. Good luck. I hope you find the boy alive.'

Sam's phone rang. 'Henry. Have you found them?'

'No reply at the house. I looked through the hall window. The cases that were there this afternoon have gone. I might be jumping to conclusions, but I think the birds have flown. I'm coming straight back. I've got the key to lock the hall up. I'll be with you in ten minutes.'

***

They gathered in Pat's lounge, Maude and Ursula concerned and quiet, and Henry itching to get going.

Miriam was unable to sit still while she listened to Sam on the phone to Charlie. Halfway through his conversation, she jumped up and started to pace the room. She said, 'It's nearly nine. We've got to get going! We'll never find him if we don't get going.'

Henry interrupted, 'Well, let's not just sit here. Let's organise ourselves. Who is going to drive, and which car? I can take Ursula and Maude in my car. Sam's got his hire car.' He looked over at Miriam, who continued to pace. 'You should go with Sam. Leave your car here with Pat.'

Miriam didn't reply. She kept her eyes on Sam, hoping and hoping for good news. He finished his call.

'What did Charlie say?' There was panic in her voice.

'They're continuing the search. There's a helicopter out with heat-seeking equipment. If he's up on the cliffs, they'll find him. They're trying to locate Olive Lander's address. So far, no luck. She may be using a different name. I've said we're on our way. If we leave now, we'll make Swanage by the early hours.'

Henry leapt up. 'OK, ladies you're with me.'

Ursula and Maude followed him to the door.

He turned back to smile at Miriam. 'We'll all meet up in Swanage. We'll find your son, I know it.' He became aware of Pat's gaze. She had a strange expression on her face. 'Goodbye for now, Pat. I wish you could come too. I'll ring you when we get to Swanage. Take care of yourself.'

***

After Sam and Miriam had left, Pat sat in her chair and allowed her head to hang forward. She thought about her stolen phone. It was the only explanation. There must have been a clue on it. Her godson was in danger because of her. She thought she was drained of all emotion, but within seconds, she found herself sobbing, and she couldn't stop.

Chapter 32

The moon was almost full, and Olive had managed to drive her jeep onto the downs without using headlights. She laid Ollie on the top of one of the larger, more inaccessible barrows as gently as she could. She muttered to herself the whole time.

'I'd call my boy Oliver, after me, so he could have been mine. Don't see why William should get him back; he doesn't deserve him. But I promised, and never let it be said that Olive Lander doesn't keep her promises. I'll come back tomorrow, and if the dear boy is still here, I will take him with me.' With that thought uppermost in her mind, she set off to drive back over the downs towards the long hill and the safety of the main road.

By this time there was poor visibility, but she didn't want to risk switching the lights on in case someone spotted her lights from the road below. Ollie must not be found. Either his father would come to take his soul, or she would collect him in the morning.

She concentrated on keeping the jeep in a straight line on the stony ground. The car lurched and rattled as if it was about to fall apart. At one point she veered off the track. She knew there was a steep slope on the other side, and she broke into a sweat. Her hands began slipping on the wheel as she wrestled with the steering.

She succeeded in getting to the bottom in one piece and cried out in relief. She had made it, although after going over so many bumps, the jeep was rattling alarmingly. She drove slowly through the town, hoping she was not drawing attention to herself.

Back in the caravan, she poured herself a large glass of Leo's expensive single malt. She recalled how he had never stinted on himself – such a mean old bastard. He hardly ever offered her a drink, and when he did, he would only give her the cheap blended brand he kept in for guests. She smiled at the thought of getting one up on him as she took a large gulp. Once she had got over her coughing fit, she settled down to sip it. She poured herself some more and sat down to think.

It had all gone according to plan. The chocolates had done their job, although the boy had regained consciousness relatively quickly. To be sure, she had injected him with a large dose of the opiate before she left. She hoped it would keep him quiet and comfortable. She didn't think there were any wild creatures living in Dorset that could drag him away. Tipsy by now, she laughed at the thought, forgetting how she had called him a 'dear boy'.

The day before, on her trip to reconnoitre, she had watched people going to and from Corfe Castle. Everyone, apart from the cyclists, seemed to keep to the tracks, and she figured out cyclists were unlikely to be riding at night. She had chosen the barrow furthest away from the main track; with luck, the boy would remain lying where he was, and if she went back for him and he was still there, she would keep him. It was compensation for the boy's father having caused the death of her sister.

She was startled out of her reverie by the sound of a helicopter passing over the top of the caravan. It was so loud it could have been in the room with her. She jumped up and went out, gazing up at its lights as it flew at low level towards the sea. They were already searching for the boy. Well, she had deceived them. They wouldn't find him there.

It was cold. She went in for a coat and torch. A walk

would do her good after all the excitement of the afternoon. Maybe Leo would come to her. She frowned as she asked herself whether apparitions could see in the dark. Maybe, like a moth, he would be attracted to her light and flutter around her.

Before she set out over the grasslands to the cliffs, she poured more whisky into one of Leo's old silver flasks and slipped it into her pocket. She skipped out of the caravan with a light heart, but within a few hundred yards, her feet were soaking wet. She had forgotten to change out of her slippers. No matter, she would keep going.

When she reached a vantage point, she stood to watch rows of lights advancing over the cliffs in the distance. People were combing the land for the boy. She did a little dance to reward herself for her cunning, but she slipped on the wet grass and fell over. She chided herself. 'Should have gone back to put your shoes on.' She broke into song. 'Slipping on a slug in your slippers.' She giggled, then swivelled round onto her knees before pushing herself up. She sat down on a wall to recover and fortify herself with the rest of the whisky from the flask.

She had nearly finished and was tipping the last dregs into her mouth when the helicopter came back. Its lights picked her up and hovered over her. She panicked. She rose as quickly as she could and looked around for somewhere to hide. There was nowhere close: no trees, only grassland. It came round again. She lurched away.

***

Ollie had lain unconscious on top of the long barrow for over four hours. The waterproof covering his puffa jacket allowed the top half of his body to remain warm and dry. The black bobble hat pulled down over his ears gave him some protection, but moisture had soaked into his jeans.

He came to, feeling cold wind on his face. He tried to make himself wake up, but he couldn't open his eyes. They had been taped over. The tape covering his mouth held. Any sound he made was muffled. He wriggled to try and get more comfortable. His legs and feet were cold and numb. His hands were tied behind his back. They felt like blocks of ice. He tried rubbing whatever was tying him against the ground, hoping there might be a stone or something sharp for him to break free.

He was so tired. He had no idea whether it was night or day. Despite the strengthening wind, he couldn't stop himself drifting off. He came to with a start. Someone was close by; he felt something brush past him. He tried to shout. A muffled sound gurgled out. He would die if that woman came back. He wriggled onto his side and rubbed his face, trying to dislodge the tape. Something cut his cheek and he wanted to cry, but he kept rubbing. He felt the tape beginning to give and redoubled his efforts. He could just see out of his left eye. He started to work on his mouth, crying now in frustration. His nose was hurting and he felt blood trickling down. He lay still again. It was hopeless.

There was movement by his ear. Not a breath, but a whisper in the wind. For the first time in what felt like days, he sensed hope. He thought as hard as he could.

'Agnes, help me. Please help me.' He repeated 'Agnes, please help me' like a mantra as he wriggled round onto his back again and continued to rub at whatever the woman had tied him with. If he could only get the ties loose, he would be able to reach the penknife in his jeans pocket.

***

Charlie was in the castle office when Sally's call came through. 'Sam has rung. He says one of the cult members has been visiting the Swanage area. Ollie might not be lost. He might have been kidnapped.'

Charlie thought rapidly. 'Have we got a description of this person?'

'Sam says he sent you a photo and a description of an Olive Lander, the woman who he believes may have taken Ollie. According to Sam, she could have been involved in Ollie's father's death, and she should be approached with caution. Is Caitlin with you? Kirsty needs her. She's very upset. I can take over from her, but please tell her to come back home.'

'Okay. We'll find Caitlin, and I'll make sure Olive Lander's picture and description are circulated. What's the news from Miriam?'

'They set off from Chester about half an hour ago. Sam says they're making good time. Miriam won't to talk to me.' Charlie wasn't surprised. She imagined how she would feel if she had a son in grave danger. Cat was going to be devastated as well. This had happened on her watch.

A police officer was there and had been listening. 'Have we got a lead, Charlie?'

Charlie sighed. 'I'm not sure. We know Oliver Marshall's father was a member of a cult. The cult tried to snatch Oliver when he lived in Chester. That was one of the reasons why his mother brought him here. A member of that cult is in the Swanage area. I'm about to circulate her name and photograph.'

The office phone rang and the officer answered. She

listened intently. 'Okay, we're on it.' She replaced the phone and turned to speak to Charlie. 'One of the helicopter pilots saw a figure running on the cliffs near the quarries. He logged it but has only just reported in. With the new information we have, Sergeant Jameson wants the search extended to the cliff top and quarry area. Can you stay here on call while I find the Durlston search party?'

Charlie nodded. 'Yes, sure. Cat's with them. Can you please tell her to come back here? Sally will take her place. Kirsty is very upset and needs her mother.'

'Will do.'

Charlie was left in peace to think. The present search could be a waste of time. If Ollie had been kidnapped, they were unlikely to find him in the Durlston area. Where would someone hide a child? In fact, why would they need to hide him here? If they were from Chester, they might be on their way back. As far as they knew, Ollie had been missing since around five p.m. It was gone nine. He might be halfway back to Chester by now, whilst his mother and Sam were driving the other way.

She tried Sam's phone, hoping he would have it on speaker in his hire car. He did. She voiced her thoughts.

'You're right, that's a possibility. However, Olive Lander is a narcissist and craves attention. Ursula and Maude, two of the cult members, are travelling down with Henry. They know Olive well and believe she will hide Ollie somewhere close to where she has been staying because she will want to go back to him.' Sam shivered at the thought.

Charlie interrupted, 'That's good to know. A pilot spotted someone on the upper cliffs running way. It might have been Olive watching the search. If he's up there, we'll find him.' She stopped. 'She might have been watching them and gloating because they were looking in the wrong place. Keep driving, Sam. Where are you now?'

'We've just got onto the motorway. We're making good progress; there's not much traffic. We'll be with you by the early hours.'

'Drive safely. Tell Miriam we are doing everything in our power to find Ollie.'

***

Caitlin had been walking slowly with the other volunteers, combing every inch of terrain they were able to cover. The police officer who had just left Charlie arrived on a quad bike and called out, 'We're extending our search to the top of the cliffs. One of the pilots spotted something suspicious near the quarries. Could six volunteers join the others up top? The others remain here. Search as far as the first marker. I'll join you soon.'

She watched as the volunteers sorted themselves into two groups. 'Could you six retrace your steps back to the road at the Coastwatch station? A vehicle will be waiting for you.' She shone her torch around the volunteers until she saw Caitlin. 'Cat, you're needed at home. Sally is going to take your place. Hop on the back and I'll take you to your car. Sorry folks, I can only take one.'

***

Sally heard a car engine; she flung the front door open and breathed a sigh of relief as she watched Caitlin's green mini pull in at the front of the house. Sally shivered as the night air hit her, and she thought about Ollie, who could be lying out there alone in the dark.

Caitlin joined her in the hall. 'Where's Kirsty?'

'She's been up and down to the flat all evening. She's up there now. Can I take your car and join Charlie? I'll be more use there than I am here. Sam phoned again. He says some of the cult are on their way and will arrive at Rock House before him. Friends, not foes.'

Caitlin handed Sally her car keys. 'I'll go up and find Kirsty. Fingers crossed we spot Ollie soon. It's getting mighty cold out there.'

Without a backward glance, Caitlin ran up the stairs, calling Kirsty. She found her gazing out of a top window.

Kirsty tried to smile when she saw her. 'Mum, look over there. There's something up in the moonlight. Like lightning bugs floating around. Not all the time. There, look, there's some!'

Caitlin stared out of the window. 'I can't see anything, love.'

Kirsty turned the light off. 'Let your night vision come. See – it's over there. Really concentrate, Mum.'

Caitlin shut her eyes for a moment, then looked again. 'Yes, I caught something then. They look as though they're dancing, but I don't think it's fireflies.'

Kirsty whooped. 'Yes, I knew something was there, and it could be guiding us to Ollie. We've got to go now! Frida will lead us to him. I've been letting her sniff one of Ollie's socks; she knows what to do. Come on, Mum!'

'Oh, darling, just wait a minute. Let's think this through. Sally's just driven off in my car. We'll have to go and find her car keys, or we could go on Dad's quad bike.' She thought for a moment. 'Yes, we'll go on the quadbike; it will be better than a car on the terrain up there. Frida will have to squash onto the back seat with you. It might just about take us up the hill; we can but try. But first, Dad. I'll phone him. Go and find yourself some warm clothes, love.'

Frida had sat watching them. One of Ollie's socks lay by her front paw. As Kirsty left the room, Frida picked the sock up in her mouth. She looked up at Caitlin as though to say it was about time, before trotting after Kirsty.

'Are you ready, love?' Caitlin called up as Kirsty came running down the stairs, closely followed by the dog. 'Dad will join us. He said to take the big torch from the garage. Let's go.'

Kirsty had dressed herself in her warmest coat and carried a blanket over her arm. She had a rucksack slung over one shoulder in which she had stuffed some biscuits, a bottle of water and the torch they always kept by the front door. She held the garage key out to her mother. 'Is Dad coming?'

Caitlin shook her head. 'He will, but he's a long way from his van. He said to take care and to ring him when we're close to where we saw the lights. He'll come up with Charlie.' Caitlin didn't tell her daughter that Sam thought it highly unlikely they would find Ollie on the downs. The search party were convinced they would find him near the quarries.

***

Caitlin hoped there was nothing wrong with the quad bike. She turned the key in the ignition yet again. It kicked in, but the engine just sputtered, then died. Bob hadn't used it for weeks. It was Kirsty who suggested checking the fuel. Maybe there would be a can of petrol for it somewhere. They searched in mounting desperation until they spotted a blue can on a bottom shelf. Caitlin took the top off and sniffed. Eureka!

This time the engine fired. 'Clever girl. Who would have thought Dad would leave the petrol in such a logical place! Hold on to your helmet, we're off.' She gunned the engine and they shot off up the drive. They had forgotten the gate fob, so Kirsty jumped down to punch the numbers in. Caitlin kept the engine revving; as soon as the gate swung open, Kirsty jumped back on and they sped away. It went fast down the hill, but Frida was the only one who enjoyed the feeling of the wind rushing by. She sniffed in delight while her ears flapped back and forth. Kirsty held on to her tightly, glad of her warm fur.

They drove through the town and made for Ulwell. At the bottom of the hill, they took a left turn onto the track which would take them up the hill. They would soon hit their first obstacle; the gates could be padlocked. But the first one was open, and they began the upward descent. It was very steep and very bumpy.

The lights of the quad bike seemed to be growing dim, but the moonlight helped them remain on the track. Caitlin dropped their speed. Frida barked and then jumped off. Kirsty, who felt as impatient as her dog, watched as Frida bounded away into the darkness, a dog on a mission.

They kept going up until the track began to level out. No sign of Frida until they heard a bark and saw the dog running towards them. Kirsty called out, 'Find Ollie, Frida.'

The dog reached them, shook herself, then took off again. She slowed down and turned to watch them following her before setting off at a slower pace.

That was when the quad bike cut out. Caitlin swore. Kirsty jumped down, pulled off her helmet, and shouting to her mother to hurry, she began to run after Frida.

'Kirsty, wait! It won't help if you fall. You need the big torch.'

Kirsty looked back and waved, but continued to follow the dog, relying on the moon to light her way. Caitlin tried to start the quad bike again, but it was dead. She fumbled for the torch. Her hands were shaking. She pressed the on switch. Nothing happened. She swore and jabbed at it with her middle finger. A bright shaft of light rewarded her. She thought to herself, *Run, woman, run as though your own life depends on it.*

She was out of breath within minutes. She had to slow down to a fast walk. Kirsty and Frida were nowhere to be seen. She felt herself panicking. Not only had she allowed Ollie to be kidnapped, now she had lost her own child. She continued to call out and broke into a jog. It was easier going now she had reached the grass track. Shining the light well ahead of her, she missed a hole in the ground. As her foot twisted within it, she allowed herself to fall. 'Ow! Oh, bloody hell!'

She sat on the ground and massaged her ankle. It was swelling already. She levered herself up, and keeping as much weight on her other leg as she could, she limped on, calling out for Kirsty. She estimated she had been walking for fifteen minutes when she saw Kirsty waving to her. She stumbled and called out, 'I'm sorry, love, I've sprained my ankle. Where's Frida?'

'She's run on. Listen, she's barking. Let me help you, Mum. Lean on me.'

They set off together. Frida had stopped barking. Then

they saw her running towards them, stopping, then running back again. They followed. Frida bounded up onto one of the barrows.

'You go, love. I can manage.'

Kirsty, as sure-footed as a mountain goat, ran up onto the barrow and shouted, 'Mum, try and be quick! Ollie's here!'

Caitlin limped as fast as she could. She figured it would be easier for her to crawl up the side of the barrow. She pulled herself onto the top and saw Kirsty bending over someone on the ground. 'Oh God, please let Ollie be alive!' She crawled over.

Ollie was tied up. He had tape over one of his eyes and over his mouth. Kirsty was trying to remove the tape from his eye as gently as she could. He had an open wound on his brow, and his cheek was red and bloodied where he must have been trying to remove the tape over his eyes. She got it off, then started on the tape covering his mouth. She tried to be gentle, but in the end she gave it a sharp tug.

Ollie inhaled and blinked his eyes; a look of relief flooded his face as Kirsty came into focus. He croaked, 'My penknife. It's in my jeans pocket.'

He shifted himself onto his left hip so that Kirsty could reach into his pocket. Her hands were cold, so she had difficulty feeling for the knife and then had to struggle to pull the blade out. At last she began to saw at the ties holding his wrists together. They were tough, but in the end they gave, and she started on the ties holding his ankles. Meanwhile, Caitlin helped him sit up and covered his shoulders with the blanket Kirsty had brought. She sat beside him and chafed his hands, trying to get some warmth into them.

As soon as Kirsty had freed his ankles, she sprang up and fetched water from her rucksack. She held the bottle to Ollie's mouth. Her voice was stern. 'Don't gulp, you'll be sick.'

Caitlin had to smile as she thought, *That's my girl, as bossy as me.* She carried on warming Ollie's hands, then told Kirsty to get underneath the blanket with him. 'Hold him, love. He needs your body heat. Might be a good idea to undo his coat – get right in, and I'll pull the blanket around you both.'

Frida sat and watched her young mistress wriggle inside the blanket. It looked fun. She trotted over as Caitlin wrapped them both up. Their legs were uncovered. Kirsty called to her, as though she needed telling; she always wanted to be part of the young ones' games.

'Come on, Frida, good girl. You can sit on us.'

Frida positioned her warm body as close to the young master as she could. She wanted to lick him, but he was all bundled up and she couldn't quite reach his face. She burrowed her nose into the blanket and found his hand to lick instead.

'Mum, Ollie's gone sort of heavy.'

Caitlin had been trying to phone Bob, but the signal kept coming and going. She could see Ollie's head resting on her daughter's shoulder, and she called out to him, 'Ollie, are you still with us?'

There was no response. 'He's unconscious, Mum. We must get him to a doctor.' Kirsty held him tight, cushioning his head as comfortably as she could. She knew enough first aid to wriggle round until he was in the recovery position.

At last Caitlin managed to get a signal. She rang

Charlie. Her words came out in a rush. 'We've found him. We're up on one of the barrows on Nine Barrow Down. He's unconscious. He needs emergency medical attention. We came most of the way on the quad bike, but it broke down near the top of the hill and I've sprained my ankle. We can't move him. Please send someone to help.'

At that moment, the big torch went out. Now all they had was the small house torch and the moonlight.

'What's happening?' Charlie had heard Caitlin swearing.

'Sorry, it's our torch; it's died. We only have a small light to signal you now. Please hurry. Ollie's in a bad way. We can't lose him.'

'Okay, Cat, we're on it. The police have just called for the air ambulance. I'll try and raise Bob. Keep Ollie as warm as you can, and keep talking to him. He may be able to hear you. We're on our way.'

***

The call went out to stop the search. The boy had been found. The volunteers started to disband, and Bob and Charlie went back into the castle with the police.

Sergeant Jameson looked mighty relieved. 'The air ambulance will be on its way within about twenty minutes. The weather conditions are reasonable. Visibility isn't bad, but the wind is strengthening. We need to get up there asap to guide them in.' He asked his colleague Constable Pritchard and Bob to take the quad bike up there. One of the volunteers had a Land Rover, and the sergeant would come up in that.

Charlie remained behind. She went into the office and

closed the door before she rang Sam. 'Ollie's been found.' She heard Miriam shout, 'How is he? Where did they find him?'

'He's had a rough time. Whoever took him tied him up and left him up on Nine Barrow Down. Caitlin and Kirsty are with him now. The air ambulance is on its way. They'll probably take him to Bournemouth Hospital. Where are you now?'

She heard Sam's voice. 'We're nearing Southampton. Not far. We could go straight to the hospital.'

'Yes, do that. I'll ring you as soon as I can to confirm what's happening. Can I speak to Miriam?'

'I'm here.' She sounded subdued.

Charlie tried to reassure her. 'He's going to be alright, Miriam. Kirsty and Cat are looking after him. The police are on their way.'

Miriam burst out, 'How could Cat have allowed him to be out on his own? She was supposed to be looking after him! I should never have left him with her!'

Charlie wanted to tell her she was being unfair. 'Don't be too hard on them. Until you phoned, none of us dreamed he could be in danger from the cult. Put the blame where it lies, Miriam. Blame the kidnapper, not Cat.'

Chapter 33

'Oh Lord, that's how Cat and Kirsty got up here. It's a miracle they got this far. I'd meant to get that quad bike repaired. Hang on. Let me shift it out the way, otherwise the sergeant won't get through.' Bob jumped down and tried the ignition. Nothing doing. He managed to push it far enough off the track. 'Okay, let's go.'

A few minutes later they saw a faint light, and then heard a bark. 'Thank God, that's Frida. Look, there they are!'

He pointed, and Constable Pritchard turned their quad bike and drove straight up onto the barrow. Against the rules, but this time they needed light. She looked at her watch. 'The air ambulance should be here soon.'

She smiled when she saw Cat and Bob hugging one another. As her eyes adjusted to the light, she saw the dark shape on the ground move.

Kirsty called out, 'Ollie's breathing steadily. I think he's gone to sleep.'

The constable knelt beside them and felt under the blanket for Ollie's wrist. His pulse was steady. His hand felt warm. 'Hello there, Kirsty, we meet again. You are doing a really good job.'

She removed her helmet. Her smile was warm and friendly. Last time Kirsty had come across her, she had had every reason to be given a good telling off. She had been riding her bike on the pavement the wrong way down the one-way system. Kirsty, who was a sensible girl, knew she had been in the wrong. It was a lesson well learned.

She smiled back at the constable. 'Thank you, ma'am'. Kirsty liked police dramas, particularly American ones.

The policewoman grinned. 'Keep yourself wrapped up

with your young man.' She patted Frida's head. 'Between you two, you've saved the day. Good girl.'

Kirsty, who wasn't sure who she was referring to, murmured, 'Her name's Frida.'

Constable Pritchard struggled to get up. As she did so, she thought it really wasn't easy getting older. Close to retirement now, she was planning to settle down to a different sort of life. But this rescue made everything worthwhile. She shook her head in disbelief. When Bob had told her that his daughter thought she had seen lights up on the hill, she too had been sceptical. So, where the hell had the lights come from? It didn't make any sense.

She looked over and saw Cat leaning heavily on Bob. She called over, 'Have you hurt yourself, Cat?'

'Yes. It's what happens when old ladies try to run.' She frowned. 'I was panicking. I thought I'd lost Kirsty as well as Ollie. Missed a rabbit hole. It's only a sprain.'

'Tell me how you found Oliver.' The constable pointed at the ties on the ground. 'Was he tied up?'

'Yes, his wrists tied. Ankles tied. Tape over his eyes and mouth. It was cruel. We think he tried to rub the tape off because his face is bruised and cut.'

'Is this the exact spot you found him? He hasn't been moved?'

'No, we haven't moved him, as such. This is the place. Right here on top of this barrow. Like some sort of sacrifice. It must have taken brute strength to drag him up here. Whoever did this must have knocked him out or drugged him. He wouldn't have come without a struggle. He was unconscious when we found him, but he came to briefly.'

'When you phoned, you said you had seen lights. Floating lights. Did Oliver have a torch? Could someone

313

else have found him first and run off?'

Caitlin frowned. 'That's the weird thing. No, it wasn't torchlight. It was faint, and the lights floated around. Anyway, even if Ollie had had a torch, he was bound so tightly there was no way he could have reached into a pocket.' She looked at Bob. 'I know you won't like me saying this. You'll think I'm being fanciful.'

Kirsty's voice piped up. 'Go on, Mum. Say it. It was ghostly. The lights were ghostly. We know who it was. It was Grandma. The lights I saw from the window were guiding us.'

Bob hugged Caitlin closer to him. 'I'm relieved you, Kirsty and Ollie are safe. I won't say more than that.'

Caitlin burst into tears.

Constable Pritchard heard the helicopter first. 'Listen, it's the air ambulance!' She scrambled down from the top of the barrow, shining her torch to guide the pilot onto level ground nearby. It came into land. The pilot and a medic jumped out.

'Where's the child?'

She pointed to the top of the barrow.

'Okay, thanks.'

Carrying her bag, the medic climbed up to the top of the barrow and knelt beside Kirsty and Ollie. Frida watched her every move.

The medic leaned over to examine Ollie and began to check him over. 'And what's your name, love? And your young man?'

'I'm Kirsty and this is Oliver. He's my friend and he's eleven years old. He was kidnapped and left up here. We found him with tape over his eyes and his mouth, and he was tied up so he couldn't move. Our dog Frida found him. Ollie told me where his penknife was so I could get him free, then he went to sleep.'

'Thank you, Kirsty. You've done a grand job keeping him so warm. We'll lift him onto a stretcher now and take him to hospital so we can check him properly.'

The medic spoke with a soft Irish accent. Kirsty thought she had a kind face. 'He's my adopted brother. Can I come with you? I'll do a good job looking after him.'

The medic smiled. 'Sorry, Kirsty. We can't take you too. We understand Oliver's mother will be in the hospital when we arrive. You don't have to worry. He'll be well looked after.'

Ollie was still asleep, missing all the drama. Kirsty leaned over and kissed him on the forehead. 'I'll come and visit you tomorrow, Ollie. You're going for a ride in a helicopter.' She wanted to cry but instead buried her face in Frida's fur.

Then Ollie was lifted onto a stretcher and he was gone. Kirsty, with her hand resting on Frida's head, watched the helicopter gain height and fly away into the night sky.

***

Charlie and Sergeant Jameson had borrowed the volunteer's Land Rover. When they arrived, the air ambulance was already ascending. The search party's silhouettes stood in stark relief at the top of the barrow, faces upturned to watch the helicopter as it returned over the downs towards Bournemouth. It was Frida who broke the spell. Despite the din of the departing helicopter, she heard their vehicle and barked. The others turned to see, just as the sergeant was pulling in at the bottom of the barrow.

Kirsty slid down, closely followed by Frida. 'Charlie, did you see the helicopter? They've taken Ollie off to hospital. They wouldn't let me go with them. I wanted to.'

Charlie held her arms out. Kirsty ran over to her. 'There was a pilot and a doctor. They put Ollie on a stretcher and said his mum would be waiting for him in the hospital. I suppose they heard it on their radio.'

Charlie held the excited girl at arm's length. 'You and Frida are heroes. You've saved Ollie from freezing out here.'

'Yes, after I got him free, Mum said to get under a blanket with him and hold him close so he didn't get hypothermia. Frida kept him warm too. I remembered to put him into the recovery position like you taught me.'

Charlie hugged her and kept her arm around her shoulder while she watched Bob helping Caitlin down. She noticed how closely Bob held Caitlin. 'Have you hurt yourself, Cat?

'Just a sprained ankle. I'm alright.'

Sergeant Jameson shouted up to Constable Pritchard, who had remained on the barrow, 'Come on down. We must take these good people home. We'll come back in the daylight.'

She shouted back. 'It might be advisable to remain at the crime scene to prevent any disturbance.'

Charlie interrupted the response the sergeant was about to make. 'Phil, there's a herd of sheep grazing on the hill. If the crime scene is abandoned, we might lose valuable evidence. Why don't you let me drive the Land Rover back down? I can radio in. It's already getting light. The crime scene should be searched and documented.'

The sergeant made no attempt to hide how he felt

about the women's suggestions. He was grumpy. It was the middle of the night and he was working on what should have been his day off. There was silence while he made his mind up whether to challenge or not. He decided not. 'Okay. I'll do as you ladies suggest. We'll remain here in the freezing cold. You'd better get a move on.'

Caitlin watched the interaction with bated breath. She had been waiting for an explosion, but it hadn't come. She nudged Bob, put her head down, and limped over to the Land Rover. She beckoned Kirsty and Frida to join her in the back seat, and Bob, who had also managed to remain silent, jumped into the passenger seat.

Charlie held her hand out to the sergeant.

He frowned, then nodded. 'Get on with it then, Charlie. As always, it's a pleasure to work with you.'

She ignored his sarcasm and climbed into the driver's seat. 'Is everybody belted up? Right, let's go.' She started the engine and drove away towards the track. They picked up some speed until they reached the slope, where she slowed right down. 'Hold on to your hats, it's going to be bumpy!'

Once they reached the main road, Charlie accelerated through dark and silent streets. 'Phil Jameson wasn't very happy with me; he likes a quiet life, but he knew I was right. We've got to catch whoever kidnapped Ollie.' She looked in the mirror. Kirsty, with her head on Bob's shoulder, looked fast asleep. 'Are you alright, Cat? You know what happened to Ollie wasn't your fault. I've been thinking about it, and I'm afraid it could have been any one of us.'

'What?' Caitlin sounded shocked. 'What do you mean?'

'There must have been something on Pat's phone. She said it was clean, but we shouldn't have taken her word for it. I know Miriam went over all their texts, but Pat was down in Swanage for Ollie's birthday, wasn't she? We didn't ask her about photos.'

Caitlin swore, then covered her mouth with her hand as she looked down at her sleeping daughter. 'Stupid, stupid mistake. I'll never forget how I felt when Ollie failed to turn up. Poor, sweet boy. I pray he's going to be alright.'

'We all will, Cat. By the way, Sam phoned as the sergeant and I were coming up the hill. He's going to wait with Miriam at the hospital, but he wanted to remind us about the others. I hope Sally's back to let them all in. Remember, there's three others coming from Chester. Quite a crowd.'

***

Miriam and Sam were already at Bournemouth Hospital when Ollie was wheeled into A&E. Miriam managed to hold his hand and speak to him before he was whisked away. They were asked to wait in a separate room, where a nurse looked in on them to reassure them about Ollie. They spent a nervous hour imagining what was happening to him behind closed doors.

Miriam was in a highly anxious state by the time the doctor came to talk to them. He smiled and shook their hands, and Sam thought how young he looked. He was tall, with short, light brown hair and dark eyes. He looked extremely tired.

'I'm Dr Ellis, Paediatric Registrar. I've been treating young Oliver. He's had a bit of an ordeal, hasn't he? He's been awake, but he has all the signs of opiate consumption. We've given him naloxone. It's a lifesaver for people who have overdosed.' He saw how horrified Miriam looked and immediately reassured her. 'Don't worry, it's perfectly safe for a child his age. We'll keep an eye on him over the next few hours. He may have some reaction, but it's likely to be minor. You can go and see him, and when the bed's ready, please go up to the ward with him. He's sleeping quite peacefully despite our ministrations!'

They were shown into another side room. Ollie was tucked up on a trolley, ready to be wheeled up to the ward. His face was pale. They noticed bruising was beginning to appear, but his breathing was steady. Miriam leaned over him and gently brushed his cheek with her finger. He opened his eyes for a moment, blinked, and closed them again.

Miriam sat down beside him. 'Thank God he's going to be alright. I don't know what I'd have done if …'

'Don't, Miriam. Don't go there. The important thing is, he's been found and he's safe.' Sam looked down at Ollie. He had a plaster on his left cheek and scratches on his nose. 'Poor little man.'

Miriam's expression hardened. 'Well, you had better go and find whoever did this to him, hadn't you?'

He put his arm around her and was heartened when she didn't try to shrug him away. Her reaction over the last few hours hadn't surprised him; she had been under so much stress. 'I'm sorry, Miriam. I know we let Ollie down. But please don't take it out on me. We'll do our very best to find out who did this.'

Her voice shook as she blurted out, 'I'm sorry. I'm not blaming you, Sam. I blame myself. I don't want you to go, but you must. Go and find whoever did this.'

As Sam drove away from the hospital, he went on thinking about Miriam. She was almost as pale as Ollie, with dark shadows under her eyes, but she had smiled, and as he was about to leave, she had kissed his cheek.

He was very tired himself, but adrenalin had kicked in. As he drove onto the main road towards Poole, he wanted to put his foot down and drive as fast as possible, until he remembered the speed cameras. He slowed down.

The Sandbanks ferry wasn't operational at night, so he had to drive round the bay to Swanage. It seemed to take a lifetime just to get through Poole, and then he was on the dual carriageway and was able to increase his speed, slowing down when he reached the road into Wareham.

He was driving into Corfe Castle when he felt his eyes drooping. He opened the window. He had work to do, and there would be coffee at Rock House to keep him awake.

He thought about Charlie, Caitlin, Bob, Kirsty and Sally welcoming Henry, Ursula and Maude. There was going to be a full house, normally something Caitlin would love, but maybe not in the early hours of the morning.

Nearly there. He must stay awake. He glanced at his watch as he hit the outskirts of Swanage. He had made good time.

When he reached Rock House, the gates were wide open, so he was able to drive straight in. The downstairs lights were on, and as he drew up to the front door, Charlie came out to greet him. He struggled out of the car. His legs felt stiff. Indeed, his whole body felt stiff. The stress of the last few days had taken its toll on him.

Charlie took him by the arm. 'You need some sleep,

Sam, even if it's just a couple of hours. Come on. You can go up to the flat. Your friends from Chester have arrived. Ursula and Maude have one of the spare bedrooms and Henry's in the lounge. Breakfast is at eight, and then we'll be ready to search for the kidnapper. Now go to bed.'

'Is Kirsty alright? '

'She'll tell you all about it later. Now go on, skedaddle. Go and get some sleep, otherwise you'll be no good to anyone. I'm going to get my head down too.'

Part 6

Chapter 34

Oswald and Enid's journey back to Dorset was mind-numbing. They had only been at home for a matter of hours before they set off. Enid dozed for the first part of the journey. When they reached Taunton, Oswald found a petrol station and stopped to fill the car. Olive was costing them a packet.

They purchased some sandwiches and cans of coke and continued their journey. Oswald allowed Enid to take over the driving so he could get some rest.

When they reached Wareham, she drove into the town and parked. 'Wake up, Oz. We'd better have something to eat. We'll be in Swanage soon.'

Oswald yawned and scratched his head. 'I'm not looking forward to this. We'll have to get the truth out of Olive somehow so we can make sure the boy's found, and then get us all to safety.'

'You mean you want us to rescue her? Why?'

'Because we're implicated too, and if the boy's dead, we all need to get away.'

Enid could hardly believe what he was saying. 'That's ridiculous! We can't just run away, and surely she wouldn't have killed the boy, would she? Not on purpose.' She took a deep breath as the implication of what she had just said hit her. 'If Olive has done something terrible, she must own up. She's not in her right mind. They'll probably lock her up in a psychiatric hospital. We're innocent. We can't possibly rescue her, or we really will be implicated. We could try to put things right. It's time we did. We must be kind to her but firm, and we must find the boy, just as we planned. Agreed?'

He nodded.

***

Olive opened her eyes and groaned. Someone was knocking on the door. She moved her head very slowly: it thumped. She had treated herself to another nip or two of whisky before she lay down, just to help her sleep. Leo had always liked a tot before bed. Now she knew why he had been so bad-tempered in the mornings. Olive burrowed deeper under the duvet, trying to ignore the knocking.

It continued. She reached over and switched on the bedside lamp. The clock glowed the time at her: 4.25. It was the middle of the night! Then she remembered the excitement of the day before and felt her heart hammering in rhythm with her head. Was it the police? She struggled out of bed. The lino on the floor was cold underfoot. She looked for her slippers, then remembered she had gone out in them last night. She pulled her purple robe over her head and padded barefoot across to the side door. 'Who's there?'

A familiar voice called out, 'It's Oz. For goodness sake, open the door!'

'Oz – is that really you?' She opened the door a crack and peered out.

Oswald pushed the door so that he and Enid could step in.

Olive slurred, 'What are you doing here? You told me you were going back to Chester.'

Oswald glared at her. 'We did go home, and now we're back here. Perhaps you'd like to tell us what

323

you've been doing?'

Enid and Oswald sat on the couch and looked up at Olive, who remained standing. She was puzzled: why were they looking at her? What did they want? Her myopic eyes looked strangely naked without glasses. Her face was paler than ever.

'This isn't a social call, Olive,' Enid enunciated very clearly. Her usual sing-song voice had disappeared. 'What have you done with the boy?'

'Whatever do you mean?'

'You know exactly what I mean. Will's boy. What have you done with him?'

Olive laughed, high-pitched laughter, as she continued to stare at them. She clapped her hands and hopped around the room, almost tripping over the robe. When she came to rest, she stood in front of them and repeated, 'What have *I* done with Will's boy? Oh, how luscious. You think *I've* done something to that darling boy? It was you who kidnapped him, not me. I wouldn't harm a hair on his head.' She laughed again, then turned on them and shouted, 'Guilty! Guilty as charged, my lord. Lock them up!'

Oswald stood and slapped her across the face. 'You're hysterical. We'll ask you again. What have you done with the boy?'

Olive touched her cheek, clenched her fist, and drove it straight into Oswald's belly. 'How dare you hit me! Enid, you saw him. It was assault! I shall report him to the police. Coming in here and threatening me. Don't you accuse me of kidnap! I would never hurt anyone.' Her voice softened. 'I'm kind and caring Sister Olive – you, you are the monsters! Child killers. You are the kidnappers. Both of you! I've done nothing.'

Oswald bent double, winded by the blow Olive had dealt him. After all the support they had given her, she was trying to frame them. He stood up straight and squared up to her. His voice trembled with rage. 'You wicked bitch. Don't try to pin the blame on us!'

Olive's demeanour changed, the fight suddenly gone out of her. Her headache was getting worse. She felt very sick. She wanted another drink to steady her nerves. She slumped down beside Enid and put her head in her hands. Breathing hard, she gulped. 'Why have you come back here to accuse me of harming the boy?'

Enid looked at her with distaste. 'Your breath smells like a distillery. Have you been drinking?'

'I just had a little drinky. A little nip of Leo's whisky. Have you got any paracetamol with you?'

Enid shook her head in disbelief. 'No, I'll make you some coffee. First, you had better tell us where the boy is.'

'How would I know? Do you think I have special powers or something?' Olive was starting to feel nauseous. She gulped, then tried to get up, tripped on the hem of the robe, and fell headlong to the floor. She managed to get onto her knees, but as she did, she started retching. They could only watch as she heaved up a stream of foul-smelling fluid. She sat on the floor, her back against the couch, clutched her stomach, and moaned, 'I think I've been poisoned.'

'More like you've poisoned yourself.' Enid went over to the kitchen unit and picked up a roll of kitchen towel, then ran some water into the washing-up bowl. 'Here. You'd better clear your mess up. Then we'll talk.'

Olive rubbed her eyes. 'I think I'm dying.'

'No, you're not dying, Olive. You're drunk.' Enid

wrinkled her nose. 'It stinks in here.' She leaned over, opened the window, and looked outside. 'It will be dawn soon.'

She watched Olive on her knees, trying to clear up her vomit. Small of stature beside Olive, Enid was as steady as a rock; she towered over her in strength of character. Oswald looked on and admired how his wife had dealt with the situation. He should not have lost his temper with Olive, even though she deserved the slap. He just wished he had had the foresight to dodge her punch.

Olive wiped the last of the vomit off the floor and rinsed the bowl out in the sink. She was defiant. 'I'm not admitting anything, and I want to go back to sleep now. You can stay in here if you like, but I'm not going anywhere. Not until I've had a sleep.' She walked over to the bedroom door and disappeared inside.

Enid sighed. 'Leave her for now, Oz. We're not going to get anything out of her in the state she's in. Quite frankly, I don't know why we bothered to come here – some sort of misplaced loyalty, I suppose. We should have left her to her own devices.'

Oswald put his arm around his wife's shoulders. 'Guilty conscience. We wanted to find the boy and save our own skins.'

She yawned. 'Too late now, Oz. I'm so tired. We could lie down too. Tackle it later.'

***

Bob had always been an early riser. After he had made Caitlin's early cup of tea, he went to wake Kirsty. She seemed none the worse for her adventure the night before. She was wide-eyed with excitement when he told her about the three strangers they had welcomed into the house during the night.

He asked her to dress and go up to the flat to call Sam down for breakfast. Kirsty was very fond of Sam, and he was very fond of Ollie's mum. She and Ollie had decided that one day they would all be together. In their minds, they had woven a story that would end, 'And they all lived happily ever after.' Oh yes, she and Ollie had it all planned. Kirsty skipped up the stairs to the flat. Sam was in the shower, so she waited for him, gazing out of the window and recalling the lights she had seen floating on the hill.

She had been brought up to believe her grandmother was a presence in the house. Two pictures of her as a young woman hung over the fireplace in the sitting room. She had been very beautiful. Unlike other children who might pray to a god, when she said a prayer, it was to her grandmother, Cecilia Roberts. She had prayed to her last night.

She was suddenly struck by an interesting thought. Ollie had told her the tragic story of Agnes Howe. Agnes, his protector. She had saved him when he encountered the darkness in Flint Castle, so maybe Agnes and her grandmother had both been up on the hill last night. It would make sense of all the lights that had been dancing around to get her attention. They had been faint but somehow they had spoken to her, drawn her to them.

When Kirsty and Sam went down to breakfast, Caitlin tried to persuade her to get ready for school. Kirsty, however, was more persuasive than her mother, pointing out her lack of sleep and how she wouldn't be able to settle.

Sally, forever the peacemaker, suggested Kirsty

remain with her while the others concentrated on investigating the whereabouts of Ollie's kidnapper. She clinched the argument by saying, 'You and I must ring the hospital this morning. Find out how Ollie is and when he's going to be discharged. I expect we'll be able to go over and fetch him and his mum later.'

Kirsty was bubbling over with enthusiasm. She wanted to tell everyone the story of how they had rescued Ollie, and her theory about the ghosts, but the adults had different ideas, and Kirsty, who was an unusually sensible girl, realised she had to be quiet and save her ideas for another time.

In addition, she was fascinated by the new people. Henry had greeted her earlier as though he knew her. He performed an exaggerated bow and then winked at her before he said, 'Sam's told me all about you and Ollie, so I feel as though I know you, but of course, you don't know me!' His face looked so open and friendly that she giggled and said, 'Who are you, then?', although she knew exactly who he was.

'I'm Henry, and I've been working with Sam up in Chester to find out the truth.'

Kirsty was interested in what sort of truth he meant. Henry struggled to find the right words for an eleven-year-old child to understand. In the end he said. 'Nasty people doing bad things. The woman who we think abducted Ollie was very nasty, but she pretended to be nice.'

'She wasn't very nice to Ollie. She tied him up really tight and put tape over his eyes and his mouth. But I suppose she must have been nice to begin with, or he wouldn't have gone with her.'

'That's right, kiddo. You've got it in one.'

Kirsty beamed at him. He'd called her 'kiddo' in an American accent. It was just like the films.

Earlier on she had met Ursula and Maude. Ursula didn't make her laugh. She was serious. She shook Kirsty's hand, and Kirsty was surprised how small she was; they almost stood nose to nose. Her mission, she said, was to catch the kidnapper. Then there was Maude, who looked very tired. She was about the same height as her mum and a bit standoffish, and she made Kirsty feel awkward. Henry was without doubt her favourite, and she was glad he was Sam's friend.

By 8.30, the eight adults and one excited child, with one grey standard poodle by her side, had finished breakfast.

Sally put her arm around Kirsty. 'You and I had better clear the dishes and let the others plan their day.'

Kirsty sighed.

'I know you'd rather be in the thick of it, love, but we don't know what's going to happen. You and I will be better off making sure Ollie gets home. It completes the circle. You and Frida rescued him, and you and Frida will bring him home.'

The remaining adults withdrew to the dining room. Without asking, Charlie sat at the head of the table and began to organise the group. 'Cat, can I borrow your iPad? Let's get a map of Swanage on the screen. Sam, can you google Swanage caravan sites? Let's see what we're dealing with here.'

Caitlin limped off in search of her iPad whilst Sam began the search. Henry reminded them of what Oswald and Enid had said about the caravan being up a 'bloody great hill'. Caitlin reappeared, and once they had the map of the area on the screen, they could see exactly where the sites were. Assuming they were looking for a static caravan, there seemed to be three main possibilities. However, there were also numerous sites that accommodated touring caravans. They were looking for a needle in a haystack.

They decided to split into three groups. Charlie checked, 'Have you all got your phones charged? We'll need to communicate with one another. I suggest Caitlin and I investigate the site in Ulwell. It could be a strong possibility, as it's the closest to Nine Barrow Down, although it's not that hilly. The other two sites are nearer Durlston and are hilly.'

Bob had been studying the map. 'Remember, the helicopter pilot was searching the Durlston area when he saw a figure on the cliff, running near the quarries. It could just have been a member of the public, but both Swanage Bay and the Coastal Park are within walking distance of Durlston. They're both large sites, quite spread out, so if Olive Lander has used an alias, she could be difficult to locate. Ursula and Maude, would you like to come with me to search the Coastal Park? Sam and Henry can tackle the Swanage Bay site.'

Sam nodded. 'We all need to look out for a white Suzuki jeep. Olive Lander was driving one in Chester, but don't assume anything; she may have come in a different vehicle.'

'Can I ask a question?' Ursula spoke for the first time. 'Why are we doing this? What are the police doing? Don't get me wrong, I want to find Olive, but are we overstepping the mark? What if our search alerts Olive and she simply disappears?'

'That's a good point, Ursula.' Charlie smiled and reassured her, 'I work with the police as a civilian investigator. Sam and I are both private investigators with the necessary qualifications. This is a case we are currently working on, but I'll check in with the station before Cat and I set off. Quite frankly, I think we have a better chance of finding the woman, particularly as some of you know her.'

She stood. 'So, to recap: Cat and I are going to the Ulwell site; Bob, Ursula and Maude, you are going to the Coastal Park, and Sam and Henry are heading over to Swanage Bay View. If one of us finds her, stay back and ring the others. You'll have to use your own judgement. Is that okay with everyone?'

Sam had been scrolling through his phone. He explained, 'For those of you who are new to Swanage, we can have very changeable weather. It's useful to check with the Met Office.' He found what he was looking for. 'Here we are. It should be fine, but there's a chance of rain this afternoon, and the wind will be northerly.' He looked over at Ursula and Maude. 'Did you bring warm clothes?'

Maude shook her head. 'I have, but Ursula, you haven't.'

Caitlin smiled. 'I was thinking this morning, you and Kirsty are very similar in stature. She's tall for her age. We've got plenty of hoodies and anoraks. Come with me and you can take your pick.'

Sam and Henry set off for Swanage Bay View in Sam's hired car, hoping they were on the right track.

***

When they entered the reception, it was packed. Henry, in his usual friendly manner, asked one of the women standing in the queue what they were all there for, to be told it was for an aquafit session. He wanted to know what aquafit was all about. Meanwhile, Sam stood at the door, telling himself not to be impatient.

By 9.30, the room was almost empty. Sam watched Henry engaging with the receptionist. He was very good at putting strangers at ease. 'We're looking for our friend Olive. We know she's staying in a caravan in Swanage, but we can't remember the name of the place she said she was staying.' He tapped his head. 'My memory – oh dear. You don't happen to have an Olive Lander here, do you?'

The receptionist frowned. 'I'm not sure we can give out that information. Data protection and all that. I'll ask in the office, but to be honest, it doesn't ring a bell.'

She came back out and shook her head. 'Sorry, we don't appear to have anyone with that name registered. You're welcome to have a look around; you may recognise her car. Very often, our owners let their friends come for a bit of a holiday, and we're not always told.'

The site was like a rabbit warren. Most of the vans were empty. There were some parked cars, but no sign of a white jeep. They got to the very top and were beginning to think they had drawn a blank when Henry grabbed hold of Sam and steered him away behind another caravan.

'If I'm not mistaken, that silver-grey BMW parked up there belongs to Oswald and Enid.'

They manoeuvred themselves closer. 'Can you see the registration number, Henry?' Sam fished in his pocket for his notebook and flicked to the page where he had recorded the details of the registered keepers of the BMW and the jeep. He read the number out.

'Yes, that's the very one, Sam. What on earth are they doing back here? Let's look around a bit more, see if we can spot the jeep.'

'Do that, Henry. I'll call the others.'

By the time Sam had talked to Charlie, Henry was back. 'There's no sign of Olive's jeep. I suggest we knock on the van door and ask them what they're doing here.' He began to walk away.

Sam hissed, 'Come back, not yet! Our instructions are to wait for the others.'

Henry retraced his steps, and they started the long walk back down the hill. Sam spotted an unlocked gate leading out onto a road.

'From memory, I think this leads to a quarry; it's possible to park up there near the top. I've walked up here with Cat and Sally. There are tracks that go all the way up onto the cliffs.' He turned to Henry. 'Let's get back down. When the others arrive, we can direct them up here. A whole crowd of us walking through the site will draw too much attention.'

They waited near the entrance to the holiday park. Half an hour later, the group was all together and had decided what to do. Sam and Henry were to go on foot, while the others had instructions to park near the quarry entrance and come back down the road and wait by the gate.

As they walked back up the hill for the second time, Henry mused, 'Was it just yesterday when we had the meeting in Chester? It seems like a lifetime ago.'

They trudged on. When they reached the top, Sam asked Henry to go and knock on the door.

Henry grinned and crossed his fingers. 'Wish me luck.' He strode round the corner and stepped up to the caravan's side entrance. He tapped and stood back. Several minutes later, a dishevelled Oswald opened the door. He stared at Henry in disbelief.

'You! What are you doing here?'

'More to the point, old boy, what are you doing here?' Henry pushed past Oswald and disappeared inside.

Sam sighed. This was not what they had planned. He hastened to the door and listened. He could just about hear Enid's sing-song voice placating Oswald. When Sam entered, he saw Enid sitting up on a sofa bed, her legs covered by a duvet. 'Keep the noise down. Olive's asleep in the bedroom.'

Sam looked around and sniffed. He spoke quietly. 'It smells bad in here. Have you all been drinking?'

Enid's voice dropped to a whisper. 'We got here late last night. We were all set to force Olive to go to the police, but she was drunk. Very drunk and sick. We couldn't get anything sensible out of her, so we thought it best to let her sleep it off.'

Henry's expression turned to fury, and in a loud whisper, he hissed, 'How could you sleep when you knew she had taken the boy?'

'We didn't!' Oswald pleaded. 'We knew the boy was missing, that's all. She said she didn't take him. You can ask her yourself. She's in there.' He pointed to the bedroom door.

Sam strode over and flung it open. The bed was empty.

'There's no-one in here, Oz. Come and look.'

Oswald scratched his head. 'She's disappeared!'

'I hardly think she's disappeared. She simply went out of the door. Look.' He pointed at what looked like French windows partially covered by a curtain. 'Clever disappearing trick, I don't think. You've let her slip through your fingers.'

Sam pulled out a couple of drawers. 'She's left her belongings.' He opened the wardrobe. 'Her handbag's in here. I don't think she's gone very far. Did she drive down here in the jeep?'

Oswald nodded.

Sam, who remembered what Ursula had said about going back to her prey, mused, 'She may have gone back to where she left Ollie.' He glared at Oswald. 'Ollie was found last night. Olive had drugged him and laid him out, tied up and gagged on the top of a barrow, as though she was sacrificing him. Hard to believe, isn't it?' His sarcastic tone made Oswald flinch.

'Oh God. Is the boy still alive?'

'Afraid for your own skin, Oz? Yes, but no thanks to you. He's recovering in hospital. If he had been left up there, he would have died of hypothermia. Was that your plan? Wait until he was dead, then deny everything? Spirit Olive away?' He walked through to the other room, followed by Oswald.

Enid, who had remained on the sofa bed, cried out in alarm, 'We came to rescue him! You must believe us; we would never have harmed the boy. We were trying to make amends, but we were so tired …'

Henry glared at her. 'It's time to get up, Enid. Time for you both to face the truth. We'll wait for you outside. You can tell your story to the police.'

Sam's phone rang.

***

There was only one space available near the quarry entrance, so Caitlin drove further down the road and pulled in close to the hedge.

Charlie got out and stood looking over the fields. 'There's a white jeep down there. I can just see it tucked into a gateway.'

Cat joined her. 'Strange, it's a very short walk up here from the caravan site. I suppose she may have been trying to conceal the jeep, but it's not a very good hiding place.'

'No, it's not. I'll stay here, Cat, in case she's close by. Can you go and see what's happening in the caravan?' Charlie walked down to the jeep and peered in before she looked round for somewhere to conceal herself.

Caitlin limped down the road to the others. She had strapped her ankle, but walking was uncomfortable, although she would never admit it. She spotted Ursula and Maude and called out, 'Olive's jeep is up there. Let's go and find Sam and Henry.'

Bob appeared from behind his van. 'I'll ring first. No need to go down if she's not there.' He listened for a moment. 'She was there, but she's gone. Oz and Enid are with them. We're to go up to where she's left the jeep and wait for them.'

**

When Charlie saw the others arriving, she beckoned to them to join her in the field.

'Enid and Oswald, I presume? Thank you for joining us.' Charlie, who didn't look very happy to see them, asked Bob and Caitlin, who knew the area, to describe the terrain.

Bob explained how some of the tracks led towards the cliffs and how some tracks diverged back towards Durlston. 'The problem is, there are loads of different ways to go. But why would she come up here at all?'

Oswald answered. 'She thinks she sees Leo. She wears that silly purple robe of his and thinks she's communing with him. I'm afraid she's tipped over the edge into insanity.' He turned to Charlie. 'She will have no remorse. She has undoubtedly got away with murder before. I don't think it will occur to her addled mind that anyone would be looking for her. What do you suggest we do, Sam?'

'Members of the Chester group, you stick together. People keep up high to commune with the gods, don't they? That's what she thinks she's doing. So, let's stay up high. Bob and Cat, you lead the way.'

'Hold on,' Charlie interrupted. 'I'll ring Sergeant Jameson: tell him we've found the vehicle and ask for backup. What does 'staying up high' mean? Which direction should we go?'

Caitlin answered, 'If I was her, I think I'd stay near the edge, where I could see the sea. When I walk up here, I see people sitting on the cliffs quite near to the gate leading out to California Farm. But anywhere along the top here, where there are well marked paths, would be a good place to "commune with the gods". I assume she doesn't know the area, so she's unlikely to walk too far away from the beaten track.'

Bob nodded. 'Yes, I'd go along with that. If she sees us, she'll probably think we're walkers. But if she sees members of the Chester group, then she's more likely to think they've been summoned to her. If Sam is right about her lack of remorse, she's unlikely to be afraid of any of us. So, should we just spread out and try to find her?' He turned to Oswald. 'You say she's wearing a purple robe, so not difficult to spot.'

'And she's unlikely to be feeling too good.' Enid's

voice was full of spite. 'She was very drunk last night. I hope she has an enormous hangover. Probably why she drove the jeep up here.'

'Okay, we have a plan. Bob, Cat and I will form one search party.' Charlie grinned. 'If we see a woman in a purple robe, we'll stay back and ring you, Sam. Meanwhile, you and the rest of the Chester group go in the opposite direction. We must try not to spook her.'

Sam was keen to get going. He looked at the group and the term 'motley crew' came to his mind. Henry was the first to go. He led the way down the track, followed by Ursula, all four foot eleven of her. She hopped along behind him, wearing a pair of high-heeled boots. She had borrowed an anorak that almost reached down to her knees. Maude clumped beside her. Enid and Oswald brought up the rear.

Sam walked along beside Caitlin, Charlie and Bob. When they reached the diverging path, the Chester group, Sam amongst them, walked straight towards the cliff and turned west. The others set off east, away from Durlston Castle.

The Chester group spotted her first. She was sitting close to the edge, as Caitlin had predicted. They stayed out of sight whilst Sam rang Charlie.

'We're going to approach her as though it's the most natural thing in the world,' Charlie responded. 'Be careful, Sam. Remember, you're dealing with a dangerous woman.'

'Don't worry. She's going to think I've come to claim her.' He began to walk towards the distant figure.

Ursula called out, 'Wait! I think we should walk holding hands. We used to hold hands during the ceremonies.' She grasped Maude's hand. 'Come on, everyone. The idea is that she'll think it's a ceremony. We'll make a circle around her. Stay close together, though.'

They did as she asked and began walking slowly towards the cliff.

Olive had her back to them. As they got closer, they could hear her voice. Closer still, and they could hear her using different voices. A deep, booming voice followed by a familiar voice, the voice of Sister Olive. 'You are the Master. Master and Supreme Being. Take me to you.' A deeper voice boomed out, 'Arise, dearest Sister Olive. Come to me.' The voice was so like Leo's that Oswald and Enid broke away from the others and stood back in horror.

Henry and Sam stood next to each other. Sam freed his hand from Henry's as Olive began to push herself up from the ground. She struggled, her legs entangled in the robe. She pulled it up to her waist. She was naked underneath. She swivelled round onto her knees to see Sam staring at her. Her face lit up with joy. Never taking her eyes off him, she managed to push herself upright. The robe fell to her feet. They stood opposite one another.

'You are all here, my beloved people, ready to witness us becoming one. Oh, dearest Brother Pascal, you have come to me too.' She held her hands out to him.

Sam stepped closer; his right hand outstretched to her. 'Yes, we've come to you. Now, be sensible, my dear Sister Olive; come away from the edge. Walk towards me.' He beckoned with his left hand, but she staggered further back, still holding her arms out to him.

Sam stepped close enough to her to grab both her hands. 'That's it. Come to me.'

Instead of advancing towards him, with a quick

movement, she pulled him to her and threw them both backwards over the edge. Sam cried out, and they heard her voice rising in ecstasy. 'My darling, we're soaring to the heavens!'

Ursula screamed.

Henry, who was closest, watched them fall. The grassy bank was very steep.

The impetus of Olive's fall kept them airborne for several seconds. Then the bank shelved, and she landed on her back, with Sam grasped to her chest. She had fallen onto a large, raised stone. Her grip loosened; Sam fell off and began to roll away. Olive lay still where she was.

Olive's body had given Sam a softer landing. However, he was winded and disorientated, and he was rolling. The bank was getting steeper. He saw a bush and thrust his left hand out to grab it. He managed to catch hold but cried out in pain, let go, and continued his downward descent until he was propelled into a mass of gorse bushes. He felt thorns tearing at his flesh, then he finally came to rest and lay looking at the sea below him.

***

Charlie, Caitlin and Bob could see the group moving towards the purple-robed figure. Caitlin led them to a path running alongside, out of the group's eyesight. They were close by when they heard a scream. Bob and Charlie broke into a run, and Charlie cursed when she saw the purple robe had disappeared. She could see Henry sitting on the edge and watched as he too disappeared. But where was Sam?

'Oh no, no, no!' Caitlin, who was still limping, caught

up with them. 'They've gone over. Sam's falling!'

She could hear Charlie on her phone. She and Bob knelt next to each other on the edge of the bank. They could see the body of Olive in her purple robe. Henry was walking crablike further down the bank. When he got to a steep area, he sat and slithered. He was close now to the bank of gorse on the edge of the cliff. They saw him kneeling by Sam. He shouted up to them, but they couldn't hear; his voice was carried away by the wind.

Bob kissed Caitlin's cheek. 'I'm going down too, love. Don't worry, I'll be careful.'

She knew it was pointless protesting, so instead she simply reached out and squeezed his hand. 'Be careful, sweetheart.' She watched him as he started to slither down the bank towards the woman lying on the rock.

Caitlin frequently walked on the cliffs and had rested on this very spot to look out over the sea towards the Isle of Wight. Sometimes she would watch the ferry sailing over to France. She knew the shape of the rock the woman was lying on. She had always thought it looked like a gravestone.

Bob reached Olive and squatted down to feel for a pulse. He shouted up, 'She's alive, but she doesn't look too good. There's nothing I can do for her. I'm going on down to check on Sam.'

Charlie knelt beside Caitlin and reassured her, 'Don't worry, you know how careful Bob is, and the emergency services are on their way.'

Ursula and Maude remained standing close by. She could see the horror of what they had just witnessed etched on their faces. She called out to them, 'What exactly happened here?'

Ursula spoke first. 'Sam was a hero. He began to

approach Olive. She'd gone loopy, talking to her dead husband. We thought we heard Leofric's voice – the voice he used when he tried to summon the devil, but it was her imitating him. She saw Sam and held her arms out to him. He meant to help her back, but she pulled him into an embrace and went over the edge with him.'

Maude shivered. 'She grunted as she hit that rock. Sam was on top of her and must have made her landing twice as hard.'

Ursula's voice hardened. 'Serve her bloody well right.'

Maude reproached her. 'Sam's a good bloke. What about him? It doesn't serve him right. And she's a fellow human being. Have some pity.'

Ursula folded her arms across her chest as if drawing comfort to herself. She gazed at Maude and nodded, then dropped down beside Caitlin. 'It occurs to me after what Maude said, Olive shouldn't lie down there alone. I'm going to stay with her until the rescue services come.'

Before Caitlin could stop her, she slipped over the edge on her bottom and began to slide down. She waved at Maude and Caitlin when she reached the flat area and attempted to wedge herself beside the stone. Although it wasn't easy to balance in her high-heeled boots, once she felt safe, she reached over for Olive's hand but immediately dropped it. Her action left Olive's arm dangling limply over the edge of the stone. Summoning her courage, she picked the arm up, laid it back beside Olive, and took the hand in hers again. She examined it with distaste. It was how she imagined a workman's hand would be, the nails long and ragged, the skin scaly to her touch.

She found herself saying. 'You really should take

more care of your hands, Olive. You need to moisturise.'
She thought she saw Olive's eyelids flicker, so she
carried on talking. 'You've got yourself into a right
pickle here. The rescue services will come soon and take
you to hospital.' She carried on talking, saying whatever
came into her head.

Bob had good knowledge of first aid. As soon as he
saw the angle of Sam's shoulder, he knew it was
dislocated. 'I can try and manipulate it back in for you,
Sam, or we can wait here for the paramedics.'

Sam grimaced. 'Shove it back in, Bob. I'll try not to
scream.'

Bob unzipped his coat, and Sam looked at him in
surprise. 'What are you doing?'

'If I can manipulate your shoulder back into its joint,
you should have it immobilised, or it might cause further
damage. I'm going to use my shirt as a makeshift sling.'
He pulled his jumper off and unbuttoned his shirt,
shivering in the cold wind. Dressed again, he knelt beside
Sam and undid his coat, gently pulling it down from his
shoulder.

Sam, who didn't want to look, held Henry's hand. He
squeezed hard as he felt the shoulder popping back into
the joint.

'Phew! I don't know who got hurt the most then,'
Henry tried to joke as he released his hand from Sam's
grip and shook it.

Bob carefully folded his shirt in a diagonal and asked
Henry to help Sam position his left arm across his chest.
He passed the sling underneath the arm and tied it around
his neck before pulling Sam's coat back up over his
shoulder, buttoning it up. The arm in its sling rested
snuggly inside the coat. 'Keep that arm nice and still.

Don't attempt to use it. Your shoulder needs checking over by a medic.'

Sam sat back while Bob felt the rest of his limbs. He protested, 'I'm OK. Scratched, battered and bruised, that's all. If you two help me, I think I can get back to the top. Let's take it slowly.' He grinned. 'It'll be less painful walking up than it was rolling all the way down.'

With Henry on one side of Sam and Bob on the other, they slowly made their way back up the bank. When Sam looked back, he shivered; he had come close to going right over the edge. The gorse had saved him.

When they reached the rock where Olive lay, Henry squeezed in beside Ursula. 'Any sign of life?'

Ursula shook her head. 'She's alive – I started talking to her and her eyelids flickered. Nothing since then.'

Sam stared at Olive. 'She may be badly injured, but she's still dangerous. This is so weird. She looks like a sacrifice laid out in that purple robe. She trussed young Oliver up and left him alone on top of a barrow. Now here she is lying on a sacrificial stone. She has sacrificed herself, and damn nearly sacrificed me as well.'

Bob put his arm around Sam's back. 'Look, we've got company above. Let's get you up to the top and into the ambulance.'

Bob shouted, 'Walking wounded coming up! The woman's alive. She's going to need your help.'

A paramedic waved and watched as Henry and Bob helped Sam by pushing him up the steep slope. Charlie and Caitlin escorted him straight to the ambulance, while Henry, Bob and the paramedic slid back down to Olive.

Ursula, who had remained with her, watched the paramedic as he felt for a pulse. 'Is she still breathing? I've been talking to her, but she hasn't responded.'

'Yes, it's shallow, but she's breathing. What's her name? Do you know how this happened?'

'Her name's Olive Lander. Basically, she let herself fall backwards and she landed on this stone, with Sam on top of her.' She was surprised the paramedic accepted what she said. To her mind, it was too fantastic. Then she thought he might be used to people falling over cliffs. She couldn't imagine herself living in a place that might compel people to do such things. The worst she could do was fall into the canal.

'Thank you. I would suggest you three go back up to the top. Search and rescue's on its way. I'll remain here with Olive.'

Henry, always the perfect gentleman, took Ursula's hand. 'Come on, old girl, I'll help you up.'

In normal circumstances, Ursula would have given him a piece of her mind. She certainly didn't need help, and she wasn't old, but nothing today was normal. In addition, seeing Olive being examined by the paramedic had affected her in an unexpected way. She couldn't grasp what she felt for this vulnerable, deranged human being, who had carried out dreadful deeds, including attempted murder; but she was shaking, so she reached out for Henry's hand and allowed him to pull her up. His hand was warm and comforting. They smiled at one another, both surprised by a friendship they hadn't realised existed until that moment.

'Do you want to watch the search and rescue team winch Olive?' Charlie posed the question, hoping for a negative answer.

Maude murmured, 'She's lucky to be alive. Or maybe she isn't. No, I don't want to watch. I hope we never have to see her again.'

Henry's expression turned to anger. 'We haven't seen the last of her. Whatever the Landers may or may not have done, there'll be plenty to clear up. If she survives, I hope the next time we see her will be in the dock, being tried for attempted murder.'

Ursula could sense Maude's discomfort. 'We know what you meant, love. We'd all like it to go away.'

Henry ignored Ursula. 'We've been members of a death cult. You two might have thought it was harmless, but it wasn't, was it? We turned a blind eye to Olive's relationship with Will. She instigated his drug use, feeding him a load of bullshit about finding himself. I remember when I first joined, Will was the cult's messianic figure, then Olive medicated him and he became a shell. I only joined the group to protect my grandfather, and that didn't turn out well. I could kick myself. I don't know why I remained and became so absorbed in it.'

Charlie spoke calmly but with authority. 'Henry, this isn't the right time to start a post-mortem. You've all had a shock. It would be best for everyone if we went back to Rock House. I noticed Oswald and Enid removed themselves after Olive's spectacular leap. I suppose they will have gone back to the caravan.'

At that moment, Sam emerged from the ambulance, his left arm immobilised in a sling. He walked towards them, carrying Bob's shirt in his good hand. 'I'm all in one piece, just bruised in places.' He grinned at Bob, holding out his shirt. 'You did a great job for a basic first aider.'

'Less of the basic, you! I'm glad you're alright, but you won't be able to use that arm for a few days. Come back to Rock House and we'll give you some ice. Best to cool the joint at frequent intervals to keep any swelling down.'

'OK, Dr Bob! I'm in your hands. Henry, will you drive me back up to Rock House?'

Caitlin offered to guide them back. 'We should go a different way. I expect the track we used will be cordoned off by now. Follow me.' She turned and limped away, followed by the others.

Charlie remained where she was. 'I'll meet you all back at the house. I want to check the jeep and the caravan. Oswald and Enid may have gone back there. Now, they would make a fascinating case study!' She hurried back up the track to where they had first spotted Olive's jeep, and as she reached it, Sergeant Jameson drew up in a patrol car.

Despite their run-in the night before, he greeted her warmly. He pulled on a pair of latex gloves. 'Let's have a look at what we have here. You reckon this is Olive Lander's vehicle?'

Charlie nodded.

He tried the driver's door. It was unlocked. 'I can see a rucksack and a package on the floor on the passenger side.' He got in, sat in the driver's seat, and reached down. 'Looks like we've found the boy's rucksack, and well, I never! A box of chocolate truffles.'

Charlie called out, 'I wouldn't eat any of those if I was you, Phil.'

He grinned at her and leaned over to open the glove box.

'Interesting array of artefacts.' He held up an empty vial and a hypodermic. 'Odd behaviour, leaving all this for us to find. It's as if she wants to be caught.'

Charlie squatted down to look at the underside of the

vehicle. 'Looks as though the exhaust has come loose. That's one bumpy track going up to Nine Barrow. I daresay you will find the jeep's tyre prints up at the top near the long barrow.'

'Right, I'll get this area taped off until we can get the vehicle moved.' The sergeant walked back over to the patrol car to radio in.

When he came back, Charlie mused, 'It's as though the woman staged the whole thing. Why would she do that? Are we missing anything?'

Phil responded, 'Forensics are at the caravan now. Maybe it will throw some light on the situation. Speaking of lights, you say Caitlin and Kirsty saw lights on the hill. Strange, there was no sign of anyone else having been there. Look, I was shirty with you last night. I'm sorry, I was having a bad night. You've been a great help. I owe you a lunch.'

Chapter 35

Bob drove through the gates of Rock House with a sigh of relief. It had been a day to remember. His passengers had been quiet on the way home, and he thought they probably felt as dazed as he did. Ursula and Maude sat in silence in the back seat of the van. Caitlin was in the passenger seat, her right hand resting on his leg. He could feel the warmth of it and felt comforted by having her close to him.

As he pulled up in front of the house, he saw Henry's car, but Caitlin's car was gone. They went in to find the house deserted. Sally had left a note to say she and Kirsty had driven over to Bournemouth Hospital to fetch Miriam and Ollie.

Caitlin looked at her watch. It was nearly 1.30 p.m.; the note had been written forty minutes before. 'They'll be at the hospital in about half an hour, so they should be back around five. Well, it's good news, but I wish we were all together again right now!'

Sam and Henry, who had initially been following Bob's van, were still nowhere to be seen. Caitlin, worried, checked again before she shut the front door. 'Strange – where could they have got to?'

'It's okay, Cat. They'll have gone to the pharmacy. You can bet your bottom dollar Sam's putting a brave face on it, but he'll be aching like hell. Painkillers are called for, big time.' Bob put his arm around Caitlin. 'Come on, let's see what we can rustle up for lunch.'

'It's very kind of you, but I'm not sure we should stay.' Ursula's clear voice had an immediate impact.

Caitlin stared at her in bewilderment. 'Where would you go? Are you intending to go back home right now?'

Ursula bit her lip. 'I sound ungrateful, I'm sorry. I spoke out of turn. We'll stay until matters are sorted out down here, but I think we should find a B&B. It's not fair to expect you to put us up.'

Bob said nothing but inwardly agreed. Caitlin might like a house full, but he found it almost unbearable. He said, 'You should be able to find accommodation easily at this time of year. Have some lunch first. Go and relax in the lounge, and I'll make you a cup of tea.'

Maude's giggle was unexpected. She pretended to frown at Ursula. 'Are you expecting me to be like Jack Reacher? We haven't even got a toothbrush between us. If we're staying for a few days, we need to go shopping.'

Ursula agreed. 'Point taken. We did come away in a hurry. How far would it be for us to walk to the shops? Quite frankly, I'm so full of nervous energy, I don't think I could eat anything.'

Caitlin explained, 'It's downhill all the way to the shops. That's the easy bit.' She grinned. 'If you want a lift back, Bob or Henry could fetch you, but I guess Henry is in the same boat as you, and he should be back any minute. Why don't you wait for him, and he can drive you all down.'

Bob laughed. 'We're going round and round.' He repeated, 'Go and relax in the lounge. I'll bring you a cup of tea.'

At that moment, the door opened. 'Did I hear the word "tea"? I could kill for a cup of tea!'

Startled, they turned to see Henry in the doorway.

Sam followed him and echoed Henry in a subdued voice. 'Tea would be good. I need to eat something too, then I can take some painkillers.'

Caitlin, seeing how pale Sam looked, was immediately

concerned. 'Sam, you can have the spare room. I'll bring you tea and sandwiches. You need to lie down and stop pretending you're OK. You only had a couple of hours sleep last night, and since then, well, I don't even want to think about it. Eat, drink, take your tablets, and then sleep. Go on up now, get comfortable, and I'll bring you some lunch.'

'Yes, boss. I'll go, but before I do, Henry, thank you for all your help, and Ursula and Maude, thank you for coming all the way down here to support us. If Olive Lander survives, she'll be locked up for a long time. We've done the world a favour today.' Sam looked over at Caitlin's face. 'Okay, I'm going right now.'

He limped towards the stairs. He had taken Caitlin's words to heart. He was hurting. He wanted to lie down. But before he reached the bottom step, he turned round to ask, 'Do you know what's happening with Ollie and Miriam?'

Bob nodded. 'They're on their way back from Bournemouth. Should be here about five. Never fear, we'll wake you when they arrive.'

With Henry, Ursula and Maude shopping, and Sam resting in bed, Caitlin and Bob snuggled up on the sofa together and fell asleep.

***

Sally, Miriam, Ollie, Kirsty and Frida came home to a quiet house. Kirsty found her parents and began to tiptoe out of the room, trying not to wake them, but Caitlin opened her eyes and called out to her, 'Kirsty, come here, my love.' She hugged her.

Kirsty wriggled. 'Oh, Mum, let go! I've only been

over to Bournemouth!'

'I know, but we missed you.'

Bob ruffled her hair. 'That goes for me too, kiddo. How's our boy Ollie?'

Ollie, who was just about to join them, heard him and grinned from ear to ear. He was *their* boy. He felt incredibly pleased. 'Hello, here I am.'

Caitlin stretched out her arms. 'Come here, Ollie.'

Kirsty sat on one side of her and Ollie on the other. Ollie broke into a beaming smile as Caitlin hugged him. Then he became serious. 'Aunty Cat, I'm very sorry I caused so much trouble. That woman told me she was your friend and seemed to know lots about you. I did think about stranger danger, but I reckoned she was okay. Not only that, but she also gave me chocolates, and the doctor said she drugged me. That's why I fell asleep and then she tied me up.'

Caitlin looked over and spotted Sally and Miriam standing at the door watching Ollie.

Miriam looked so pleased. She called out to Ollie, 'Well done for apologising. Unfortunately, that woman has fooled lots of people.'

Miriam and Sally joined them, but Sally sat apart and listened in silence. Miriam looked around. 'I haven't heard from Sam, and where are all the others?'

Bob answered, 'Sam's upstairs asleep. Henry, Ursula and Maude went off to do some shopping and to fix themselves up with accommodation. They said if they find somewhere to stay, they won't see us until the morning.'

'Ollie's told me what happened, but have they caught the woman who kidnapped him yet?' Miriam's question was followed by silence as Caitlin struggled to figure out how much to tell her.

'Yes, it was Olive Lander; all the evidence points towards her being the kidnapper. She was located this morning. Oswald and Enid left the scene and we haven't seen them since. Maybe we should let Sam tell you what happened next, when he wakes.'

Bob frowned at Caitlin. 'Cat, I think I'd better tell Miriam. We can't leave it all up to Sam. There was an accident. Sam has a minor injury. His shoulder got dislocated, but don't worry, he's in pain but alright. Olive Lander on the other hand ...' He tailed off. 'Well, we don't know whether she's dead or alive. She was winched up by the rescue services from a steep incline and taken to hospital. Charlie's over there now. We'll hear more as the evening progresses.'

Kirsty could hardly contain herself. 'Did Ollie's air ambulance come back again? That's so cool. You were asleep, Ollie, but you should have seen them flying in to rescue you. It was awesome.'

Bob stopped her. 'No, this time it was air-sea rescue, but we'd left the scene by then.'

'Did they take Sam as well?' Miriam looked a picture of misery.

Bob went over to Miriam and put his arm around her shoulder. 'No, I promise you, he's upstairs asleep. Kirsty, take Miriam up to the spare room to see Sam. It's probably time he woke up, and he'll want to see her. And when you've shown Miriam where he is, come straight back down. Alright?'

Kirsty gave her father a knowing look.

Caitlin's phone rang. She listened intently for a few minutes. 'That was Charlie. She's about to head back here. Olive Lander hasn't regained consciousness. It seems she's sustained a major head injury. Her spine's injured, she has broken ribs, a broken tibia and a compound fracture to her right leg. They don't know how bad the spinal injury is yet. Charlie says it doesn't look good. There's nothing we can do now but wait.'

Bob looked at his watch pointedly when Kirsty came clattering back in. 'Sam's awake. He's kissing Miriam.' She held her thumb up and winked at Ollie.

'What did I say about coming straight back down, Kirsty?' Bob shook his head. 'I propose I fetch us fish and chips for our supper tonight. It doesn't look as though Henry and the others are coming back, so we can have a quiet evening in together.'

***

After they had eaten, the children could hardly keep their eyes open. Ollie, who had remained close to Kirsty and Frida all evening, asked his mother if he could sleep in Kirsty's room. She felt the same frisson of jealousy she had experienced before but told herself it was perfectly natural for him to want to be with Kirsty and Frida. They were his rescuers.

Sam had eaten a few chips, then returned upstairs to sleep, and by the end of the evening, Caitlin and Bob were upstairs together and Sally had disappeared with Charlie. So, Miriam ended up on her own in the flat, and exhausted as she was, fell asleep almost immediately. She woke again sometime in the middle of the night, when memories of the last few days came flooding back. Will was dead, and try as she might, she could hardly recall what he had looked like before the demons got into his head. The memory of the last time she had seen him was too deeply imprinted in her mind.

She had yet to say goodbye to him. She thought how she would go back to Chester and attend his inquest, and afterwards she would lay his ghost. The phrase 'lay his ghost' hung in the air – all that had happened kept coming back to ghosts. Would poor unhappy Will begin to haunt their home? She remembered Pat's revelation about Agnes Howe: the story of Agnes's son being murdered and how she had been blamed and killed by a merciless society.

She spoke out loud. 'Ollie's father meant to harm him, didn't he? I'm not sure if Will was murdered in the house, but if you can hear me, Agnes, I hope all that's happened since wasn't your revenge.' She stopped herself and shivered. *Oh God, what am I saying? Why am I thinking like this? Agnes protected us. Will may have been helped along, but he died willingly, because in his addled mind, he thought he would be reborn. The woman who gave Will drugs and who kidnapped Ollie is surely as good as dead. So I mustn't think like this, not now, not ever.*

Some hours later she fell asleep again.

Chapter 36
Chester

Pat had lain awake all night thinking about her friends. When she received a call from Sam to reassure her that Ollie had been found, she shed more tears, but this time, tears of joy. Later another call came, to say Ollie was recovering well in hospital and Miriam was with him. She felt as though a world of worry had been lifted from her shoulders.

However, Pat had always been straight with Miriam, maybe too straight sometimes, and yet hadn't plucked up the courage to confess to her part in helping the cult pinpoint Ollie's whereabouts. She had realised too late: it was the photos on her stolen phone. She had forgotten all about taking them until a sudden memory popped into her head. Ollie's birthday treat. The worry and guilt came straight back to hit her between the eyes.

The school day passed by in a haze. Back at home, she still felt sick with fear. For the umpteenth time, she wished she had gone to Dorset with the others. Despite knowing Ollie was safe, she now had the worry of Sam and Henry pursuing dangerous criminals.

It was almost a relief to hear a tap on the front door, until anxiety took over again. What if something even more awful had happened? She rose from her chair and walked over to the window. The light over the front door shone on a slim young woman with long blonde hair – Sandy.

'Can I speak to you please, Miss James?'

Pat noticed Sandy's tawny eyes were shining with something like elation. She invited her in, glad of the distraction, and showed her into the lounge.

Sandy began immediately. 'I've been having tea with my aunt and uncle. They live close by Mr and Mrs Marshall's house. We were reading the report on Mr Marshall's death in the local paper and got talking. My aunt and my uncle told me something that might be of interest to the police.'

'Why have you come to me, not the police?'

Sandy's brow furrowed. 'We've never had anything to do with the police and we weren't sure what to do. I thought you might like to hear what they'd seen, and we hoped you'd give us some advice.'

'Forgive me for being so brusque. Of course you can run it by me.'

Sandy began her tale. 'My aunt often walks past Mr and Mrs Marshall's house because she takes the short cut to town via the tow path. She recalled how on the 26th of January, she had arranged to meet her friend by the canal. She knows the exact date because it was her friend's birthday, and they were going into town for lunch.

'She saw a woman riding up to the house on a bike. She was a tall woman wearing a black jacket. My aunt thought she was a community nurse because she was carrying what looked like a medical bag. Anyway, she had a key and she let herself in. My aunt thought it all very strange because she'd seen the bike leaning against the house a couple of times before.

'It gets even more interesting, because not long after that, my uncle was coming home from the pub and saw lights on in the house. The front room curtain wasn't closed all the way and he saw people in there. He figured Mr and Mrs Marshall must be having a party. Later, he was taking the dog out and he saw an ambulance parked outside. He and my aunt asked a couple of neighbours whether they had heard anything about Mr or Mrs Marshall being ill, but no-one had.'

'That *is* interesting, Sandy. Mrs Marshall and young Oliver had already left Chester by then. I had popped round to the house once or twice to pick up Mrs Marshall's post, but then she had it redirected, so I didn't go again.'

Sandy continued, 'The report in the paper said he'd been dead for some time, but it was vague. Do you think my aunt and uncle should report what they saw? They don't want people to think they're busybodies.'

'Yes, definitely. They should report it. Do you think your aunt would be able to give a description of the woman she saw?'

Sandy grinned. 'Oh yes. You see, she thought the woman was odd, so she had a good look at her. When she took off her bicycle helmet, she had a red scarf tied round her head, which my aunt said framed her face as though she was a nun. She said she'd remember her face if she saw her again.'

Pat smiled with satisfaction. At last, the evidence Sam had been looking for. If Sandy's aunt identified the scarf Will was holding when they found him, it would prove beyond doubt that Olive had been with him. She got up. 'Thank you for coming to tell me, Sandy. Please encourage your aunt and uncle to go to the police. Now, let me take you home. It's getting late.'

'Thanks, Miss James, but Mum is outside in the car, waiting for me. I hope we can help the police nail whoever hurt Ollie's dad.'

***

Miriam gazed out of the window at Nine Barrow Down lit up in the early morning sun. It looked beautiful, fresh and green, and above all, normal. It was from this very window that Kirsty had spotted the mysterious lights floating around, drawing her to the barrow where Ollie lay. The lights had saved Ollie's life. Miriam's head told her they were a natural phenomenon, but in her heart she thought otherwise. Ollie had said he heard Agnes whispering to him, and Kirsty was convinced the ghost of her grandmother had also been on the hill. Miriam realised that at last, she too was beginning to believe.

She looked at her watch; it was after nine, and here she was being philosophical and still in her pyjamas. Time to get ready to face the day. When she emerged, showered and dressed, Ollie, Kirsty and Frida were waiting for her. Frida bounded over, sat next to her, and stared, a baleful look in her eyes.

Miriam squatted down. Despite her previous fear of dogs, she found herself laying her dark, curly head onto Frida's grey curly fur. Frida licked her cheek with enthusiasm. 'You are such a good dog for finding Ollie. Thank you, Frida.'

Miriam looked over at the two children watching her. Was that a smug look she could see on their faces?

Ollie called over, 'You looked sad when Frida followed us last night. Now Frida loves you, and we're all part of the same family.'

Miriam didn't know how to respond. The course of her life with Ollie had turned onto an unfamiliar path. She wasn't sure whether she had any choice but to accept this new direction. 'You two have been scheming, haven't you? Don't think I haven't noticed!' She grinned at them. 'I've seen you watching me.'

Ollie did have the grace to look a little ashamed. 'You look so happy when you're with Sam.'

'I am happy, love.' Miriam sighed. 'But there are things I'm going to have to do before we can settle into a new life. Come here. Let's live for the moment. I want us to be happy.' She stood and reached her arms out for the two children.

Sam pushed the door open in time to see their group hug. Frida wagged her tail but stayed where she was. Sam was puzzled. 'Hello, all. You look very cheerful. What's going on?'

Miriam reached towards Sam. 'Join us. We won't hug you too hard.'

Kirsty and Ollie began to giggle. They broke away and said in one voice. 'We're going to get some breakfast,' which started Miriam giggling.

'Enough of your mischief! Just go, you two. We'll be down in a minute.'

Sam was still puzzled. 'Am I missing something?'

'It seems they've got our lives planned out for us. It's quite a responsibility, don't you think?'

Sam wasn't quite sure what Miriam meant, but he hoped she was beginning to share his feelings. He gazed at her. Despite the trauma of the last few days, she was fresh-faced and her eyes twinkled. He said, 'I had a phone call from Henry this morning. They've decided to go straight back home. It seems like a lifetime ago, but remember the group meeting, when Paul's mother Eira couldn't stop coughing? I'm afraid she's tested positive for Covid. I sat down the other end of the table, but Ursula and Maude were close to her, and they're both anti-vaxxers.'

Miriam frowned. 'Oh hell. It's easy to forget Covid. Have you been vaccinated? Ollie and I have.'

He nodded. 'Yes, I'm up to date. We should be alright.' In response, a smiling Miriam took his hand and led him to the sofa. She put her arm around his good shoulder and drew him to her.

***

Downstairs, Caitlin was busy setting the breakfast table. She wondered whether Olive Lander had survived the night. It would be simpler for them if she died, but Caitlin had no faith in anything being simple. Her reverie was interrupted by the children, closely followed by the dog. Kirsty asked where her dad was.

'He'll be back in a minute. He's gone to buy fresh bread and some more eggs. I'm going to make scrambled egg and bacon when he gets back. Are you two hungry? Stupid question! There's juice in the fridge, help yourselves.'

Caitlin watched Ollie. She marvelled at his resilience. His ordeal hardly seemed to have affected him physically. However, whether he had been affected mentally remained to be seen. Since they had returned together from Bournemouth, Ollie had not wanted to be separated from Kirsty. Another day off school for Kirsty, but she must go back tomorrow.

'Kirsty, can you go up and call Sal and Charlie? Tell them breakfast will be ready in half an hour.'

Kirsty turned for the door, and Ollie began to follow. 'Stay and keep me company, Ollie. Kirsty won't be long. I want to know how you're feeling.'

'I'm okay, Aunty Cat. The kidnap's like a dream. I didn't like being in hospital much. I prefer it here. Do you think Mum will agree to us staying here?'

'I can't answer that, love. Mum has got a lot of sorting out to do before she can think about the future, but you can stay here for as long as it takes. Mum knows that.'

Ollie looked very serious. 'Do you think she'll marry Sam? Kirsty does.'

Caitlin tried to look equally serious, but the twinkle in her eye gave her away. 'I can't answer that either! Give them time and let them sort themselves out.'

Ollie was happy with that, as long as he was with them. He wanted Sam to stay with his Mum in Rock House. 'Do you think Mum will have to go back to Chester?'

Caitlin shook her head. 'You must ask her, Ollie.' She stopped to think. 'Do you know what a powwow is?'

'It's something to do with native Americans, isn't it?'

Caitlin smiled. 'Yes, and it's a good word for holding a meeting, don't you think? We've had lots of powwows in Rock House. I think the adults will need one after breakfast, and Ollie, take my advice, don't go mentioning marriage.'

Neither Kirsty nor Ollie was happy to hear that they were to be excluded from the meeting, until Miriam explained the natural history project she had in mind for them.

'I want you to record as many creatures, plants and fungi as you can find in the garden. Start with soil for today. Kneel and study a small area, then dig some compost out of the compost box and examine the contents. Look at the soil under the hedges, beneath trees and in the rose garden. When you've finished, compare results from the different environments. Use your laptops to research and then write up what you've learned.'

Bob winked at Kirsty. 'Sounds more enjoyable to me than being inside listening to us grown-ups.'

The children weighed up the situation and came down on Bob's side. He waited until they had left the room before saying, 'I could help them with the soil samples.'

Caitlin smiled. 'Of course you could, love. Only, you must let them find out for themselves too. Don't spoon-feed them.'

'I won't. I'll just point them in the right direction.' With that, Bob put his coat on and joined the children.

Sally and Miriam cleared the breakfast table while Caitlin made coffee. Charlie was on the phone. Sam, ignoring the action all around him, remained at the table.

Miriam was unable to disguise her concern for him. 'You could take some more painkillers now you've eaten. Shall I fetch them for you?'

Sam smiled gratefully. 'Thanks, I've got paracetamol with me. I'll take a couple now.'

As he fumbled in his pocket, Caitlin joined in. 'If Bob hadn't escaped into the garden, he'd probably advise a couple of ibuprofen as well, to keep the swelling down. Do you want some?'

Sam sighed and nodded his head. 'Yeah. My shoulder's horrible, but I'm not going to complain. I thank my lucky stars I'm alive and kicking.'

Caitlin searched through a kitchen drawer and handed him a box. 'Here you go; take two with a glass of water. Do you want a coffee as well?'

He nodded.

'Once Charlie is off the phone, maybe we could discuss arrangements.'

It was Miriam's turn to sigh. 'I'll have to go back to Chester.' She looked over at Charlie, who had finished her phone call. 'Is there any news?'

Charlie grimaced. 'Olive Lander is certainly a survivor. She's unconscious, but her vital signs are good. The police are with her, hoping to get a statement when she comes to.'

Sam grunted. 'They'll be lucky. I hope they realise what a dangerous woman she is.'

Charlie took a sip from her mug. 'I'll finish my coffee, then I'm going to join them at the hospital. Lander's injuries are life-threatening; she's dangerous, but she won't be going anywhere. We'll gather any evidence we can from our end, but don't hold out too much hope of the police being able to charge her yet, given the physical and mental state she's in. Do you want to come with me, Sally?'

Sally's face brightened. 'Yes, please. I feel a bit of a spare part here. Let me do something useful.'

'Okay, we'll make tracks, and Sam, you rest, get better.' She looked at Miriam and Caitlin. 'Don't let him do too much.'

As Charlie and Sally left, Sam saluted them with his good arm. 'And then there were three.'

Which was when Miriam's phone rang. It was Pat. Miriam switched to speaker so they could all take part in the conversation. 'Morning, Pat. Are you on your break? Can we talk? Caitlin and Sam are here with me.'

'I can't talk for long. I just wanted to let you know what's happening here. Several witnesses have come forward, one who remembers seeing a woman who looked like a nurse letting herself into your house. Another witness saw people in the house and remembers seeing an ambulance parked outside. How are you doing down there? Has the woman survived?'

Sam answered, 'Yes, she has, and thanks, Pat – good news about the witnesses. I presume they'll be able to give approximate dates as well as descriptions?'

'Absolutely, and all the dates are when Mimi had already left. How's Ollie this morning?'

Miriam answered this time. 'He seems pretty much back to normal. His tummy was sore yesterday, but he's just eaten a good breakfast.'

'I'm going to have to go, but I'll ring tonight. Let me know when you're coming back.' The phone went dead.

Miriam repeated, 'Let me know when you're coming back.' She shook her head. 'Oh God, I don't want to go back. Face the police, face an inquest, face my poor house.'

Caitlin leaned across the table and reached for her hand. 'You must face it before you can truly start again. We'll help you, and it won't be as bad as you think. Trust me, it never is. I remember you saying Pat had arranged for the house to be cleaned.'

'Yes, she has.' She smiled at them both. 'I can't do anything until I've had a heart-to-heart with Ollie. I don't want to second-guess what he'll say.' She reached for Caitlin's hand. 'We can all see how much he feels part of your family. I felt I was losing him at first.'

Caitlin reassured her, 'If I was in your shoes, I'd have felt the same. But listen, Kirsty is used to Rock House being a sanctuary, but she has never taken to anyone as she's taken to you and Ollie. I love having you here. I knew we'd be friends from the moment we met.'

Miriam's eyes filled with tears. She brushed them away, irritated with herself. 'Thank you. You're right,

Cat. With your help, I can face it all, and Ollie and I will settle here or somewhere close by so we can remain part of your family.'

Just for a moment, Sam wanted to cry out, 'But what about me? You haven't mentioned me!'

Miriam must have sensed how he was feeling. She put her arm around him and drew him to her, burying her head in his good shoulder. He tried not to wince. Her voice was muffled, but he heard what she said distinctly, and with it all his aches and pains seemed to disappear.

'I love you, Sam.'

Miriam had driven Sam's hire car back to Chester, despite his protestations that his arm was out of the sling and his shoulder relatively pain-free. But it had seemed important to Miriam that she take control. The plan was to drop the hire car off in Chester and return to Rock House in Miriam's car.

They had all agreed they would have a memorial for Will in Chester during the Easter holidays so their new family and friends would be able to come. Miriam had been relieved when Ollie said he would stay in Rock House whilst she travelled up this time. He wanted to see their old home, but he wasn't ready. He would do so after he had said goodbye to his father at the memorial.

Neither Miriam nor Sam had developed any Covid symptoms. Henry had subsequently gone down with it, and along with Ursula and Maude, was still testing positive. Miriam felt a sense of relief. One less thing to face. She didn't want to see them and be reminded of the cult. She preferred to forget the memory of the meeting she had witnessed with Pat on the awful night when Ollie was taken.

***

Now she was back in Pat's house, she kept experiencing a feeling of déjà vu. Pat had prepared a meal and was in the kitchen peeling vegetables. They were having a steak casserole, one of Pat's signature dishes.

Miriam looked over to the corner of the lounge where

the Christmas tree had once stood, its lights flicking on and off. She mused out loud to Sam, 'It was just before New Year, and I was sitting on this very sofa, with Pat beside me, and I found the courage to tell her what had been happening with Will. Three months, and it seems a lifetime ago.'

Pat appeared in the doorway with a bottle of champagne. 'There's some flute glasses in the cabinet. Could you get them for me, Mimi, while I wrestle with this cork?' She sat down opposite Sam, put the bottle on the coffee table, covered the cork with a tea towel, twisted it, and bang, the cork popped off. A few bubbles escaped down the side of the bottle. Miriam put three glasses on the coffee table, and Pat poured.

'Here's to you two. I can't tell you how delighted I am to see you together. It was meant to be.'

Miriam smiled, but then her expression changed as she thought about Will. 'I don't know if it's appropriate, but will you join me in a toast to Will? He wasn't always a bad man.' She turned to Sam. 'Our marriage ended years before you and I met, Sam, and I don't think I was ever as happy with him as I'm going to be with you.'

Sam raised his glass. 'To Will. I hope he can rest in peace.'

Pat took a sip from her glass before speaking. 'Difficult to believe he will ever rest in peace.' She saw Miriam's look. 'It's true, Mimi, but I hope he will. There, I've said it.' She raised her glass. 'To Will. Now, enough of that. I'm more interested in you two and what is going to happen to Olive Lander. I have a confession to make, Sam. You know you left those papers behind?'

Sam was puzzled. 'I don't remember leaving anything here with you.'

Pat paused, looking as puzzled as Sam, then tapped the side of her head. 'Stupid, of course it wasn't you. It was Henry. He had some papers from the Lander's house. He picked them up just before you left and forgot he had them. He gave them to me for safekeeping. I've read them – just a few loose pages from Olive Lander's journal, but they might throw some light on what happened. How about we have a look at them tomorrow?'

Miriam's glass was empty. Pat leaned over and topped all their glasses up. 'Let's drink up and be merry this evening.' She raised her glass again. 'It's over, Mimi. It's good to see you smiling again. Drink your bubbly.' She raised her glass again. 'To the start of your new lives.'

***

Extracts from the Journal of Olive Lander

18 November 2019

When I answered the advert for Family of Hope and Rebirth, it crossed my mind it was a scam. It takes one scammer to know another, and I had unfinished business with the contact, William Marshall.

I expected our first meeting to be awkward. I thought he might recognise the resemblance to my sister, but there was only a look of delight on his face. Conversation was easy – ideas burst out of him. I admit I found his grey eyes bewitching, and I began to understand how he had trapped Sara.

He didn't have a clue who I was; I'm good at playing games. We went to a hotel room. He drew up a chair and asked me to sit opposite him. He said he wanted to hypnotise me, to help me understand how to shift reality.

I had no idea what he was talking about. So I smiled at him and started to pretend to unbutton my blouse and said in play. 'You don't have to hypnotise me, William, I'm more than willing to have sex with you.' You should have seen the look on his face.

He ignored what I had said and told me to sit, reached over, and removed my glasses. I swear his eyes became darker. He told me to concentrate. Secretly amused, I did as he commanded. He spoke in a soft voice and despite myself, my eyes became heavy.

I heard laughter and loud voices, and when I looked around me, I saw people sitting at long tables, dressed in clothes from long ago. I waited for them to ask me who I was, but they seemed unaware of my presence. It was only when I looked at the top table that I saw a man who stared straight at me. He nodded in recognition. To my astonishment, he had William Marshall's face. I don't know what happened then, but I remember struggling until I found myself being pulled back into reality.

That's how I became Sister Olive, adrift in a heroic new world with a man who calls himself William Marshall, Knight Templar and friend of kings. He thirsts for power, fame and fortune. He has no idea what I know, or what I want, and he thinks he's mesmerised me.

3 January 2020

William has led me into his darkness. I have seen things I can't explain, and he has made me pledge myself to him. He says two must become one to solve the mystery. He calls it The Demon Paradox. I think I am beginning to understand, and when his end comes, as it surely will, it will be all the more delicious.

29 January 2020

A drunken evening and I told Leo about William Marshall. Big mistake, he wants it too.

4 February 2020

Leo has taken control. Tonight, he and William talked together as though I wasn't there. How dare they. I will not play the little woman.

31 March 2020

We are in lockdown. I have learned how to access the dark web.

14 July 2020

Free again and Leo has become the leader, but it is William who fascinates the group. His eyes draw them in until they become putty in his hands. He takes them out of their reality into other realms, but he might as well make the most of playing the messiah, because it's not going to last. I can sense his weakness.

4 August 2020

Leo's friends, Oswald and Enid, have joined. I thought they had more sense. They've taken to calling William Marshall the marshal. Oh, really! It's just a play on words. It's become Brother this and Sister that, as though it makes any difference.

5 November 2020

Just as the group were getting to know one another, we're in lockdown again. Leo says we'll use Zoom. As William sinks, Leo rises, and he is tightening his grip on the group. He has begun to use it for his own greedy ends. Mark Williams has nearly destroyed his wife and son by taking his own life, just like my Sara did. There is no doubt now that William Marshall was the cause of my sister's death. The group still wait in vain for their lives to be transformed.

Miriam read through the extract twice before giving it back to Sam. 'This doesn't make sense. May I use your computer, Pat? Will's student was called Sara. I remember the local paper reporting her death. I don't remember anything about her having a sister.'

The newspaper article they found contained a grainy picture of Sara Lawrence. Sam and Pat noted the resemblance between Sara and Olive. The same round, moon faces and large glasses.

Miriam, who had never met Olive, remarked, 'If you ignore the glasses, you say the face shape is similar, but what other resemblance is there? I remember Sara being a lively teenager. Not beautiful, but attractive. There is no mention of her having a sister, and anyway, the ages are all wrong.'

Sam peered at the picture again. 'Olive's eyes are a different shape. She could be a relative, but certainly not a sister.'

'I only met Olive once,' Pat chipped in. 'But she struck me as very odd. What if she saw the photo and saw the resemblance to herself, then wove a fantasy around having a sister called Sara? She may have constructed a whole imaginary life for herself. It fits in with the attraction to the reality-shifting she mentions. Shall we look that up as well? I think I've heard of it.' She stopped and keyed in the words *reality shifting*.

'It says it's a belief that you can alter the reality you

are experiencing through intentional focus and visualisation. Some people believe they can enter their desired reality that way. Maybe that ties in with Olive saying Will was offering to hypnotise her, and her willingness to play along with it. Did he ever try to hypnotise you, Mimi?'

Miriam sat back, folded her arms, and sighed. 'I remember an argument we had about it, but it was years ago. He said he could take me back in time, but I ridiculed the whole idea. I liked my reality – I had no wish to inhabit another one. It was around the time he lost his job at the university. We had a huge bust-up. He wouldn't accept any responsibility for what happened to Sara – he said there was no evidence, and he played the victim because he'd lost his post. But she had lost her life. It sickened me, and I never saw him in the same light again. Our marriage, which was already shaky, never recovered.'

Sam scanned the extract again. 'She says she answered an advert and the contact was William Marshall. Then she says she was afraid he might recognise her. I think we are on the right track – your theory of a fantasy sister makes sense. She was out for revenge.'

Pat frowned. 'That's a bit extreme, isn't it? Revenge is a very personal thing.'

They stared at one another, each of them trying to get a sense of what it all meant.

Miriam murmured, 'I think I'm beginning to understand. It's mad, but try this. Will loses his sense of reality. He's met new people who think like him, and they've formed a group. He becomes isolated during the Covid lockdowns, but he can't turn to me because I'm hostile, so he begins to try to influence Ollie – which is when the haunting begins.'

Pat interrupted, 'That's possible, but then what? Why didn't he just get on with it? He had people to support him. Why did he want Ollie? He must have known that you would never allow him to have custody.'

'Yes, but remember he was mentally frail by then, and he set his dogs Oswald and Enid on to Ollie. Meanwhile, Olive Lander was playing him. She was savouring his destruction.' She shivered. 'If this is how it was, I can't help but be sorry for Will. He didn't stand a chance. He had already gone too far by influencing poor Sara Lawrence. He refused to believe he had a part in her suicide, but with the knowledge we have now, who could possibly doubt it? We should give the journal extract to the police. They might not accept our theory, but who knows?'

Sam was embarrassed. 'The problem is, there's no signature, and I'm afraid Henry acquired those papers when we broke into the Lander's house. It isn't permissible evidence.'

Miriam asked, 'Did you take anything else?'

'No. We were looking for contact addresses and hoped to find something to back up Henry's explanation for his grandfather's accident and lost savings. I tried to gain access to their computer, but it was password protected and I couldn't crack it. I think we should contact the DI we met. I've forgotten her name. Do you remember, Miriam?'

'There was one who was very grim, and the other, let me see … I think she said her name was Wallis. Does that sound right?'

'That's it, yes, DI Wallis was the one with the red hair.'

***

Miriam and Sam were shown into the same small interview room in the police station, but this time they were not kept waiting. Detective Inspector Wallis joined them within minutes of their arrival. Miriam was struck by how, on this occasion, she looked and acted the part of a senior police officer. Her red hair was pulled back from her face into one thick plait, and she wore a black suit and crisp white shirt. Her handshake was firm and her expression serious, although Miriam thought she detected a slight twinkle in her blue eyes.

'Thank you for making an appointment. I'm pleased to see you both. I'm afraid I can't discuss the details of the investigation with you, but we are making progress.'

Before the DI had a chance to continue, Sam cut in, 'We have a story to tell you. It might be helpful, but I'm afraid we can't offer any proof.' He began to tell the DI about the origins of the cult and Olive Lander's conviction that Sara Lawrence had been her sister. 'We think Olive Lander's motivation was revenge, entangled within a belief that it is possible to transform into a different reality. Trapping Oliver was in part revenge on the whole family, but also connected with a pact she had made with William Marshall.'

DI Wallace frowned. 'How have you come to this conclusion?'

Miriam answered, 'We've been talking about it and put two and two together.

We admit we might have made assumptions, but we're basing our theory on Will's actions, and I don't think we're far off the mark. His mental anguish began when a student of his committed suicide. Look up Sara

Lawrence's photo. There is a marked resemblance to Olive Lander. We think she wove a fantasy around Sara and set out to trap Will. We also believe she persuaded him to take drugs, spinning him a lie that they were harmless and would lead to self-realisation. Then she abandoned him to his fate.'

DI Wallis sat back in her chair, contemplating what had been said. 'That's quite some theory, and it begs the question – when does exploitation and neglect become murder? Difficult to prove. We have interviewed the witness who saw the person the cult call Sister Olive entering the house, and the witness's husband, who, some days later, saw people in the house and the ambulance outside. We have also interviewed some cult members. They too believe Will was given drugs but took them willingly. We've also searched the Landers' property, looking for evidence. There was nothing, not even a computer.' She spotted Miriam and Sam glancing at each other and raised her eyebrows. 'There wasn't even a paper trail, which does seem odd.'

'Have you talked to Oswald and Enid Hughes? They were close to the Landers. I know they helped when Leo Lander was in hospital. I bet they have a key to Olive's house.'

'Thanks for that information. We are currently looking into the Landers' attempt to defraud some of the cult members. I can also reveal that Olive Lander has been diagnosed with a personality disorder. She is likely to be physically disabled, although I believe she is recovering some mobility. She will certainly be charged with the kidnap of your son, Mrs Marshall, but whether she will ever be well enough to stand trial is debatable. She will be kept in a secure unit whilst our investigations continue.'

Miriam sighed. 'Thanks for sharing that with us. I hope after all the suffering she's caused, she will stand trial one day. We all deserve justice.'

The DI smiled and stood. The interview was over. Miriam was relieved. They had told their story as they had wished. The DI had seemed to be genuinely interested, although she had not recorded their conversation. However, when they discussed the interview together, Sam suggested it had been observed through a two-way mirror. They could only hope they had been taken seriously.

The humanist memorial event Miriam and Ollie had arranged for Will was a quiet affair. Will's mother had died, but Miriam and Will had always visited her grave on her birthday. It seemed fitting, therefore, to hold the memorial in the small hall at the cemetery, and for Will's ashes to be with his mother in death.

Will's father and mother had divorced when he was ten. Miriam had met the father once, but he had made it very clear he wanted nothing to do with his son. She had almost forgotten his existence, so when he turned up at the memorial, she barely recognised him. He refused to join them, even when she pointed his grandson out. His only comments were, 'I'm here for his mother's sake. Not surprised Will came to a bad end. You want to watch that boy or he'll end up the same way.'

All Ollie saw was an old man who shuffled into the hall wearing a trilby and a black suit, which hung on his body as if he had shrunk. When Ollie's mother went over to speak to the man, she pointed over to their seats. Ollie was relieved when the man shook his head and sat down at the back. When they all gathered afterwards, he was gone, and Ollie forgot all about him. He was only to discover that the man was his grandfather years later.

Miriam had expected more people from the cult to come to pay their respects, but only Henry attended. Ursula and Maude sent their apologies. Oswald and Enid had not been seen since they left Swanage, although Henry said there was a *For Sale* sign outside their house. Poor Eira Williams had died. Covid had claimed her.

Paul was grieving, blaming the cult and swearing to get revenge for his parents. He said that once his mother had realised what a charlatan Will had been, she had turned her face to the wall, her heart broken. It hit Miriam then. Why would they come to mourn a man who had ruined so many lives?

***

With the memorial over, Miriam felt her energy returning. Together, in Miriam's old home, they made short work of clearing the house. By the time they had finished, they were all tired and hungry. Pat and Henry had had the foresight to book them into a restaurant for an evening meal, and that is where they were headed after Miriam and Ollie had turned to take one last look at their home. It was up for sale, and Ollie hoped a new family would move in. Although he believed Agnes had helped him on Nine Barrow Down, he didn't think she would be able leave Chester permanently, but his model railway would always be a link to her. His mum and Sam had had ghostly experiences with it, so maybe a small part of Agnes would remain.

Martin, Miriam's cousin, was flying back from New Zealand at the end of April. He and Janey had been reunited, her contract had been renewed, and Martin had been offered a job with the NZ Civil Aviation Authority. Their flat in Bristol had been sold, and Martin proposed to rent Swallow Lodge to Miriam for a peppercorn rent. Although Ollie wasn't keen to leave Rock House, he knew the flat was too small for his mum, Sam and him.

***

After their meal, Miriam, Ollie, Sam and Henry went back to Pat's house, and the others to a hotel in the town. One more night, then they would be back in Dorset. Pat and Henry had promised to help in any way they could whilst the house in Chester was being sold. Miriam was delighted to see them working so well together, until she reprimanded herself for matchmaking. Happiness was clearly in the air. After the holidays, Ollie would be going to the same school as Kirsty. Everything had worked out perfectly.

Chapter 39
Swallow Lodge, Studland
20 September 2024

Sam was catching up on some paperwork when his phone rang. After he had listened for several minutes, his expression changed to one of shock.

'Can you repeat what you just said, please?

'I said I'm about to have my book published about the cult, but don't worry, I've changed all the names.'

Sam almost shouted, 'No, not that, Maude – what did you just say about Olive Lander?'

'I said she disappeared from the secure unit last month. Didn't you and Miriam know?'

This time he did shout. 'No, we didn't!' He held the phone away for a moment and breathed hard before speaking again. 'She was in a wheelchair. How could she have gone?'

Maude was impervious to Sam's distress. 'She's good at play-acting. She tricked them all. She must have been laughing at them behind their backs the whole time. Anyway, since the news broke, I've had a woman on the phone who wants to use the story in a podcast. I'm ringing because she asked whether you and Miriam would participate.'

'For God's sake, Maude! After all the suffering that she caused, I'm shocked you can even ask. A book is one thing. A podcast quite another. I'm not even sure it would be legal. Olive Lander was never charged.'

'Never mind that, Sam. Just ask Miriam, could you? It'll help my book sales no end. You never know, the podcast journalist might be able to track Olive Lander down, and we'd get some answers at last.'

'I'd like to tell you and your podcast friends to go take a running jump, but I guess the whole story is going to get out now, whether we like or not. Thank you, Maude. I'll get back to you.'

He put the phone down.

Acknowledgements

I owe a debt of gratitude to Michael Jacobs, who has given me valuable constructive feedback and who was generous enough to edit my initial manuscript.

And a very big thank you to my long-suffering husband, Phil, who understands my need for solitude. When I talk about the characters I've created and what they go through, he even seems to enjoy it. He's also an excellent proofreader, my best friend and an all-round good egg!

About The Author

Gill Calvin Thomas has retired from academic life and lives with her husband in Swanage, Dorset. She finds inspiration while walking in the Isle of Purbeck. Here, she is able to escape into a world of her own making, getting to know her characters whilst she plans the next twist and turn of a plot.

As writing has become a major part of Gill's life, she has withdrawn from taking a leading role in many community volunteer activities, although she has retained her interest in local and national politics. A lifelong feminist, Gill likes nothing better than a spirited debate on the issues of the day with family and friends. As her writing career develops, she hopes to explore those issues in her stories.

www.blossomspringpublishing.com